MY GIRLFRIEND BITES

Also by Doug Solter

My Girlfriend Bites Again (Feb 2023)

My Girlfriend Bites Me (March 2023)

The Gems Young Adult Spy Series

Skid Young Adult Racing Series

MY GIRLFRIEND BITES

BOOK ONE OF THE MY GIRLFRIEND BITES SERIES

Doug Solter

Brain Matter Publishing

My Girlfriend Bites. *Copyright © 2013 and 2022 Doug Solter.*

All right reserved. Published in the United States by Brain Matter Publishing. This book is a work of fiction. Names, characters, and incidents are either products of the author's imagination or used fictitiously. Any resemblance to actual events, or persons, living or dead, is entirely coincidental. No part of this publication can be reproduced or transmitted in any form or by any means, electronic or mechanical, without permission in writing from the author except in brief quotations embodied in critical articles and reviews.

Second Trade Paperback Edition

ISBN-13: 978-1-4912753-3-7 (CreateSpace)

Cover Art Design by Travis Miles

Website: www.probookcovers.com

*To Joe, who convinced me to finish this book.
I'm so glad he did.*

MY GIRLFRIEND BITES

CHAPTER ONE

AIDEN

I brace for the most insane thing that I've ever attempted, telling a girl that I'm in love with her. But that's only one fire pit I have to jump over. This wasn't any girl. Hell no, I couldn't fall in love with the standard girl I could borrow a pen or a piece of paper from. A standard girl I could maybe fool into having a burger with me after school. I couldn't make life that simple for myself. I had to fall in love with the hottest girl ever conceived by the Almighty...Pamela Osterhaus. She laughs with some friends standing around her locker as school wakes up for hour number one of this amazing Monday morning.

Well, I'm hoping my Monday will be amazing. It could be a disaster of Death Star proportions. Do you ever wonder about all those millions of stormtroopers that died when Luke Skywalker nailed the exhaust ports with proton torpedoes and caused a gigantic artificial moon to explode? I do. That must have sucked. Imagine you're a stormtrooper taking a relaxing dump in the bathroom or playing cards with your buddies in the barracks when the world around you explodes into flames. And then you get tossed into the vacuum of space with zero oxygen, suffocating to death.

Pamela touches the shoulder of the girl she's listening to. I imagine that smooth hand touching my shoulder. Or maybe my hand. Or better yet, my face. I bet her skin feels like silk.

Wouldn't it be so cool to have a girl touch you like that? Not on accident. That happens a lot in the hallways when you accidentally bump into a girl or step on her shoes. That's not what I mean. That's not a special kind of touch.

Pamela Osterhaus. Don't let that husky-sounding German name fool you. Pamela is thin and shapely with this long, strawberry-blond hair. Her perfume smells like a dryer sheet. You know, the ones your mom would toss in the dryer to prevent static cling? Light and flowery. A scent a girl loves to soak herself with.

Pamela doesn't know me. We did have two classes together last year, but I don't think she remembers. But I sure as hell remember her. I couldn't stop remembering her.

My stomach swims in acid. I can't make my feet walk over to talk to her. I did plan this out. Knew exactly what I wanted to say. Even memorized it. I went through the words over and over again in my bedroom, talking to a poster of Bat Girl substituting for Pamela.

Don't laugh. I would ask Bat Girl out in a second if I knew her real identity. I only wish I had Bat Girl's guts.

"Excuse me." The pissed-off voice comes from my right. It's Cave Girl. Her eyes glare from under a curtain of long, straight-black hair. The girl is scary weird and about as friendly as a tiger with rabies.

"You're blocking my locker," Cave Girl says. Even the sound of her voice creeps me out.

I move down the hall to give Cave Girl her space and then continue my mental build-up. The minute-hand descends like a hammer, ready to crush my opportunity to bits when the first-hour bell sounds. I can't say what I want to say with Pamela's friends still hanging around. It's intimidating enough saying them in front of Pamela. I could wait for a better time.

No, I'll chicken out. If I don't do it now, I'll be thinking about it all damn day and — screw it. I'm doing this.

But not with her friends there.

Would you guys please leave? I'm dying here.

The bell sounds again. Kids start heading for first-hour

classes. I should be heading to my class now. But I wait.

This will kill me if I don't...

Pamela's friends leave for class. My beautiful target selects a book from her locker and slips it inside her backpack. She slams her locker shut with a metallic clunk and turns back around to look up into my eyes.

"Hi, Pamela. What's up?" I say, trying to sound smooth, but my voice wavers. Her soft green eyes squint as she tries to place me. "I'm Aiden Jay. I took Economics with you last year?"

Pamela pauses, calling up the class in her mind. "Oh yeah, you sat in the row next to me."

"That was me," I say, much too loud. Losing my cool. I settle down. "How did you do in that class? The final was tough, but I tore it up."

"It tore me up. That's why I'm taking Economics again this semester."

Damn it. Now I made her feel stupid. *Way to go, Aiden.*

"I kind of accidentally tore up the final. It was a fluke because I didn't even study for it. And I was high."

I was high? What am I saying! Now she thinks I'm a druggie.

"I'm only messing with you. I don't do drugs. Not unless Red Bull counts."

Kids rush off to class all around us. Pamela's eyes dance from the kids to me and then back again. "Did you want something?" she asks.

"Oh, yeah. I wanted to —"

The saliva in my mouth turns to sand.

Damn it. This was so easy with Bat Girl.

Pamela fidgets. She wants me to hurry.

And I'm failing.

It's like I'm hanging off a cliff. My fingers slipping off one... By one...

So I push through it before I fall.

"I...I like you." The sentence loosens my tongue. I feel a sudden rush of emotion as the words come flying out. "Over the summer I kept thinking about you. The way you laughed and the way you smiled in class, it's really amazing. And you're like the nicest girl ever. A guy would be lucky to have a girlfriend as nice as you. And...you're really cute too. I mean, you must have guys coming up to you and asking you out all the time. And why wouldn't they? You're, like, everything a guy would want in a girl."

Pamela shows nothing. I can't even tell if she's happy, pissed, or even moved by what I'm saying.

I keep going. What else can I do?

"If you only want to be friends, I understand, and that's cool with me. It really is. I'm so sorry to stop you like this, but I had to tell you face-to-face or it would destroy me." I swallow and take a deep breath. "I only wanted to let you know how much I like you."

F-me. I did it. I went up to a girl and said it. It's like this huge weight squashing my skull for weeks is now dissolved into air. Amazing. Did I kick ass or what?

I search Pamela's face for a clue. Did she like what I said?

She laughs.

Laughs?

Laughs. In my face.

"Are you being serious?" Pamela asks. "I, like, barely know you. Do you think I would instantly fall in love with you because you like my smile?" She slings her backpack over her shoulder. "The only thing I remember in Economics was that you would stare at my legs like some perv. I'm so not interested in spending time with a guy who creeps me out. And any guy who's too dumb to notice I have a boyfriend is too dumb to waste my time with. And if you don't stop talking to me, I'll whisper a suggestion in my boyfriend's ear and have you killed."

Pamela removes her claws from my chest. Then she moves down the hall with her back to me. "Sorry, but I don't want to be your girlfriend." She yells that last sentence on purpose. The kids in the hallway stare and laugh. Soon their fingers tap out text versions of my social disaster for their friends to enjoy and share with the entire school.

The floor tiles I stand on explode into flames as I tumble

into the vacuum of space.
I'm now a pathetic stormtrooper.
And my Death Star just blew up.

* * *

My sneakers crunch fallen twigs and pine cones as a breeze nudges the trees above, making them creak and groan. The full moon punches through the forest, putting out more light than I want tonight. I can't wait to throw this cheap yellow rope over a branch, wrap the other around my neck, and put a final period on the most worthless sentence ever created. My life.

Pamela could have let me down easy by saying, "Thank you, but I already have a boyfriend." Maybe acknowledge the fact I poured my heart out to her, opening up something inside that's hard enough to dig out and say in front of a girl you've worshiped for months.

"*Are you being serious?*" The sentence still hurts. Like a recent burn on my skin. I can't believe her. She laughed. It was funny to her. *My feelings were funny to her.*

After school, I went home and shut myself inside my room, letting the darkness in. Darkness is a best friend, one I've lived with for so long. I thought Pamela was the answer. I thought being with her would lift me out of this crap. Give me something to hope for in life, not crush it to powder. I'm sick of waiting. I'm sick of hoping things will get better. This stupid idea that if I keep hanging on, my life will become something amazing. Something worth staying around for. But life is cruel. Not beautiful. It's painful and it's ugly and I've been lied to and I'm pissed, but not enough to fight back.

I want to give up.

So I found this yellow rope in Pop's garage and knew what I should do with it. Now I'm happy. I'm finally going to die.

I find a strong pecan tree that should work. I toss one end of the rope over a thick branch that looks good. It should support my weight. To anchor the rope, I tie one end around the trunk of the pecan tree and make sure it's tight. On the other end I make a great hangman's noose courtesy of the Boy Scouts. That's back when I gave a crap about the Boy Scouts. The scout leaders didn't teach us this particular knot, but one of the guys in our troop knew how and showed us.

I use a borrowed steak knife to stick my suicide note to the rotting tree trunk I'm using to jump off of. A patch of wild mushrooms form an uneven ring around the trunk. I hate mushrooms. Nasty tasting things. Mom would fry them in butter for Dad and the smell made me gag and wanna barf.

I step on top of the rotting trunk. Wrap the noose around my neck. Tighten it. Soon the rope is snug against my throat, and its straw-like surface irritates my skin. But the rope over the pecan branch looks tight and ready to do what I need it to do.

Okay. All I have to do is step off. Take one step, and I can be happy again.

I wonder if Pamela will feel guilty about me dying. I hope so.

They all should feel guilty.

A wolf howls through the trees. The sound pierces the silence of the forest as a warm breeze gives me a final kiss goodbye. Sounds like I'll be a free meal for some lucky wolf tonight. I feel tears racing down my cheeks. I don't want to cry. Real men don't cry when they're about to face death. I try to stop because I don't want to go out like this, but I can't stop.

Damn it. I can't even die like a real man.

I'm so pathetic.

I breathe in.

And jump off the stump.

CHAPTER TWO

AIDEN

So how did I screw that up? I remember the rope biting into my neck. I blacked out. Then I woke up in this stupid hospital. Alive. What the hell? The hospital staff filled in some of the missing pieces. Late that night, someone brought me to the ER when things were going crazy. A huge apartment fire swamped the place with twelve burn patients and their grieving families. The staff didn't remember any details about the person who brought me in and disappeared. They never left a name. Whoever this good Samaritan is...I want to thank them for being an asshole.

"Ready to go?" A male nurse rolls a wheelchair into my tiny hospital room. He raises the shades, letting in all that bright sunshine I want kept out.

I peel myself off the sticky leather chair I've been waiting in, gather my stuff, and nod. The male nurse wheels the chair next to me.

"Do I have to use that?"

"Yes, sir. Hospital policy."

Whatever. I drop myself into the chair, putting my backpack on my knees. The nurse slaps down the foot rests. I divert my eyes from him, catching a glimpse of myself in the mirror. The wheelchair completes the I'm-a-total-loser look that is so me right now.

We take an elevator down to the first-floor lobby. The

nurse rolls me past walls decorated with buffaloes, Indian art, and other Oklahoma-related crap. Through the front window, the morning sun paints the hospital lobby this weird shade of orange. It almost fools me into thinking this will be the happy day when I come back to my happy life that I failed to escape from.

Dad waits in the lobby, wearing his familiar Liberty Airways t-shirt that's permanently stained with hydraulic fluid and wheel grease from a Boeing 737-800. He follows as the male nurse wheels me up to the old Dodge pickup. I get out of the stupid wheelchair and lift the door handle. Locked. Dad climbs in, reaches over, and unlocks it.

Johnny Cash sings from the old country radio station Dad likes to listen to as we drive home. He's the only guy who listens to the radio anymore. I bought him a digital music player for Christmas, but it's still in his bedroom. Unopened. Whatever.

"How about pizza for dinner?" Dad asks. "Want the usual?"

"Sounds fine," I say, wondering when he's going to say something about *you know what* again.

"Bought you an electric razor."

"Okay."

Dad nods. Hesitates. "Hid the scissors, too."

I don't answer.

"Catch you trying that again and I'll ground you."

Ground me? That's funny. He's acting like I broke a window or lied about my grades.

"I'm being serious, Aiden."

I nod. "Okay."

Dad guides the pickup into the driveway. I stare at our sad, one-story house that I hoped I would never see again. We step on the porch causing Fatso, the neighbor's dog, to bark its head off. Stupid dog. All it does all day is bark. And it knows that we live here. If it can smell us, why does it keep barking like that?

I'm glad we never got a dog.

* * *

The outside of Wiley Post High School reminds me of a slaughterhouse. The hooks ready to plunge into my skin and take me down the conveyor belt to the rotating knives disguised as classrooms. The inside has few windows. Only an endless criss-crossing of sanitized hallways with smooth white walls, red classroom doors, and shiny, white-tiled floors. The shine comes from the janitors mopping up all the blood the school takes out of the students.

Yeah, okay, I'm getting way too dark. But I'm not looking forward to school at all. It's going to suck. I bet everyone knows what I tried to do with that rope. And if they put that together with what I did in front of Pamela, then everyone will figure out *why* I tried to kill myself.

"Ignore that bitch, A-man."

Issy and I wait for the lunch line to stir. Issy Bishara is my sensei. My guru. My wingman for life. His comment makes the old lady serving the mac and liquid cheese glare.

"Sorry. That wasn't a reference to you, ma'am," Issy says. "You seem like a finely distinguished woman for your age. Clint Eastwood would definitely want some of that."

I bust up laughing. I can't help it. Issy's funny.

Issy flashes an innocent smile, one he'd perfected during junior high. Issy is short for Ishmail. I met him in seventh-grade Life Sciences class when we dissected a real chicken leg with veins and nerves all over it. Disgusting. After that class I couldn't eat fried chicken for a year.

Issy burps. "Pamela Osterhaus wasn't worth your time. You shouldn't have said anything to her."

"Thanks for the help; that doesn't help me at all," I say.

"Wished you told me you were going to do it. I would've talked you out of it."

"Next time I'm in love with a girl, wanting to pour out my love for her in front of the south-side lockers again...I'll check with you first."

"Good. Friends always get each other's backs. Just saying."

Issy glances at the next lunch lady behind the fogged glass. "Cheeseburger."

"Chicken nuggets," I say.

Issy grabs his burger. "You don't need the perfect girl to be happy."

I take the paper raft full of chicken nuggets with two packets of honey mustard, then move along the line for drinks. "What's wrong with finding the perfect girl?"

"Hey, I'd love it if Hermione sat on my lap and taught me awesome magic tricks while I seduced her, but that's not realistic."

"Hermione?"

"The girl in the Harry Potter books? How do you not know this?"

"Because I have zero interest," I say. Which is true. "Anyway, that's a character from a book. I'm talking about finding a real girl who is perfect."

"Impossible." Issy selects a can of Coke.

"No. I'm saying, perfect in my eyes." I snatch my standard grape soda.

"Still impossible."

"How do you know?"

The cashier rings up Issy's tray as he motions towards the wide-open cafeteria filled with students. "See all those girls? They're not perfect. But A-man, they're girls. They're still soft when you touch them and they still have those wonderful girlie parts. And when they kiss you, they'll still build a tent inside your pants."

The female cashier sighs. "That's a nice image. Thank you for that." She gives Issy back his change, and we find an empty table.

"So did you have the flu last week?" Issy bites into his greasy cheeseburger.

"Hmm?" My mouth is full of chicken.

My friend sucks down his Coke. "You said you were sick last week. Was it the flu?"

I swallow. I didn't tell Issy about the forest, or the yellow rope around my neck, or the hospital visit, or about the therapist I have to go see now. "Yeah, it was the flu. Kicked my ass all week."

Wish I could tell him the truth, but he wouldn't understand. He would just tell me how stupid I was. Like I don't already know this.

I'm early to fifth-hour Algebra. Don't know why. Guess I'm bored, and sitting in a huge vacant classroom is something new and different. A handful of voices echo from the hallway. The second hand ticks on the clock above the white-board with faint stains of past math problems. I unzip my backpack, remove my stuff for class, then wait.

The AC kicks on. Air rushes through the vent in the ceiling, brushing a page of my open algebra book.

The room does nothing else to entertain me.

This coming-to-class-early thing was a stupid idea.

My pencil is worn down to a dull bump, so I get up and jam it in the pencil sharpener. The smell of grinding wood and tangy lead fills the room as I note a girl pausing at the doorway.

Cave Girl.

Today she wears jeans and this pink T-shirt. Her hair is long and dark and covering her face like a window curtain. Amazing. It's so long the ends reach her belly-button. Cave Girl has only been at Wiley Post for a few weeks but her "fame" is already the talk of the school. Cave Girl never talks to anyone. I mean, if you're standing in front of her locker she will, but usually she doesn't talk to girls or dudes. She will talk to a teacher, but only if they ask her questions.

Cave Girl grunts a lot too. Swear to God. When we're working on a test or some other assignment in class, I can hear her grunting. Like she's working hard on an algebra problem and her Cave Girl mind is on overload. From what I hear, she does this a lot in her other classes. One girl swears that she heard Cave Girl growling in the girl's bathroom.

The story goes that scientists cloned Cave Girl using DNA taken from a pre-historic teenager they found frozen in some icy mountain in northern Canada. Sounds like crap to me. I mean, why would adults bother with cloning a teen since they have plenty of us around to ignore already?

Today, the girl who's never friendly to anyone, the girl who doesn't acknowledge my existence unless I'm blocking her locker, that girl stares at me. I mean, really stares. I've sat behind her for weeks and she's never made eye contact with me whatsoever, and to be nice, I did the same.

I grip the razor-sharp pencil in case Cave Girl attacks me with that spiked-club that she carries in her backpack. The one her ancestors used to bring down dinosaurs for food. That's if you believe the rumors.

But Cave Girl moves to her desk. I take the long way around to mine and sit behind her. She then twists around.

She's turning around? Why is she doing that!?

"Hi." Her voice is light and just above a whisper.

Why is she talking to me? What did I do wrong?

I nod and pick up my sharp pencil again.

"Happy to see you back."

She is? Why? Don't make me stab you, Cave Girl.

"Thanks," I say, trying not to sound too grateful.

Hiding through those strands of black hair, Cave Girl smiles, making her cheeks flex. Her skin is so clear and soft. Her lips part as her mouth hangs slightly open. She doesn't wear lipstick or any makeup at all. Still, those lips have this natural roundness to them. A roundness that begs...well, I wouldn't mind taking my mouth and...the girl does have nice lips.

Amazing. I never noticed this before, but Cave Girl is... kinda hot. Her eyes have this unusual amber tint. Maybe it's the way the fluorescent lights hit them.

"You're welcome," Cave Girl says as she stares with this weird intensity that makes me want to squirm under my desk and hide.

But I grab another pencil and get up to sharpen it. While grinding more wood and lead, I sneak a peek at Cave Girl. Her eyes stay fixed on me. Like that's not weird or creepy.

I end up grinding the new pencil until it disintegrates.

Two more girls walk in and talk about some dumb television show that was on last night. Cave Girl opens her algebra book and reads. I take the long way around to my seat again, but this time Cave Girl doesn't turn around for the rest of fifth hour.

After school, I meet back up with Issy at the Taco Pronto by his house. The small dining area sits empty, with a television bolted up in a corner and switched to a sports network we never watch. You do have to be careful walking on the hard Mexican tile. Swear to God. Sometimes the employees mop it and forget to put up the little plastic sign that warns you about it being wet. How do I know this? Because I got a free burrito out of falling on my ass last month.

"Cave Girl said that to you?" Issy looks shocked.

"Yeah." I suck my drink through a straw.

"Why did she talk to you?"

I shrug.

"Were you flirting with her?"

"I was sharpening a pencil."

Issy grins. "Maybe she wanted to play with your huge pencil before class."

Yeah, right.

"Don't know if I want her touching my pencil. She might break it."

Issy loses his grin. "That would blow, wouldn't it?" He considers the horror. "Do you think they can break like that?"

"It's a bone, right? So if you can break an arm or a leg..."

"Nah, it can't be a bone because it shrinks. A bone can't shrink."

That makes sense.

"Then maybe they can't break," I say.

"Did you hear about that girl in New York or New Jersey? The one who got pissed off and cut her boyfriend's pencil off?"

"The whole enchilada?"

"Sí."

"No way."

Issy nods. "Serious pencil breakage there."

My mind tries to form an image, but it's so ugly I flush it out of my brain. "How does he take a piss?"

"I guess they rearranged his plumbing. Maybe he pisses like a girl now." A sadness clouds Issy's face. "If that ever happened to me, do a bro a favor and kill me."

Yeah.

"Sign me up too," I say.

Issy shows me a fist, and I bump it.

I crunch on some gooey cheese nachos that taste awesome. Issy chomps on a giant deluxe beef burrito. His face changes as he glances through the window behind me.

"What is it?" I ask.

"The legion of doom. They're here."

My stomach free-falls. That's Issy's nickname for...them. I swivel around. Kirk Cummings and two of his henchman fall out of his black sports truck. Mooney has this military buzz cut, and Jack wears this stupid fedora that he thinks looks GQ. The three walk inside our restaurant.

I so don't need this.

"Are you ready?" I ask.

"I'm not leaving because of them," Issy says. "Just ignore them."

Bad idea. But I don't say anything. My ears go into sensitive-hearing mode as I listen for Kirk's voice. There might be a slight chance that he's getting his order to go.

"For here," Kirk says to the cashier.

Or not.

These nachos were tasting so good. Too bad I won't be able to finish them.

The legion of doom finds a table near us. It doesn't take long.

"Blow Jay." Kirk waves at me. "How's it going?"

Mooney and Jack smile. Blow Jay is a name variation of a sex act that Kirk wants everyone at school to think I do, but I don't. I'm more virgin than olive oil. Blow Jay isn't very original as a put-down, but it does fit Kirk's stunning creativity. I don't need this.

"Hi, Lizzie. How's Allah treating you today?" Kirk asks.

Issy hesitates, but then keeps eating.
Assholes.
"You know Jesus would kick Muhammad's ass," Kirk says.
Issy stops chewing, shakes his head. Issy's family is from Pakistan, and they're serious Muslims, but not in some wacko-militant way. They've always been kind to me, but there are some things you don't make fun of, and Kirk better shut his pie-hole.
"Don't say anything," I whisper.
But Issy ignores me.
"Did your parents actually want you, Kirk? Or were you a botched abortion?"
We are dead. Our bodies will be turned into meat for the burritos.
"Shut up, you stupid sand nigger," Kirk says.
Damn.
Issy's eyes burn. His mouth tightens. It's weird. I never see Issy get this mad. Leave it to Kirk to draw out the worst in people. Issy bends in his seat to face the other table. "Want to know something interesting? I'm the dude who ratted you out to Mr. Echohawk."
Kirk squints. "You what?"
"I saw you prying that vending machine open and stealing the change out of it."
I can't believe he's telling him this. Does Issy want us both slaughtered?
Kirk processes the info. His brain still runs on Windows 98. Finally it stirs. "I got suspended for that." Kirk stands and moves to our table.
I still don't need this.
Issy tightens up. My stomach churns. With nachos inside, this could spell disaster.
"I should kick your ass," Kirk says.
Issy says nothing.
Kirk glares at Issy, then leans over my nachos and snorts. He spits out a glob of saliva which gravity pulls down on a long string that hangs in mid-air…before breaking and coating my nachos.

Kirk smiles. "Mmmm. Delicious."

"Number thirty-four?" the girl at the register calls out.

Kirk flashes another wicked grin and heads over to the counter to pick up his order.

Issy checks with me. I nod. Time for the escape pods. I dump my nachos into the trash, toss my plastic tray on top, and get halfway out the door before I realize Issy's not with me. I whip around and see him hesitating inside the doorway.

What's he waiting on? We're almost free.

Issy watches Kirk, who's now at the condiments bar gathering peppers and salsa.

Issy thinks for a moment. And then heads straight for Kirk.

WHAT'S HE DOING!

Issy hesitates behind Kirk. When the guy turns, Issy slams his hands down on his tray, and spills the deluxe enchilada platter all over the shiny Mexican tile.

Damn.

Issy sprints towards the door. I'm way ahead of him, hauling my happy ass outside to my bike. I hop on and pedal like crazy, getting halfway across the parking lot.

Issy jumps on his bike, but takes time to point it in the right direction before pushing off.

Kirk rushes out the door, snatches Issy off his bike, and slams him to the ground. "You owe me lunch, Lizzie!" He kicks Issy hard in the stomach, and he twitches in pain.

My legs lose their will. I come to a stop a few feet away from the entrance to the parking lot. Mooney and Jack come outside to watch the show. Kirk smiles at them and kicks Issy in the gut again.

I can't move. A part of me wants to help out Issy, but if I do anything, I'll get the same beat-down. They might even kick me in the face or my groin or some other bad place I can't think of right now. I catch my hands quivering on the bike's metal handle bars. Fear shoots through my bones. It's totally paralyzing me.

Mooney yells at me, "Pissing in your pants yet?"

Kirk and Jack laugh. Issy moans on the cement while holding his stomach.

What should I do?

Mooney takes a few steps in my direction. His hands form fists. "C'mon, chicken."

My nerves break like glass. I swing my bike around and pedal as hard as I can.

I hear them yelling...

"Look at him go!" Mooney laughs.

"I'm gonna find you, Blow Jay. We ain't done yet," Kirk yells.

The sounds from them fade as I round a corner and race for home.

CHAPTER THREE

AIDEN

On the morning route I'm the first stop, so I always get my choice of seats on the empty bus. Plus as one of the few juniors still riding, none of the younger kids give me any crap since I'm older. It's like the only time during the day I get any respect.
    The orange sun burns my side of the bus as we make the turn into Issy's subdivision. Fresh air sweeps into the open windows as I grip the ripped-leather backing of the seat in front of mine, wondering what my friend will say. I haven't talked to him since yesterday. Maybe I should have sent him a text, but Issy didn't text me about it so — I don't know. Maybe he's pissed. Well, I'm not the one who kicked him or the one who pissed Kirk off. I wanted to leave, but no, Issy had to piss off three guys who could kick our butts blindfolded. It was stupid. So in a way, Issy deserved it. Right?
    After we make stop after stop, the bus fills up with kids and gets noisy as we reach Issy's stop.
    The bus groans to a halt. The doors flip open. Issy mopes up the stairs, his face tired and weak, like he hasn't slept. Issy's one of those annoying people who once they're awake, BOOM, they're up. Believe it or not, he never looks this groggy in the morning.
    Issy makes his way up the aisle. I notice a sling on his

right arm. Is it broken? He hesitates.

What's Issy doing? Looking for a seat? Every day I save him a seat. So what's this? We're not friends now?

The bus moves forward. Issy has to choose. There's never any seats available by the time he gets on the bus. That's why I save him one. Realizing this, Issy surrenders and plops right beside me like he always does.

The bus accelerates as the automatic transmission shifts gears. Issy says nothing. Doesn't even look over or acknowledge that I exist. Should I bring it up? Should I wait for him to bring it up? Should I shut up? Damn. Should I, like, apologize?

But I didn't do anything wrong.

"How could you do that?" His words drip with acid.

I don't know. Call it my survival instinct? I avoid the question.

"Are you okay?"

"Do I look okay, asshole?" His eyes glare.

"I thought about calling 911."

"But?"

I hesitate. "He had two guys there. What was I gonna do against them?"

"Stick up for your best friend?" Issy's words kick me in the stomach. Or is that guilt?

"Did you go to the doctor?"

"My parents went mental. I told them somebody jumped me and took my wallet. They called the cops, and I had to fill out a report."

"Did you snitch on Kirk again?"

Issy laughs, not because he thinks it's funny. It's more of a nervous type of laugh. "No," he says.

"Why not?"

"Guess who came over to take the report? Kirk's dad. You do know he's a cop, right?"

"Dude, that sucks."

"No. Do you know what sucks? Getting the stuffing kicked out of your intestines while watching your best friend scrambling away on his bicycle, leaving his wingman on the

ground like a used jock strap. Now THAT sucks."
Issy doesn't have to act like that. I know I suck. I know I ran. I was scared, damn it. Did Issy want me to get beat up just so I could prove that I'm his friend? His eyes say yes. That's exactly what he expected from me.
I suck.
"You should have backed me up," Issy says. "I still can't believe you hit the eject button to save your own ass."
I close my eyes. I do believe it. I'm a turd. A joke. I don't deserve a good friend like Issy.
Hell, I don't deserve any friends.

Four and half hours later and Issy sits with me at lunch. Amazing. It's weird, almost like this morning didn't happen. I say almost because Issy's more calm than normal. But on a day like this, I'll take it. It gives me hope our friendship isn't doomed. During lunch I talk about cars, knowing full well that Issy's a car nut, and if anything will bring him out of his hatred towards me, it's that.

"What about a Volkswagen Beetle? Those look kinda pimp," Issy says.

"That's a tampon wagon," I say.

"No, it's not."

"Dude, they have a built-in flower vase on the dash."

Issy frowns. "Yeah, you're right."

"I thought you liked Mustangs?"

"I see too many girls driving those. The car doesn't reek of man like it used to."

"Reek of man?" I ask.

"My first car should ooze man juice. Be a real dude's car."

Ooze man juice. Car companies should hire Issy to come up with sick sales slogans. "The Ford Mustang. It oozes man juice."

"How about a Ferrari?" I ask.

"Yes! But my dad would laugh in my face if I asked him for one."

Issy flips through his phone, searching cars on the web. "Hey, what about a Volkswagen Jetta?" He shows me a picture of a bad-ass looking black four-door sedan with dark-red racing stripes. The car hugs the ground thanks to a modified bag suspension. Sweet-looking black tires with red brake calipers match the striping. Sex on wheels.

I whistle. "Yes."

"Yes?"

"Now that's a pencil wagon," I say.

Issy grins from ear to ear. "I could buy a used one and modify it. My dad would go for that because he crushes on saving money." Issy's eyes grow big. "After school you want to hang at that custom shop? I need some ideas for the...what are you staring at?"

Kirk Cummings slowly moves behind Issy. The asshole draws a finger across his neck. That's a signal for me. I'll be dead sooner than later. It's like high noon in an old western movie. Two-thirty in the afternoon means I better get the hell out of school or I'd get another trip to the hospital. Maybe instead of Issy's sling, I would get a broken arm. Or worse.

Suicidal Aiden wants that. Maybe in his rage, Kirk could end my life with a lucky kick in the head. Or a swift kick in the chest. Hard enough to stop my heart from beating or make it pop like a balloon. That would be quick and painless, right?

Issy twists around and catches the tail-end of Kirk's hand gesture. "Damn," he says under his breath.

Yeah. I'm screwed.

I think about death during sixth period Biology as Mr. Neil lectures us on Darwin and natural selection. How only the strong animal species survive and the weak species fade into history. Are my genes defective? Do they have bad code written inside them? Making all future copies of me act like scared little turds? Is my sperm so bad that I shouldn't spread it? Maybe Kirk should kill me. Then it wouldn't be my fault. It would be an act of nature. Something that should happen naturally. That way my life was sealed the moment I was born. I've had no control over it since day one.

Thunder rumbles through the walls of the school. Sounds

like a storm's moving in.

When the final bell rings, everyone rushes out to get home while I stay put and play a game on my phone for a few minutes. Then I rise from my chair, leaving the safety of my Biology classroom for the more dangerous hallway, where I keep looking around for an ambush. On the way to my locker, I pass by one of the few windows we have at school. Rain pounds the glass and the pavement outside. It's like an ocean falling from the sky.

Kirk would have to wait outside in this typhoon-like rain to kick my ass since trying to attack me inside school with all the security cameras would get him thrown out of school permanently. This sliver of hope pushes me to my locker. I transfer the stuff I'll need for homework tonight and seal the zipper on my backpack tight since it's raining. I reach the big double doors that lead outside to the bus loading zone. I hear the roar of the downpour through the glass as I grip one of the release bars. The metal feels cold.

I hesitate. Other kids rush around me and head into the downpour raging outside, using their hands to shield themselves in a useless attempt at keeping dry. Some use their backpacks. Others are smart and have an umbrella. I scan the glass for any signs of an unwelcome surprise in this wet, gray mess. Kirk wouldn't be out in this junk, would he?

He would. Kirk waits under an awning near the bus loading zone. The overflowing gutters above him dump this blanket of water that hides him a little. But I can still see him. Kirk doesn't ride the bus anymore. That means he's waiting for someone to appear. He looks pissed. Like making him wait in this rain is an insult. Like Kirk needs more of a reason to destroy me. I'm so dead.

But I want to be dead. Right?

I don't know what to do. Take death like a man, or run away like a coward.

My hand pushes the metal bar. The door gives way. At least my hand wants to be brave, but my cowardly body takes over and cements my legs to the floor. Now my brave hand shakes on the bar.

You wuss. You coward.
You still can't die like a man.
I duck back into the school and hide in an empty classroom.

An hour passes. I test the hallway.
It's empty.
Good. I follow the hallway, turn the corner, and reach the big double doors again. The glass shows the rain still punching the ground with fury. The busses are gone, but there's nothing standing under the awning besides a wall of bricks. The student parking lot is almost empty. Kirk's black sports truck isn't there anymore.
The fist that grips my heart relaxes. Looks like I have one extra day to enjoy.
R2D2 chirps from my phone. A text from Issy. *Where r u?*
I hit him back. *Still @ school. Miss the bus.*
Kirk was lookin 4 u.
Really? Fell sleep n biology. I reply.
Did u miss bus on purpose?
My finger hesitates over the phone, then I type. *I fell asleep. Can u grab ur mom's car & pick me up?*
Mom has her car at work.
Damn.
Pick me up with ur bike.
In the rain w a bad arm? Nope. U can walk.
I'll drown n the rain.
U fell asleep. Not me.
What a dick. I wouldn't be in this situation without his "help."
No, that's not right. I've been on Kirk's radar ever since junior high. This is only a new chapter of hell.
I stare out the doors. The rain hasn't let up for two hours. I rest my cheek against the cold glass. The water drizzles down the side. It looks like the water and I will become good friends for the next hour. My skin will absorb so much water that it might liquefy into slime.
A locker slams shut. It's my fifth-period neighbor, Cave

Girl. Is someone picking her up? Or did she drive to school? I watch her bend over to rearrange things inside her backpack. Gravity pulls her blouse down, and I can see...amazing. She's got nice boobs.

    I watch them.

    She hesitates, as if she can feel...

    Her eyes jump to mine.

    I turn away and clean the window with my hand, buffing it to a shine. The glass feels cold but quite smooth.

    Cave Girl gathers her things and heads for the doors. Black hair still covers her face. I think she's giving me an evil stare, but it's hard to tell under that hair. How bad do I need a ride?

    I flick my eyes to the wet outdoors. The odds that the rain would stop don't look promising.

    Well, she is a girl. Kinda. Maybe a girl would take pity on me.

    As she heads for the door on my left, I step in front of it. Cave Girl halts and examines me. What's this girl's real name? I can't remember. B-something, I think.

    "Hi, Breanne."

    She doesn't react.

    Not Breanne. Damn. Okay. Um...

    "Bella?"

    Her mouth twitches to the side. I'm screwing this up.

    What was her name? Didn't it sound like...

    "Dee?"

    "Bree." She corrects me.

    "How's it going, Bree?" I ask with too much excitement.

    "All right."

    "Awesome."

    I run out of vocabulary. Bree moves to the other door.

    "Do you have a car?"

    She stops. "Why?"

    "I missed the bus. I could walk home, but..." My eyes point at the rain hitting the door window.

    Bree checks the rain, then checks me. Is she thinking about it? Sitting inside a dry car would be sweet.

    "Sorry, but there's no way I can give you a ride." The door

bar clunks as Bree sprints out into the wall of rain. I watch her climb into a black, two-door car. It's huge. Issy would know the make and model. I bet it was made in the 1960s or '70s. They made huge cars back then.

The rain smacks against the double doors. I push against the cold release bar one more time.

Okay, life. I surrender to your crap.

CHAPTER FOUR

AIDEN

The rain stings me like a horde of angry bees as I slog across the bus loading zone. I do the short-cut across the baseball field and reach the concrete jungle...this huge block of retail stores and shopping centers with tons of heavy traffic. I have to cross in the middle of all this junk to get home. My shirt and jeans are soaked and glued to my skin. My bones feel like popsicles.

When I reach the main intersection of the jungle, I push the cross-walk button. I have to fight liquid misery for two minutes before the stupid traffic light changes. Finally I get the flashing green man and start to jog across three rows of stopped cars. The car in the middle lane slows me to a crawl.

It's huge, black, and nasty looking...but in, like, a sick way. That's Bree's car.

I glance at the windshield. The metal wipers swoosh back and forth in perfect rhythm. The rain makes it hard to see through the glass, but I know it's her car. Four round headlights shine against the grayness, with a long metal grill that separates the headlights into groups of two. The flashing-red hand now warns me to get my ass to the other side. I clear the crosswalk and continue along the sidewalk, making my way along Mingo Road.

There's a huge puddle nearby. This Lexus rolls towards it. The lady driver talks on the phone while oblivious to what she's about to do. Her tires plow through the puddle, launching a big wave that strikes me in the face. I'm so wet now I shouldn't care, but that lady should be paying attention to us poor pedestrians who don't have our license yet. Girls suck at driving anyway.

A distant horn sounds. I ignore it. With all the traffic and the rain, I bet a few drivers are laying on their horns because they're stressing. Guess I'm lucky I crossed the street when I did.

The horn blares again. Weird. Doesn't sound like a normal high-pitched car horn. You know, like one from a Honda or one of those little South-Korean cars. It's much deeper. Old-sounding.

My curiosity peaks the third time it goes off. My gaze crosses the busy six-lane street and finds the black two-door waiting in a strip-mall parking lot, its round lights burning. The wipers swoosh back and forth.

I stop.

Bree's honking at me? Why? Did I piss her off at the crosswalk?

The driver-side window drops to reveal Bree's long hair. She waves me over.

She's giving me a ride? Amazing.

The inside of Bree's car smells like leather. It's roomy too. I tug hard and pull the large, heavy door shut, then put my wet backpack on the floor between my feet. The swishing noise made by the wipers continues, but now I hear and feel a low rumble that vibrates my seat. Bree's hand twists a large steering wheel with three spokes coming out from the center. The large center console stretches across the entire dashboard like a giant Band-Aid. The inside of this car is as huge as the outside.

I grab for my seatbelt and feel only air. I look and don't see one attached to the side of the door. Searching lower, I see the metal tab near the bottom of my seat. I sling that belt across my lap and click it together.

"Thanks for the ride," I say.

Bree only nods and turns her attention outside. The motor

growls when she touches the gas, but Bree drives the muscle car back on to the wet, rainy street like a cautious grandma. I look around. The inside has silver-trimmed black leather, a silver dash with this old-school FM/AM radio, and a round tab labeled LIGHTER. Is that for a cigarette? They had those in cars? A red badge above the radio identifies this car as an Oldsmobile, which I've never heard of. It's in good condition for an old car. How did Bree get a car like this? Is it her dad's?

Bree's backpack sits on the backseat next to...stuffed animals. What the hell? One looks like a moose and the other a squirrel wearing some kind of blue aviator's cap with goggles on top of its head. Both have happy little expressions stitched on their faces with a lap belt holding them in place like kids. That's kinda weird.

"Where do you live?" Bree's voice sounds tense.

"8438 North Bison. It's just off 91st street. I'll show you where to turn."

Bree bites into her bottom lip, like she's nervous about something. Maybe she hasn't been driving for too long. I've only taken a couple lessons myself, and it's overwhelming.

"Is this your dad's car?"

"Huh?"

"The car. Is it your dad's? Because it's sick."

"Could you please be quiet? I have to concentrate," she says.

I watch the wipers swoosh back and forth for a while. Then I watch Bree for a while. I wonder how soft her hair is? Would a girl let you touch their hair if you asked? Or would they freak out? It's not like you're touching their boobs.

A sharp, gurgling sound moans from Bree's stomach. Wow. That was loud.

Cave Girl grunts and holds her stomach. She has this look of horror, like I caught her naked. Don't know why girls get so embarrassed about farts and burps. It's natural human exhaust. Why hold a fart in when you can let it loose and go on with your life? Sounds simple to me. I love farting. It's a fun way to make your friends laugh.

Bree swings the big steering wheel, pointing the car into a

convenience store. We park and she shuts off the engine. Bree reaches behind the seat and grabs her wallet. "I'm hungry."

"Okay. I'll wait in the car," I say.

Bree's mouth twitches to the side. She shoots a quick glance to her fluffy passengers in the back seat.

What? Does she think I'm going to steal those? Whatever.

"You don't want a drink?" she asks.

I have zero money.

"I'm not thirsty," I answer.

Bree doesn't like what I said. Her eyes squint. "You're not hungry at all?"

"Nope."

"Bathroom?"

What's this girl's hang-up? Can't I just wait inside the car? Is she that paranoid?

Bree climbs out and shuts her door. But hesitates. She steps up to the curb. Hesitates again. Her eyes just won't leave me alone.

Whatever. Fine. I pop open my door and follow Bree inside the damn store.

There's only a handful of customers inside the big convenience store. Must be the rain outside. Rows of potato chips, chocolate candy, and crap people forget to buy at the grocery line the shelves. Bree passes them and heads for the cold sandwiches. She opens a glass door, and chooses a deluxe roast beef and a chilled bottled water. Interesting snack for a girl. I drift over to the row of self-serve fountain drinks and spot my favorite grape soda in the world next to the 89-cent plastic cups. I dig into my pocket and feel coinage. Sweet. I examine my hand. One quarter, three dimes, and a ball of lint. I try the other pocket. One more dime.

I hate being poor.

Bree places her sandwich, water, and a Texas-sized package of beef jerky on the cashier counter. Amazing. She's no vegan, that's for sure. Bree pays with a five-dollar bill and gets back change.

"Hey...um, Bree?"

The girl freezes, like she's forgotten I'm with her.

"Can I borrow twenty-five cents?" I show her the coins I have in my hand so she knows I'm legit.

Bree scoops up her change. Her thumb caresses a bright, shiny quarter. She then places the quarter in my hand. I feel her soft, delicate fingers rubbing against my skin. Bree's lips part and form a shallow smile before she leaves the store.

Sweet, I have money. I better hurry. I fill a plastic cup full of grape soda, pay, and run outside. The rain is lighter but still makes me wet. I open the heavy door and climb back into the car. Bree starts the engine, grabs her sandwich, and rips the plastic wrapping off with her teeth.

She freezes and looks me over again.

What did I do?

Bree shakes off whatever she's thinking about and bites into the sandwich. But not like a normal girl. You know, nibbling on it? She puts a big hurt on that sandwich. Bree even grunts a couple times as she chews it. I stop myself from laughing. Gotta love Cave Girl. Bree chews slower, as if she realizes I'm watching her performance. She holds the sandwich in her mouth while shifting the car into reverse to back out.

We turn on to 91st street and approach my subdivision. I tell Bree to turn at the second left, and she does, weaving through the streets and bringing the car to a halt in front of my house. The engine idles. Must be a V-8 since the car growls even when it's not moving.

"Is this the right house?" Bree asks.

"Yeah." I grasp the metal door lever. I want to stay in the car and observe Cave Girl. See what more bizarre things she does in her daily routine. But then I'm still kinda scared of her so...I shove open the passenger door. "Thanks for the ride."

Bree stares through a natural split in her black curtain of hair. Why does she look so sad? Is it because I borrowed a quarter?

I climb out of the car and slam the door shut. I run towards my house as the rain strikes my hair and cheeks.

When I reach the dry porch, I notice the big black car hasn't moved. The wipers still swoosh back and forth.
  I don't go inside.
  The car lingers...
  I linger.
  I then wave at Bree.
  Why are you doing that? You'll look stupid.
  Bree waves back.
  Amazing. She waved back.
  The massive car rumbles down my street and disappears around a curve.

CHAPTER FIVE

AIDEN

"Cave Girl drives that black '67 Oldsmobile?" Issy's mouth drops open like the spout on those little milk cartons we had in kindergarten.

Our bus creaks and groans while making another turn. The morning sun slaps my eyes, so I blink and look away. "And I saw three numbers next to the name. 442. What do those numbers mean?"

"Her car is a 442?"

"Yeah. What the hell is a 442?"

"It means four-barrel carburetor, four-speed transmission, and two exhausts. Only the best muscle car Oldsmobile ever made. I'll look up the specs and send them to you. What else happened? Did you make a move?"

"On Cave Girl? No. Should I have?"

"She's crazy, but she's still a girl. What do you have to lose?"

"I tried that theory once, remember?"

"That was Pamela Osterhaus. She's not a normal girl," Issy says.

The pain kicks my chest as Pamela's laugh echoes in my brain.

"Can we drop Pamela?"

"Done. Gonna ask Cave Girl out?"

"I don't think she likes me," I say.

"Then why did she give you a ride after she said no the first time? She felt sorry for you. I'm telling you, pity is a great in."

"A great in?"

"A great excuse for a girl to hang with you."

"Could we think of another way that doesn't make me sound like a total failure?" I ask.

"Look, she trusted you enough to be inside her car. Trust is a big thing for a girl. I think you have a shot." Issy pauses. "Be straight. Did this girl give you a seriously stiff pencil?"

I'm not telling Issy that.

"She did! Look at that face of yours."

I shake my head, but I can't hide the smile.

We all stream off the bus like refugees, hiking across the loading zone toward our beloved school waiting to embrace us within its loving walls.

Someone shoves me to the pavement hard. The rough concrete scrapes my skin, and now my hands are sore.

"What's up, Blow Jay?"

My stomach churns out more acid. It's Kirk. Is today the day?

Issy touches his sling and keeps walking. I don't blame him. Guess I'm on my own.

"You made me wait in the rain, douche bag. I don't like waiting in the rain for little punk-asses like you."

I watch the crack in the sidewalk.

"Ready for your ass-kicking now?"

I close my eyes and swallow. I'm sick of worrying about this.

Let's get it over with. I wait for it.

And wait.

A minute passes. I open my eyes as a bunch of kids gather to see the show. Kirk savors his new audience. "I have a great idea. Since you made me wait, Blow Jay. I'll make you wait." He laughs to himself. "That's right. I might kick your ass tomorrow, next week, next month...who knows? One thing's for sure. You'll never see it coming." Kirk spits on my face. His mucus trails down my cheek as he disappears inside school.

All day my brain recycles all the vicious ways Kirk can physically hurt me. I replay his attack on Issy over and over, putting myself in the place of my best friend. I feel every kick to my stomach. To my face. To my groin. Would Kirk do more than that? He said I pissed him off for avoiding him. Does that mean Kirk's going to hurt me worse than Issy? Like going-to-the-hospital-ICU worse?

I drag my body to Algebra and stuff it in my seat. Bree flicks a glance my way, so quick you could blink and miss it. Her long black hair shines. For the first time today, I forget all about Kirk.

"Hi," I say.

Bree doesn't say anything. Whatever.

"Hi," she finally answers, but with zero enthusiasm.

I reach for my wallet and pull out five one-dollar bills. I jam my hand in a pocket, feel a quarter, and take that out too. "Here's the money I owe you." I place the wrinkled paper bills and a shiny silver quarter on top of her desk.

Bree twists around slowly. Her amber eyes dart to mine, then inspect my offering. "You just owe me a quarter."

"That's gas money."

Bree touches the bills. "Thanks." She hesitates a moment before folding the money and slipping it in her pocket.

I watch her during class. Strands from her long hair flirt with the top of my desk. Bree wears shorts today. She crosses her legs, and they look awesome. Why didn't I notice them before?

Jesse from across the row has. He stares at Bree's legs, totally mesmerized. I mean, dude, don't be so obvious. You'll screw it up for the rest of us.

Amber, the girl behind Jesse, notices his near catatonic state. She checks out Bree and rolls her eyes. Whatever. Don't judge us. Amber's only jealous we're not looking at her legs.

I sneak my finger close to the back of Bree's chair and let her hair brush against my skin. Her hair feels soft.

Bree stiffens. Did she feel that?

Mr. Strickland babbles on and on about some theorem I should be writing down, but I'm watching Bree's hair as it brushes against my desk. I like a girl with long hair. Don't know why, but I've always thought it was kinda cool. I slide my hand closer to those tempting little strands, wanting so bad to touch a girl again.

"Stop touching my hair," Bree shouts.

My heart stops. The classroom stops. And I think the entire north wing of the school just stopped.

"What's going on back there?" Mr. Strickland's burly voice asks.

Damn. Jesse laughs at me while Amber shakes her head. Everyone in class smiles because they love it when a kid gets singled out and ridiculed by Strickland. He's everyone's favorite show after lunch.

"Is Mr. Jay bothering you, Miss Mayflower?" Strickland never calls us by our first names. The man still thinks he's teaching at some expensive prep-school.

"No," she says.

"Your previously unsolicited comment seemed to negate that answer."

Bree hides behind her sheet of hair.

"Mr. Jay? Are you fondling this young woman's hair?"

Snickers and repressed laughs slip from the class.

I swallow. "Her hair. It keeps brushing the top of my desk. It bothers me."

That's not true, but it sounds better than getting nailed for fondling. Whatever that is.

"Mr. Jay, learn to live with life's little inconveniences. And, Miss Mayflower?"

Bree lifts her head.

"Perhaps wearing your hair in a ponytail configuration would allow better management of your straying hair. And I for one, would appreciate gazing upon your eyes for a change. I'm sure they look quite splendid indeed."

After the last bell, Issy and me follow the kids squeezing through the double doors to freedom. Soon the warm afternoon sun heats my face as we head for our yellow-and-black chariot parked at the end of a long bus line.

"Aiden!" Bree closes in. The long hair I fondled bounces with every quick step. "Don't ever embarrass me in front of class like that." Her mouth twitches to the side as her amber eyes sizzle. "Plus don't ever touch my hair again. Never... touch it...again." She sucks in a deep breath and releases it, making the strands of her hair dance in front of her face. Bree hesitates, as if wanting to yell at us for doing something else. Her eyes bounce to Issy, who grins like a clown, and then back to me. But the girl drops whatever she wanted to say and marches back inside the school.

Wow. That girl was pissed.

Issy steps forward. "That was so hot. I always tagged Cave Girl as this little wallflower who lost touch with reality, you know? But that look...that girl's a ball of uranium. She's mysterious too. There's something more going on there besides the extra-long hair and the growling. So what did you do to her in class?" I fill him in, and Issy grins. "Getting your game on with the flirting. I like it."

"I was only touching her hair. Guess I shouldn't have done it."

"You totally should be doing it. How does a girl know you exist if you don't do stuff to get her attention?"

I wasn't trying to get her attention. I was only messing around, but Issy's right. There's something more to that girl.

Issy rambles on. "You should go apologize. Oh, wait, better still...you should apologize before she drives off. But, like, draw out the apology, right? Make it long and gushy. Girls love that. And if you waste enough time, you'll miss the bus again and she'll be forced to give you another ride out of kindness."

Wow. That's a lot to remember. Wish I had more confidence going into this since the last girl I tried to ask...I shouldn't think about that now.

"Seriously? Do you think that will work?" I ask.

"The girl will melt under your apology."

"What if Bree says yes? What do I do then?"

"You keep talking. See if she wants to go get a burger," Issy says. "Or if your coconuts feel mucho solid, ask her out."

"So wait, you now want me to ask Cave Girl out?"

"I thought you liked her?"

I don't answer because I'm not sure. She's interesting and the girl is kinda hot in this weird way, but after what happened with me and Pamela—

"Okay, forget it." Issy heads for our bus.

I follow. My brain debates the question. Do I like Bree? Do I want to ask her out? She does have nice legs. And her hair's soft. And her voice sounds nice when she's not pissed. I glance at the student parking lot. The chrome on the black '67 Oldsmobile gleams in the sunlight, tempting me to climb back inside.

"Are you coming?" Issy waits on the bus stairs.

My feet don't move.

Issy moves away from the bus and follows my eyes over to the glistening car. He smiles. "Do it."

"Yeah?"

"Absolutely."

CHAPTER SIX

AIDEN

The large student parking lot bursts into action. Cars and trucks zoom through the wooden exit gates to escape from school. A line of cracked pavement traces my walk to Bree's car. She's not here, so I wait. I rub my palms and find sweat all over them. I wipe my hands on my pants to dry them. I try a few different looks to make it seem like I'm cool and relaxed when my stomach's tight as a fist.

Pamela Osterhaus struts towards her yellow Honda, with two friends trailing her. She blows a fake kiss my way, and her friends crack up. My confidence takes a direct hit and takes on water. I'm not fooling anyone. The cutest girls in school laugh at me because they know I'm a joke.

Damn it. Now I can't even fake being cool. Look at me. I'm a disaster in sneakers.

"What do you want?" Bree crosses her arms as she squints in the sunlight.

Where did she come from? I watched the double doors like a hawk and...guess it doesn't matter. I suck in air and lift my chest.

Don't fail. Don't say the wrong thing. Don't embarrass yourself. Don't...just do everything perfectly, and don't suck.

"Sorry if I embarrassed you in front of class today. I only touched your hair because...you know what? It's, like, your hair and only you should enjoy touching it."

I don't know what I'm saying.

"I mean, I don't enjoy touching your hair. I don't like touching my own hair because I don't wash it much."

That's information I don't think she needs to hear.

"Only kidding. I do wash my hair because it gets really gross if I don't."

Nice. I'm a disaster.

"I guess...what I'm asking is...can I have a ride home?"

"No," Bree says.

"But I missed the bus again."

Her eyes trace the long, yellow line of idling busses over my shoulder.

"Sure about that?" she asks.

Damn it. I'm supposed to stretch this apology out. Seducing girls is tricky.

"I thought you would like some company?" I ask.

"I don't." Bree circles me and unlocks her car door.

"I'll pay for gas and throw in a roast beef sandwich at your favorite convenience store."

Bree slips behind the wheel and slams the door shut. She rolls down her window. "Still no." Bree fires up the V-8. It's too late. She's leaving. Fail number two. I'm a loser. I will always be a loser.

No! Think of something, you idiot. Don't let her leave.

The transmission clunks into reverse. I run behind the Oldsmobile right as the white lights shine on the tail lamps. Bree notices I'm blocking her way. She revs the big car and it sounds loud and dangerous.

"I don't understand," I yell over the racing engine. "I'm only asking for a ride. You acted like it was no big thing when you gave me one yesterday."

Bree kills the engine, pushes the massive door open with little effort, and steps into the sun with her arms crossed. "I gave you a ride because it was raining. That's it. A random act of sympathy with no strings. You don't owe me anything, and I don't owe you anything. Go hop on your bus, and leave me alone. Okay? Thanks."

What? She took pity on me? Seeing me as some sad little

loser that needed saving?

A hot flash of anger curls up in my throat and spews out. "Well, I thought you'd like a friend since everybody here thinks you're a grunting freak with zero intelligence. The school's resident psychopath. The girl who creeps everyone out. Seriously. You should feel lucky that *I'm* even talking to you."

Her mouth twitches to the side as those eyes rip into me.

Whatever. No girl is worth this much work.

I walk back to the loading zone.

Issy waits near our bus, observing my fail from a distance. "Not good, huh?"

I shrug.

"But you went for it, A-man. I admire your—"

An engine roars and tires squeal as they take a turn too fast. I listen as the tires slide against the pavement and leave a strong scent of rubber.

Issy's mouth hangs open.

I glance over my shoulder. The black car rumbles near our bus. Bree motions me over with her finger.

I insulted her. Why does Bree still want to talk to me? I don't understand girls.

"Why are you not moving?" Issy asks and nudges me forward. My legs take over, and I reach the passenger-side window of the car.

"Get in. I'll take you home." Bree sounds calm and reserved. Not pissed at all.

I hesitate. That scene in the movie *Return of the Jedi* flashes in my brain. The part where the rebels attack Death Star number two and rebel Admiral Akbar turns around and shouts. "It's a trap!"

"Change your mind?" she asks.

I shake my head.

"Door's unlocked."

I scan her eyes again. Bree comes across much calmer now. Maybe she thought about it and then realized how amazing I am. Sweet! I'm going in.

I hop inside the car and slam the door shut. Bree pulls the

lap belt across her waist and snaps it close. She raises her eyebrows. Hint. Hint. I pull my seatbelt across and click it into place. A north breeze sweeps into the car. Bree's nostrils flex. Something in the air invigorates her. She slams the smooth metal shifter into first gear. A wicked grin spreads across her face. "I hope you brought gas money because I'm about to waste a lot of gasoline."

I don't like how she said that.

Bree stands on the gas. The engine roars as she pops the clutch and launches the Oldsmobile past the buses in a cloud of white smoke. The large car scrambles up to Mingo Road and skids into a right turn.

The posted speed limit on busy Memorial Avenue is 45 miles per hour. The thin red needle on the round speedometer inches towards 70. Bree weaves the car through three lanes of traffic, throwing around the big steering wheel like it's nothing while constantly shifting gears and stomping on the clutch. Bree does it all so fast I'm having a hard time believing she's not a pro race car driver like that girl Samantha Sutton.

Bree twists the wheel, sandwiching the car in front of a semi-truck that gives her an air horn. She then guns the engine and makes the needle go up to 72...before she slams on the brakes to avoid a flower delivery van.

Funny thing is that Bree hit the brakes *before* the man swerved into our lane. How did Bree know the other driver would do that?

This is insane. This girl is insane. I'm insane for getting into the car with Cave Girl. She obviously doesn't want me anywhere near her, and I get the message. I so get the message now.

Bree whips around a city bus before it applies its brakes to take on passengers. Again, how can she anticipate what the other drivers are going to do *before* they do it?

I watch her face. She's in this deep concentration, almost like a trance, as she focuses all her senses on driving.

Bree races around a box truck, and there's this intersection in front of us. The green light turns yellow.

The girl floors it.

I'm sixteen and about to have my first heart attack.

We fly through the red light. Bree flicks her wrist for a quick wheel correction to miss another car moving through the intersection.

That was too close. How can she react so quickly? That car came out of freaking nowhere.

The car skids through a turn and pours on the speed as we race down a two-lane road. Bree catches up with a slow-moving car that forces her to back way down, but she pokes the Oldsmobile out just enough to see if she can pass.

My nerves crack like dry spaghetti. I can't take this anymore. I want out of this car. Bree is totally insane, and I've made a huge mistake.

"Am I scaring you?" she asks with this innocent inflection that's so fake.

Is Bree making fun of me? Saying I'm a wuss?

My brain screams. *"Yes! You are! Accept this so she'll stop torturing us!"*

But my coconuts don't want to give any girl that satisfaction.

"Not at all," I lie.

Bree's mouth twitches to the side.

I grip the leather strap attached to the door.

Bree shifts into overdrive and swings out for a pass. An SUV comes towards us in the opposite direction. We clear the slow-moving car, but instead of moving back into her lane... Bree stays in the left lane.

The SUV flashes its lights.

Bree doesn't move over. The girl fires off this crazy look. Her burning eyes tell me she'll kill us in a heart-beat. My stomach tenses into a fist. Cave Girl will do it. She'll kill us both.

Why am I scared? Didn't I try to hang myself a few weeks ago?

That helpless feeling returns and floods my chest. That darkness that swallows up all the light and leaves me empty. Like a black hole in the pit of my stomach. Bree is giving me a way out.

It's perfect. I'll be killed in a traffic accident. Something ordinary. Something that happens every day. Something that won't embarrass Dad when he hears the news.

Now I only have to do one thing...

I press the release tab, and my seat belt retracts with a loud-metallic snap.

"What are you doing?" Bree asks, her voice wavering.

I close my eyes and prepare. The pain will be sudden, but quick. Think about it. No more Kirk. No more hurting Issy with my stupidity. It'll be great. Much better than hanging myself.

I'm so ready.

The horn of the SUV blares. It shouldn't be too long now.

CHAPTER SEVEN

AIDEN

The car swerves under me. The horn of the SUV sounds loud, almost on top of us. Airbags didn't exist in 1967, so I wait for the dashboard to slam into my face. Would I hear the impact first? Would I hear Bree scream? Would I hear myself scream?

I press my lips together. Not me. For once I'm going to die like a man. I wait for the impact.

And wait.

Nothing.

No skidding tires. No crunching glass. No screams. The noise of the V-8 drops to a purr as Bree releases the gas pedal.

I open my eyes. The road is clear ahead.

Bree slows way down and whips the car into a parking lot. She brakes to a stop. "Why did you do that?"

I don't say anything.

"Why did you take off your seat belt?"

"Why were you trying to kill us?" I ask.

"I wouldn't hit another car on purpose."

I shrug. Sure fooled me.

Bree pauses, thinking about something. "You wanted me to do it, didn't you?"

"No, I didn't."

"Why do you want to die?"

I feel naked and vulnerable. Exposed to a world that wants to laugh at my joke of a life. The pain surges through me, and it hurts. I don't want anyone to know because it's no one's business. I unlock the door and push it open. "I'll walk home from here." I grab my backpack and jump out of the car, slamming the door shut.

"Please come back here." Bree's voice sounds light and gentle. It tempts me to follow it.

"Don't worry. I won't bother you anymore." I walk, and the engine cuts off behind me. A car door groans open.

"Aiden." Her voice sounds stronger.

I keep walking.

Bree suddenly appears in my path. Whoa. How did she...? Did she run up here? That's way too fast.

"Stop walking...please?"

I make a move to go around her. Bree thrusts her arm across my chest. Whoa. Her arm is like this iron girder. It doesn't give an inch. Does Bree work out at a gym?

"I'm sorry I did that." Bree's crazy amber eyes that threw our lives into danger vanish. Warmer eyes replace them as her hand relaxes against my chest and lingers there a moment before she lowers her arm. "The thrill ride is officially over." Bree flashes a smile to reassure me as she drifts back to the car. The driver's door groans open as Bree slides back behind the wheel.

Her gentle voice gives me this weird comfort, like I could trust her. That weird comfort draws me back inside the car.

* * *

The night floods my bedroom as I try to close my eyes and sleep, but I can't. I keep replaying the afternoon over and over in my head. How nervous I felt waiting for Bree in the parking lot. The fear that she was going to run me down. The fear she that was going to kill us. The fear that turned into a painful embarrassment, but Bree didn't make fun of me. She didn't turn on me like Pamela did when I opened up to her.

Bree sort of cared. I don't know why, because she hardly knows me. I'm some loser who sits behind her in Algebra. Bree is so weird, but, like, awesome weird. The I-want-to-know-more-about-her weird.

My tired body wins and pulls me under. I fall asleep and dream...

Bree's long, black hair spreads out from her head, like she's floating on top of water, but there's no water. She's drifting on this layer of air, her body gliding over it like the wings of a seagull. She smiles and glares at me, like the girl can't decide which side of herself she wants to show. Bree is naked, but not in some slutty way. She's more like a sculpture you see in a museum. Her skin is almost like white marble, shiny and pure.

I try to reach out to her.

Bree's amber eyes darken and turn to the color of blood. Her long, black hair grows and grows like an out-of-control plant. The hair covers her body like a blanket. Insulating her. Protecting her. The hair keeps growing and growing. The strands wrap around my neck. I don't notice this until they press against my throat and tighten.

Tighter and tighter they squeeze.

I gasp for breath.

The hair's soft texture changes to the rough texture of rope. The black strands turn yellow.

I choke. Gasp. Struggle for oxygen.

But nothing is there. I can't breathe. My chest aches from the strain, but it's no use.

Life falls away from my grasp.

I wake up gasping for air.

***

"Are you resistant to time constraints in school, Mr. Jay?" Mr. Strickland's critical gaze follows me as I slip into Algebra late.

No, sir, my bladder resists emptying quickly.

I would love to throw that brilliant comment back at him,

but I take my seat and shut up instead.

"Hope your tardiness doesn't affect your preparation for today's algebra test."

Damn it. I completely forgot we had a test today. Guess I was occupied with other things.

Bree smiles, as if I cued her with a tap on the shoulder. Her curvy cheeks and the face that goes with them look a little brighter under those black strands of hair. I think about the dream and the fantasy girl that occupied them. Now she's so close. Inches away.

Bree tilts her head. "Aiden?" she whispers.

"Yes?" I whisper back.

"Take one."

"Huh?"

Oh. The algebra test. The one I'm about to fail. I take one copy and pass the stack to the guy behind me.

Mr. Strickland then gives us the green light to start.

Thirty minutes pass.

I don't believe it. I dropped a scholastic miracle out of my butt. Not only did I complete all the problems, I think I got most of them right. Amazing. Once in a great while I can amaze myself. I do a victory march up the aisle to Mr. Strickland's desk to turn in the miracle I have created. Walking back, I pass Bree wearing this clinched face, like someone is using a vise grip on her head.

Most of the class finishes their tests. Only Bree is left. Her anxious finger taps on the desk like a small woodpecker on eight cans of Red Bull.

"Time has expired," Mr. Strickland announces. "Writing utensils down, please."

A small growl escapes as Bree slams her pencil down, breaking it in two. Her growl makes some of the students hold in their muffled giggles. Bree collects herself and turns in her test. The bell rings, and everyone gathers their stuff. Bree doesn't move, her mind occupied.

"How'd you do?" I ask.

"Not good," she says. "What about you?"

"Think I did all right."

"I studied six hours for this test," Bree huffs.

"Six hours? That's some dedication."

"Still didn't help."

"What parts of the test did you have trouble on?"

Bree sighs. "I got my name right."

"You couldn't have done that bad, not with six hours' worth of cramming. You're being too hard on yourself."

"I'm not too optimistic." Bree gathers her things.

I bet she only needs a tutor. I know millions of guys who would love to help a cute girl with...hey, I love math.

"I'm not a math professor or anything," I say, "but math is easy for me. I could help you. That's if you want some help."

She slings her backpack over her shoulder. "What kind of help?"

"Study together. Check each other's work. That sort of thing. A math buddy."

"A math buddy?" Issy shakes his head.

The lunch line moves like an earthworm.

"I know. I know. It was a disaster. I acted like Bree and I were in fourth grade and I wanted to go over our multiplication tables."

"Is that her real name? Bree?"

I nod. The line moves one foot.

"Using math as a pick-up line has failure stamped all over it," Issy says. "One time I acted like a clueless guy in Home Economics. You know, hoping one of the girls would feel sorry for me and help me out? But they figured out I was faking."

"Isn't that the class you failed?"

"Yeah. I killed my baby."

"Killed your...what?" I ask.

"That stupid fake baby they give you. The one you're supposed to take care of? I put mine in the refrigerator."

"Why?"

"It had a fever so I figured, why not put him in the fridge to cool off and...I failed the class, okay?"

"Baby killer."

"Shut up, math buddy."

I blow off Issy and let my eyes drift over the same lame cafeteria food. The same students in line. The same boring lunch I have every day.

Is that Bree?

She's on the opposite side of our huge cafeteria. Bree isn't hard to miss because there's this sea of heads tilted in her direction as she moves across the room. Bree wears a normal pink T-shirt with jeans, something lots of girls wear. But everyone still watches her. Some of them laugh because she's Cave Girl, the student they make fun of because everyone else is doing it.

But for others...there's something different about Bree. The way she moves...it's so fluid and graceful. Like a dancer in complete control of her body. Every step calculated and precise with this sway and confidence that many students would try to hide so they wouldn't stand out.

Bree has the same lunch period as us? I've never seen her in the cafeteria before. She scans the lunch tables. Who is she looking for? The girl's nostrils flare up and down, like a police dog sniffing a suspected drug house. Bree did the same thing in the car when the windows were down. Maybe she smells that over-fried chicken with instant taters the old ladies cooked. Amazing. It's like Bree trusts her nose more than she does her eyes.

More kids in the cafeteria snicker and laugh as Cave Girl gives them another free show of weirdness.

Bree ignores them and continues sniffing.

Her eyes then snap in my direction. I hold back the urge to jump.

Bree walks up to the lunch line. "What are you doing for lunch?"

"Um...standing in line. It's fried chicken day," I say.

On the word chicken, Bree's mouth twitches to the side.

"Did you read chapter twenty-two for Algebra?" she asks.

"Yeah."

"Can we go over it before class? Like now?"

"You want to go over it during lunch?"

Lunch is for stuffing your face and goofing off. Not for studying. This girl is mental.

"I'll drive us to the mall," Bree says. "We can study in the food court while we eat."

The mall is expensive. But those cute eyes hook me. I do have enough money for a grape soda.

"Okay."

Issy's mouth hangs open like a mailbox. I know, right? A girl asking me out to lunch? Amazing.

"Oh...Bree, this is my friend Issy. Issy...Bree."

She cracks a half-smile. "Hi."

"Your car kicks serious ass. I want to steal it," Issy blurts out. Maybe he didn't mean to say that last part.

Bree squints, trying to figure Issy out. This isn't the first time a girl has tried. Bree brushes him off and moves towards the outside doors.

I hesitate. Leaving Issy in line feels awkward. We've eaten lunch together since seventh grade.

"Sorry," I manage to say.

Issy tries to smile, but it doesn't take. "No foul. I completely understand. Bree has boobs. I don't."

CHAPTER EIGHT

AIDEN

The dome-sized food court at Wood Creek Mall overflows with noisy juniors and seniors who have cars and the money to eat here. Carved into the ceiling, a large skylight brings in the sunlight. A trapped bird chirps as it flies from one synthetic tree to another, trying to escape the grove of fake trees that all the chairs and tables circle around.

I follow Bree to the Greek gyro place, but I can't afford one of those. There's the Tex-Mex place next to it. I could buy a beef taco and a courtesy water. I pull out two worn-paper bills.

Bree watches. She must think I'm on welfare. Or too poor to buy my own lunch.

"Sorry...I totally blanked in the cafeteria. Forgot to mention I'm paying for lunch," she says. "It's the least I could do after trying to kill you yesterday."

Bree and I find a table under a fake tree. I dig into my cheesy nachos while Bree sinks her teeth into a plain gyro with extra meat and no sauce. The girl grunts as she chews, but I don't laugh. We eat for a while, and through the entire meal I have this weird feeling she's constantly watching me. I try to catch her doing it, but the girl skillfully tosses her eyes away milliseconds before my eyes can get there. It drives me insane. How does she do that?

So I stare at her. I dare Bree to look and not turn away.

Her eyes take the bait and snap on to mine.

I don't flinch. I don't look away. I keep my eyes trained on hers.

Bree stiffens. Leans forward. Her eyes grab on to mine. Pulling me.

My heart races. I feel the cold wood tabletop under my fingers as I grip it tighter and tighter.

Bree doesn't move a muscle. Her cheeks are still. Her lips separate, showing off her finely-polished teeth.

She's moved closer. How did I miss that? Is Bree creeping towards me? Or am I seeing things?

No, she's moving towards me. Amazing. So subtle you can barely tell.

What is she doing?

Bree snaps out of it. Leans back and smiles. "Ready to get started?"

I relax my death grip on the table and open my textbook.

We review chapter twenty-two. Bree asks a few questions, and I point to a problem.

"A rational function is the division of one polynomial function by another."

Bree's eyes glaze over.

"When graphing a rational function, you look at the x and y intercepts."

"Intercepts?" Bree asks, still not getting it.

"Yes, the intercepts. See the y intercept? This function doesn't mean anything because in this case, x equals zero. So there's no y intercept."

Bree absorbs my explanation.

"Does that make sense?"

Bree tenses up. Her mouth tightens into a sneer. Her arm blurs as it flings her algebra book off the table and across the floor. It slides about forty feet away from our table.

"None of this makes sense," Bree huffs with frustration.

Everyone in the food court watches. I fetch Bree's textbook and her notes from the floor. Bree stews as her body quivers. Amazing, I've never seen anyone get this upset over math.

"Let's take a break." I close my book and concentrate on cheesy-good nachos.

Bree opens her book and stares at the pages. "No, I must learn this."

"You're obsessing. Let your brain chill for a few minutes."

Bree thinks about it and then shuts her book. She grabs the gyro and plunges her teeth deep into the lamb. More grunts as she chews. She swallows. "What?"

"Nothing."

"Do I eat wrong?"

Eat wrong? That's a weird question.

"No, I just...I've never saw a girl eat so much meat. You're not the salad type."

"Meat is good for you because it has all that protein. A girl needs her protein." Her eyes study me. "What? Do I act too weird?"

"No."

"Do I live up to my nickname?"

Her nickname? Oh, damn. Does she know about the Cave Girl thing?

I act as innocent as a little puppy. "Your nickname?"

"Cave Girl?" Her lips press hard together.

I munch on a nacho. "Who calls you that?"

"Really, Aiden?" Bree crosses her arms. "That's your answer? Do you think I'm that stupid?"

There's no laughter in her eyes. Only a coldness that sends a chill up my spine. I don't want to test those eyes.

"I...I'm sorry I called you that," I blurt out. "Now I feel like an asshole."

"Why do they call me that?" Bree sounds more hurt than pissed.

"Um...I guess because..." I stall. This feels so awkward, like I've been called out on a lie, and all that guilt is punching me in the gut. I know what it's like when people make fun of you.

Damn. Was I acting like one big hypocrite?

"I won't bite your head off. Promise," Bree says.

I drink some liquid grape courage first. "I guess...um... because of your long hair and because you don't talk to anybody. Guess they think you're a freak or something."

"Does everyone think I really come from the Ice Age? Or that scientists cloned me?"

Hearing the rumors coming from the subject's mouth does make it all sound stupid and unbelievable.

"Not that, exactly. But some kids might think you carry a spiked club in your backpack to attack dinosaurs with."

Bree freezes.

I nod to confirm.

Bree shakes her head. "That's so stupid."

I laugh because it is stupid.

"What?" she asks. "Do you think I'm a freak?"

"No, I think you're...interesting."

A tiny grin flexes those lips of hers. "Thanks for the honesty."

"Thanks for not throwing your algebra book at me."

Bree laughs. And it's the sweetest laugh I've ever heard.

* * *

A purple sky paints the world outside my bedroom window. The clock reads 6:16 a.m. I stretch against the cotton sheets and flop over. I want more sleep but I so need to piss. I roll out of bed, and the smell hits me in the hallway. The whiff of alcohol, that all-too-familiar scent that always makes my heart deflate. I flush the toilet and head for the living room, knowing already what I'll find there.

Dad lies across the black leather recliner, which has rips all along its arms and back. Like me, the chair has seen better days. Dad snores. His body reeks from a mixture of Budweiser, Kentucky bourbon, and vomit courtesy of a half-eaten Big Mac on the table next to him. Dad only had a couple beers last night before I went to bed. But while I slept, he turned that "snack" into a full Thanksgiving dinner with all the alcoholic trimmings.

I shake Dad, and he mumbles. He's way out of it. There's no way he can go to work like this. Better call again. My thumb searches and finds Dad's supervisor in my phone contacts. I hit call, and it connects.

"Mr. Flynn? Hi, this is—"

"Hello, Aiden," Mr. Flynn says. He knows my voice all too well.

"Oh...hi. Um...Dad has a stomach bug. He's throwing up big time."

"Throwing up? Sounds bad."

"Yeah, he can't keep anything down...so...he won't be into work today."

"I see." Mr. Flynn sounds skeptical. I so suck at lying, but I can't let Dad lose his job. How are we going to live if he gets fired? My dad doesn't believe in savings accounts.

I have to make this work. "If he doesn't improve, I'm going to take Dad to the hospital because I'm worried about him," I lie. "But I'm hoping he recovers enough to be at work tomorrow."

"If he's bad enough to go to the hospital, he's not going to be better by tomorrow."

Dad can't miss any more days. The airline might realize they can get on fine without him.

"You never know," I say. "These things can straighten themselves out in twenty-four hours sometimes."

"True," Mr. Flynn says. "It always depends on the amount of sickness that person drank in the last twenty-four hours. Tell your Dad I hope he feels better. If he needs to go to the hospital, tell him he better stay there for at least two weeks before coming back to work. Hospitals are good places to get help."

"Okay. I'll tell him that."

I'm not sure what Mr. Flynn means. Does he want Dad to stay away from work? I guess that's better than getting fired, right?

I put away the phone and find an old dish rag. I soak it in water and use it to clean the vomit off Dad's mouth and chest before putting him to bed to sleep it off.

CHAPTER NINE

AIDEN

I get off the bus and start the walk home like I've done every afternoon since starting my academic career in first grade. I listen to the wind rustling through the trees as they dump their leaves for fall. The neighborhood surrounds me with the same old houses. The same old cars. The same old fences. The sun casts a dark shadow of me against the crumbling pavement. It's amazing to watch another version of yourself mimicking every movement of yours perfectly. A doppelganger that makes his sneakers slap against the pavement like yours.

A low rumble reaches my ears. It increases in volume.

Coming closer...

And closer...

A massive new shape overtakes my shadow. A car.

I glance up to see the Oldsmobile rolling next to me. Bree smiles through the open window, her black hair now in a long ponytail.

I stop walking. "What's up? Missed you in class."

A massive understatement. When I didn't see Bree in Algebra, my afternoon felt empty.

"We had a family emergency," Bree says. "I was up most of the night."

"Everything okay?"

"Only a scare. Thank the goddess Lu..." She stops herself

mid-sentence. "Can I get your notes from class?"

Why didn't Bree text me? She didn't have to drive all the way over...oh, wait, she doesn't have my number does she?

"You didn't miss much. Mr. Strickland graded our tests."

"What did you get?"

"A ninety-six."

"Really? And you didn't study for the test at all?"

"Nope."

"I so hate you." But Bree grins when she says it.

"We did get some homework." I slip my backpack off and unzip it to pull out my notes.

"Hop in. I'll take you home."

Awesome. I go around the front of the car and jump in. Bree drives while I grab the piece of paper with the assignment written on it. I place it on her thigh. My fingers hover there a moment. Bree's hand comes off the steering wheel and bumps into mine. I flinch and take my hand away.

"Could you copy that for me?" she asks.

"You can have mine."

"Don't you need it?"

I tap my forehead. "It's all up here."

"You're impressive."

Bree stops the car in front of my house and we shoot each other glances. I don't want to get out. And she doesn't ask me to leave. So we sit there with the motor running. My notes clinging to her thigh. The thigh my fingers brushed against.

A new confidence nudges my voice. "Can I...have your phone number? In case you miss class again. That way you can text me instead of wasting gas."

Her hand touches my notes. "I don't have a phone. Can I give you my email? I check it every day."

Wow. She *wants* to give me her email?

I give Bree a pen. She finds an old gas receipt on the floor and writes down her email.

Moonluver@zmail.com

Bree hands me the slip of paper. "See you at school."

Oh. I have to get out of the car, I guess. I hesitate, then roll out of the car and take a few steps up my driveway. The car idles in the street. I twist and wave goodbye. Bree returns my wave. My warm chest turns hot. I want to jump on top of the car and beg her not to drive off because I don't want my afternoon to be normal.

What excuse do I use? We need milk. Maybe Bree could give me a ride to the store.

That's so lame. Think of something! Now! She's going to drive off any second, and this chance will be gone forever!

Why don't I just ask her? Come right out and tell her?

You did that with Pamela Osterhaus too, dumb-ass! Remember that disaster?

The black car rolls forward.

I run up to it, and the tires jerk to a stop. I grip the steel door and poke my head through the open window. "What are you doing right now?"

Bree pauses. "I don't know. Why?"

"Do you want to go hang out at the mall? Like wander around and contemplate the meaning of life?"

"Contemplate the meaning of life? Sounds important."

My stomach twists into a knot. Can't believe I'm doing this again. This girl will destroy me like Pamela did. I'm crazy for even trying this again.

Bree's fingers dance on the steering wheel, as she thinks. I went too far. She only wants to be friends, and I'm screwing that up by forcing her to go on a date.

"All right," she says.

Huh? Did she...? Amazing.

The upper and lower levels of the Wood Creek Mall spread out in two directions as skylights in the ceiling let in more natural sunlight. The place is open enough that you don't feel trapped or fenced-in like that Promontory Point Mall in midtown Tulsa.

I run my fingers along the cool, smooth, metal railing on the upper level as we drift inside a spacious department store with soothing guitar music playing from the speakers. We coast through all the different departments. Hardware.

Kitchenware. Appliances. Children's clothing. Bedding. Soon we pass a working display of a brand new GameMasterMax system with wireless controllers, body detection modules with emulators, and the game Go Kart Madness loaded up and begging for us to play it. This store has officially become kick-ass.

I pick up a controller. "Race me?"

Bree doesn't seem too sure about this. "How do these work?"

"The controller? It's easy." I pick up the wireless controller and gesture toward her hand. "Can I put this around your wrist?"

Bree offers her hand and I gently slip the holding strap over her wrist. My fingers stroke her soft skin which feels like thin cotton. I slip the controller into her hand and squeeze it closed. I guide Bree's hand, showing her how the car moves where her hand moves. I lightly squeeze her finger on the buttons, showing her how to operate the gas and brake. When Bree turns to ask a question, her hair brushes my cheek. I get a strong scent from her. It's not like a girlie smell. You know, perfume and hair spray? It's more like a hint of mint or honeysuckle. A scent you would get from outside.

I hope Bree keeps brushing against me like that.

We start a brand new game on Go Kart Madness. I pick a fat Grizzly Bear as my driver while Bree goes with a pink fox. 1...2...3...Go! Bree laughs as her kart spins out. I play Go Kart Madness at Issy's place all the time, so I'm super good at it. But I let Bree take the lead a couple times since she's still learning the game. Then she cheats! When I try passing her, Bree bumps me with her hip and I lose my concentration.

So I bump her back, and this makes her laugh.

Bree starts to get too cocky about her driving skills so I stop holding back and really smoke her tail in the next two races.

Bree holds her mouth wide-open in mock shock. "You were so hustling me."

"Hustling you?" I laugh. "What do you mean?"

"Holding back your skills to mess with me. I want your best game. Don't hold back."

I puff out my chest. "Are you sure? Think you can handle it?"

Bree's eyes narrow. "I can handle anything."

We start another game. This time Bree shoots her hand over my eyes, and I can't see anything. I try pulling down her arm...but it's like a piece of granite. I can't budge it. I try peeling back a finger, but even that finger is so damn strong. Bree giggles and removes her hand.

I bring my hand up to blind her and...

Ouch. She grabs my arm, holding it in mid-air.

"Oh no you don't." Bree grins.

I can't move my arm. I'm trying to and...damn.

"Do you lift weights?" I ask.

"No," Bree says.

"Why are you so strong? Does Superman know you swiped his vitamins?" I joke.

Bree releases my arm. Her cheerful face disappears. "I'm not that strong."

"Whatever. You're strong for a girl. Do you do a lot of weight training to get bulked up like that?"

Bree slips the controller off her wrist. "I'm tired of playing this." She walks off. Her pink fox crashes into a tree and dies.

She wanders into the cosmetics area with its six oval service counters. Their glass cases lit from the inside, making the yellow liquid inside the bottles shine like pieces of fine crystal. I follow Bree as she skims the displays, touching the polished wood slats that separate different brands of perfume. Guess I pissed her off with my comment.

"I should take you back home." Bree's attention lingers on the perfume, like even she doesn't want to follow her own suggestion.

"Okay. If you want to," I say.

Bree peels herself from the glass. "My parents will freak if I'm not home soon."

"Hi! Would you be interested in trying some samples?" a sales associate asks. Her store tag reads Holly. The woman gestures toward a nearby chair with a lighted mirror.

"Not really."

Bree giggles. "I think she's talking to me." She glances at the associate. "No, thanks."

"Please?" Holly asks. "It's been a slow day, and I'm bored. Besides, it'll make you feel good. Consider it a free makeover."

Bree hesitates. "I don't wear cosmetics."

"I noticed that. Why not? Your face has such great bone structure and nice symmetry." Holly glances at me. "Wouldn't she look fantastic?"

I shrug.

Like I know anything about makeup or bone structure, or symmetry...whatever that is.

Bree stares at herself in the mirror.

"I'll give you some extra samples to take home," Holly says.

"All right." Bree slips into the chair, and Holly cleans her face. The woman then applies something called a base. I scan the long line of makeup products Holly lines up for Bree to try. If I stay and watch this, I'll kill off every man cell inside my brain.

I leave Bree with Holly and wander over to the guy side of the service counter. I find some samples of men's cologne. I sniff one called Metro. Yuck. Too fruity for a dude. I spray another one called Right Hook. The scent makes my eyes water. Too strong. I recover a little before trying sample number three, Wild Forest. This one smells better. Very outdoorsy with hints of pine in it. I'd wear this one. Hmmm. Does Bree like guys with cologne? What the hell. I squirt a bunch of it around my neck and chest and on both arms. Next I walk around the store to waste more time.

After a few laps, I return to the perfume counter and...

Whoa.

"What is it?" Bree asks. Her mirror shows me frozen in place behind her. "Does it look that bad? It looks completely awful, doesn't it?"

Bree's face looks...amazing. Like a model. Her cheeks have

color. Her eyes are highlighted in light blue, and her lashes are full and dark. The combination makes her eyes pop. Her complexion is creamy smooth. Her deep-red lips look so kissable. Bree looks like a girl that men would fight wars over. I can't believe the change. This use to be Cave Girl?

Bree reads my face and gets it wrong. "Please take it all off."

"Are you certain? But...you look gorgeous." Holly acts shocked. "I would kill to have a face like yours. And your complexion is so clear. For a teen that's amazing."

"You look beautiful." The truth escapes my lips.

Bree's mouth twitches to the side. "Really, Aiden? You better not be lying."

"I'm not."

"I want it off," Bree says. "I can't go home like this."

"Only if you're absolutely positive," Holly says.

"Can I take a picture?" The question slips out, and I regret it immediately.

"Why?" Bree asks with suspicion.

Because you're so beautiful that I want to stare at that face for the rest of my life. I should say that, but I shrug instead.

"I agree. You should preserve this moment," Holly says. "Oh, and you should take it together. That would be fun. Let me see your phone."

Nice save, Holly.

I set up my phone to take a picture and hand it over to Holly. Bree hesitates, but when I stand close to her, she gives in to the idea and scoots closer. I try placing my arm around her waist, but I stop myself. I don't want to make Bree feel weird about this. But she squeezes her body against mine without hesitation, causing electricity to sizzle up and down my skin. I try to act normal as I put my arm around her waist. I resist the urge to pull her closer.

"Smile," Holly says.

I'm already there.

Thirty minutes later we're back at my house. The black car idles near the curb. I know Bree has to go home and I should let her...but I don't want to.

So we sit.

The motor hums.

I imagine my hand coming up and touching her face. My fingers running through her soft hair.

Bree twists the steering wheel. "I better get home."

"Yeah, okay." It's hard but I push myself out of the car and close the door.

Bree's gaze lingers on me a moment. Then she puts the car in gear and moves up the street. And just like that...she's gone.

I stomp across the tall grass. I need to cut it before Dad gets on my case. I hope he's not pissed at me for calling his boss. That thought makes my feet hesitate on the porch. Will Dad give me a lecture? Or will he give me something worse?

Way to ruin the best afternoon of your life, loser.

My ears pick up the far-off sound of screeching brakes. Then...I hear the Oldsmobile's distinct engine racing while its tires squeal under protest. The V-8 grows louder and louder. Is Bree coming back?

My heart beats faster. It's hungry for her.

I move across our front lawn again. The tall blades of grass brush against my jeans.

The black car rounds a corner and slides to a stop, leaving puffs of burnt rubber in the air. Bree steps out of the car and stands there. Motionless. Like when I did that staring contest at lunch with her. Did Bree forget something? Did I do something to piss her off again?

I open my mouth to ask.

But in a blink of an eye she lingers next to me. Her breath stroking my face. Her lips hesitate over mine. I breathe her in and can smell honeysuckle. Not mint at all. It's definitely honeysuckle.

Why did Bree come back? Does she want me to kiss her?

Well, if that's what the girl wants.

Before I can even lean forward...Bree hugs me, resting her chin on my shoulder. Her body tightens around me like a soft comforter. The girl's hug is so strong there's no way I could break out of it.

Bree releases me. Her eyes are so warm and soft. The girl smiles and skips back to her car without a word. The engine fires up, and she races back down the street. The noise of the engine fades.

My heart pounds in my chest like a mallet. It's so intense that I have to sit down on the driveway to chill.

CHAPTER TEN

AIDEN

Excited, Issy rushes up the stairs and bumps into kids as he moves down the middle of the aisle. My wingman drops next to me, and the bus moans forward with the sulfur-egg scent of diesel.

"Do you know what my dad told me this morning?" Issy asks.

Huh? Damn. It's like what...eight in the morning? My sleepy brain doesn't even want to consider questions at this time. I grunt a reply.

"He's taking me this weekend to pick out a car."

"Oh."

"Oh? That's all you can say? 'Oh.' I'm getting a car? Our days of traveling in this yellow motorized box are numbered."

"That's awesome news. It really is."

Issy sags. "Guess you don't need a ride from your wingman since you already have a girlfriend for a chauffeur."

I wipe my face. "Bree's not my girlfriend. I think we need to go on a real date to make that sentence true."

"So ask her."

I hesitate. "For a real date?"

"Absolutely."

"Do you think this weekend's too soon?" I ask.

"Hell no, you have to seize the day. Go all-in. Play for all the marbles. Go with the flow. Take the hill. Shoot all your bullets...I've run out of clichés. But you know what I'm saying."

The engine coughs and wheezes like an old man. Our bus needs to be retired. It's going to fall apart one day, and I hope I'm not on it when it does.

"Thinking about taking her out to dinner and maybe a movie or...?"

"Dinner and something else," Issy says. "Everyone does a movie. You need to do something different. Unexpected. Something that'll surprise Bree and show her how awesome you are."

"I could take her to the zoo."

Issy tilts his head to the side. "The zoo?"

"Yeah, they have HalloZoowen all this week. At night, they put up cool lights all over the place, and people dress up in Halloween costumes. My parents took me to one when I was little, and it was fun. That'll be something different."

"Girls like plays and musicals, crap like that," Issy says. "When I think different, I don't think zoo."

"But it would be dark, and we would be alone."

Issy perks up. "I like where this is going. It's dark outside and maybe scary. Hold on...when a girl gets scared they want you to hold on to them. Yes! I'm liking this zoo idea now."

"Yeah?"

"Scary Halloween stuff. A dark night. She'll be holding on to you. This is good. This is very good. Oh, you know what you should do? Make the zoo a surprise. Ask her out to dinner and tell her the next part of the date is a surprise, somewhere special. Girls eat that up. When are you asking her?"

"At lunch. We're studying for an algebra quiz," I say.

"Fantastic. Think of it. This weekend I will have my first car and you will have your first girlfriend." Issy waits for a fist-bump.

I thump it. This will be an amazing weekend.

Off campus for lunch, Bree and I get lucky and nab a corner table at the tiny fast-food beef place that's shoved into a large strip mall near school. Bree pays for a triple roast beef sandwich combo and gives me her deliciously-greasy fries. That way I can buy a three-dollar sandwich and a courtesy water to create the poor student combo.

We crack open the algebra books, and go over some problems that might be on the quiz today. We sit close together. Every breath tastes like honeysuckle and reminds me how close she is. We finish our cram session as lunch time disappears, along with my chance to ask Bree out. I take in a deep breath...

"So...what are you doing this weekend?"

Bree finishes her sandwich. "My parents want to go camping."

Damn. That means she's busy. No, wait. Better make sure.

"And you're going with them?" I ask.

"Oh yeah, it's so fun." Bree lights up. "The nights are super beautiful. Sleeping under the stars and the moon. It's the best thing in the world. You feel so alive."

Guess this date isn't happening. I slurp up the last of my grape soda to sooth my rejection.

Bree studies my face. "But I don't have to go. Why?"

"Oh...um...I wanted to...ask you out. Like, on a date?"

Bree tenses up like a skeleton. She only wants to be friends. I knew it. Damn, I knew it. I'm done. Steak-so-burnt-you-feed-it-to-your-dog done. She's about to freak out.

"Don't worry about it. Forget I said anything." I glance at the door with the red EXIT sign glowing above it.

"Aiden, don't apologize." Bree softens. "I'm flattered."

"But you only want to be friends." The oldest rejection said to losers like me for centuries.

"It's not like that at all." Bree hesitates. "You'll have to meet my parents first before you can ask me out. They have to give their permission." Bree closes her eyes and sighs. "My dad is super strict about who I can hang with. In fact, I shouldn't have gone to the mall with you the other day. And I shouldn't be giving you rides home." Bree sighs again. "Piss on the sun."

Piss on the what?

"I'll have to tell Dad about you," Bree says.

"How super strict is he? Your dad isn't, like, serial-killer violent, is he?"

Bree hesitates.

What? Does that mean yes?

"When I drove you home that first day, I should have told my dad. That's my bad." Bree leans back and runs her fingers through her hair. "Which means I should tell my parents about you. I need to call Mom first. She'll be receptive and help me out with Dad. Does five o'clock work for you?"

"What happens at five o'clock?" I ask.

"I'll pick you up then so you can have dinner with me and my parents tonight."

CHAPTER ELEVEN

AIDEN

Bree maneuvers her big car into a brand-new housing addition that's been freshly cut from the forest. Some of the completed wannabe-mansions stand against the falling sun. Wooden skeletons of other houses under construction fill up more of the lots. Mercedes are parked on some of the new driveways. I'm right. Bree's family must shower themselves in hundred dollar bills.

Bree parks in the driveway of an expensive two-story house with a large flower bed that has zero flowers. She flashes a reassuring smile, but her face says the opposite. Bree's nervous about this dinner, too. I follow her to a gold, stained-glass door that opens into this huge entryway. A flight of walnut-colored stairs leads up to the second floor. A circular, crystal light hangs next to a large skylight at the top of the ceiling.

A woman enters. Her sandals clip-clop across the polished-wood floor. Her hair is long and dark like Bree's. The woman smiles. "Welcome, Abe."

Bree raises her eyebrows. "It's Aiden, Mom."

"Oh, my apologies, Aiden. Would you like something to drink?"

"No, I'm good."

Mrs. Mayflower escorts us to the kitchen, where there's no dinner table, only a big center island with four empty plates.

A strong scent of broiled steak flavors the air and makes me hungry. The kitchen itself opens up into a cavernous living room with both sections making up one huge room. The big windows in the living room show the large forest surrounding the Mayflowers' small backyard.

Bree shows me the couch and switches on the satellite television. She excuses herself to help her mom in the kitchen. I flip through channels and end up watching this show about prisons in Russia.

I catch some movement in the backyard.

What is that? It intrigues me enough to stand up and look through the glass window. I see a large man in a business suit standing on the porch. His chest is wide and thick like the front of a semi. A beard covers the man's face, but I can see his eyes as they glare in my direction.

Is he a burglar?

Before I can act, the massive intruder opens the back door and rushes inside. "Who are you? Why are you in my house?"

I jump over the couch, stumble over a table, and almost take out a lamp, before grabbing the light shade and setting it back up.

"Daddy, no!" Bree races into the living room like a blur and stops the man in his tracks. "This is Aiden. I invited him for dinner."

The man looks me over. "Invited who for dinner?"

"His name is Aiden, and he goes to school with your daughter. Isn't that nice, dear?" Mrs. Mayflower appears and kisses her husband's cheek before shooting him a look that says something, but I have no clue what.

Mr. Mayflower sighs. "What a relief. I thought that..." The large man stops himself and loosens the tie on his suit. "Someone want to explain what's going on here?"

Bree and her mom exchange looks. Mom nods and guides Mr. Mayflower into another part of the house.

I start breathing again. That was intense.

Bree flashes this embarrassed smile. "That's my, dad."

The Mayflowers gather around the kitchen island. Mrs.

Mayflower takes out three steaks, their sides blood-red with a thin brown crust on the top and bottom. Doesn't that need more time in the oven? Guess Mrs. Mayflower isn't much of a cook. She gives the undercooked steaks to her family and then moves to a second oven, where she takes out a fourth steak. This one looks medium-rare, which is still too raw for me.

She places the steak on my plate. "Please let me know if that's cooked enough for you."

I take a knife and saw into the steak. It drips blood. Yuck.

"Um...maybe a few more minutes if that's okay."

Her mom smiles and removes the steak.

"Meat loses its taste the more it's cooked," Mr. Mayflower says.

I give him a polite smile. "I can't eat steak if it looks too raw. Grosses me out."

Mr. Mayflower shoots a quick look to his daughter. Her mouth twitches to the side. What was that about? Sorry if I don't want to risk food poisoning.

A few minutes later, Bree's mom pulls out the steak. It's still pink, but I don't want to hold up dinner so I thank her. "Do you have any steak sauce?"

"Steak sauce?" Mr. Mayflower asks, treating my question like it was a stupid thing to say.

"We're out," Bree says. "Sorry."

"I almost forgot." Mrs. Mayflower opens the microwave and takes out a clear-plastic tub of mac and cheese from a grocery store deli. She sinks a big spoon in the cheesy goo and places it in the middle of the island. "To go with our steak. Help yourself, Aiden."

I spoon out a big helping of mac and cheese and pass it to Mr. Mayflower, who doesn't even look at it before passing it over to his wife. Mrs. Mayflower smiles and moves it over to her daughter. Bree glances at my plate, then spoons out a small portion before sliding it back to me.

The steak tastes delicious. The mac and cheese goes great with it, too.

Bree nibbles on her mac and cheese and makes a face, but

when the girl sees me watching, she throws up a fake smile.

As Bree eats the steak, her white dinner plate fills with red juice, reminding me of blood. My stomach turns queasy, so I make myself look away.

Mr. Mayflower gnaws on his steak using his fingers while red juice drips all over the place. Wow. That's disgusting. And he grunts like a bear eating something it killed. Like father, like daughter.

Mrs. Mayflower clears her throat loudly.

Her husband stops eating, glances at me, then rests his meat back on the plate. The man cleans his hands and picks up the knife and fork.

Amazing. This meal feels like one of those old black-and-white *Twilight Zone* episodes my granddad loved to watch. He got me hooked on their bizarre stories that messed with your head, but in this amazing way.

After dinner, Mrs. Mayflower makes coffee using some high-tech gourmet coffee brewer that does individual cups. I'm enjoying my double-chocolate cappuccino when Bree puts me on the spot.

"Mom? Dad? Aiden has something he wants to ask you." She tosses me a grin.

I do?

Oh, yeah. Dinner had me so occupied, I completely forgot.

I put my elbows on top of the dark slate counter, trying to make myself appear mature and serious. "Mr. and Mrs. Mayflower? I would like to ask your permission...um...to take your daughter out this Saturday."

Mr. Mayflower gets quiet. His stare hardens.

"To study algebra?" Mrs. Mayflower asks.

"No, I want to take Bree out to dinner and maybe to a museum or maybe to a bowling alley. I don't know yet." I catch Bree's eyes. "But I promise it'll be something fun."

Bree's cute face fills with hope.

"A date?" Her father does not sound happy. "That's out of the question."

"I agree," Mrs. Mayflower says in a nicer tone. "Bree is only sixteen. She's not ready to date boys yet."

Bree's hope wilts along with her body. I wait for her to get mad and yell at her parents. But their daughter doesn't argue. Doesn't give them even a dirty look. That disappointment on her face kills me. Wow. Maybe she did want to go out with me.

"Um...I promise to take excellent care of your daughter," I say. "My hands will not touch your daughter's flesh." Did I say that? Oh my God. Sounds like I promised not to rape their daughter. I suck at talking. "What I meant to say is...I will respect Bree at all times, and you don't have to worry—"

"Not the point," Mr. Mayflower interrupts. "Point is, we think Bree is too young to date. Not too crazy about my daughter having a friend either."

Bree frowns.

"It's not you, Aiden. It's us," Mrs Mayflower says. "I agree with my husband. Bree is far too young. However, I think it would be fine if you still wanted to be friends." The woman checks for her husband's reaction.

The large man huffs, and shakes his head.

A tear slides down Bree's face. Why is she crying?

"Can you at least allow your daughter to have one friend?" Mrs. Mayflower whispers to her husband.

Mr. Mayflower crosses his arms and stands his ground like a marble slab, but he notes the tear on his daughter's cheek. This causes the man's rigid body to melt. His arms fall to the sides. "Damn it. You can have one friend. But he's it."

Bree wipes the tear away and smiles.

"But no dating."

So that's it? No dating? I find this awesome girl who's hot and beautiful and wants to hang out with me, but now her parents won't let us go out? Screw that. I want to go out with this girl.

"You could come with us on the date," I say. "Both of you could act as chaperons if you want."

"You want us to come with you?" Mrs. Mayflower asks.

"I'm taking Bree out one way or the other. The particulars don't matter to me just as long as I get to spend time with your daughter."

I'm pushing the envelope by saying that. It might piss them off, plus it scares me that I'm laying it all out again for a girl. This backfired with Pamela.

Bree's eyes sparkle. She must have liked what I said.

Mr. Mayflower twists his mouth to the side, like his daughter. "You challenging my decision, young man?"

Maybe? The coward in me gets ready to jump over the couch if Bree's dad decides to chase me again.

Mrs. Mayflower clears her throat. "Our daughter knows how important it is to behave herself in public, and so far she's done an outstanding job. Hasn't she, dear?"

"Yes."

"And we can't expect to keep Bree in the house like she was a prisoner."

A prisoner? They must be strict parents. I mean, giving her permission to have a friend? That's messed up. I can't believe a girl like Bree would put up with that.

"Daddy, I promise to be super careful."

Mr. Mayflower's eyes linger on his daughter, his mind still turning, his mouth still cracked in a frown.

"It's just one date," Mrs. Mayflower says.

"Dangerous out there. She's safer here."

What are they worried about? What danger is out there?

"And yet we let Bree go to school every day without hesitation. Why? Because we agreed it was good for her to be around other kids."

Amazing. Did they, like, home school Bree? Why don't they want her around other kids?

Mr. Mayflower squeezes Bree's hand. "You must be vigilant and be aware of your feelings at all times. If you feel like..." Mr. Mayflower glances at me, then whispers something to Bree, who nods a few times.

"I will, Daddy. Absolutely."

He kisses Bree on the forehead, then shifts his attention to me. "Three-hour date. I will be timing you. Bring her back on time or you will see my wrath, young man. Believe me."

My stomach drops to the carpet. I believe him.

CHAPTER TWELVE

AIDEN

My stomach does cartwheels as I shower. The cool water attacks my skin, my face, my chest, my legs. And I scrub everything that's attached. My good hygiene efforts do nothing to calm the nerves dancing inside. I don't know why I'm this nervous. I hung out with Bree at the mall and that wasn't weird or awkward. We felt comfortable together. But this is an official date. An official statement that we're heading to a new level.

This'll be my first date with a girl. I know. I suck. I'm still trying to figure out how this works.

Will Bree let me kiss her? Does the girl ask first? Does she give you a sign that says, "Hey, dude, please suck my face off?"

Bree will expect me to kiss her, right? But how do I know when? It's not like reading a girl's mind is simple.

Hope she kisses me first. That way, I'll know.

I dry myself off and put on some nice clothes, not all dressed-up crap but still nice, and wait in the living room for Bree.

"Going somewhere important? You're all dressed up for it," Dad says, trying to be funny.

"I have a date," I say.

Dad's eyebrows lift up in surprise as he plops down on the sofa. I can still smell the wheel grease staining his fingers even after he washed them. "What's her name?"

"Bree."

Dad points the remote. The television comes to life. The dishwasher runs through the next part of its wash cycle.

On television, the second baseman throws a man out at first. The crowd goes wild inside the ballpark.

"When does this adventure start?" Dad asks.

"About an hour. She's picking me up."

Dad shifts his body. "The girl is picking you up?"

I nod.

"Son, men don't let women drive on dates. You're her escort. You must show your woman right off the bat that you can take good care of her."

Real men, Dad...don't vomit on themselves after drinking enough beer to supply Oktoberfest. Wish I had the guts to say that.

"Well, this young man doesn't have a car to pick her up in," I say instead.

Dad absorbs my answer as the next batter strikes out on television. Then he digs into his pocket, bringing out the keys to the truck. "Go to her house, and pick her up early. She'll appreciate the gesture." Dad throws me the keys, and I miss the catch, but they drop in my lap.

Why is Dad all of a sudden being so generous?

"Um...but I need you to come with me, don't I? I only have my learner's permit."

Dad chuckles. "You drive better than I do. Just take it slow, and don't get caught."

The sun sets over the horizon as I guide the Dodge Ram pickup down the same route I remember from my dinner with Bree's parents. I park the truck beside the curbside brick mailbox and hike up Bree's driveway, passing by the black Oldsmobile. The front door of the house opens, and Bree steps outside.

Amazing.

She's wearing a sleeveless cotton dress that stops a few

inches short of her bare knees. Bree's stylized hair twists down over her shoulders with curls, like she had it done at a salon. Her dress hugs a lean and firm body that looks like it belongs to an Olympic athlete. Her toned muscles blend wonderfully with her feminine curves. Bree did a wonderful job mimicking Holly's makeup work. Bree's face looks stunning. Just like it did in Holly's mirror. I can't believe this beautiful creature wants to go out with me.

"I'm super confused," Bree says. "I thought I was picking you up?"

"I'd like to drive for once. If that's cool."

A smile parts those beautiful red lips. "All right." Bree waves to her mom and dad, who spy on us from the big front window. Mr. Mayflower holds up three fingers. A reminder. Three hours I have with Bree and no more.

Thanks. Like I need more pressure tonight.

The brick walls inside the big Italian restaurant amplify all the background noise by a factor of ten. I do my best to concentrate on Bree, who raises her voice to tell me what music she likes.

Our conversation then dies.

I smile.

Bree smiles.

I don't know what else to talk about. The restaurant? The tablecloth? Ask Bree if she can speak Italian?

That's stupid. Don't ask her that.

My ankle itches so I bend down and scratch it. At this new angle, I can see a small, crescent moon tat on top of Bree's foot. Never noticed that before.

She flexes her ankle. "Do you like it?"

"Yeah, I do. Why the moon?"

"Because the moon is magical. It gives light to the darkness," Bree says. "Can't you feel its energy in the air when there's a full moon? The night becomes so alive. So vibrant. You can always feel it." She pauses. "I find it super hard to sleep during a full moon. How can you sleep with all that energy seething through your body? Sometimes you have no choice but to run through the woods."

Wait. Is Bree telling me that she runs around in the woods in the middle of the night? That's so Cave Girl weird.

"Do you do that?" I ask.

"Do I do what?"

"Run around in the forest in the middle of the night?"

The hint of surprise on her face gets covered up quickly. "I didn't say that. No, I'm saying that I *understand* why some people do. The hospital emergency rooms have busy nights on a full moon because people run around in the middle of the night and bump into things. That's what I meant. I wasn't talking about me at all."

"Okay, cool."

"I'm super serious. I just like the moon. That's all." A weird nervousness comes over Bree that I haven't seen before.

"So you're only a moon enthusiast and that's all."

"Yes." She giggles. "A moon enthusiast. I like that." Bree gulps down some water from her glass.

"There's a lot of suicides during a full moon." The words roll off my tongue, and I instantly tense up the moment my brain catches it. Suicides? Why did I bring that up? Like that doesn't make me sound depressing to be around.

The table falls silent.

My stomach burns. I've destroyed this date. Blew it up in my own face. Why do I keep saying stupid things? I should have printed a list of awesome one-liners I could say and slip those into my pocket because I suck at improv.

Bree's eyes search mine. "Even the moon can't cure everyone's darkness."

Why is she looking at me like that? Does she suspect that I tried to...no way. How could Bree possibly know that?

"I don't believe in all that witches and wizards stuff. I think it's a bunch of old superstitious crap made up by people to scare other people. And to sell them Halloween junk at grocery stores."

Bree sips more water. "You don't believe myths could be based on the truth?"

"Nope. I don't believe in Bigfoot either."

Our waiter comes over. I order fettuccine Alfredo and salad.

Bree takes more time, scanning the menu as her mouth twitches to the side. "I'll take the veal Parmesan."

"Our chef's signature dish. Excellent choice," the waiter says.

"But I want it without the sauce and cheese on top."

"Breaded veal without the Parmesan?"

"Yes, and what side dish comes with that?"

"A side order of pasta marinara with our vegetable of the day."

Bree's eyes wince. "I want meatballs instead."

"Side order of spaghetti and meatballs? We can do that." The waiter writes it down.

"No pasta. Only the meatballs. And can you leave off the veggies and just add more meatballs?"

The waiter shoots me an unhappy look. I pretend to look out the window. The man rips off an order slip, crumples it up, and starts again. "I have a breaded veal without sauce or cheese with a double order of meatballs. What dressing would you like on your salad?"

Bree bites her lip. "No dressing, but can you put an obscene amount of bacon bits on it?"

"Bacon bits instead of dressing?" The waiter looks at Bree like she's gone insane.

"An obscene amount. Yes."

"I'll put your order in right away," he says with a slight hint of mockery in his voice as he takes away our menus and leaves.

Bree leans forward. "What's the plan for after dinner? You said something about a surprise?"

CHAPTER THIRTEEN

AIDEN

Bree bombards me with questions about our destination. I play cool and tell her to be patient. I guide the truck on to the highway that curves around the northeast part of the city, take the first exit after the airport, and roll it past the entrance of Mohawk Park.

Bree's nostrils flare. "Are we going to a zoo?" Her nervousness at dinner comes back. "Isn't the zoo closed at night?"

"Not for HallowZooeen," I say, trying to make it sound as awesome as I can.

Under the lights, the parking lot overflows with cars as I circle and manage to find a spot. I shut off the engine and climb out of the truck. But when I open her door, Bree doesn't move. I must have totally blown her away with this zoo idea. That's a good thing because girls love surprises. Bree faces the direction of the zoo, her nose twitching and flexing.

"Something wrong?" I ask.

"I've never been to a zoo."

"Seriously? Like your parents never took you?"

Bree shakes her head.

"You'll love it. With all the lights at night, it should be amazing." I do the gentlemanly thing and offer her my hand.

Bree hesitates again. Does she hate my idea? I thought

she'd like the zoo at night. It's something different. Something outside the box. She must think it's the dumbest idea ever. But before I go into full-panic mode, Bree accepts my hand and steps down. She lightly cups her hand around mine, flashes me a nervous smile, and we head for the main entrance.

Pockets of orange and white light punch through the darkness, revealing the animal exhibits and most of the walkways in the large zoo. Families, as well as the staff, are dressed up in all kinds of costumes. There's, like, pirates, wizards, cowboys, werewolves, fairies, super heroes, ballerinas, and vampires moving around the zoo. Lions roar in the darkness. Elephants call out for attention. Animal sounds of all types echo over the night air. When the sun goes down, this sanitized kiddie zoo in the daytime takes on a more ominous vibe.

This is awesome. Bree should have a strong urge to cling to my arm, and since I'm her escort, I must hold her tight so she feels safe and warm, her body leaning against mine all night long. What a brilliant idea this was!

A tiger roars as we walk along the concrete path.

"Spooky hearing that at night," I say, trying to set up the right mood for some body-warming action. "It's like being alone in the jungle with all the animals watching you."

Bree squeezes my arm. "I wouldn't let anything happen to you."

"What are you going to do against a charging tiger? Throw your shoe at him?"

"Only to distract him."

Bree's funny. I'd love to see this small girl confront a tiger.

"And then what? Run away screaming?"

"Me or the tiger?" Bree asks.

We step inside the primate building, which smells musty-old. It consists of a simple but long hallway that has windows to the cages on both sides. Kind of plain and boring. Ten monkeys fling themselves across wood beams placed inside their cages. They swing from place to place with such ease. I think it's fun to watch them mess around, doing what monkeys do. A few toss fresh poop at each other, and Bree laughs. The way her cheeks lift when she smiles is kinda cute.

Three of the monkeys wander up to the glass close to Bree and stare at her with this intense curiosity.

Bree moves further down the large glass.

The three monkeys follow her. They're mesmerized by Bree.

That's weird.

Bree moves way over to the other side.

The three monkeys follow her there.

I see another exhibit on the other side of the hallway so I guide Bree over to it.

I throw a quick look over my shoulder...

Now all ten monkeys are staring at us.

They're absolutely still.

Absolutely quiet.

Absolutely creepy.

Next is an indoor replica of a rain forest with real plants, real humidity, and real animals who live there, minus the dangerous ones. Bree and I move through it and see creatures squirming all around us. This is so much cooler than watching them inside cages. Bree's nostrils flare as she slows way down, almost to a stop. Her body tightens up. Those firm muscles underneath her dress flex, as if they're moving under her skin.

No. It must be the strange tropical lighting they use inside here.

"It feels real, doesn't it?" I ask. "Like you're in a real rain forest."

Bree heads for the exit without answering me.

The elephants wander through their enclosure as we reach their wooden observation deck. When the male elephant sees us, the huge animal stops abruptly. It backs away and rotates completely around, choosing to stay on the opposite side of the enclosure. Do I smell bad or something?

"That elephant's huge," I say.

"The lions have their work cut out for them," Bree says.

"Yeah, they hunt elephants, don't they?"

"The lions attack them like a team. Like a pack."

The lights around this exhibit give Bree this soft orange glow that I wish I could pull out my phone and take a picture of. But I don't want to break this excellent mood.

"Are you having a good time?"

Bree moves closer and smiles. "Yes, I am."

I lean against the wood rail. Bree touches my back, and her fingers slide down my spine. Only a thin layer of cotton separates her fingers from my skin. Wow. That feels so amazing.

Bree leans against my back, holding on to my waist as if I was the boy she dreams about. The heat from her body toasts my back and neck. She feels so warm. So soft. So comfortable. Her hair brushes against my neck, and I smell the honeysuckle again.

I close my eyes.

Enjoying the moment.

Wanting it to linger...

Forever.

The small, motorized zoo train whistles as it pulls us along in the last car. Two young girls hold on to each other and laugh in the seats ahead of us. Bree's curly hair flips around in the wind. Her nostrils flex in and out. Her hands rest on her lap. I follow my urge and place my hand over them. To my surprise, Bree opens her hand and accepts them with a squeeze. The glow from the giraffe exhibit snags my attention as the train passes by it.

Something touches the side of my neck. It's Bree. She nuzzles me like a friendly dog. My neck tingles when she touches it. Damn. This is so cool. The best night of my life.

I feel something sharp against my neck. A bite?

It's more like a nip than a bite, pulling my skin rather than cutting. Bree releases my neck and licks my ear. Wow. My body revs up like a Ferrari burning at 7,000 RPM. If I don't release all this pressure, my engine will blow and I will embarrass myself all over these new pants.

To my relief, the little train slows down for our stop. I lead Bree through the turnstile and follow the signs pointing to some bathrooms located near the wolf exhibit. I excuse myself and hop into a stall inside the men's room while Bree waits. I splash freezing water across my face, rubbing it all over my skin. I repeat this several times to calm myself down. Soon my Ferrari drifts back down to idle. After about ten minutes, I feel confident enough to button up my shirt and head back outside.

Only to find out that my date is gone.

I search the area around the bathrooms and don't find Bree. She might be in the ladies' room so I wait for her to come out. A long howl echoes across the zoo, drawing my eyes to a sign-post. That howl came from the nearby wolf exhibit. Maybe Bree wandered over there. I walk down the tree-lined sidewalk that flows into an open, grassy area. I now have a perfect view of the wolf habitat, which is all lit up for HallowZooeen. I recognize the two girls who were on the kiddie train with us. They point at something on the other side of the habitat. I follow their eyes and see five wolves. Two of them black. Two of them snow white. And the last one has dark fur with a red tint to it.

All five wolves concentrate on Bree.

She watches them from the sidewalk opposite the habitat. Something about her fascinates the wolves because I can see the top of their fur twitching. Like they're excited. One black wolf howls into the dark sky with this strange, wild shrill that crawls up my spine. The other wolves start whimpering and whining. They pace back and forth with this nervous energy. Whatever it is, they can barely control themselves. Why are they acting like that?

I step closer to the habitat and another wild shrill hurts my ears.

That shrill came from Bree.

What?

Bree opens her mouth and another strong howl roars from deep inside her. She mimics the wolves' cries with perfection. Seriously? This is not happening. That waiter must have been pissed and slipped a drug into my fettuccine because those sounds can not be coming from my date.

The two little girls giggle. They think Bree is hilarious. I think my date needs mental help. Cave Girl is seriously crazy.

The wolves hug the ground with their ears down, tails glued to their stomachs, and snouts lowered. The dark-red wolf rolls on its back, exposing his chest and groin towards Bree. The other four wolves flop on their backs too.

What the hell is going on?

I jog towards Bree. She sniffs the air, and her head snaps in my direction with a look of total panic on her face. Are the wolves scaring her?

"What are you doing?" I ask.

Bree's eyes dance around like she's losing her mind. "I...I was playing around." She steps away from the habitat. "I'm ready to go now if you are." Bree snatches my arm and almost pulls it off my body. Her grip is like a vise.

"That hurts."

Bree releases my arm. "I'm sorry. I don't want to get in trouble."

The dark-red wolf rolls to its feet and trots deep inside the exhibit. The animal returns with a piece of raw meat in its teeth with blood dripping from it.

"Please, Aiden. We have to go now." Bree sounds desperate.

The wolf carries the meat up to the edge of the drop-off that separates the habitat from the public fencing. Bree follows my gaze and looks over her shoulder. On cue, the wolf drops the meat to the ground and whimpers at Bree, treating her like...she's one of them.

Damn. A new possibility slams me in the gut.

But that possibility is impossible.

That's crazy. Something a nut would believe. I don't believe in that stuff. Myths are not real. I don't live in Tolkien's Middle Earth or in a galaxy far, far away. I live in Oklahoma. We're lucky to get a Star Trek convention every year.

But the side of my brain that churns out answers to math

problems analyzes the evidence.

Bree's all-meat diet. Those animal-quick reflexes of hers. The way she uses her nose to detect things. That bite on my neck and the way she nuzzled me. The way she howled at the wolves and got a free dinner out of it. There's always been something weird about Bree, and now it all fits. The girl I've fallen in love with is a...

No, I still don't believe this. Mythical creatures don't sit in front of me in Algebra. They don't pick up guys walking in the rain. And they don't drive an Oldsmobile.

Or maybe they do.

Bree reads my face like a web page. "What is it?"

It's fear, and I swallow as much of it down as I can.

"You're right," I manage to say. "It's time to leave."

I concentrate on driving the truck along the dark road. My stomach fills with acid. I'm sitting inches away from a...I can't even think the word. I have to somehow keep it together for a while longer. At least until I can figure out what the hell to do.

"Really? Are you not going to tell me?" Bree's mounting frustration doesn't calm me down. She must smell the stench of fear I'm giving off. I'll have to do the best I can.

"Tell you what?" I try to sound casual, but I suck at it.

"Whatever it is that's making you sweat."

"I'm not sweating."

Bree wipes my forehead, and shows her shiny hand. "What are you stressing about?"

I don't answer.

"Aiden?"

I watch the road.

Her hand touches my leg, and I feel it twitch.

"Tell me. What is it?" Bree asks. "Is it about the wolves?"

"I don't want to know."

"You don't want to know, what?"

"I'm not sure."

"So you're not sure about something that you don't want to know about?"

"I'm...confused right now."

"Can I help with that?" she asks.

The traffic light ahead turns red, so I stop the truck. Now I don't have a reason to look away. I peek over at Bree. Her mouth twitches to the side as her eyes continue to try to get through my wall.

"Can I just take you home and we can talk about it later?" I ask, but my voice sounds more like I'm begging.

"No," Bree says.

I stare at the glowing dashboard. "How do I ask this?"

Her voice softens. "Easy. Just ask."

"You'll think I'm crazy. I think I'm crazy." I notice my hand twisting on the steering wheel, like Bree's hand did when she picked me up that rainy afternoon. I can't look her in the eyes. My stomach burns so bad the acid must be eating through the lining. A part of me doesn't want to hear the answer to this question, but it's too late to stop.

"Are you some kind of animal?" I throw it out there quickly, getting it over with.

Silence.

"Yes," Bree says.

I search her face for any sign of joking or sarcasm, any sign that this was one huge joke on me, but there's none.

My brain goes numb.

"The light's green," she says.

I stick my eyes on the road and drive across the intersection.

"There's a park up ahead. Make a right," Bree says. "We need to have a talk."

Is Bree planning to kill me now? Is that nip she gave me on the train going to be a full bite that rips my neck and throat out? Letting me bleed to death in some city park to be discovered by some hipster out on his morning jog? I think the stomach acid has seeped into my vital organs now.

I maneuver the truck into the parking lot and switch off the engine. One single street lamp casts a weak, hollow glow inside the cab. A dark shadow covers Bree's face, disguising that cute girl at the restaurant. The silence inside the truck is the loudest I've ever heard.

We sit there for a moment.

Or two.

"Up for a walk?" Bree opens her door and steps out.

I close my eyes. I have this awful feeling that I know something that I shouldn't know about. Something dangerous. Something that will reveal its scary self and rip my body apart like Christmas wrapping paper. My door pops open without me touching it.

"Come. Walk with me." Bree offers her hand.

I hesitate.

"I won't hurt you," she whispers.

My shaky hand grasps hers, and I climb out of the truck.

Then Bree leads me into a dark grove of trees.

CHAPTER FOURTEEN

AIDEN

What is Bree up to? I'm still nervous because I don't know what in the hell is about to happen. But I have to make sure I don't freak out when she shows me...whatever it is she wants to show me. Bree has gone crazy. That would answer a lot of things. My early idea that she's a wolf is too insane. It's obvious that Bree thinks she's some kind of animal, but that must be a sign of mental illness. Okay. If I want to be her real friend, I should tell someone that my new girlfriend needs to see a psychiatrist.

Bree guides me through the grove of trees and down this path that twists inside the park. We pass two empty basketball courts shining from a quad of lights above. We pass a playground full of swings and slides.

Bree squeezes my hand and gives me a reassuring smile. Okay. I need to act confident and support my girlfriend. I won't laugh at her or make fun of her. I'll keep telling myself that she's a girl who needs help and I want to help her. So in response to Bree's smile, I squeeze her hand.

The girl's face lights up, and she pulls me along as our stroll turns into a run.

I'm panting when we reach a lighted picnic area with four metal tables and a public grill with pieces of used charcoal caked inside. This area of the park is pitch-black, making the lighted picnic area stand out like an island in a sea of dark.

Bree releases my hand, leaps up on a table like a gymnast, and then swivels around to face me. All with perfect balance and grace. "Grab a seat."

I hesitate.

Bree jumps off the table and holds my hands. "Don't freak out. No matter what happens, always remember...I will never hurt you, Aiden. I so promise that."

No matter what happens? But what is going to happen? And why do I have to worry about getting hurt?

Those words don't help.

"Everything will be fine," Bree purrs, her voice soothing. "Now grab a seat."

I sit and place my hands across the cold, iron top of the picnic table so I can steady them.

Bree hops up on another table and hesitates. "Could you like, turn around?"

I spin myself around and face the darkness surrounding us. I hear a zipper going down. Is she taking off her dress? I peek over my shoulder just as Bree steps out of her dress. She wears only a pink bra and panties. Amazing. This night has officially become the best of my life. Bree stands there a moment, hesitating. Her lines are so soft and curvy. I can see all her muscles clearly now. Bree is so gorgeous.

"Hey!" she yells. "No peeking."

I watch the darkness again. "I thought I heard you call my name."

"Yeah, right."

I hear more clothes sliding off her body. Suddenly the entire world seems to be trying to pull my chin to the side so I can look, but I resist. I will not destroy this fantastic event that's happening to me of all people. My first date with a girl and she takes off all her clothes. Issy will freak when I tell him, if he even believes me. I should take a picture. I hold my phone over my shoulder without looking.

"Aiden!" Her voice booms like deep, rolling thunder.

I almost drop my phone. What's with her voice? I slip my phone in a pocket and hear this low, deep groan. Is that Bree?

A bone cracks. What? That sounds bad. I twist to look.

Bree crouches naked on top of the table. Her eyes closed. Her face tense. More bones twist and crack as her skin moves. Her body convulses. Oh, crap. Bree's having a seizure. I need to call 911, right? What's wrong with her?

"Bree?"

"This is...normal." Her voice sounds deep and hoarse. "Be done...in a minute. Don't freak out."

Don't freak out? All I'm doing is freaking out!

Gray fur pushes up through her skin, sprouting all over her back. Her arms. Her legs. Her jaw slides forward as large, sharp teeth puncture her gums and set themselves into place.

I'm standing, my cowardly legs not even asking for permission.

Bree's nose forms a snout. Her hands grow into paws, and her fingers form into razor-sharp claws. Wolf-like ears rise from her head. The gray fur grows thick and covers her completely. A low, final growl escapes from the creature's mouth. The thing looks like a wolf. No...it's like half-wolf and half-monster.

I notice my hands quivering like jelly, and my legs have taken this opportunity to move away from the picnic area.

The creature sprawls across the table, its body covering the entire thing. Its jagged teeth shine. Its amber eyes watch every move I make.

I take a few backward steps.

The creature whimpers.

I move further away from it.

The monster hops off the table, and I run.

My legs pump harder and harder as I race down the path as fast as I can go. I'm not looking behind me. When a victim does that in a horror film, they fall down and get killed. Screw that. I keep my eyes forward and fly past the basketball courts.

A distant whimper calls out behind me.

I don't stop.

I plow through the grove of trees. Leaves smack my face and clothes. My toe catches something on the ground, and I stumble forward, but I keep my balance and use the awkward momentum to push myself ahead. It's so dark in here. I hope I'm fleeing in the right direction.

Sharp animal cries bounce around the trees. The monster must be chasing after me.

I clear the grove of trees. There's the parking lot. The Dodge pickup waits. I unlock the driver's door to my life-boat and tumble inside, slamming the door closed. My chest pounds as I struggle to breathe.

The truck bounces. Something's on the hood.

The monster glares through the windshield, its teeth wanting to rip me into shreds. That face looks horrible, more vicious than a dog or even a wolf. It's like a mash-up of an animal with Satan.

I lock the doors and try to calm down. Okay. The girl from my Algebra class is a demon. Oh my God. I sat inches away from that in Algebra! I wanted to touch its hair. I wanted to... kiss that thing!

The creature jumps off the hood and crawls up to the driver's side. I move away from the door as the monster paws at the window, its sharp claws tapping the glass, and it whimpers.

"Go away," I yell. "Leave me alone."

It growls and shows its teeth.

I have to get out of here. I fire up the truck and shove it into reverse. A howl makes me turn around. The creature stands behind the truck, trying to block me in.

Like hell you will. I stomp on the gas. The truck squeals backwards, making the creature leap out of the way. I race the truck out of the park in full reverse. I don't even bother to turn around until I hit the first traffic light. Then I do a U-turn and speed off to my house.

I bounce the truck into my driveway. Run into my house. Lock the front door. Rush inside my room. Shove that shredded-cloth sofa I have against the door. Not good enough. I drag my desk over. Pin one end against the sofa and the other end against my bed, creating a brace. I dig out my baseball bat and sit on the edge of my bed.

For the rest of the night, I listen for noises.

CHAPTER FIFTEEN

AIDEN

The morning sun pours out my window. It reminds me that I've been up for seven straight hours waiting for Bree to rampage through my house, kill my dad, and then hurl herself against my barricade like a fang-wielding maniac.

I did an on-line search about werewolves. How the moon affects them. How they are similar and different from normal wolves. How they can turn others into werewolves. How humans can kill them. All this knowledge does nothing to calm me down. I should have never accepted that ride from Bree. From now on, I will never accept car rides from strange girls. Even if I think they're cute.

I need to piss, but I'm too scared to move back my protective layer of furniture to go to the bathroom.

A shadow blocks the sun from my window.

Bree stands inches away from the glass.

Oh, crap. I back away from my desk. That thin layer of glass won't keep her out. Why didn't I think of the window? I should have covered it with duct tape or something. Where's my bat?

I scoop it from the floor and grip it. The hard wood surface gives me a shred of confidence. I'll keep swinging the bat at her and hope I can knock her unconscious, then I can fetch Dad and get out of here.

Bree's gaze burns through the window.

I run into my desk. I can't back up any more. I won't have enough time to pull the desk and the sofa out of the way before Bree attacks. I'm trapped. Bree will change into that monster again, crash through my window, and turn me into a werewolf.

Wait. Do I want to be a werewolf? That sounds kind of cool.

Maybe I should think about this.

Bree taps the window and motions me to open it.

Seriously? I shake my head. No way.

Bree rolls her eyes and then holds up a rock. Her eyebrows lift. Well?

Well, I don't want to get in trouble for a broken window so I release the lock and open it. Bree climbs into my room with little effort and leans against the window-sill. I stand with my back pressed hard against the desk. My Death Star wall clock ticks off the seconds.

Bree studies my homemade barricade. Her mouth twitches to the side. "Really, Aiden? A barricade?"

"Are you going to eat me?"

Bree cocks her head. "Did you really just ask me that?"

I don't answer.

Bree blows off my question. "We need to talk. So let's go grab some breakfast."

"Breakfast?" I ask.

"I'm super starving right now, so grab your wallet and let's go eat."

"Why do I need my wallet?"

"Last night you left your date stranded miles away from her home, without her purse, without her phone, and basically forced that poor girl to walk all the way back to her house on the other side of town. So throw me some respect. I think you owe me that."

"What if you just left me alone and we pretended that last night didn't happen?""It's too late for that." Bree crosses her arms. "Look, I want to be cool about this. I want us to chill, eat some breakfast, and relax. You can ask me anything you want to about last night. Seriously, anything. And I won't lie to you. So are you down with that?"

My eyes tell me it's only a girl so why should I be afraid of her? But my brain screams to stay away. I know what she is, and I don't want any part of it.

"Aiden? Werewolves aren't known for their patience."

Okay. Guess I'm buying breakfast. Better than me being breakfast, I guess.

I check my wallet. "I'll need to go borrow some money from my dad."

Bree drives us into mid-town Tulsa to the outdoor shopping center of Yale Circle. Manicured shrubs, groomed trees, and pampered flowers decorate the landscape. This place has hundreds of specialty stores that require a shopper to wave their Visa gold card before entering. I know because one time I tagged along with Issy when his mom brought us here to find him some clothes. The only thing I could afford to buy was a piece of candy at the Russell Stover's chocolate shop.

Bree parks her car and leads me to an open-air restaurant. The hostess guides us to an outside table at Bree's request. The linen feels silky, and the silverware is polished to a shine. The prices on the menu are insane. This is only breakfast. Two eggs, bacon, and toast. How expensive is that to whip together? Lucky for me, Dad wasn't pissed about Bree visiting so early. He gave me thirty bucks and said I would need it to impress my girlfriend for the whole day. First the truck and now money. I still don't know why Dad is being so generous.

The air stirs. It's chilly this morning. I can tell because I'm only wearing a T-shirt.

"Would you like to sit inside?" the female server asks.

Yes, I would love to.

"No, we like it out here. Can we order now?" Bree waits for the waitress to break out her order book. "I want the regular pancakes with three orders of sausage."

"Three orders? That'll be extra."

"That's all right." Bree grins at me. "He's paying."

"And you, sir?" the server asks.

"I'm not hungry."

"Yes, you are," Bree says. "I could hear your stomach on the way over."

Think that's more nerves than hunger, but I've been up for hours, so maybe I am hungry.

"Okay, I'll take pancakes too."

The server leaves. Standing in the tree-covered courtyard next to us, a large clock chimes a happy little melody as birds fly from tree to tree. Minus the dead one rotting a few feet away from our table.

"Why did you run away from me last night?" Bree asks, her words sprinkled with a little hurt. "I told you not to freak out."

My fingers pick at a tiny hole in the table-cloth. "I was scared."

"That's still no excuse for abandoning me."

"It is when my cute date suddenly turns into this giant, snarling animal with huge teeth, seriously blowing away every pre-conceived notion I have about the universe. So cut me a break if I wasn't following all the dating rules during the greatest moment of terror in my life." I take a big sip of ice water. I lost it there, but it's the truth.

Bree smiles. "You think I'm cute?"

I almost choke on the ice cubes. "That's all you got from my last two sentences?"

"Sorry." Bree brushes her hair back with her hand. "Last night must have stressed you out."

"Yeah. I mean, you can't tell someone not to freak out, change into a monster, and then expect them not to freak out."

"Hey, werewolves aren't monsters. We're animals. Just like humans are. Really...there was no need for that whole chase scene. And what's with trying to run me down with your truck?"

"What do you want me to say? You freaked me out. People do stupid things when they freak out. You growled and showed your teeth at me. When a dog does that I usually take it as a personal threat. Have you ever heard of a pit bull attack? Same thing." I pause. "You scared the piss out of me last night."

Bree stares at her water. "What about now?" She shoots her eyes up to catch my reaction.

I stare at that stupid dead bird again, its sides flat because of decay.

She continues. "It's not like I don't have control over it."

"What about those movies? Werewolves always change during a full moon and then go crazy and kill people because they can't help themselves."

Bree rolls her eyes again. "Super piles of crap. We're nothing like that."

I don't believe her.

"Aiden, you're my friend and I won't hurt you." Her eyes beg me to believe her. "Do you know why I shifted in front of you?" Bree pauses. "It was because I trusted you. Out of all those kids in school, I wanted to believe that you were different. That you liked hanging out with Bree Mayflower. Not Cave Girl." Bree strokes her long hair. "I assumed you could handle this. But I assumed wrong, huh?"

I don't answer.

The server brings us our food. Bree pours a tanker-load of maple syrup over her pancakes and the small mound of sausages. She attacks the pancakes with this nervous energy, devouring it with a few grunts that she doesn't bother to hide. As we eat, both of us throw glances at each other as our breakfast turns more and more uncomfortable. Frustration builds on her face minute by minute. Bree empties her glass of cold water. Her body stiffens.

"You can't tell anyone. You can't tell a living soul for the rest of your life. It's too dangerous for me and my family. Even if a rumor got started at school, it would be super devastating."

"Okay."

"This is serious. I'm not joking. If you try to tell someone… I might have to do something that I don't want to do. I love my family and will do anything I can to protect them."

I freeze.

"I like you, Aiden. I really like you. So please don't make me choose."

So much for the I-won't-ever-hurt-you-Aiden. The acid returns to my stomach. The chill in the air seeps through my skin and into my veins. The closeness we shared at the zoo and the way Bree touched me on the train seems so far away. A memory of someone else's life, not mine. We both thought we knew each other.

And now we don't know each other at all.

CHAPTER SIXTEEN

AIDEN

For dinner I toss a frozen lasagna into the oven and bake it like the instructions say. The block of pasta and cheese turns out decent enough for both Dad and I to polish it off. Dad has two cans of beer to go along with his lasagna. After I wash dishes and switch on our noisy dishwasher, I join Dad in the living room. There's a football game on so we watch that for a while.

Dad finishes beer number three, puts it on the side-table, and clears his throat. "Good lasagna. Still miss your mom's cooking, though."

Me too. Mom could bake, grill, sauté, puree, marinate, fry, and wrap these edible masterpieces that would give my mouth spastic fits of joy. She used her kitchen like a master swordsman would use his blade.

I push the dark thoughts away. Thinking about Mom always makes me sad. It's been a long time since she passed. I should toughen up and not let it bother me. Real men don't cry over stuff like that, blubbering about things like a loser who can't take it. Dad didn't cry. Sure he was sad. That face I remember couldn't hide the grief, but he never cried. He took it like a man. I cried day and night because I couldn't do anything else. Dad would then yell at me to stop. Men don't cry like that. They keep it inside. Build a cement bunker around it. Dad said life will throw you a lot of punches so you're better off fighting than sitting on your ass and crying about it. Men always need to be strong.

I must be the biggest disappointment of his life.

A metal snap makes my eyes flip over to Dad. He's opening another can of beer. That's number four in an hour and a half. I know what's coming.

I go to my room because I hate being around Dad when he's drunk. If luck is on my side, he'll pass out in the living room and not bother me. I have no idea what to say if I have to again call Dad's supervisor in the morning. I'm running out of plausible excuses. Using mad cow disease sounds too fishy.

Three hours later.

"Aiden? Aiden? Get over here, son." Dad yells from the living room. His voice slurred and thick. I can barely understand the words.

I ignore him.

Dad's fist pounds my door. "Aid..." He can't even say my name. My stomach tightens. I'm sick of dealing with this. I wish he would leave me alone.

Dad opens my door without asking. The sour, beer-laced air that rushes in makes me want to hurl. It's disgusting. God help me I will never drink beer for the rest of my life. Dad sways like a tall sailing ship riding a stiff wind. His face tells me he's still trying to understand something, so I wait for him to catch up with the real world.

"Grass...needs ut," Dad blurts out.

I sigh. It's hard to understand and speak Drunk, a language composed of slurred words and mumbling. But over the years I've mastered the language.

"Okay, I'll cut the grass tomorrow."

"Now," he says. "Cut grass now. Too long."

"But it's 10:30 at night. It's too late to cut it."

"Now," Dad yells.

"Won't our neighbors get pissed?"

Dad towers over me, his eyes flaming. His arms and fists tighten. Damn. He's too angry and too drunk. Fear inches up my spine.

"Get up."

"Dad..."

"Get up," he yells.

I force myself to stand and brace for it. Dad throws a punch, knocking me on my ass. I taste iron in my mouth. Blood. I feel tears forming. The wuss inside me wants to cry because it hurts. But I can't cry. If Dad sees one tear, he will beat that emotion out. He expects me to take a punch like that because I'm a man.

I fight off the tears. I'll have to put gas in the mower. Maybe I could get away with only cutting the front yard, enough to satisfy him tonight and only piss off the neighbors for an hour instead of two. I change into some sweat pants and put on some old crappy sneakers.

Dad leaves and goes inside his bedroom, closing the door. I don't hear anything from his room for about ten minutes. Maybe he fell asleep.

I wait to make sure.

I blow off the grass and go to bed. But I go ahead and set my alarm for six o'clock in the morning. Not that I want to get up that early, but I better cut the stupid grass before school just to be safe.

* * *

The alarm screams. I get up, groggy as hell, but I still put on the sweats, pour gas in the mower, and rip up some grass. I finish about a third of the front yard before Dad comes outside, squinting his eyes at this morning's brilliant sunrise. He says something but the sound of the mower drowns him out. I kill the engine.

"What are you doing?"

Duh.

"Cutting the grass," I say.

Dad rubs his messed-up hair in confusion. "Why? You cut it three days ago."

Doesn't he think I know that? But he ordered me to...here

we go again. Whatever. It's like the beer absorbs Dad's memory.

"Put this stuff away. You'll be late for school."

I do what Dad says. Then I shower, change clothes, and rush out my front door because I'm now late for the bus. I get halfway down my driveway before I slide to a stop.

Idling by the curb is a 2008 Volkswagon Jetta, a gleaming beacon of independence.

Issy pokes his head out the window. He's wearing aviator sunglasses which look sick with the Jetta. "Get in this car, A-Man. We have the need for speed. But first we're stopping at McDonald's because I have the need for eats."

Hell yeah. We're not chained to a bus route now. I hop in the Jetta, and Issy spins out. We scarf down breakfast with plenty of time to make it to school. I love this. Getting up and having breakfast with your friend before you go off to school. Like an adult. This was impossible when I was taking the bus with a bunch of children.

A group of cheerleaders hang out in the student parking area so Issy decides to show off his new ride. He accelerates and tosses the car into the parking lot like a Hollywood stunt-man.

But Issy doesn't make it.

The Jetta slams against the cement curb, making us jump in our seats. That can't be good. Issy pulls the Jetta off the curb with an unceremonious plop. There's now a flop-flop sound coming from one of the wheels as the poor Jetta lumbers along like a sick buffalo. Issy parks, and we get out to examine the damage. The front driver's-side tire now has this big dent in it. We hit that curb so hard I think Issy bent the rim. Oh, and there's a new crack spreading up the fender.

Issy cusses at himself as we head inside to start our day.

The cafeteria fills up for lunch, but my wingman saves me a spot in line. Issy plays down the injuries to his Jetta. He wants to buy a body kit for it anyway, so he'll get the money to replace the fender at the same time. No problem. I point out that he should worry about getting a new tire and rim first because his dad won't be happy when he finds out his son can't make a right turn.

"Thanks for trashing lunch," Issy says.

"Dude, you're the one showing off your driving skills." I use my fingers to make fake quotation marks around the word skills.

"I have driving skills, but they're not fully-developed yet. Becoming a master in the art of driving takes time. It's like aging a fine wine."

"Awesome. So you'll master the art of turning right by the time you're what? Thirty?"

Issy throws me the finger. My focus drifts through the crowd of lunch tables with all the social groups represented: the goth table, the soccer table, the sci-fi table, the football table, the band table, the theater table...

Then I see Bree. She leans on a wall near the outside doors, watching every move I make. Is she spying on me? Making sure I don't "out her" to Issy?

No, I don't think it's that. There's something else in that look of hers. More of a want. A desire. Those eyes want to pull me towards her, like a tractor beam from the Death Star that pulls in the Millennium Falcon. Bree is cuter than the Death Star, but they're both extremely dangerous.

I bet she wants to do lunch again. Act like nothing is different. How can I do that? How can I forget she changed into a scary wolf-thing with large teeth that can rip open my arteries? Why did Bree pick me anyway? Out of all the guys in this school why did a...werewolf...decide I should know who she is? If it's supposed to be so secret, why tell me? I didn't want to know all this. I only wanted a girl. A normal girl. Why can't Bree be like Pamela? Pamela isn't this complex. She's a simple girl with a simple brain. Pamela's normal. Pamela is the *type* of girl I should be with.

"Bree's staring at you," Issy says as the lunch line stirs.

"I know."

"You never did tell me about your date Saturday, *like you promised*. Did Bree let you touch her boobs?"

Bree's mouth twitches to the side. She can hear us from way over there.

"Let's not go there."

"That bad, huh?" Issy asks. "That sucks. She should have let you take a peek at them, if only to be nice."

She did. I got an eyeful of wonders that night, but not all of them awesome. But I can't tell Issy any of it without Bree's wrath. I wouldn't put it past her to leap across the cafeteria and attack me in front of the entire school.

After we pay for our lunches, Issy searches for a table while I watch Bree. She still hasn't moved, but the corners of her mouth wilt as she notices my lunch tray. The girl was hoping I'd change my mind. Bree's amber eyes soften and look wet. Werewolves don't cry, do they?

Issy whistles and puts his tray down on a vacant table right next to a second chair with my name on it.

I hesitate.

Bree fights off her sadness and releases a weak smile in my direction, still trying to show me that she's friendly, still wanting to be my friend, still wanting to be the girl I thought she was. But I'm not the guy she thinks I am. I join Issy at the table. Bree's smile melts, and her eyes drop to the floor. I know. I'm such a horrible person, but I don't want to deal with her "issues" right now.

The sound of girls laughing flips my attention to the next table over. Pamela Osterhaus and her friends giggle and snort, but for once their attention isn't on me. Instead, they focus all their destructive power on Bree.

"I so want to burn her wardrobe," Pamela says.

"Walmart has not been kind to her," a strawberry blonde says.

Pamela laughs. "More like Goodwill."

The whole table laughs.

Bree glares. She can hear them too.

"And that hair. Oh my God," Pamela says. "Someone needs to kidnap Sasquatch Girl and drop her off at a salon."

"They'll probably throw her out. Too much work," another girl adds.

"She should be waiting more than a month to wash her hair," the strawberry blonde says. "Check this out, I saw her once at the mall, and she ate this giant, triple cheeseburger. Seriously, it must be like 5,000 calories, right? So I watch her take down this burger, and all the juices were dripping down and coating her chin and her neck—"

"Oh my God, that's so disgusting," Pamela interrupts.

The blond continues. "I know, right? She looked like a lion trying to devour a moose."

"I think the poor girl has mental problems," another girl says.

Bree's eyes fill with pain. Each comment stabs her like a knife. I can see that on her face because I know that feeling. That painful feeling you get when someone makes you feel like dirt. Pamela did the same thing to me after I told her that I loved her. That witch laughed at me too. Making me feel small...

Alone.

Unimportant.

Rejected.

Bree feels that now. Rejection from me. Rejection from everyone at school. Rejection from humans. Bree revealed something deep and personal to her, and I rejected her because of it. I revealed something deep and personal to Pamela, and she rejected me.

Amazing. I'm a hypocrite. I've become Pamela.

Bree plows through the outside doors.

"Where are you going?" Issy asks.

His question makes me realize I'm standing up with the lunch tray still in my hands.

"Can you watch my food?" I put down my tray.

Issy glances at the outside doors, then holds up his fist. "Never give up. Never surrender."

I fist-bump him and run outside.

Rows and rows of vehicles fly by as I run through the student parking lot in search of the black Oldsmobile. I must find Bree. I don't want her thinking I'm like the hundreds of kids at school who judge her. I'm no hypocrite. And I won't let them turn me into one. I see the black car and notice two empty front seats. Where did she go?

A head pops up from the back seat. It's Bree. She smells me. Her eyes look swollen. Her cheeks glisten with tears. She's been crying. All of a sudden I feel weird, like I'm disturbing her privacy.

Maybe she wants to be alone. I back away and swivel around.

A door groans open.

"Did you want something?" Bree sounds upbeat and hopeful.

I stop. "Oh, I..."

Should I be honest?

"I wanted to see if you were okay."

"I'm great." Bree wipes her cheeks, totally negating the answer she gave me.

A car rolls by.

The wind teases Bree's hair.

"Okay. Um...I'll go back inside. Issy's probably waiting for me so..."

Bree frowns. "I understand if you want to eat with your friend."

"I don't have to. I could hang if you want."

Bree brightens and climbs back into her car, leaving the door open. I climb into the passenger side and close the metal door with a solid clunk. Bree climbs in back, carefully picking up the moose and squirrel, which she places on her lap as she props herself against the back side-window. Her fingers fiddle around with the moose's ears.

"Do they have names?" I ask.

"Rocky the Squirrel and Bullwinkle the Moose. They're from this old '60s cartoon that my dad has on DVD. He got me into it when I was a kid."

"So no stuffed wolves, huh?"

Bree pauses. "Having a stuffed animal that looks like you is sort of creepy."

Yeah, that would be creepy. I swing around and rest my legs on the driver's leather seat so I can face Bree. "I take it you heard what Pamela and her friends were saying."

Bree gets quiet. "It's hard for me to hold back. I'm not use to it. Where I come from, if a girl says crap about me like that, we go at it. Do you know what I mean? We shift. We fight each other. One of us submits to the other, and we're done. The girls here...I so want to take Pamela and throw her through a wall."

"I know what you mean."

"Really, Aiden, I'm seriously that strong. Flinging a girl through a wall is easy. But I can't do that because I have to pretend like I'm this frail human girl, and it's awful." Bree glances at me. "Do I really scare you? Honestly?"

I don't answer.

"So I do."

"You overwhelmed me that night," I say. "On a night when my nerves suffered through dinner and then I had to keep acting mellow as I walked around a zoo with a pretty girl that I wanted to impress...that's a crap load of stress for any guy."

"So I stressed you out way before the park?"

"Seriously, yeah. But, like, in a good way."

Bree smiles to herself. "You were successful."

"At what?"

"Impressing me." She points to herself. "This girl doesn't shift into a werewolf for just anybody."

I relax against the leather seat, letting myself get comfortable. "You mentioned 'where I come from.' Now where is that?"

Bree hesitates, like she's not supposed to say. "Colorado. Our pack had a small compound up in the mountains where we all lived together."

"Like a group home kind of thing?"

She nods. "We all took care of each other. Each family had a house, and we had a community building where we did all kinds of pack-related events. All the adults had jobs, and they would pool everyone's income together and share it. My dad was the pack treasurer since he was the chief financial manager for a huge bank in Denver. He made the pack a lot of money with investments." Bree sighs. "I so loved it there."

"Why did you move here? Did your pack disband or...?"

"I could eat a buffalo. Are you starving? Let's stuff our faces before Algebra." Bree quickly hops into the driver's seat while gently pulling my legs back so she can squeeze in. I drop my question as she starts the car, and we take off for a quick lunch.

* * *

After school lets out, I help Issy put on the Jetta's spare tire in the student parking lot. Some kids laugh and point as they roll by, acting like having a flat tire would never happen to any of them. Wish I could flip them off. Bree parks next to us and volunteers to stand by if the spare tire isn't going to work, which is decent of her.

Issy thumbs through the Volkswagen owner's manual, finds the changing-tire procedure and follows it step-by-step.

"That's wrong," he says.

I stop loosening a bolt on the bent tire. "Why does it matter how the bolts come off?"

"They say to do it like an X. Do the two opposite bolts, then the other set of bolts."

"That's when you're tightening the bolts on, not taking them off."

"Do it anyway. Just in case."

"Whatever, dude."

"I don't want my tire nuts to get all screwed up," Issy says.

His tire nuts. That's funny.

"I'm not tightening anyone's nuts."

Issy grins. "You better not whack my nuts either."

"That would suck. Because you can't drive with whacked nuts."

"Don't I know it."

Bree rolls her eyes.

Issy catches it. "You don't want to whack my nuts, Bree?"

Wow, Issy. And he wonders why girls can't take him seriously.

MY GIRLFRIEND BITES

A mischievous grin curls up Bree's lip. "Issy, I would love to. Aiden? Can you hand me that tire iron?"

She's calling him out! That's amazing. I have to see this. I hand the girl what she asked for.

Bree's fingers grip the black metal. She raises an eyebrow towards Issy. Well?

My wingman frowns and shields his coconuts.

I laugh so hard I almost throw up. My reaction puts a huge smile on Bree's face as she gives me back the tire iron. It takes me a minute to stop laughing. Then Issy follows me to the trunk so we can get the temporary-spare.

Something pulls me away from the trunk. I catch a glimpse of Kirk before he throws me against the pavement.

"Remember me, Blow Jay?" Kirk asks. "I'm the guy who's scheduled to kick your ass."

My body jolts to full-alert status. A shot of instant adrenaline races in my veins, preparing me to run for my life. So is it today? Would I be visiting the ER at St. Francis Hospital this afternoon? Would I be getting the crap kicked out of me like Issy? Would I get a broken jaw? A broken nose? A broken body?

Kirk drags me to my feet, and glares for a moment or two. Makes me wait for it. Makes me dread it. Makes me hate him. God, I hate him so much. I shouldn't hate a person like this, but I do. "That's only a friendly reminder that your days are still numbered," he says.

"Leave him alone," Bree shouts. Her feet are apart. Her eyes cold. Her body stiff as a brick wall. I can see her muscles moving under the fabric of her T-shirt. Damn. Is she going to change in the school parking lot?

Kirk looks surprised. "That's breaking news. Blow Jay has a girlfriend?" He wraps his arm around my neck like we're friends. "You're in love with Cave Girl?"

"That's like disgusting-sick," Mooney says to Jack. Kirk's henchman surround me. I don't have a chance.

"I hear you don't bathe," Kirk says to Bree.

She sizzles with anger, but doesn't answer.

"Does Blow Jay satisfy you? Does he know where the key

goes?"

Mooney and Jack laugh.

Bree squints, like she's straining against the monster pushing against her. My fear of Kirk disappears as I worry more and more about what Bree will do.

"Tell you what. When you're ready for a real man, come see me. I'll show you how it's done." Kirk bites his bottom lip and pretends like he's doing it with Bree.

"Keep her out of this." The words sound weird coming from my lips, but it's my voice ordering Kirk to do something. I'm going to die.

Kirk faces me. "Or what?"

I hesitate. No, I can't make myself do it. I can't demolish the piles of fear. I rip my eyes away.

Kirk pushes me to the ground again.

A low, throaty growl makes everyone turn to Bree. She crouches on all fours, her hands digging into the pavement. My heart races. The monster will come out again.

"That bitch is crazy. Look, she thinks she's a dog now." Kirk backs away as he laughs. "You two weirdos are perfect for each other." Kirk joins Mooney and Jack as they all head for Kirk's truck. Guess they're bored with us already.

I kneel down beside Bree. Her hands and arms shake. Her breath is raspy and hoarse like the night she changed. Issy watches Bree with amazement. There's also a small crowd that's formed around us. If Bree changes in front of them...I wrap my arms around Bree and guide her to the Oldsmobile. I feel her skin quivering against mine, her body shaking to its core. I stroke her long, black hair and open the driver-side door. I don't know how to drive a stick, but maybe Bree can at least drive away from the parking lot. I help her inside the car and run around to the passenger side as everyone watches.

"Is she having a seizure?" Issy asks.

"I'll tell you later." I jump into the car.

Bree grips the steering wheel tight. Her head is still slumped over the wheel, her body still quivering.

I stroke her long hair again. "Relax. You'll have to drive.

Every thing's okay. Kirk is gone, so take deep breaths. Let yourself relax."

Bree sucks in more air, doing exactly what I tell her. She rises halfway up in her seat and starts the engine. Bree peels out of the parking lot. I fall into her lap when she whips the car around and heads south-bound, but I pull myself back into my seat. Bree slows down and parks the car near a bank.

She leans back in her seat. "I was going to kill him."

"You wouldn't have hurt my feelings," I say.

"No, really. *I was going to kill him.* Crush his skull in. Throw him against the pavement. I couldn't control myself. I was shifting, and I couldn't stop it."

"But you did stop it."

"Only because you held on to me. Only because the thought of hurting you on accident...made me chill out." Bree rolls her face towards mine. "You were the only thing holding me back. If you weren't there, I would have shifted and killed him."

So why did I hold her back?

Because murder is wrong. Even if you're killing an asshole like Kirk.

Bree closes her eyes and relaxes. Her breathing slows. "Why does that guy mess with you? What did you do to him?"

"Nothing. He's been messing with Issy and me since junior high. I have no clue why. I wish he would leave us alone, you know?"

"It's because he thinks you're weak."

He would be right, too.

"You should fight him," Bree says. "Make him think twice before he messes with you again."

"Easy for a werewolf to say."

"You could take him."

"In a fight? Thanks for the confidence boost, but I don't see that happening," I say.

"I don't doubt it for one second," Bree says, her eyes dead serious.

Why does she say that? What does she see in me that I don't? I look at me and see a failure. A guy not worth anything but a kick in the ass. But then Bree lets me step into her secret world, trusting me over everyone at school. Then I got scared and ran away. I'm sick of being that Aiden. The one who's scared and runs away all the time. I want to be the Aiden that Bree thinks I am.

Bree waves her hand in my face. "Yo, can you still hear me?"

"What?"

"The Hideaway? For some pizza? I'm craving the double-decker meat pie."

"Can we do it tonight?" I ask.

"I won't make it that long without food. This wolf girl needs her pizza."

"No, I mean, pizza right now sounds awesome...I was talking about tonight as in...I want you to take me out to the forest again."

Bree hesitates. "Seriously?"

"I promise not to run this time."

She checks my face to see if I'm for real.

I am.

Bree's smile lights up the car.

CHAPTER SEVENTEEN

BREE

Aiden wants to check me out naked tonight...as a wolf. I was blown away when he asked because this was the same boy who ran away like a chicken with his head bitten off when we tried this before. Aiden acted so silly that night. Barricading his bedroom door? Really? I, like, only wanted to vent and let my friend know that he pissed me off. I did come super close to killing Aiden that morning. Really close. Within a stack of pancakes close. Oh my Goddess, those pancakes were so yummy. The grease from the sausage links mixed with maple syrup...it's like the best. Totally serious. It's like my one guilty pleasure in the world. Human girls have ice cream or chocolate. I have pancakes smothered in syrup and sausage grease.

What was I talking about? I so have to stop obsessing about food.

Aiden. That's right. Tonight I bring him to a remote place called the Buffalo Mountain Wilderness Area, which is only a hill full of trees on the west side of the Arkansas River. The park's closed, but some kids from another school chill in the parking lot and smoke weed. I should mess with their heads by shifting, jumping on their car, and howling. They would so freak and scatter like deer, and the weed would make them so out of it they would stumble around the forest bumping into trees. So hilarious.

I giggle to myself. Wish I could do something fun like that, but if I did, Dad would chop my tail off.

"What are you laughing about?" Aiden's green eyes blink as they watch me under his mop of red hair.

I tell him my plan for the weed smokers, and the boy cracks this nervous laugh. Poor guy is so uptight. He better not skate on me again. Better take the keys to the car and slip them inside my shoes in case Aiden bails.

That's super negative, Bree. Think good thoughts instead, all right? Like the fact that Aiden's trusting you again. He's gotta be serious about me, right? Why else would he ask me to do this again? He likes you. He said you were pretty.

Aiden's right. I am pretty. As in...pretty awesome.

Oh, there's a good place. I steer the car off the lonely road into this small dirt turnout and kill the engine and lights. Darkness drops over the trees. Fall ravaged their leaves and turned them into these prickly skeletons of sad wood. The north wind teases the branches, which scrape against each other. The air is scented with rabbits, a raccoon, and... mmmm, deer. A fawn, I think.

But I'm so not hungry. The large, double-decker meat pie this afternoon gave my stomach some much-needed love. This girl should be good for another hour or so. Lucky my metabolism is like a V-12 engine with the pedal stuck to the floor. Food, like, evaporates inside me. Same with my parents. It's how we werewolves roll. If I was a human girl, I'm convinced that all this eating would make me weigh like 500 pounds easy.

Aiden's nervous eyes scan the dark trees, and I smell sweat on his skin. My ears pick up his hand twisting the leather handle on the door. Wish this boy would relax. How many times can I say, "I won't hurt you," before he believes me?

I slip out of the car, and Aiden follows, staying close to the fender, running his hand against the steel like a blind man without a cane. What's up with that? Oh, piss on the sun. I forgot to bring a light. Humans can't see five inches in front of their face in the dark. It's so laughable how blind they are without their artificial lights.

Almost forgot. I twist my key in the lock and lift the trunk lid. Dad put an emergency road kit in my car, and I think there's a...yes! I dig enough and score a battery-operated lantern. So glad Dad splurged for the deluxe emergency kit. I grip the lantern in my left hand and lightly squeeze Aiden's hand with my right as we move into the dark forest. I snake through the trees and prickly bushes, blazing my own path. I know where I want to go, but since the parking lot is full of pot-heads, we'll have to go a different route. No biggie, though.

"How can you see?" Aiden squints into the blackness, using his poor human eyes as best he can.

"I just can," I say because it's true. I see extremely well in the dark. I didn't do it tonight because Aiden was with me, but I've driven at night without head-lights before. Those lights mess with my eyes so bad that I like to leave them off when I can. But I still have to be careful when I do it since human drivers can't see my car and they freak and get all road-rage on me. But since Aiden is here...

I squeeze the rubber button, and the lantern blasts the trees. Ouch. It's like the forest blew up. So much light. It's ridiculous.

Soon we enter a small clearing shaped by a natural break in the forest. The clearing isn't much bigger than a large bedroom, but the trees leave enough room to see the stars and sky. The light pollution from Tulsa makes the stars dull and the sky so milky. I miss Colorado. There the stars crowd the mountain skies like a dark blanket with millions of jewels sewn into the fabric. Bright little jewels that dazzle the eyes. So vibrant and beautiful. A link that binds us close to the universe.

What sucks is that our Mother, our Goddess of light, our precious Moon hides from us tonight. I can feel when she's gone. It's like this emptiness inside that all werewolves feel. Like something's missing from our soul.

"Where do you want me to sit?" Aiden asks, interrupting my deep thoughts about the universe.

I flash him a smile. "Anywhere is fine." I place the lantern near the center of the clearing and face him. "Ready?"

"Is there anything I should know?"

"About what?"

"Werewolves. Like, is there something I shouldn't do?"

"There is one thing. Don't run away again."

"Okay." Aiden smiles with a hint of embarrassment, and it's so cute.

I kick off my sneakers and slip the keys of the car inside them so quick that I don't think Aiden noticed. I hesitate. Should I make him turn around again? It's not like I'm ashamed of my body. Running through the forest without clothes has this way of breaking down a girl's modesty. Still, I would be lying if I said I wasn't nervous about exposing myself to Aiden again. But if Aiden wants to be my friend, he has to accept this with zero conditions. That means he has to get use to me shifting. That means...I can't hold anything back from him.

I pull off my shirt and jeans. Then off go my bra and panties. My skin feels the chill in the air, and the craving to shift becomes stronger. I glance at Aiden, and he hides his eyes, still trying to be a considerate guy. His human morality is cute.

"Really, Aiden...you can watch if you want."

His eyes rise to mine. "That won't bother you?"

"Not at all."

Without the moon, I have to totally focus on stirring the wolf deep inside me to come out and play. The animal wakes and stirs. She floods into my body, applying pressure on every inch of it. She's ready to spring from her hiding place. So I release her.

The animal takes control. My beautiful fur grows. My snout presses outward from my face as my powerful jaw forms, and my teeth extend, spreading out and down. Bones in my body grow and crack. My fingers and hands sprout claws. My legs and arms rip and tear as my muscles swell. My body stretches along the axis of my spine. The pain feels so wonderful. And here comes the final release as my wolf body relaxes into existence. Shifting is super awesome. It's like a drug. The only drug a werewolf girl needs to keep her happy. Aiden sits still. His eyes now see how truly beautiful I am. On impulse, I jump and land two feet away from him. He backs up and stumbles over a branch that tosses him to the ground. Clumsy human.

I crawl up to him, and Aiden shakes like a terrified puppy. Wish he would chill out. If I wanted to attack him, he wouldn't have time to quiver. Better calm him down. I plop down on my stomach and roll over, holding up my paws, surrendering to Aiden like a submissive wolf, and wait for him to make the next move.

Aiden collects himself, drinks in some air, and then moves his hand towards my fur. I wag my tail. See? I'm not mean. I'm super friendly. Aiden gently strokes my side, and I close my eyes to encourage him. His tender fingers sink deeper and deeper under the fur and massage the skin underneath. Aiden pets me now, his fingers pushing against my skin and combing through my fur. It ignites my body like a fireball. A whimper escapes. I can't help myself. This boy knows how to pet a girl with fur. Aiden scratches my stomach, which brings out another whimper from me as I open my eyes, flashing him a friendly look of appreciation. Aiden calms down. I'm so winning him over.

I roll to my feet and tip-toe beside him, flopping my body against his.

Aiden puts an arm around me in a hug. I rotate so I can look at him. I lean my snout in closer, and Aiden tenses up. Must be my long, sharp teeth. I shoot my tongue out and lick the side of his face. Aiden laughs really hard, like he's relieved I wasn't going to bite him.

Don't worry, Aiden. I could never bite you. Not now. Not ever.

Aiden strokes the side of my face. His touch feels gentle and caring, so wonderful. It's in those lovely, gorgeous eyes of his that I can tell he's accepting me. I'm not some hideous monster. I'm something beautiful. Something worthy to be loved. Something special.

An exciting impulse shoves me into a stance. I want to play with my best friend tonight! I leap back and forth a few times. Aiden stands with this clueless look on his face. I bark and run around him in a circle, constantly glancing back at him. *Dude, I want to play now!*

He's not getting it. I nudge him in the stomach and jump back. Then I run to the edge of the trees and look back. *Chase me!*

He still doesn't get it.

I circle around and shove him gently from behind. He stumbles forward but doesn't fall. I sprint a few feet and skid to a stop, swiveling my head around to grin at him, which is not easy with fangs.

"Um…do you want me to chase you?" he asks.

Finally! I nod.

Aiden grabs the lantern and rushes towards me.

Awesome! I sprint into the woods. The fallen leaves crackle under my paws as the trees whiz past. I duck and jump and swerve around branches and trunks. The world of the forest knows I'm here. The rabbits run. The raccoon climbs higher into the tree, and the fawn bounces away. I'm not hunting so being quiet isn't important tonight. Having fun definitely is. Aiden chases me as best he can, stumbling around bushes and trees. The light he carries is like this huge bonfire that marks his location. For a boy, he's not running that fast either. I lose him in the trees with so little effort on my part. I circle around and snuggle under a bush to spy on him.

Aiden slows, takes a few more awkward steps, and halts. He wipes sweat off his face. "Bree?" His voice bounces off some nearby trees and falls away.

I stay put.

"Bree?" he calls out again, showing his back to me.

A tiny urge, more like an instinct creeps up in me. The hunter inside the werewolf sees her meal standing there vulnerable, not paying attention to its surroundings. Showing me your back is like waving something red in front of a bull. You're so tempting me to strike. Huge mistake, Aiden.

I leap into the open, racing towards him as fast as I can push myself. I jump and go airborne, crashing into Aiden's back and knocking him to the ground. I prance away with my tail in the air. Aiden never moved his head, never yelped, never suspected I was coming. Bet I took him completely by surprise. I change direction and trot up to the boy I ambushed. He still lies on the ground, making a weird wheezing-type sound. Why is Aiden doing that? The boy grunts and gasps like he can't breathe.

Aiden? Oh my Goddess. I use my snout and push him on to his back. His mouth stretches open, as if trying to suck up every ounce of oxygen as he struggles to get air into his lungs.

Did I crush his windpipe? Did I squeeze his lungs against his ribs? Why did I have to run so fast? Why did I have to show off? He's a human boy not a werewolf. He's cute and delicate. Oh, please let him be okay. I lick his face all over to say I'm sorry. I better shift back to human because Aiden might need another ride to the hospital.

Aiden huffs. "Wow...you knocked...all the air out of me." He gasps for more oxygen, but not as bad as before.

Relief pours over me. Thank the Goddess Luna he's okay.

The boy takes a seat on the grass. I relax and plop down across his lap.

"Take it easy on the wrestling moves, okay?" he asks with a hint of a smile.

That cheers me up as I wait for my friend to catch his breath.

Aiden climbs to his feet. I bounce to my paws and wag my tail. I'm so ready for another chase. But Aiden picks up a thick broken twig and waves it in the air.

Really, Aiden? Are you going to...? No, please don't do that to me.

"Want to play fetch?"

I so don't believe he said that. I show him my teeth and growl.

"What's wrong?" he asks.

Before Aiden can twitch, I rip the stick out of his hand

with my teeth. To make my point super obvious, I wait a second before spitting it to the ground.

"What? I thought you wanted to play?"

Hello? Do I look like a golden retriever to you?

Aiden doesn't get it. I sigh. The fun is over. I close my eyes and focus. I tuck the animal back inside me once again. The fur recedes into my skin. My snout collapses back into my face. My arms and legs shift back. The animal inside tightens back up into its little ball. I step over and put on my clothes.

"Did I do something wrong?" Aiden asks.

I slip on the bra and panties first. "I'm your friend. Not your pet," I say, my voice slightly hoarse. I step into my jeans and zip them up.

"Oh...yeah." Aiden pauses. "Guess you're not a dog, huh?"

I stuff my head through my T-shirt. "I'm not *anyone's* dog." I take out my car keys and slip on my sneakers. I steal a glance at him. "I'm sorry about that back shove. Are you all right? I was scared that I really hurt you."

"It's okay. Only hit the ground hard. I'll live."

"Still. I feel bad."

"It's nice to know that werewolves care."

"I'll always care."

Aiden hesitates. "Why?"

"Because we're friends."

"So it's not like you feel...sorry for me, right?"

"Feel sorry for you?"

Aiden scratches his neck and lets his question drop.

My head soars above the clouds like an eagle. I so love this. No more secrets to hide. No more acting like something I'm not. This boy likes Bree the werewolf. A best friend who likes me for who I am. It's the best feeling in the world. It reminds me of when Dawn was alive.

My heart twists. I miss my bestie so much. No one in our pack deserved to be shot down like that.

Thank goodness for Aiden. He makes the loneliness in me disappear. Werewolves don't make good loners. We need companionship and to be a part of a large family that sticks by you when things in life go bad. If my family has to stay in Oklahoma forever, having Aiden here would make that sacrifice completely bearable.

"Turn your lights on!" Aiden shrieks.

Lights? Oh, yeah. I flick on the car's headlights, and they reveal a truck coming from the opposite direction on the winding, two-lane road. I wish Aiden would chill. My ears picked up that truck long before I saw it come out of the darkness. I hold in the clutch and shift into fourth gear to speed up. The sound of an arm brushing against the seat makes me glance over in time to notice Aiden placing his hand over mine on the gearshift. His warm hand makes my skin tingle. My heart shifts into tenth gear, and my body hums.

I'm in love with a human boy.

And I think I like it.

CHAPTER EIGHTEEN

BREE

A silver pike strikes Chevalier's chest and pierces his heart. His eyes feel the silver as it poisons his tissues. The attack is so quick and blatant that our Alpha has no time to react. Our mighty Chevalier drops to his knees and shakes as the silver attacks his bloodstream, eating him up from the inside and laying waste to his body. He rolls to the ground and dies right in front of the entire pack.

"Bree! Run!" Mom yells.

I can't move. The sight of his death shocks me, and I can't rip my eyes from the scene. The murderer stands over the body of Chevalier. The thing came out of nowhere. I never got a whiff of it, and judging by the reaction of the twenty werewolves standing around me, neither did they. Fear chills the air inside our little community building.

The murderer is a...human? Really? Is it human? The intruder's face is stitched together with pieces of human skin. Like some gruesome jigsaw puzzle. Its eyes black. Its stare cold and lacking any hint of emotion. This creature wears a layer of chain mail composed of pure silver. I can tell by the way the tiny, interlocking rings glisten under the lights. A huge belt of weapons bristle across its hips: knives, throwing stars, and a pistol.

I force my terrified legs to move away as the werewolves around me shift. My own skin burns, fear pushing my natural instincts to kick in and shift so I can fight like a wolf.

Windows shatter all around us, tossing glass everywhere as more of the creatures swarm into the building.

Again, no scent. No sound. No warning. How can they not have a scent?

Mom shoves me at the door. "Get out."

Dad's back legs and torso have shifted. His gorgeous black fur is unmistakable. Mom's snout forms, her teeth growing over her bottom lip. Her yellow eyes glare at me to leave.

No! I want to stay and fight.

Mom barrels into me at full speed and knocks me clear through the wooden front door. I hit the ground outside and roll about twenty-five feet along the dirt before stopping. Only my pride hurts. I should be fighting along with my pack because Chevalier was my Alpha too. I scramble to my feet and think about disobeying Mom. The burning feels intense, and I want to release it and shift.

But then I hear all those painful yelps coming from inside. I've never heard werewolves cry out like that. There's also a strong scent of blood in the air. Those sounds and smells make my stomach sick. I sense that my pack is dying inside that building. I still want to race inside and help, but I'm not as big as the adults. And judging by the sounds I'm picking up, the adults aren't big enough for these creatures either.

So I run.

Weaving through the vehicles parked inside the compound, I pass by our Ford Expedition and stop. I need keys. I run to our house on the far side of the compound and slam into the front door, almost forgetting to turn the knob first. I search frantically for Mom's purse. Where is it?

The kitchen counter. I snatch it and Dad's laptop and then race to my bedroom. Rocky and Bullwinkle grin at me from on top of my bed. I can't leave them behind.

I stumble out the front door with Mom's purse, Dad's laptop case, and two stuffed animals tucked under my arms. I waddle up to the Ford and dig into the purse for the keys.

My ears pick up barks and growls coming from about 250 feet away. A handful of werewolves scatter into the forest that surrounds our compound. Some are wounded. All of them yelp in some degree of pain. The attackers chase them with shotguns, pistols, and an assault rifle.

I see Dawn. I'd recognize my bestie's dark-reddish fur anywhere as she dashes to the edge of the forest. I need to help her.

One creature aims a silver pistol in her direction.

NO!

A loud crack fills the air. Dawn falls and disappears into the tall, straw-like grass.

DAWN!

I watch for any hint of movement. Any hope that my friend is still alive, but the grass doesn't move an inch.

Dawn?

I can't believe this is happening. Why are they killing us? Why is my best friend dead?

Mom's words scream inside my head, "Bree! Run!"

My hand shakes as I insert the key fob and hit the start button. The Ford Expedition roars to life. Through the windshield, I spot Mom and Dad along with Luther and Taz. The four werewolves create a rough, protective ring in a small clearing beside the damaged community building. Ten creatures surround them.

My heart races. Those things will kill my parents. Like they killed Chevalier. Like they killed Dawn. I can't leave them behind to get slaughtered, and I won't sit here and watch them die.

I shift out of park and hit the gas. The vehicle roars backwards and rams into Chevalier's Corvette. Piss on the sun. Wrong gear. I put the Ford in drive and floor it. The big vehicle moves forward this time, and I aim it towards the ring.

One of the creatures blocks my way. I steer the Ford right at him. The creature doesn't blink as it raises a shotgun. I rev the engine to try and scare the thing, but it's like trying to scare a wall. The creature's expression doesn't change. Same cold eyes. Same cold look. The gun fires...

My windshield explodes into glass shards that poke my

skin.

I hold my foot down, and the big vehicle plows into the creature, flinging it to the side with a hard thump. I check the side-mirror to see the damage.

The creature rises, its right arm freakishly bent behind its body. A human couldn't take that kind of pain, but this thing reveals no sign it's even hurt. Using its good arm, the creature whips out a pistol and runs after me.

I gun the Ford again and bounce it off-road as I circle around the clearing to search for my parents. The ring of werewolves disappears as creatures swarm all over the place. Bullets ding the body of the Ford Expedition like hail stones as the creatures use me for target practice.

Pain shoots up my shoulder as silver bites into my skin. Oh my Goddess. It burns so bad that I can feel my eyes watering. I check my arm. Looks like the bullet only grazed me. I'm lucky.

I see my parents. Mom's on the ground, and her creamy fur is stained with lots of blood. Dad stands on his hind legs, flashing his large teeth and guarding Mom from another attack. A creature with silver knives in both hands runs straight for my dad.

I squash the accelerator. The creature spins its head in my direction. Too late. I feel the SUV lift as it climbs on top of the thing and crushes whatever bones it used to have. I stand on the brakes, causing the big vehicle to shudder to a stop.

"Mom! Dad!" I yell out the window.

Dad scoops up Mom and lumbers toward the SUV. I check both side-mirrors for unwanted company. Clear.

I peek down at the truck's back-up camera. Four creatures close in fast. Three of them have knives. One has the assault rifle.

Dad places Mom in the back seat and hops inside. I stomp on the gas pedal and spin the vehicle back around to leave the compound. The loud snap, snap of automatic gunfire makes me duck out of sight. But I can't see where I'm going, so I try to keep the SUV as straight as I can so I don't hit anything hard enough to stop us.

Soon the rifle fire stops, and I pop up just in time to see...a large tree ahead.

I yank the wheel hard to the left, and we miss the tree. But the sounds of popping wood and metal scraping off make me grit my teeth as the tree branches rake the side of the vehicle.

I wrestle the SUV through the compound entrance and point it down the access road as fast as it can go.

My brain overloads with questions. What are those things? Why did they attack us? Is Mom going to die?

Dad slips into the passenger seat next to me.

"Daddy?" I want him to answer all my questions. I want him to make this all disappear. I want him to heal Mom. I want him to tell me this is really a dream.

"Not now...drive," he says.

"But Daddy..."

He leans over and kisses the side of my hair. "Need you to be strong right now," his deep voice whispers into my ear. The little girl in me feels warm and comfortable again. Dad's calm voice always did that. "Need you to be my rock. Can you be my rock?"

"Yes," I whisper back as I feel the tears wet my cheeks.

I steer us on to the state highway that leads to Glen Haven. Dad squeezes my arm with reassurance.

We're safe now.

And then a creature lands on the hood with a silver knife in its hand.

What!?

The knife strikes my chest before I can scream.

I yelp and wake up.

The darkness of my new bedroom chills me out. Another stupid nightmare. I so hate it. I hate reliving that awful moment over and over. It's like I did some terrible crime and the great powers of the universe are punishing me for it one night at a time. Every detail of the nightmare is real. Too real. Minus the end because I was never stabbed by a Demon Skin. (That's what we call them now.) I think it's my subconscious adding its own spin to my awful reality. Why can't my subconscious pick something happy to add? How about me kicking that creature's butt?

I move around in bed and notice gray fur. My fur. I check my hand and see a paw. Piss on the sun, I shifted in my sleep again. Now I'll have to wash my sheets or Mom will know I had another nightmare. She over-worries about that stuff.

I nuzzle Bullwinkle's stomach and then rest my head next to my furry friends. Rocky and Bullwinkle have been my friends since I was four. It's silly for a sixteen-year-old wolf to keep them this long, but it's hard to give them up because they remind me of the good times. The times when the pack thrived. We were all so free and alive, and I so want to live like that again. Someday.

I snooze in bed until the morning welcomes my nose with the strong scent of fresh deer, which rolls me out of bed. Slipping on some clothes, I bounce down the stairs and reach the kitchen. Dad couldn't sleep last night so he did some hunting in the woods. His insomnia brought us a juicy buck.

Mom asks about Aiden as we enjoy our breakfast. I tell her about hanging out with him at Hideaway Pizza and mention how easy it was to talk to him. I don't mention the shifting in the woods part. If my parents ever found out that Aiden knows who we are...that would cause massive problems.

But hey, I have it under control. Aiden will never tell a soul. Besides, my parents don't need to know everything that happens in my life.

I gnaw on a deer leg as Dad warns me again about how important it is to keep our secret. Dad gets paranoid sometimes. I humor Dad by nodding a lot and contributing an example from school when I was following his orders.

"Aiden's only a friend, correct? Not falling in love with him, are you?" Dad asks, with a little fear behind the words.

My personal life is not any of his business. It's not like I'm keeping Aiden a secret, but the details of our relationship should be.

I give him a sweet smile. "I haven't said anything to him."

"Not what I asked."

I pick some deer cartilage out of my teeth. "We're close

friends, and I care about him, yes."

"He's not one of us. You do know that you could never mate with him," Dad says, always willing to pour a bucket of reality over my head.

Right now I could care less about mating. It's not like I don't think Aiden is super cute enough to mate with. It's just...right now I'm in love with having a best friend again. Does that make sense?

"I know that, Daddy. Don't worry about it."

"Aiden's a nice young man. I like him," Mom says, dabbing her mouth with a cloth napkin stained with deer blood.

See? Mom gets it. Here's a human we could trust. Someone who wouldn't betray us. I wish Dad could see that.

"Boy doesn't have any guts. Can't protect you. Need a boy who can protect you. Might be a nice guy and say nice things, but he'll run away in a fight. I sense it in him."

Dad's right. Aiden isn't much of a fighter right now, but I think the boy has the heart of a fighter inside him. I really do. All he needs is a friendly nudge, and I could be that nudge. I could toughen him up and give him encouragement to boost his confidence. If Aiden and I are going to be together, he needs to be able to defend himself in case the Demon Skins find us again, which I hope they never do.

Hiding seems to be our only defense against them.

CHAPTER NINETEEN

BREE

I hate this movie. It's so dark and depressing. Why do humans torture themselves watching characters who see life as this dismal hole that leads nowhere? I don't get it. They live so inside their heads. They never stop and take a look around to see how beautiful the world is. They never live in the moment. All they do is treat life like this huge burden they have to carry instead of the awesome gift it really is. It makes me so sad. But Aiden wanted to see this dark movie about a French circus clown who's sad and hates his life. The English subtitles drive me crazy. I read books not movies.

Aiden chomps on his popcorn while I snack on some beef jerky that I hid in my purse. But we do share a grape soda together, and so far that's been the highlight of our movie night. The clown on the screen walks across a winter wasteland. Snow falling against smoke-colored skies. He's sad again. Boo-hoo. Who gets sad playing with little kids? They're jumping and running and playing and laughing like super-cute baby wolves. I don't get this clown.

I concentrate on the snow instead. The beautiful snow. Little frosty pieces of heaven that remind me of Colorado and the mountains and the home I had to leave.

And then the nightmare rushes over me. Dawn's long, red hair blowing in the wind. My best friend's laugh. The crack of the gun that killed her.

I shake off the image, and a yawn takes over my mouth, but I close it as quick as I can.

"You hate this movie, don't you," Aiden whispers.

He caught me.

"I don't hate it," I whisper, "but I don't like it all that well."

"I'm sorry."

"Why? Like, you didn't make the movie."

"Still." Aiden checks the aisle. "We're blocked in on both sides, so it would be kind of awkward to try and leave now. Can you wait until the end?"

"Sure." I can't hold back a sigh.

Aiden nods and steps back into movie world. I watch his green eyes follow the screen as his mind sinks back into the movie. Wish I could share this experience with him, but I rest against his warm chest instead and settle in for a tiny nap.

The movie gets quieter now...the wail of the wind and the sound of the clown kicking up snow as he walks. You could hear a feather drop. Wouldn't it be hilarious if someone shrieked and made the audience jump? An idea forms. An idea that would be an awesome way to clear a crowded theater and get me out of this depressing movie.

I snuggle up to Aiden's ear. "I'm going to do something. Don't freak out when I do it, okay?"

"What something are we talking about?" Aiden asks, looking worried.

"Something hilarious." I pat him on the cheek and sit back in my chair. I cup my hand around my lips, breathe in really deep, and then...I wail.

The blaring sound cracks against all four walls of the theater and fills the room with the best howl I've done in like forever. Popcorn flies in the air as people jump to their feet and scatter for the exits. Girls scream. People start freaking out and climbing over rows of seats to get away. It's like someone hit a switch and put a gazillion bolts of electricity through all of them.

I stuff a wad of paper napkins in my mouth to muffle my laughing. Aiden's eyes are huge. He can't believe what I did, but he's also grinning, too, because it's hilarious. We both lean against each other, trying to hide our guilty faces from the handful of people still in the theater trying to figure out if the howl came from the movie or if there's something furry running loose around them.

"I think I swallowed my tongue," Aiden whispers.

That makes me laugh all over again. "I warned you."

Our cheeks touch. Our faces side-by-side. I smell the popcorn on his breath.

"That was insane," Aiden says, his voice delighted.

"Should I do it again?"

"No, they'll figure out where you are. We should act scared and run out."

"Sell it! Awesome idea."

Aiden and I flash serious faces that say we're not happy about our movie-going experience being interrupted. The theater empties out. A manager and some of his minions come in and search with flashlights. They don't even bother to stop the movie or turn on the main lights. I've made everyone crazy.

"Did you kids see anything running around the aisles?" the manager asks us.

I almost answer but Aiden beats me.

"I saw a dog. Big pit bull. He ran down the row in back of us and then down the stairs. Ugly looking thing."

"Pit bull?" The Manager makes a face. "Oh boy. You kids better leave."

Aiden takes my hand, and we hop down the steps. The manager and his minions continue their search in the dark for the phony intruder. I release Aiden's hand and stop. He throws me a confused look.

I smile.

"No. Don't," he whispers.

I wail the second-best howl I've ever done. Flashlights fly in all directions, and the manager freaks out and yells a few choice obscenities while convinced he's about to be attacked.

I laugh so hard my eyes water.

Aiden tells me about this cool bridge that spans over the

Arkansas River. So I park my car, and we take a walk across this old railroad bridge that the city rebuilt for people to use. A cyclist rides by; her wheels roll over each wood plank and make this cascading rumble that follows her to the other side of the bridge. Large wooden crossbeams hold up the old train tracks above us to make this open-air ceiling.

Aiden holds my hand as he peeks over the railing. I so love this. It's nice to be out in the crisp night air with the moon radiating its love on our skin and giving its wonderful light to show us this beautiful world. The wolf inside stretches. She would love to shift and race up and down this bridge to see how fast she could do it. Aiden says this bridge links to some huge trail system that circles all of the city.

Aiden lets go of my hand and grips the railing, staring down at the dark water that rushes under the bridge. I rest my hand next to his.

"I wonder if anyone has jumped off this bridge," he says.

"Why would they do that?"

Aiden stares at the water. "To commit suicide."

Is he still thinking about that? He wouldn't jump, would he? I don't like it when Aiden thinks like this. Must be that stupid, depressing movie. Maybe he's still wondering if that French clown did commit suicide at the end. Maybe it's a good thing we left early because that movie must remind Aiden of the night when he...piss on the sun. That's why he wanted to go see that movie.

Suicide still fascinates him.

"That's a good way to do it. Dropping yourself into the water. Letting the current take you down the river. Letting the water enter your lungs as you sink deeper and deeper. I bet it doesn't hurt."

Really, Aiden? Do we have to talk about this?

"Is this about that stupid movie?" I ask.

Aiden's silence means yes.

"It was so depressing. All that clown thought about was killing himself and how the circus would miss him if he were gone, and it was so awful. Who wants to watch that?"

Aiden faces me. "But for him, death would be a release. He

was just occupying space and not doing anything for a world that didn't want him to exist in the first place."

"How does he know that the world doesn't want him? Did the clown ask every kid at the circus who watched him? Maybe those kids were happy because he made them laugh, and maybe some of them needed to laugh."

"What if he wanted something more out of his life than to be laughed at?"

"Then why did he become a clown?" I ask.

"Maybe he was forced to be a clown."

I stop myself from laughing. "How do you force someone to be a clown?"

Aiden stares into the distance. The gentle rush of the water below drowns out the awkward silence. The strong smell of algae and fish tickles my nose. A distant sound of two cyclists rolling along the planks on the other side of the bridge.

Aiden watches the river again. This boy worries me. If he tries to kill himself again, I might not be there next time to save him. Why would he want to leave me anyway? Am I not worth staying for?

"Aiden?"

He hesitates, then shifts his gaze to me.

"Promise me. Don't ever try to kill yourself again."

"You don't have to..." His mouth freezes in mid-sentence as surprise grips his face. "How did you know about that?"

"Know about what?"

Aiden pauses. "That I...tried to kill myself."

Piss on the sun. I forgot. Should I lie? Should I tell him the truth?

Aiden softens. Embarrassment makes his cheeks turn red. It's so sad.

"You told me about it," I lie, making one final attempt at making this less awkward than it already is.

"I haven't told anyone," Aiden says, his voice lower. "Issy doesn't even know."

He caught me, but maybe this is a good thing. "All right." I pick at a loose splinter of wood on one of the beams. "I saw

you that night. The night you tried to hang yourself."
Aiden gets quiet.
"I was hunting in the woods. Alone. I didn't catch a thing to eat that night, and I was super bored. But then I caught your scent and decided to stalk you."

I leave out the part that his scent was super sexy, a mix of hot-boy sweat and a juicy burger. Maybe Aiden ate a bacon cheeseburger for his "last" meal, but the combination was irresistible to this girl. I check his eyes to see if he's mad about the stalking part, but he only shows a blank stare.

"I wasn't going to hurt you. I was only curious about what you were up to, and it was fun to stalk a human for once. Anyway...you strung up that yellow rope, and I didn't know why you were doing that, so I sat there in the bushes and watched. I saw you put a noose around your neck, and then I knew exactly what you were planning to do."

Aiden's lips tighten. His eyes squint. He looks pissed.

"I started to panic. What do I do? My parents didn't want me to interact with humans. They would have told me not to interfere, but you looked so sad. So broken. And then you jumped off that stump, and the rope bit into your neck, and you were choking, and I...I couldn't bear to see you die. So I took you down, but you were already passed out, and I was so scared that you were going to die that I shifted, put you in my car, and drove you to the hospital. The nurses noticed the rope marks and asked me if you had tried to kill yourself, and I said yes. When I knew they were taking good care of you, I left."

Aiden's fingernails dig into the wood rail.

"Why did you try to kill yourself?" I ask.

"It's not important."

"I don't understand any of it, but I want to." I rest my hand over his on the rail. I want Aiden to know I'm here for him. I'm someone real he can talk to. I'm someone he can trust.

"I said it's not important."

"Really...even if it's trivial, I want to know. I want to help"

"Bree."

"Whatever it is, I'll understand. Werewolves are great

listeners." I smile. That's a good joke.

"I take it werewolves don't get depressed, huh?"

"Grumpy, yes. Depressed? I've never met one like that."

"And why would they be depressed? You're all so strong. Even in human form you're all so damn strong. And you're all so nimble and fast. And you have this happy family with a mom and a dad who loves you. And you all live inside this nice, big house. And you have your own car. How could you ever be depressed, Bree?" His mocking tone boils in anger, and the suddenness of it overpowers me.

"What do you have to worry about?" Aiden yells. "No one can hurt you. You're a damn werewolf. What can actually hurt a werewolf? Nothing. You've never had the world come crashing down on you and then you realize that you're not strong enough to fix it. And the only thing you know how to do is to escape from it by killing yourself. And then you can't even do that right. If that ever happens to you, Bree, let me know because I would love to see how you deal with all that crap without completely losing it."

His words stab me like they were laced with silver. All I can think about is Dawn and Chevalier and all the butchered wolves of my pack dead on the grass. The helplessness I felt. None of us were strong that day. The sadness bubbles up in my throat, and I can't push it back down. The tears stream out of me like someone opened a valve to a dam, releasing all the pain and the grief. It's so powerful I have to lean against a bridge support so I don't fall into the river.

Aiden hugs me tight. "I'm so sorry. I didn't mean to make you cry." He brings me to his chest, and I wet his shirt with tears. It's been building for a while, and now I can't stop wailing. Aiden cradles my head, and I feel him holding on. Not letting me go. "I suck. I really suck for making you cry." He lets me sob into his chest for a while.

It takes time, but I gain back my composure. I keep my cheek glued to his chest. I like the way the fabric feels against my skin.

"I tried to kill myself over a girl," Aiden says, quiet and honest.

I peel myself off him. "A girl?"

"Pamela Osterhaus. Told her I was in love with her."

I try to hold back a sudden laugh. "Pamela Osterhaus?"

"It's not funny."

"Sorry." I bite my lip. Aiden droops like a dead flower. He's hurting, and I'm laughing at him. I get serious. "What happened after you told her?"

Aiden clears his throat, almost like he's holding back from crying. "She laughed in my face. I felt like a loser, and...I got sick of everything. School. My dad. Everything." He sighs and checks my reaction. "I know. It was stupid."

"If there's anything in this world worth dying for, Pamela Osterhaus is so not it."

"I figured that out."

"Aiden Jay, you should be kissing the ground I walk on for stopping you from throwing your beautiful life away for that witch."

Aiden grins to himself and nods. He kneels down to the bridge floor and bows to me like I'm a princess in a Disney movie. He kisses the wood plank by my shoe. Aww. That's so cute.

I playfully touch my toe on the next wood plank and pull it back.

Aiden leans over and kisses that plank too. Super sweet.

"Are you kissing every plank from here to the car?" I ask.

"Oh...um...do you want me to do that?"

"Maybe." I tease and toss my eyes to the river, which glistens under the full moon, its powerful rays calling me to come out and play.

CHAPTER TWENTY

BREE

The woods reek of animals as I dash through the trees using my four powerful legs, the glowing moon fueling my desire to run and hunt. On my back, Aiden grips a handful of fur and hangs on. I told him to yell if I went too fast or if he got too scared, but the boy holds on tight and doesn't complain as I race through the bushes and trees. I've never hunted with an audience before, but the prideful wolf in me likes all this extra attention.

I dip under one tree, and the branch smacks Aiden in the face.
Oh, I'm sorry, Aiden. Wish I could talk.
Wait. Is that a deer?
The strong scent slows me down to a trot.
Yes, it's a male, and he's close by. Smells like my late-night snack.
"Do you smell something?" Aiden asks in his loud human voice. The one I told him not to use.
I growl.
"My bad," he whispers. "I won't bother you."
Dude, I told you to whisper. I didn't say you couldn't talk. Communicating as a wolf can be so frustrating.
"Is it a bunny?" he asks, using his quiet voice this time.
"Really, Aiden? Why are you asking me questions when I can only grunt, growl, or whimper?"
I ignore him as I approach my prey and go into stealth mode,

picking each step carefully. Like my paws are big marshmallows. Soft and quiet.

Breaking one twig.

Crunching one pecan nut...

Is like blasting a loud speaker at a deer.

Aiden's breath strokes my fur. He's breathing faster, the anticipation causing his pulse to race like mine. It's like we're both sharing the same adrenaline. The same thrill for the hunt. He grips my fur tighter as he waits for me to attack.

This is so awesome!

I see the deer, and he's a big one. Fifteen points on those antlers. I'll have to go straight for his neck and snap it before he has a chance to gore me with that pointy head gear of his. But with Aiden clinging to my back, that might be tricky. I don't want Aiden to get speared, so I'll put myself in the way if the deer charges. I can take an antler in the stomach with no problem. Unlike a human.

I sneak a few more steps towards the deer. The dark shadow of the pecan tree shields my whereabouts, but he should smell me soon, so I can't hang back like this forever. I tense my muscles and prepare them like a runner waiting for the starter pistol. I cock my body back, ready to throw it at my target. My animal instincts take over. Waiting for just the right moment. That tenth of a second...

To attack my prey...

And take it down.

"Should I get off?"

Aiden whispers his question, but it's too late. The deer sprints. Piss on the sun!

I leap after it, pushing myself as fast as I can go. Dodging left. Dodging right. This buck is fast, but I can take him. I grit my teeth and push harder.

The deer sprints into a narrow gully. I throw myself into the air and land on the other side of the gully to cut him off from scampering out. The deer bolts along the length of the deep bottom. I give chase by running along the top so he can't leap out without me getting a piece of him.

The deer races towards the end of the gully. He'll have to jump out or stop at the bottom, but I don't wait for him to

choose. I go with my instinct and leap over the gully.
The deer jumps to get out.

I catch him in my jaws, and we roll back into the gully. The male struggles, and I keep his head away so those antlers won't strike my skin. This deer has spirit, thrashing back and forth, anxious to stay alive, but he's not strong enough to shake me off.

I'm so sorry for this.

I snap his neck, and his body goes limp as the life escapes from his body. I always snap the neck first because I want to make the animal's death quick and painless. I can't stand to see another creature suffer.

I gently lay the deer across some dead leaves. Thank the Goddess Luna it was a clean break. He shouldn't have felt too much pain. I whimper and howl out of respect for the deer's spirit. Respect for the precious life that I've taken to nourish me and my pack. Then I rip into its flesh and taste the delicious flavor of a fresh kill.

"Did you break its neck?" Aiden asks, his voice coming from behind.

Did he fall off my back? I was so focused on the deer I forgot he was clinging to me.

I stop eating and give him a nod. Dry, brown leaves cling to Aiden's hair and parts of his long wool coat. He must have tumbled off when I jumped. Hope he's okay.

"You killed it. Just like that." Aiden steps toward the kill, his eyes fascinated by my prize. "That deer didn't have a chance, did it?"

The gully confined his movements and made him easier to chase. That was a mistake on his part.

"That was beautiful." Aiden touches the deer. "The way you jumped and tackled that deer in mid-air. Bringing it down like that. And snap. It was over."

It was a great tackle and so worthy of praise. Maybe a part of me wanted to show off for my one-boy audience.

"That's the clean way to do it, snapping the neck. If you're going to die, you would want to go out that way. Quick."

I wish Aiden would stop obsessing about it. Death isn't beautiful. I've stolen the most precious gift this animal had so

I could satisfy this deep and selfish need I have. I'm so not proud. Ashamed is more like it. Everyone has a side to themselves that they hate. A side to themselves they wish they could shake off like water. A side to themselves which pulls like a weight, dragging them to places they so don't want to visit.

I cried after my first kill. I was twelve. Puberty is when the werewolf gene matures enough to let a child do a full shift. I was hunting in the mountains with my pack. A gorgeous summer sun, with the smell of pine in the air. I was so excited about my first hunt and wanted to impress our Alpha, Chevalier, and my dad. Chevalier instructed me to go in front of the pack and lead the hunt with the understanding that the first animal I find would be my first kill. So I proudly went to the front and lead the pack down this one remote valley.

I found nothing for awhile, but then a small fawn leaped into view. She couldn't have been more than a few months old. A baby wandering too far away from its mother. Excited, I caught up way too easily and attacked the poor little thing. Even as a tween werewolf I towered over the little fawn. The baby didn't have a chance against me.

I remember...the doe's eyes frozen in terror. That young face begging me to please stop.

Those eyes of hers did it. I had a major break-down. Once I realized what I was doing to that poor doe, I lost it completely. I was so upset I shifted back right on the spot and cried. I shamed my parents in front of the entire pack, but Chevalier still took me under his paw and worked with me. Through his guidance, he helped me to accept who and what I am.

"Why did you stop eating?" Aiden asks.

My appetite disappears. The deep need to hunt has been satisfied, but now I can't eat. Maybe it's Aiden. Maybe he's reminding me of what I am. Putting a mirror to my face and forcing me to look at myself. Tonight I don't like what I see.

I close my eyes and shift. My bones crack. The snout tucks back into my face. The sweet burn from my skin as my fur retracts.

"Why are you changing? Your clothes are back in the car."

I cough. "This isn't beautiful. Death is an awful thing.

Killing is awful." I kneel right next to him. The cold air chills my skin and makes me shake, but I still must tell him. "Please stop talking about death like it's this great thing. It's not. It's the most awful thing ever. Don't glamorize it."

Aiden frowns. "Okay. Sheesh, you're freezing." He pulls off his coat.

"Seriously. Life is precious, and what I've done here is savage and awful, and I hate it. But I can't stop myself."

Aiden places his coat over me. "You still worried I'm going to kill myself?"

"Yes." I'm being honest, and I don't care.

Little snowflakes fall. Clouds cover the moon and drop flurries into the cold December night.

"Bree?"

I glance into these soft green eyes that watch me like I'm a Hawaiian sunset.

"Why would I want to kill myself," he says, "when I have you?"

Aiden pulls the coat with me wrapped inside closer to him. I hug him tight so he can stay warm too. We're touching cheeks again, like in the movie theater just after my most-excellent howl. His scent floods my nose, and I love it. He smells better than roses. Smells better than fresh deer. Smells better than chocolate.

He leans in and hovers over my mouth.

Yes.

I want you to do it.

Take me. Seize the moment.

Be a wolf.

And then, his lips touch mine. He's gentle, but hesitant. I open my mouth, and Aiden accepts my invitation and presses harder against my lips. A bolt of lightning goes through my body. My skin forgets how cold it is.

Aiden pulls back to check my reaction.

I smile and kiss him again. Aiden brightens, and we kiss and kiss and kiss. We then stop, and Aiden holds me against his chest, our warm bodies keeping each other toasty. I tuck my bare feet and legs under his long wool coat and become a little ball wrapped up on Aiden's lap.

The forest settles down, becoming quiet and peaceful as we watch the snowflakes drift down like feathers, changing the dark forest into a white one.

* * *

Aiden stands by his open locker. I sprint over the floor tiles and glide my sneakers to a perfect stop next to him. "Where to for lunch? I'll let you pick. I'll even do Chinese." I just discovered Mongolian beef and so love it. Why is Aiden frowning?

He stuffs his backpack in his locker and shuts it. "Do we have to eat out again?"

"No biggie. We can eat here if you want."

Aiden heads off, and I follow. I sense something weird going on. I try to hold Aiden's hand, and he accepts it as we move to the school cafeteria. I smell the pasta and the meat sauce the lunch ladies prepare. I also smell the crispy veggies on the salad bar and the tangy salad dressings and the cubes of ham and bacon I'll have to pile on top of my spaghetti to make it half-way edible. But if Aiden wants to eat here, I will sacrifice my lunch to make him happy. Why did he stop walking? I backtrack. "Are you okay?"

Aiden hesitates. That would be a no.

"I...I promised Issy that I would go out to eat with him today."

"Oh," I say.

"I think he's been feeling left out since we've been hanging out so much."

"But we sometimes eat at the table with Issy."

"*We* eat at the table." Aiden points out.

We meaning *me*.

"Are you pissed?" Aiden asks.

He heard me sigh.

"I'm fine with it." I stick up a smile.

Aiden steps into the cafeteria and then circles back around. "Oh...um...Issy wants me to come over and play a couple levels of Death and Valor with him after school."

"Do you need me to drop you off at his place?"

"No, I'll ride with him after school. If that's okay?"

I don't love this idea of sharing my boyfriend. Why can't he hang out with me? You know, that girl he kissed? Girl werewolves don't provide him with enough excitement? Blowing up digitized pixels gives Aiden more excitement than being with a fantastic girl like me?

"Sure. Go ahead," I say, not really meaning it.

The final bell rings, and I head outside with Aiden. He keeps glancing at me, trying to read my mood. I don't say anything. During Algebra I didn't talk to him much because I'm still miffed about lunch and I want to make him feel guilty about ditching me for a stupid game.

Issy's scent rushes out the main doors.

Aiden grips his backpack. "You're still cool about this, right? It's only for this afternoon."

I watch the horizon. "Have fun playing your game."

"You're doing that thing with your mouth."

"That thing with my mouth?"

Aiden motions to his lips. "You know...that thing you do when you don't like something?"

Ugh. I'm twitching my mouth to the side. It's this stupid habit that always gives me away, and I can't stop doing it. I keep my mouth straight and stiff.

"A-man." Issy fist-bumps Aiden. "You ready to blow away some terrorist scum?"

Aiden hesitates.

"So you're not ready to blow away terrorist scum?"

Is Aiden cracking? Bending to my will? Feeling mucho guilty about leaving his girlfriend all alone? He should.

"I forgot. I promised Bree we'd go to the aquarium today," Aiden says. A huge lie, but it works nicely.

Issy looks hurt. The boy doesn't hide his disappointment and even fires a look in my direction that's too aggressive. The wolf in me doesn't like it.

"Later, then," Issy grunts and mopes off to his car.

Aiden gives me a smile as flat as a dead fish. "What do you want to do?" he asks with a hint of surrender as he moves towards my car.

Will he be acting like this all afternoon? Making me feel guilty and awful for breaking up his play date? Fine. I get the message. No girls allowed.

"Do you want to spend the afternoon with Issy?"

"No, it's okay," Aiden lies.

No, it's not okay, and that's so obvious. He's making me feel like a witch who's putting a control spell on her boyfriend that forces him to do things against his will.

"Go ahead. Call Issy before he leaves. Tell him I can't go to the aquarium today."

Aiden slows. "Are you only saying that? Or do you mean it?"

"I mean it. You guys have fun," I say.

He gets out his phone, hesitates, and checks with me one more time.

"It's fine."

Aiden calls and catches Issy still in the parking lot. That smile on my boyfriend's cute face soothes my disappointment. A little. He puts away his phone. "Thanks, Bree. I promise to make it up to you."

"You better." I lean in a couple inches and part my lips. An awesome thank-you kiss would be an excellent move for him at this point. I'll even forgive Aiden if he gives me a good one.

But he sprints towards the parking lot to find Issy.

Really, Aiden? Seriously? My boyfriend still needs more training.

I open my car door and toss my backpack in, then say hello to Rocky and Bullwinkle in the backseat. They'd so never ditch me for a game. I start the car and wind down both windows for the warm southern breeze to sweep inside. But something makes me pause. A faint scent. It's Kirk Cumming's scent. Something about it makes me feel uneasy. If my fur was out, it would be bristling right now. I concentrate on the scent and wait to put the car in drive.

Now I detect Aiden's scent. Both their scents mix together.

MY GIRLFRIEND BITES

They're close to each other. Is Kirk harassing Aiden again? I kill the engine.
And then smell human blood.
I jump out of the car and bolt towards the far side of the parking lot.

CHAPTER TWENTY-ONE

BREE

Blood pools near Aiden's mouth as his body lies over the rough pavement. His cheeks glisten with tears as Kirk slams his foot into his gut, making Aiden flinch in pain. Kirk's two friends watch and enjoy the violence.
"Told you this was gonna happen, asshole." Kirk struts around his victim with this false confidence.
"Stop it!" Issy yells from the ground as blood drips from his nose and lips. I bet he tried to help and was hit too.
"Shut up, Lizzie." Mooney the skinhead fakes a lunge at Issy, making the boy scoot back.
Kirk's cowboy boot strikes Aiden in the stomach again. He coughs and dry-heaves. Hate burns in me. The wolf wants to come out and fight to protect a member of my pack.
That's not quite right. My feelings for this boy...consume me. They go deep. Deeper than protecting a member of the pack. It's much more personal than that. It's protecting my mate. Kirk is attacking *my mate*. The boy I love more than anything in this world. The boy I can't stand to see getting hurt.
The wolf strains against the girl. It wants to attack and kill the threat to my mate.
No! Suppress it. Stay human. If anyone sees you as a wolf, it will put your family in danger, and you can't risk their safety.
Piss on the sun. These stupid boys...don't they realize that

I'm a bomb? Hurt what I love and I will go up like a warehouse full of fireworks, damaging everything within the blast radius. I can't stop this fury. If I don't release it...the fur and the claws come out.

"Get off of him," I growl as I march towards the three boys. "Leave the parking lot now or I'm calling the cops." I'm trying my best to give Dumb, Dumber, and Dumbest an escape route. They don't want to test me right now.

Kirk folds his arms. "Fantastic. It's crouching-dog girl. You here to bark for your boyfriend?"

Mooney and Jack laugh.

Kirk stares at me. "Yuck. Do you actually kiss this, Aiden?"

These guys need to stop and run away right now. I can't hold her back if they—

"She's nasty looking," Jack says.

"Her body's okay," Mooney says. "Just have to put a bag over her head."

Kirk slams his boot into Aiden one last time. "Is that what you have to do before you touch her, Blow—?"

I slam Kirk hard against the ground. So fast no one even realizes what's going on. Kirk blows out all the air in his lungs. He'll be down for a moment or two.

I plant my feet as Mooney and Jack slowly realize Kirk is down on the ground.

Mooney takes hold of my T-shirt and pulls me in a hold.

I rip the boy off like a glove and throw him fifty feet as he shatters the window of a parked car. Mooney screams in pain. I think he broke some bones.

Good.

Jack backs away from me, his eyes terrified. But it's too late for mercy now. I shove him as hard as I can, and his butt skims the surface of the parking lot for about seventy feet before his back strikes the curb. Jack rolls over in pain.

I close my eyes. The fury still boils like a pond of lava.

Calm down. You have to stay human. Keep it inside. Don't let it out.

"Wow, Bree."

I know that voice, and now I get a whiff of his scent. Issy

watches my public audition for Super Girl. Why is he holding his phone up? Is he taking pictures!?

Kirk stirs, and I leap over him in a flash. The boy pushes against me, trying to get to his feet, but it's too easy to keep him down, like he's a fly trying to push back a bookcase. The boy struggles and struggles and struggles. That fake confidence changes to shock as Kirk realizes I'm not some frail girl. I'm a werewolf, and he's a pitiful, weak, and useless human being. Kirk is the one who's frail and vulnerable. I know how to break his neck. One hand across his throat and one little twist of my wrist and snap.

I hate this boy. After what he did to Aiden, snapping his neck would be too merciful. I could puncture an artery. The kind that bleeds forever and will leave him in agony before killing him.

Kirk gasps as he struggles for air. I now see my own hands around his throat, squeezing the life out of him. The wolf senses his weakness and goes in for the kill. It's automatic. A reflex.

I've lost control.

The wolf is killing him. Eliminating the threat to her mate. One way or the other she will have her kill.

Something clutches my arm. I ignore it. Whoever it is, they won't be able to peel me off my kill.

"Please stop," Aiden says, his words labored.

Kirk sounds like that sucker tube at the dentist's office that slurps up water and spit. The boy under me struggles to find any pocket of air.

Aiden squeezes my arm, and his breath tickles my ear. "It's over. Let him go, Bree."

His touch, his scent, his closeness brings me back. I shove the wolf to the side and take back control. I make my fingers release Kirk's throat, and he coughs like crazy as he rolls over.

I turn away and help Aiden stand up.

"Do you need to go to the hospital?" Issy asks.

Aiden leans against me. "Just take me home."

"At least let my mom take a look at you," Issy insists.

"Is she a doctor?" I ask.

The inside of Issy's roomy house has this interesting Middle-Eastern-mixed-with-Ikea look. A beautiful lamp shines across the microfiber couch that Aiden rests on. The Persian rug tucked under us has these beautiful animal patterns interlaced with golden trees and landscape. So gorgeous. It must be worth a lot of money. Wish I could talk Dad into buying one of these.

"Swallow this. It should help ease the pain." Issy's mom gives Aiden a pill and some milk to wash it down with. She's done a great job stopping the nose bleed and treating the cuts inside Aiden's mouth. After a full examination, Issy's mom tells us that Aiden is only bruised.

"You should report this to the principal in the morning," Issy's mom insists. "Those boys need to be expelled."

Aiden flicks his gaze to me. "I don't think they'll be a problem anymore."

I'm so happy to see that relieved look on his face, but I'm totally embarrassed because I let things get way out of control. I could have killed those boys. Thank the Goddess Luna that Aiden talked me down from that cliff.

But now there's a giant problem which needs fixing. I swear I saw Issy taking pictures of what happened, which is not good. I need to find out.

"Would you like something to drink? Tea? Coffee? Ginger ale?" Issy's mom asks.

This would be a good time to get her out of the room.

"Would some hot tea be too much trouble?" I ask.

"Not at all. I could use some myself. Ishmail, do you want some tea?"

Issy nods, and his mother floats into the kitchen. She's graceful for a human. All right. Now it's time for some answers.

"Did you take pictures of the fight?" I ask.

Issy smiles. "Better. I shot video."

Video? Issy whips out his camera and joins Aiden on the couch. I squeeze beside Issy to get a better look. His fingers dance across the buttons and bring up a menu and the video player. He hits play. It's shaky, but the view looks up from the ground where Issy fell after getting punched. There I am. It's so weird seeing myself standing there. Look how pissed I am. I wouldn't want to mess with that girl. She pushes Kirk, and he flies out of frame. Good. Issy didn't get video of how far I tossed Kirk. The camera then moves higher as Issy scrambles to his feet. He now frames the camera better as I pick up Mooney and fling him into the air like he's a Frisbee.

"How did you do that?" Issy asks. "Mooney plays varsity football, and he's three times your size. That's crazy."

My huge feat of werewolf strength captured perfectly on video. So not good. Now it's Jack's turn. Issy shoots this part extremely well, getting great shots of my angry face and following Jack as I fling him like a bowling ball. The kid skims the ground and crashes into the far-away curb.

My stomach twists. This is a major problem.

"Again. How did you do that?" Issy asks.

And here comes the "awesome" part of the video. Me trying to choke a boy to death. Kirk gasping for air. The girl choking him has the cold, heartless face of a killer. It's like I'm watching this insane girl on video who doesn't act like me at all. But it is me, and I'm doing every single one of those awful things.

"I thought you were going to kill him," Issy says.

"Me too," Aiden says.

That makes three of us.

"Could you please erase that video?" I ask.

"Erase it? But it's awesome. The best video ever made. A girl kicking Kirk's ass? It's priceless. Do you know how many hits this will get on YouTube? This will go viral."

Viral? I can't let viral happen. Viral will endanger everyone I love.

"Please, Issy?"

"Tell me how you threw a football player in the air like that and I might erase it."

It's because I'm a werewolf, and I'll throw you out a window if you don't...oh, piss on the sun. There must be some ancient

fighting technique I could fake black-belt knowledge of.
"I know Sho-mo-shi-a," I say.
Or I could create one.
"Shomo what?" Issy asks.
"Sho-mo-shi-a. It's an ancient fighting technique the Aztec Indians used against the Spanish. It's a combination of weight distribution, pressure points, and an expert knowledge of mass, gravity, and velocity."
Not bad for being total crap.
"That sounds more Japanese than Aztec," Issy says.
"That's what they call it," I lie. "My father taught me. He wanted me to be able to defend myself."
"Against who? The 101st Airborne Division?"
Aiden laughs.
"All right. Now I told you how I threw that boy so how about erasing that video for me?"
Issy hesitates and then pushes a few buttons. "Done."
"Thank you. Really, I appreciate that."
"Sure, but can I leave it up on YouTube?"
I swallow my tongue. "What? It's up on YouTube right now!"
Aiden sits up. "You uploaded it already?"
"Yeah, in the car on the way here." Issy brings up his phone. "Let's see how many hits it has."
Disaster. Epic fail. You name it, I've just done it. Right now millions of people are watching my werewolf coming-out party.
Aiden comes to my rescue. "Dude, if her parents see that video, Bree will be grounded for the rest of this decade. You have to delete it."
"Do you realize what this video will do to our social lives? The rest of junior year will be awesome. Everyone will love this video."
Who cares about being popular? I'm trying to protect my family from getting slaughtered. Anything that even suggests that I'm a werewolf could ruin everything.
I grip Issy's leg. "Delete that video."
"C'mon, it's so awesome. You should be proud of it."

I tighten my grip.

"Ouch," he quips.

"Take it down." I let a little werewolf creep into my voice.

"I have tea," Issy's mom announces as she comes out of the kitchen. A silver tray and tea set with steam rising from the spout. She places the tray on the coffee table and pours three cups.

I take my hand off Issy's leg.

"Sugar?" she asks.

I fake a smile, "Two please."

"Bree?" Aiden asks. "I need something from your car. Can you come unlock it for me?"

Huh? I put his backpack in Issy's car so why would he ask me to...? Oh. Maybe Aiden wants a private chat. Good idea.

We step outside, and the bright sun makes me squint as I wait for Aiden. He takes it easy coming over because his gut is still sore and tender.

"Do you have an idea?" I ask.

"Yeah, I think you should tell him," Aiden says.

"Tell him what?"

"Tell him what you are."

"That's not happening."

"Bree, you can trust him.

"How can I trust him? He just uploaded a video about me behind my back and without asking."

"You should tell him because the longer Issy hangs out with us, the more suspicious he'll get."

These are the times I wish I was a witch. I could then cast a memory spell to make Issy forget everything.

"So you don't think he buys my fighting technique story?" I ask.

"Not really. It's kind of stupid," Aiden says.

Stupid? It's not stupid. Well...not incredibly stupid. Lightly stupid maybe. Oh, piss on the sun, that's not important. What am I going to do? Seriously? And not just about Issy. What about Kirk, Mooney, and Jack? Will they tell anyone? Like the principal? Or the police? Or the FBI?

I don't know if I can fix this.

CHAPTER TWENTY-TWO

BREE

Issy becomes way too excited when I ask him to load up Death and Valor 4 on his GameMaster because I want to play this game that he and Aiden seem so obsessed over. We slip into Issy's room, and Aiden quietly shuts the door. As Issy boots up his GameMaster, my wolf ears follow his mom's footsteps. I want to make sure she's nowhere near her son's bedroom. Dishes clang, and water pours into the sink. Sounds like she's in the kitchen. Good. This conversation needs to be private.

Issy loads the game and hands me a machine-gun shaped controller that provides "realism," according to him. He explains the start of the game and what to expect on the first level, and that's when I stop him.

"Can I trust you?"

"Totally," Issy says. "We'll be playing on a team, and I won't let you get lost or surrounded. Right, Aiden? Am I a good squad leader or what?"

"I'm not talking about the game."

"Oh." Issy squints. "I'm not following."

"Bree needs to tell you something," Aiden says. "A secret."

"A huge secret," I add.

His eyebrows lift. "A huge secret? This sounds good." He puts down the controller.

"So...the parking lot today," I begin. "You asked me how I

threw those boys."

Issy nods.

"All right. You might think this is...totally out-there. But I swear it's the truth. For real. No faking. The most honest I could ever be with you." I take in a deep breath. Here we go.

"I'm a werewolf."

Issy blinks.

"My family moved here a few months ago after my pack was attacked and murdered. My family is hiding out from our enemies, and that video you uploaded could lead them straight to us. And if they find me and my family, they'll kill us. They will not stop chasing us until we are all dead."

Issy takes another moment.

And laughs. "That's the most insane thing I've ever heard. You actually think you're a werewolf?"

"I've seen her change into one," Aiden says.

Issy shakes his head. "You two are messing with me. Are you serious? Nah, I think you're both messing with me."

"Could a normal human girl my size do those things you saw in the parking lot?"

Issy frowns, thinks, checks me, checks Aiden. Checks me again. "No."

"Then how do you explain it?"

Issy shifts a little on his bed, checks me out one more time. He's still not sure.

"Maybe you should change in front of him," Aiden says.

"No way! Not here. Not with his mom walking around," I say.

"Hold on. You want to change into a werewolf, here? In my bedroom?" Issy asks.

"I can't. It's too dangerous."

"He's not going to believe you unless you show him," Aiden says.

"A-man...so you're telling me that this girl...the one standing here...is a werewolf? And you've seen this?"

Aiden smiles and nods.

"And, Bree...you can change into a werewolf like right now? Don't have to wait for a full moon?"

"I could, yeah," I say.

Issy crosses his arms. "Do it."

My ears search for Issy's mom. She moves around the house, going in and out of rooms. My instinct says this is way too dangerous. But Issy won't believe me if I don't do it. Piss on the sun. I have to get that video off YouTube.

"Turn around," I say.

"Why?" Issy asks.

"I have to take off my clothes."

"Well, how do I believe you if I don't see the whole process?"

Aiden snatches a folded blanket on a table. "I'll hold this in front of you."

"No, Issy's right. He has to see everything happen."

Aiden leans in and whispers, "But does he have to see you naked?"

"I'll rip my clothes to shreds if I leave them on, and this T-shirt is too cute."

"I'll buy you a new shirt."

A guy volunteering to buy me new clothes? I like this.

"I love these jeans too."

"Okay," Aiden says, not thrilled.

Really, Aiden? You should be happy. I'm so worth new clothes.

I stand, kick off my sneakers, and pull off my socks. I unbutton my jeans...and notice Issy holding up his phone. "What are you doing?"

"C'mon," Issy says. "A girl turns into a werewolf and I can't record it?"

"Give your phone to Aiden."

"But..."

"Now."

Aiden holds out his hand.

Issy frowns, rolls the phone in his hands, and then gives it up. "You better not be messing with me."

I force the wolf out of its hiding place. Concentrate on my bones as they crack. My fur as it sprouts. My snout as it forms. The threads pop and rip as my cute pink T-shirt splits and falls away. My jeans hang in longer since the material is stronger. But then they, too, split and fall to the carpet. Finally that sweet, aching pain as the bones set and my fur settles.

Issy's mouth hangs open.

"You okay?" Aiden asks.

Issy doesn't move.

"Whatever you do. Don't run away," Aiden says. "When I first saw her, I freaked and ran away because I was scared half to—"

"This is awesome!" Issy yells.

"Seriously, Issy. If you feel scared, I understand."

Issy doesn't look scared. If anything, he's fascinated. The boy rises from the bed and lingers right near my face. The wolf finds this intimidating. A threat from an animal wanting a fight. But the human me keeps the wolf in check. "Is that really you, Bree? Can you understand what I'm saying?"

I nod.

"Awesome," Issy says under his breath, like he's in church and witnessing a divine miracle.

The chrome door knob jiggles. "Ishmail? Why is your door locked?"

Piss on the sun. Issy's mom. I whimper at Aiden.

"Give me a minute," Issy yells and then lowers his voice. "Change back, quick."

"It takes her a few minutes to change back," Aiden says with desperation. "We have to hide her."

"I have cookies for your friends," Issy's mom says.

"We don't want any cookies," Issy says.

A pause. "What is going on inside that room, Ishmail."

Aiden gestures to go under Issy's bed, but there's no way I can fit under there. I shake my head and dash into his bathroom.

Issy whispers, "Closing the door to the bathroom is too obvious."

This is so ridiculous.

Issy opens the sliding doors to his closet. "Get in here."

"Open this door," Issy's mom says. "If you are doing

anything inappropriate with that girl, your father will become unglued."

"We're playing Death and Valor. I have to wait for a stopping point," Issy calls out.

I leap inside the closet. Big, bulky werewolf-me can't quite fit comfortably inside, but the two boys stuff me in as best they can. Aiden slams the door shut, and it pinches my tail. A yelp comes out, and I cover my mouth with a paw.

"What was that noise?" Issy's mom asks.

"This level of the game has wolves in it," Issy lies.

Aiden opens the closet door, pulls my tail out of harm's way, and shuts it.

I'm in darkness. I focus on shifting back. I feel my snout shrinking. My fur pulls back into my skin. My bones retract back into place.

I listen as the bedroom door opens. "We have a rule, Ishmail." His mom's voice booms into the room.

"I know, but you know we hate getting distracted during the game."

"What are those sounds?" Issy's mom asks.

"Those cookies look good, Mrs. Bishara," Aiden says. "May I have one?"

"Where is that girl?" she asks.

"Bree had to go home," Aiden says.

Another loud crack comes from my shifting body. Shhh. I wish my body wasn't so noisy.

"What is going on inside your closet?" Issy's mom sounds too close to the door.

"It's the house settling," Issy says with panic in his voice.

The closet door slides open, and the darkness flashes into light. Issy's mom gets an eyeful of a naked me in her son's closet. And she doesn't look too happy.

"Get up, young lady."

I pull one of Issy's shirts off the hanger and cover myself as a sudden rush of human modesty takes over.

"You boys go into the living room," Issy's mom says.

"Mom...I can explain."

"Ishmail." Her voice doesn't mess around.

Issy and Aiden evacuate the room.

The older woman folds her arms and levels this glare that makes my heart freeze. "I don't know who you think you are. Coming into my son's bedroom and trying to corrupt him and his friend. Tempting them into making a bad decision in their lives. Perhaps you enjoy using your body as an amusement park, but I think it's disgusting, and I should call your parents and tell them you need to learn how sacred a woman's body is. How she should not use herself in this way."

I hate lectures, especially from adults who are not my parents. This woman doesn't know me, and I resent that she thinks I'm some slut. I know that finding a naked girl in her son's closet would lead to some awkward questions, but I stand there and accept my accuser's role of a teen temptress trying to corrupt nice boys into doing bad things.

* * *

I have this nervous twitch in my stomach as I drive myself to school the next morning. I took care of the Issy situation, but Kirk and his buddies still saw me act like SheHulk in the parking lot. What am I going to do about that? Will those boys just blow it off and leave us alone? I have no idea, and that's what makes me nervous. If we're discovered, my family will have to move and become gypsy werewolves again, migrating from city to city. Alone. Without a pack. Wolves need a family. We need our packs. We need our own woods and our own place to call home. I don't want to move again. Aiden is here. How can I leave him?

Maybe Dad would let him come with us if I asked him.

That's not happening, and you know it.

Dad would order me to forget about Aiden, and since Dad is now the Alpha, I would have to obey. It would kill me inside, but I would have to obey.

A car horn snaps me back to attention. The traffic light is green. I hit the gas and fling my car through the intersection.

Aiden holds my hand as we move down the hall to Algebra. He apologizes for Issy's inquisition at lunch. I drove Aiden and Issy out to the cheap pizza buffet on Mingo Road since I also promised Issy that I would buy him lunch if he took my video off YouTube. But what sucked about lunch was Issy and his insane werewolf questions...

"If you bite someone, do they turn into a werewolf?"
"No."
"Do you always change on a full moon?"
"No."
"Can you howl? Show me."
"Yes and no."
"How do werewolves have sex?"
"Next question."
"Do you know any single girls who are vampires?"
"Next question."
"If Jason from Friday the 13th hunted you down and hacked off your arm, would it grow back?"
"Yes."
"What if it was your head?"
"Don't know."
"Is it true only silver can kill you?"
"Yes."
"Have you ever killed a human?"
"No, but are you volunteering?"

Things went downhill from there. I ended up having to stop the Q&A because secretly I was so ready to bash my head against the table.

Aiden squeezes my hand. "Sure you're okay?"

I breathe in his emerald-green eyes. "I'm perfect."

Mr. Strickland starts Algebra with a new theorem on the white board that appears so complicated I think it must be the answer to how the universe was formed. It's times like these I'm so glad to have a math whiz for a boyfriend. Halfway through class a senior comes in with a paper slip.

Mr. Strickland reads it. "Aiden and Bree. You're wanted in

the office."

My stomach drops. The office. Those two words sound so simple. So non-threatening. What bad thing could happen inside an office? In my case, it could be the start of Armageddon.

We stand, and twenty-four pairs of eyes watch us leave class and follow the senior who holds our office summons. Aiden shoots a worried look in my direction. I wish I could fake a confident smile and tell him things will be okay. But the truth is...I don't think it will be okay.

We enter the school's administration office and bypass the large wood counter that most students see when they come to get school information or to correct some school-related paperwork. We go deeper in the gut of the administration office and pass a couple office cubicles before reaching the big office. The Principal's Office.

The large office contains no windows, only lights that shine on a walnut desk. Behind that desk is Principal Echohawk, who is pure Pawnee Indian with a body as big as a haystack. But what snags my attention are the three students waiting in front of him. Mooney wears a large bandage attached to the back of his head with fresh cuts and bruises on his face. Both of his arms are held up by slings with a brace hugging his neck. Jack wears a cast over his shoulder and arm. Kirk gets off easy with only a neck brace. When they notice I'm in the room, the boys hide their eyes. The wolf can sense it. They're afraid of me.

"Please come in," Principal Echohawk says, his hands pressed together. "We need to discuss what happened in the parking lot yesterday."

CHAPTER TWENTY-THREE

BREE

As instructed by Principal Echohawk, Aiden shuts the polished-wood door that seals our fate inside the office. There's no place to sit, so we're forced to stand to the side. This is it. I'm so dead. Mr. Echohawk will ask me all kinds of questions I can't give him good answers to, and he won't be satisfied, and so he'll dig deeper into my past. *Where did I live before coming here? Who did I live with? What exactly are you?*

Piss on the sun. What if Mr. Echohawk contacts the police? Their investigation would be more intense and would complicate things by tossing suspicion on my parents. *Who are they, and where did they come from? Where did my father get all that money we have?* Dad can't tell them it came from a Colorado werewolf pack investment portfolio. That would go over big.

"Miss Mayflower?"

Principal Echohawk waits for me to address him. "These young men tell me that yesterday after school...you jumped them in the parking lot. Is this true?"

Jumped them? What a bunch of vampires. I gave them the weregirl butt-kicking they were asking for. But I have to lie, of course. Always protect the pack.

"No, I only watched."

"She's lying," Kirk says before grimacing as his neck tilts.

"She jumped us from behind and did some crazy karate shit—"

"Language," Echohawk interrupts.

"Karate...stuff to beat us up for no reason at all."

"You've been bullying us all year," Aiden says. "You even threatened to beat me up."

"Is that true?" Echohawk asks Kirk.

"I haven't touched the guy. Maybe I told him to go f—"

"Language."

"Yeah...maybe I told him to go pleasure himself after school. Sure. But I didn't threaten to beat him up."

"Now *you're* lying," Aiden says.

Kirk throws out another F-bomb.

Echohawk glares. "Keep swearing, and I'll be adding detention days on top of whatever else I decide to throw at you."

Kirk folds his arms across his chest and pouts.

Echohawk waits for the room to settle. "I took the liberty of pulling video footage from the school security cameras located in the parking lot."

Security cameras? Oh no. No. No. No. There's more video of me? I hate this stupid age of technology.

On his face, Aiden has the same worry I do. The principal knows the truth, and I'm doomed. My body revs up to full panic mode as a knot forms in my stomach. It's a strange sensation that I don't get too often. The last time was that day in the compound when the Demon Skins attacked. It's fear. Real fear. Suddenly I'm a deer caught in the cross-hairs of my killer.

Echohawk loads up a video file on his laptop and swivels the screen around so we all can see and hits play. "The video clearly shows Aiden getting jumped by you three." Echohawk levels his finger at Kirk, Mooney, and Jack.

The security video fills the screen. A digital clock records minutes and seconds in the right bottom corner. The small lettering on top identifies it as *Student Parking Lot NE Corner*. There's Aiden in one corner of the video. Kirk, Mooney, and Jack run into frame and attack him. My blood boils all over again as the boys punch and kick Aiden while he's helpless on the ground. I feel every hit his body takes, as if it was directed at my own stomach. A dark-skinned boy appears in frame. That must be Issy.

"Another boy tries to intervene," Echohawks says. "And then, Kirk, you attack him and put him down."

Kirk wails on Issy and beats him to the ground. Aiden tries to crawl away and only makes it behind a parked SUV before Kirk notices and runs over too. Mooney and Jack follow and disappear behind the SUV too as the center of the action shifts behind it. Funny, I don't see myself on the video yet.

There I am, coming out of the right side of the frame. My hands make little fists as I sprint behind the SUV.

Mooney then flies from behind the SUV and smashes into the car I put him in. Glass twinkles as it spreads around the impact. A moment passes. Jack's hat flies off as he skims the pavement and bangs hard into the curbing. The video freezes.

Echohawk addresses the three boys in front of him. "Judging by the way you two are thrown around in this video, someone is fighting back. Although I wish I could see who that someone is."

"That was Bree," Kirk says. "She's the one doing all that. I swear to God."

Echohawk's eyes drift over to me. "Please forgive me if this question is a bit too private, but how much do you weigh? Approximately."

Two hundred and forty pounds. I'm serious. Werewolves have lots of mass due to all that extra bone structure packed tight inside us. My body is like a small paperweight. You try picking it up, thinking it's small and light, only to find out it's dense and really heavy.

I hesitate on purpose. Human girls are sensitive about weight questions so I should act like I'm this waif of a girl who is so gentle that a breeze could knock her over.

"Oh...um...I weigh...about ninety-five pounds," I say, pretending that I think I'm too fat.

Echohawk rises from his chair and examines my face. Why

is he doing that?

"Could you please hold your hair back for a moment?" he asks.

I comb back my long hair and hold it up.

Principal Echohawk inspects my neck, ears, and the sides of my face. It's so strange. He then takes his seat. "Kirk? So you're insisting that a ninety-five pound girl was able to beat up three boys, one of whom is a defensive lineman, and come out of that fight with no bruises. No cuts. No scratches of any kind?"

He so doesn't believe them. Awesome. But Echohawk still needs the identity of the person who fought back...so I'll give it to him.

"It was Aiden," I say. "He totally freaked after they attacked him and got so crazy mad that he beat the crap out of them. I've never seen him so pissed."

Aiden flashes a what-are-you-doing look.

"I'm sorry, Aiden, but they should know the truth. You snapped when you saw Issy getting beat up again." I turn to Echohawk. "The boy in the video who tried to help Aiden? That's our friend Ishmail Bishara. A boy that was also jumped by Kirk and his friends earlier this—"

"I didn't beat up Issy," Kirk interrupts.

"And you didn't jump Aiden either," Echohawk adds, his tone sarcastic and suspicious. "Is what Bree saying true?"

Aiden hesitates, then nods.

"So you retaliated for the attack on your friend?"

"Yes, sir." Aiden plays along. Sacrificing himself to save his girl from getting exposed. This boy is so awesome. I'd love to kiss every inch of his face right now.

"I see what's going on here," Echohawk says.

The anger swells inside Kirk. "This is bullshit. My dad has a good lawyer, and he'll sue this school." Kirk points at me. "And he'll sue your parents too."

"Your father has the right to do anything he wants, Kirk, but the evidence shows you three boys started the fight," Echohawk says. "Now I will have to decide if you get a suspension or if I should expel you from school."

Principal Echohawk dismisses Aiden and me so he can deal with Kirk and his idiots in private. My heart deflates as the stress and the anxiety floats away. I think my lie will stick, but Echohawk still might want to talk to Issy and get his side of the story. I don't have Issy's phone number so I'll have to tell Aiden to warn his friend. But I can't do it now because of the senior escorting us back to Algebra as our human hall pass.

"Heard about what happened yesterday so I copied the video." The senior smiles. "Classic. Kirk has been bullying my little brother for months, and I'm so glad somebody finally kicked his ass."

Aiden blinks, like he can't believe a senior is giving him a compliment.

"He was amazing," I say. "I was so scared, but Aiden stood up and went all Batman on them. He was fearless." I slide my arm across Aiden's back and lean on him, selling this as best I can.

We arrive back to class and finish the rest of Algebra. Aiden texts Issy about what to tell Echohawk about the fight. Lucky for us we catch him en-route to the office. Issy tells Echohawk about the fight at Taco Pronto and names Aiden as the boy who fought back. Kirk, Mooney, and Jack get what they deserve, a long suspension. But justice comes with a price.

Aiden gets suspended one week for fighting.

CHAPTER TWENTY-FOUR

BREE

Word about the fight spreads like a hurricane through Wiley Post High School. On Aiden's first day back from suspension, our normal walk down the hallway is anything but. Aiden receives fist-bumps from everyone. Seriously. Kids stop Aiden every few feet and thank him for getting Kirk suspended for an entire month. Seems like there were a lot of students totally sick of Kirk and his bullying. Even a few seniors stop Aiden. One calls him Bruce Wayne...Batman in disguise.
"Don't ever piss off Bruce Wayne," another senior adds. "Or you'll get Kirked."
Getting "Kirked" becomes the new verb at school.
Aiden smiles the whole morning because he can't believe this is happening to him. I have to pitch myself, too, because this situation turned out better than I could have hoped. Not only did I wipe out the problem, I also found a way to boost my boyfriend's confidence. I'll have Aiden jumping off a cliff in no time, becoming the fearless boyfriend I can rely on. But this new Aiden and his sudden popularity that I created does come with drawbacks.
I leave Aiden at his locker while I head for sixth hour, making that old familiar turn around the corner, when my wolf instincts slam on the brakes and slow me to a stop. Something feels different. Something that shouldn't be in my

vicinity. Kind of like a piece of dirt stuck on a white bed sheet. What am I feeling? It's not danger, but something feels off.

I turn and a strong scent smacks my nose. Voldemort mixed with Chanel.

What is *she* doing on this side of school? I peek back around the corner. The long hallway swims with students shuffling to get to class. Voices call out while others chat with their friends. Lockers open and close. Nothing out of the ordinary. Maybe I'm...no, there she is.

Pamela Osterhaus meanders down the hall, a female slug digesting the floor polish off the tile as she slithers along it. Her elephant hips sway like a pontoon boat on a lake. She angles herself towards the left side of the hallway, near a set of lockers where a cute boy is searching through his locker for a book.

My cute boy.

Pamela leans those hips against the locker and tries to act seductively. Flames tickle my stomach as the wolf stirs, wanting to put down the threat. I should move over there and pretend that I forgot something. Then give Aiden a kiss on the cheek or hug him extra tight to give Pamela an ice-clear message to back off.

But the human wins. I stay back to spy because I want to see what my boyfriend does. There was a time when Aiden was so in love with this girl that he tried to kill himself. Does he still have deep feelings for her? Will Aiden be loyal to me?

I strain my wolf ears to hear what they're saying. It's not easy with all this hallway noise. Aiden shuts his locker with a clank, and his eyebrows twitch up in surprise. A smile rolls out.

A smile? Why are you smiling at her!

"Hi," Pamela purrs as her body shifts like a cobra ready to strike. "I heard about what happened in the parking lot. Are you all right?"

Is she only being nice? Showing gratitude like everyone else? I could be wrong about her.

"Yeah, I'm okay." Aiden's shyness keeps his eyes down.

My heart sinks. *Don't disappoint me. I couldn't take that now. Please don't let me down.*

"Kirk is a douche bag," Pamela says. "I dated him once, and it was tragically awful. Did you really take on all three of those boys?"

Aiden slings his backpack over his shoulder. "Um...yeah... didn't have much of a choice. I don't like fighting."

Pamela slips closer. "It was still brave." She flips her blond hair back and lets it settle on her shoulders. I get a strong whiff of her hair product, which reminds me of toilet bowl cleaner. I step forward...but stop myself. No. I want Aiden to do this. I want him to show me that Pamela is past history.

"Something has been bothering me for a while." She pauses and sighs. "I want to apologize for saying all those awful things to you and for making fun of you after the fact. Basically I was a real bitch to you." Pamela brushes back more of her hair. "I thought I had you all figured out. What type of guy you were. However, you proved me completely wrong." Pamela leans in close, but only enough to force Aiden to look at her. "Do you still have feelings for me?"

Aiden's green eyes search hers.

I will kill them both.

Pamela brushes against him, as if it were spontaneous and not planned. "Are you and Bree hooked up?" she asks while picking off a hair or a piece of lint from his shirt.

I can't take more of this. Tell her no. Tell her that you have a super girlfriend that you love and would never ever cheat on. That human girl can't change into a werewolf. Or run fast. Or treat you as awesome as I would.

My boyfriend hesitates.

Really, Aiden? You better say something or I swear I'll march over there and...

"Yeah, I'm going out with Bree right now," he says.

Yes! Thank you! You get a kiss for that.

Pamela's smile weakens. "I see." She traces her finger across his chest. "Let me know if that ever changes because... I don't want to lose my place in line."

Keep this up and she'll lose her place in life.

Why is Aiden grinning? He so better knock that off.

Pamela slinks down the hallway. I want to run up to Aiden and strip off all his clothes and hose him down to wash her disgusting scent off my boyfriend, but I shove myself around the corner and sprint off to class.

Walking out of school with Aiden, I wrap my hands around him like a gift I don't want to share on Christmas morning. I rest my chin on his shoulder and cling on to him because I'm not letting him go. Soon his cheek leans against the top of my head, and his closeness turns up the sweet burn inside. I'm on the edge of mating season...a month when werewolves get extremely frisky. The intensity increases every year as I get older. In Colorado my pack enforced separation between the teen boy and girl werewolves during mating season. The Lycan Commandments dictate that both a girl and a boy must be eighteen before they can officially mate, but the pack encouraged young werewolves to choose a mate within the pack, wanting the love and the companionship between them to be strong before anything else was allowed.

During my mating separation last year, Mom bought some magazines of cute beefy boys with no shirts on that I could focus all my feelings on. Most human girls can satisfy their cravings with chocolate or a pint of Ben & Jerry, but I don't think human girls could deal with the intensity a female werewolf goes through when it's her time of the year, so to speak.

Aiden squeezes my hip, and that sweet burn rages into an inferno. I bite my lip so the pain can distract my hormones. Poor Aiden might have to fight me off with a stick.

CHAPTER TWENTY-FIVE

BREE

The sounds coming from my parents' bedroom down the hallway are...hugely awkward. I think I know what they're doing in there, but then again, I don't want to know. I press ear buds to my ear holes and blast music to drown the noise. I want to forget all about cute boys because I can't lose control.

The dance club songs I blast into my ears are way too suggestive in content as they talk about shaking one's butt or grinding it against...I change the play list to Beethoven. Thank the Goddess for Ludwig. His music calms me. It's so beautiful and not at all sexual. I listen to the complete Ninth Symphony, pulling myself into the world of music and letting it take me away for a while.

Dad ordered me to limit my time with Aiden for the next few weeks. I can only see him during school hours, and it's so hard, but I have it under control. We can still snuggle at lunch in the back of my car, which is so nice. Aiden cuddles me in his arms, and I nuzzle his ears with my nose and then rest my cheek against his chest and listen to his heart pumping and...

Piss on the sun! This isn't helping.

I roll on my bed and curl up into a ball. The burning pulsates through every piece of me. How many more weekends of this burning do I have to suffer?

I flip through a new set of magazines Mom bought. Some

of the half-naked boys are cute and would be exciting eye candy for human girls. But for me, they're only boys on paper. I don't know them. Not like I know Aiden. I can't smell their scent or feel their presence in a room. They can't tell me how beautiful I look. They can't twist a strand of my hair with their finger, or brush my cheek, or hold me tight, or kiss me good night.

I so have to get out of here.

Firing up my car, I drive over to the bookstore and wander around, taking in the sights and smells of paper and wood. Some days I like to come in here and walk around. Any stress that builds up at school can be easily released here. Books don't care if someone called you Cave Girl, or made fun of your hair, or laughed at your clothes, or said hurtful things that made you want to kill. Books accept you just the way you are.

I glance through the romance section because I need a sexy book, like girl-friendly sexy not sleazy. Something that could last me a few days and make me concentrate on a fictional mate, one I could load all my passion on. But there's so many books to choose from that I can't decide. Do I want historical romance? Romantic thriller? Romantic mystery? Paranormal romance? Ugh, not that one.

I pull one novel off the shelf that looks promising and scan the first chapter. Oh, this will so work. I order a ham sandwich in the café and read for a half hour. Then I go into the bathroom to splash cold water on my face. This book is perfect. The cashier rings up my purchase, and I'm out of there for some late night reading.

***

Breaking Wild Stallions gets me through the weekend. I even highlight the extra sexy parts and keep the book in my backpack in case I need to distract myself at school. Today will be so hard, and I don't know if I can get through it without embarrassing myself.

I fail even before school starts.

I'm kissing Aiden before he even says hi to me in the parking lot. Issy doesn't know what to do. I'm making him totally uncomfortable, and I so can't help it. This is my boyfriend, and I've missed him over the weekend. Really missed him.

Aiden grins. "Please do that every morning."

At lunch I cling on to Aiden like a baby monkey. I know it's too obsessive, but I can't stop myself. I nip his ear and start licking it. Seriously. I know! I'm so shameless, and I don't care. So what if humans don't do this in public. They should free themselves from all that puritanism they love to hold on to.

Issy has enough and carries his tray over to the band table. I'm so glad he's leaving us alone.

"Bree...cut it out," Aiden whispers.

He doesn't mean that. I bet he loves all this attention. What boy wouldn't? I'm beautiful, and he's gorgeous and all mine. I lick Aiden's cheek and nuzzle his hair.

"Stop it. Everyone's staring," he whines.

Staring? And then I notice all the kids in the cafeteria. They're all pointing and laughing at us. Or I should say laughing at me and my ridiculous acts of public affection. Embarrassment tucks me behind Aiden, and I so wish I could shift into a tiny bug that could fly away. I should fake being sick and go home to read *Breaking Wild Stallions* again. But I do the wrong thing...I stay at school and go to Algebra.

But I prepare myself. *Think mind over matter, Bree. Focus on algebra. Equations and theorems, right? Even if you have to do all the problems in the back of the book or memorize your multiplication tables again. Whatever it takes, don't turn around or make eye contact with that cute boy behind you. Yes, you can do it!*

Aiden sabotages my plan by messing with the ends of my hair. His touch radiates through me, and I get so drunk on it that I ease back in my seat and rest my head on top of his desk and treat it like a pillow. I watch Aiden upside down and

plead for more attention with my eyes.
"What are you doing?" he asks softly.
"Don't stop," I moan. "Please, don't stop!"
"Oh, I won't stop, Miss Mayflower. This new theorem is quite thrilling," Mr. Strickland says in a mocking tone.
A laugh bursts from all the kids as I shake off the lustful fog in my head. I snap straight in my chair, which gets a new wave of laughs. Aiden hides his face behind his algebra book.

School mercifully ends. I pounce on Aiden as soon as he hops into my car. I rub my hands all over his shirt and kiss him everywhere I can find skin. Soon I find his lips, and the burning only increases. I so can't stop. We kiss for a couple minutes, and I'm sweating like the heater is on but it's not.

Aiden stops me and asks in this gentle, sweet voice, "Do you want to do it?"

The wolf wants to so bad that she's pushing me into it, fully committed to satisfying my urges. He's a boy and I'm a girl and we love each other. That's all that matters in this scary world with so much evil. Evil that slaughters your entire pack and leaves your broken family in search of a new life.

But I should resist. I don't want to hurt my family. They mean everything to me, and doing this would be a sin, and I would shame them, especially my father. Oh yeah...and there's the small issue of Aiden being human and not werewolf. That union is unforgivable in my world.

But this cute boy lingers so close to me, still waiting for my answer.

I so want to give in. I want to be happy. I want this boy. And I want him now!

"I need a milkshake," I blurt out.

Aiden pauses. "A milkshake?"

Cold, creamy, chocolate ice cream smothering the fire inside, yes, that's exactly what I need. I rip myself from Aiden, turn over the Oldsmobile, and speed through the student parking lot. Aiden struggles to get on his seat belt as I race to the nearest burger place and suck down a large chocolate shake so fast the frozen headache almost turns my brain to ice. But I hold it together as I drive Aiden home and bring the car up to the curb.

Aiden twists the door handle. Why is he stalling? Bet he's sad I didn't answer his question. I'm so sorry if he feels bad, but this is such a good thing. Yes, resisting the urge is good for both of us.

"Do you want to hook up tonight? Rent a movie or something?" he asks.

Yes!

But...ugh...no, I can't.

"Some other time. My parents want me to stay home," I say.

Aiden can't hide his disappointment as he climbs out of the car and moves around to my open window. "See you tomorrow." He leans in and kisses me full on the lips.

My lips burn. My heart burns. My body heats up. No. No. No!

Aiden jogs up his driveway. My resistance turns to cotton candy and dissolves into nothing. I leap out of my car and catch up with Aiden, hugging him tight. He touches my chin and raises it. Our eyes meet.

"My bedroom is a little messy, but is that okay?" Aiden asks.

I give him a smile and nod.

"Are you sure?" he asks. "I want you to be absolutely sure."

"Absolutely."

Aiden's fingers close on my hand. His grip is soft and reassuring as we head inside his house.

Together.

CHAPTER TWENTY-SIX

BREE

An aviation theme decorates the small living room of Aiden's house. Paintings of jets and prop planes hang on the walls. A heavy curtain blocks the afternoon sun from the main window, and a floor lamp is on, showering one corner of the room with light. A smooth wood mantel displays plastic models of aircraft over a fireplace that has never been used. A two-barrel shotgun hangs above the mantel.

The scent of sour liquor comes from the man slumped in a recliner. The half-bottle of Jack Daniel's he's been enjoying waits on a coffee table to be finished. The man's head slowly rolls toward us. "Aiden, wha...who's dat?" The man's words slur together.

Oh my Goddess. Is this Aiden's dad?

"Could you wait for me outside, please?" Aiden can't even look at me. His body slouches as if all the life were sucked out of it. He's horrified I'm seeing this.

I back away like I've walked into a crime scene and don't want to destroy any evidence. There's vomit on the coffee table, and I trace it to his father's shirt. I didn't know his father was such an alcoholic. Aiden never talks about his family much, and now I wish he would have. Why does his dad drink like that? Tossing his cookies over his own furniture and making his son feel embarrassed in front of his girlfriend. Why?

I don't understand this human need for alcohol. Numbing your senses on purpose sounds so stupid to me. Life is to be enjoyed in the moment, and your senses bring that world to you. I would be depressed if I couldn't sniff the air or run as fast as I could, jumping and rolling and living, but people like Aiden's dad choose to block those senses. I don't get humans sometimes.

Outside, I lean on my car and wait for about twenty minutes before Aiden comes back out with his hands in his pockets and his shoulders drooping. I still put up a big, friendly smile. I don't want Aiden to think I'm judging him because of his dad. That's so not fair.

"Well, I guess you've met my dad now," he says, trying to push it off as a joke that no one can laugh at. "Usually he only has one drink on days like these. Today it got out of hand. But he doesn't do this a lot."

Something tells me Aiden's lying to protect his dad, which I totally understand. Still, I wish he would trust me.

"Guess we'll have to get together some other time," Aiden says.

Some other time? My hormones wail with grief. But Aiden feels awful. I should respect that.

"What about the back seat of my car?" My hormones slip those words out before my brain can put a stop to it.

He squeezes my hands. "Are you sure? Don't you want this to be more...special?"

I do. And it should be, right? In the back seat of my car does sound gross. So that only leaves one other place. A place that's far too dangerous, but my hormones don't care.

"What if we went to my house?"

I park the car in my driveway and then pull Bullwinkle and Rocky out of the car. I do a quick sniff and detect no recent scent from my parents. I unlock the door and put in the alarm code, then lead Aiden up the stairs to my bedroom. I place Rocky and Bullwinkle on top of my dresser.

"So what's the story on those animals?" he asks.

"The story?"

"Yeah, you always have them in the car with you, and you take them up to your room. I'm wondering why because it's... how do I put this...?"

"Psycho?"

His face changes, like he thinks he's embarrassing me. "I didn't mean it to come out like that."

"I know what you mean." My fingers stroke Bullwinkle's soft fur. "These are my good luck charms." My mind falls back into the nightmare. I can't help it. Should I tell him about the enemy that nearly destroyed us? A part of me wants to confide in Aiden. A part of me wants to share the scariest moment that's ever happened in my life. My two furry friends smile. Their cheerful faces nudge me to trust this new friend in our lives.

I gently pull Aiden, and we sit on my bed's spongy comforter. I tell him about my old pack in Colorado. Our Alpha Chevalier. The vicious attack of the invincible new enemy called the Demon Skins. The killing of my friend Dawn. My mom almost dying. Our desperate escape.

"Dad was never sure where to go. We would go to other small towns that had a forest nearby, but my father was concerned that if the Demon Skins could find an out-of-the-way compound in the mountains, they could easily find us in a small town. Finally my dad came up with the last place a werewolf would want to live...right in the middle of a big city filled with humans. No offense."

Aiden holds on to my every word. "Why are they hunting you?"

"We have no clue. They're attacking packs all over the world and driving all the werewolves into hiding. But these Demon Skins still find ways to hunt us down. It's so scary. Even the Elders don't know what to do."

"And you don't know how to kill these Demon Skins?"

"They have silver in their blood so if we try to bite them or rip off a limb, it's like biting into poison. And you can't kill them like a human either."

"Are they alive?"

"Somehow they are, but honestly I'm still not sure. They don't seem to experience pain. I hit one with a car and broke its arm, but the thing didn't feel anything, only went back on the attack like nothing happened. You know those Borg aliens on that show Star Trek? They act like those things."

"They sound like soldiers of some kind," Aiden says, thinking about it, as if he wants to help. I'm so glad I'm telling him this. I should have done it much earlier. "Who created them?"

"No one knows who wants us all dead. Someone created those awful things, but it's a huge mystery, and we might not live long enough to solve it."

Aiden holds me closer, as if he can feel how much talking about this upsets me. I rest my head against Aiden's chest. He would fight for me, wouldn't he? If the Demon Skins ever came, Aiden would do his best to protect me. I know he didn't put up much of a fight with Kirk, but if the girl he loved was in danger, Aiden would fight for her, wouldn't he? Yes, I have faith in him.

I close my eyes. The heat of his body warms my cheek. Aiden kisses my hair. His fingers knead my skin and that turns up the sweet burn inside. The wolf nuzzles his neck, and the human kisses it. Aiden hesitates. His eyes linger on my forehead. My nose. And finally my lips. He leans in, pauses.

That pause draws me closer.

Aiden smiles at the gesture, and it gives him the confidence to touch his lips to mine. He's tender. And the kiss is beautiful, sweet, and so lovely.

The sweet burn swells to an inferno. The wolf shoves the nice girl aside and locks her in a closet.

I fling Aiden off the bed, and his back smacks the floor. Hard. His face betrays his pain.

"Bree?" Aiden sounds confused.

I ignore him and rip his cotton shirt wide open, scattering the plastic buttons everywhere. The seams pop and split as I claw at his shirt like it's skin because I want his clothes off. Next I break off the brass button holding his jeans together

and pull them all the way down to his ankles.
The fire consumes me.
I want him.
I want him to mate with me. Now!
Aiden looks dazed, like he's unable to understand what's going on. He tries to lift himself off the floor.
But I slam him back down.
"What...what are you doing?" Aiden rises again.
This time I force the boy wolf to stay down. He wiggles and struggles against me. Why is he resisting? Doesn't this wolf want to mate? Am I not playful enough? Doesn't he want me as much as I want him? Bet this boy is playing a game to get me so excited that I won't look at another wolf. I smell the sweat coming off him so he must be excited too. He wants me.
"Get off of me, Bree."
Show me you're an alpha. Push me off, then. Make me chase you. I want to play!
Why is this wolf acting so weak? He's not aggressive at all. Am I not worth the challenge?
I check his green eyes. The boy wolf inside those eyes looks...
Terrified?
I...I don't understand. Why would he be terrified?
Aiden?
The girl inside peeks out. My friend doesn't want this. He doesn't understand what I'm doing. His eyes plead for me to stop.
I can't stop.
The wolf won't let me stop.
I've lost control over her.
Oh, please forgive me.
I can't stop her as she pulls down his underwear.
Aiden, I'm so sorry.
Then I feel two giant hands grab me and rip me off Aiden. My nose picks up the familiar scent.
Dad's home.

CHAPTER TWENTY-SEVEN

BREE

Dad takes me down the hallway as if I'm a light dishrag. There's no way I could get away from the tight hold he has on me. I haven't been carried like this since I was a little girl and burned down a house. That's a long story.

Dad almost tosses me into the bathroom. "Take off your clothes. Get into that shower." He's in full Alpha mode, and I comply without hesitation. He shuts the door, and I disrobe and put myself under a steady stream of freezing-cold water. The burning drains away from my skin and my body as I shiver. The human part seizes control while my brain replays every awful thing I did to Aiden, my guilt pressing the rewind button over and over again.

If Dad hadn't pulled me away...

Poor Aiden.

He wanted me. And I wanted him. But instead of that sweet girl he kissed on the bed or the girl in the forest who curled up under his warm coat as the snow came down, he got some werewolf slut who nearly...I can't even think about it. Did I try to force Aiden into...?

No. No. No, I could never do that to him. I love him. If Aiden would have said no, I would have...kept going.

I hate myself. I want to claw my insides out and bash my head against a brick wall. I treated my best friend in the whole world like an object instead of a person. I feel so sick.

The first time I shifted in front of Aiden I swore to him that I wasn't dangerous, that I was always under full control of the wolf.

Am I fooling myself? Can I have a normal relationship with a human boy without hurting him or doing something against his will, simply because I can? The chill from the icy water sharpens my mind and brings this clarity to it.

No, this was different. This was all caused by mating season. That uncontrollable fire. That's why I couldn't stop myself. Normally I would never let things get that far out of hand. I would never have pushed Aiden like that. Yes, that's it. I'll have to be more careful in the future, that's all. When mating season returns next year, I will lock myself up in a concrete bunker if I have to. This will never happen again.

I dry off, and the fire has been purged from my body. I wrap myself in a towel and pad my way down the hall to my room. I'll have to apologize to Aiden.

What if he doesn't forgive me? Have I killed our friendship?

I go in and brace myself for the consequences.

Aiden is gone.

Dad waits on my bed. His face is reserved, and I bet, pissed. "Boy's in the car. I'll take him home."

"The feelings are gone now," I say. "I can throw on some clothes and—"

"You're not leaving this room for a while."

"Daddy, I'm fine now."

"You could have hurt that boy."

My heart sinks because Dad's right.

"Why did you disobey me? Did I not tell you to stay away from Aiden? Particularly during this month?"

I nod.

Dad pats the comforter next to him, and I sit. "This is why I wasn't thrilled with you having a human friend." Dad rubs his face and eases out a long, drawn-out breath to calm himself.

"Does he know?"

I know what Dad is asking, and if I answer with the truth, he might get super angry.

"Bree?"

What will Dad do? Will he hurt Aiden? Threaten him? Kill him?

Dad wouldn't do that. Would he?

I can't take that chance.

Dad sighs, "Aiden knows, doesn't he?"

Lie. Tell him anything. Tell him you fit in so well at school that Aiden and everyone at school is clueless.

"He doesn't know." I sound like the worst actress ever.

"Final answer?" he asks.

I make the mistake of raising my eyes. Dad's face pinches together like a prosecutor grilling a suspect on the stand, throwing that last ounce of contempt before throwing her to the mercy of the jury. I can't do it. He's sees right through my words as if they're crystal.

"No," I waver.

"You told him, didn't you?"

"No, I didn't tell him." I hesitate and see Rocky and Bullwinkle watching me like they were sending me all their love and support. "I showed him."

"Bree." His voice sounds so disappointed.

The secret is out now. Might as well give it all up.

"Aiden's friend Issy knows too, but that's all. Only the two boys, but they've been really cooperative. Much more than I thought they would be."

"Child, Humans can be just as great of an enemy as the Demon Skins."

"But these humans are good. I trust them. They're my friends."

"Can *I* trust them?" Dad asks. "How do I know they won't say something on accident to the wrong person? That could jeopardize more than just our family's safety. With all these random Demon Skin attacks, our people are vulnerable now. This is the one time when we can not afford to ignite another human crusade against our kind."

"You can trust them, Daddy."

"Be easier if I killed them."

"No!" I scream. The intensity of my voice shocks my dad. "I won't let you! I won't let you touch him!"

"Bree..."

"I will hate you. If you ever harmed Aiden, I would hate you forever."

Dad's large arms swallow me up in the familiar bear hug that would always calm me down when I was a child. "Shhh. Don't jump to conclusions now."

I surrender and bury my face, soaking his shirt with tears. "I love him. Don't hurt him, please. I love him." Everything hits me at once, and I lose it. I sob and pour out everything to Dad. How Aiden and I met and became friends, and how wonderful he treats me, and how wonderful I feel around him, and how he's the most important thing in my life.

Dad lifts me from his chest. "Don't suppose I could talk you into taking a break from Aiden, could I?"

How can Dad still ask me that after pouring out my soul to him?

Dad squirms because he knows I'm glaring at him. "Fine. You love him, and that's that."

"Yes, Daddy. And that's that."

CHAPTER TWENTY-EIGHT

AIDEN

Darkness swallows up the forest. The wind has died. My hope has died. And now I will die. Bree's Sasquatch-sized father trails behind Issy and me, prodding us deeper into the forest behind their house. Deeper into the darkness where he can hide our bodies and let them decompose for years. Or maybe he will eat us and not tell Bree. Somewhere in the back of my mind I knew this would happen. I knew Bree was too good to be true. I'm an idiot for trying to think I could handle a werewolf for a girlfriend. That I'm this macho dude that could handle anything a girl could throw at me. But pinning me down to the ground and ripping my clothes off? Normal girls don't act like that.

Yes, of course I've had *that* dream. The dream where all the hottest girls in school, plus a few random super models thrown in, chase me down the hallways, wanting to rip my clothes off because they want my sexy bod. Don't get me wrong. It's a great dream, but when Bree tried it for real...it honestly scared the crap out of me.

In my dream, I loved all those girls pawing over my clothes. Those dream girls giggled and acted like...you know...normal girls would. It turned me on. But then Bree acted like some crazed, female demon bent on my annihilation. She held me to the floor like she was going to kill me, eat me, or force me to...none of it was sexy. None of it was like my dream. I wasn't trapped in a room with a beautiful girl. I was trapped in a room with an unpredictable wolf who would either lick me or kill me with a blink of those burning red eyes. Super models don't have burning red eyes.

I mean, if I forced Bree down, took off her clothes, and prevented her from getting up, wouldn't that be rape? Forcing yourself on a girl and she doesn't want it, isn't that rape? Is that what Bree tried to do to me?

I'm confused.

"Keep going," Bree's father says from behind me. He noticed I've slowed down.

I increase my pace and catch up with Issy, who looks like he's about to piss all over himself. When I told him that Mr. Mayflower wanted to talk to us in private, Issy got jazzed about meeting another werewolf. But now that excitement has turned to butt-loads of anxiety. Both of us don't like the way Mr. Mayflower acts. He's not telling us why we need to go deep into a dark forest to talk. Why can't we talk in their nice, comfortable house, since his wife and daughter went to the mall? Something's wrong.

"Only a little further now," Mr. Mayflower says. The glow from his camping lantern creates a strange shadow across his face. Like a dark mask.

The forest lies quiet. The animals must have decided to get the hell out when they saw two teens being escorted by a gigantic werewolf. I don't blame them.

We soon reach two big rectangular holes cut deep into the earth. They're over five-feet long.

"Think I have the dimensions right." Mr. Mayflower examines his handwork with the lantern. "Go ahead. Try 'em out." He gestures down at the holes with the lantern.

Why does he want us to stand in a hole? And why do each of us have a...damn. Oh, damn.

Issy and I turn. Each reads the other's face. Mr. Mayflower has dug our graves. I knew it. I knew that he was leading us down here to kill us. My chest hurts. The icy feeling of helplessness jabs the back of my neck.

"No way. I'm not going down there," Issy says.

Mr. Mayflower stands still. "I insist."

Issy checks to see if I'm going to do anything, like run for my life.

"Losing my patience here, boys."

I don't want to die like this, getting mauled by a werewolf and becoming fertilizer for a bunch of trees. I'm not sure I even want to die. But I know I don't want to die like this. And why does Issy have to die with me? My wingman didn't ask for any of this. Issy is a new car owner and was so looking forward to being a senior. Now I've condemned him. I'm about to ruin his life because I picked the wrong forest to commit suicide in.

No, I don't regret what Bree did. I would have never met her if she didn't save me. But by saving me, did she only prolong my death? Was I always meant to die?

Issy waves his hand to grab my attention. He mouths something I can't make out. Then he does sign language by pointing at himself, then me, then to the forest. He shouldn't...

"Run for it!" Issy yells as he hauls ass towards the forest.

That's not going to work.

Mr. Mayflower pounces on him in a second, grabbing Issy off the ground and carrying him back to the holes. Issy rattles off a host of obscenities, saying his dad will sue him for murder and kidnapping. How killing children will get him multiple life sentences. Mr. Mayflower ignores Issy and places him back next to me.

"Get in the holes. This can be quick and painless or long and excruciating. Which one do you two want?"

What else can we do? There's no use fighting him, and we can't run away.

I step down into one of the holes. I touch the sides, and the freshly cut dirt feels cold. Mr. Mayflower wouldn't bury us alive, would he? Suffocating on dirt would suck, but he did give us a choice. I'll take quick and painless, then.

Issy watches me and hesitates. He glances over at his own hole. Doesn't move.

Mr. Mayflower towers over Issy. "Let's go, son. Into the

hole."

Issy hesitates. His eyes are glassy. He's scared. Extremely scared. I should be scared like him, but I'm not. I'm ready for it to end. Maybe Bree was a gift. A final gift from the universe before it takes me away. This is my future. To die my junior year has always been my future. I can't escape it. Bree only set back the clock. But now the clock moves forward, and the alarm is about to go off again.

"Why are you doing this?" Issy asks, his voice trembling. "I won't tell anyone about your kind. I swear."

"Can't take the chance. Into the hole," Mr. Mayflower says, simple and direct.

A tear races down Issy's cheek, but he holds it in. Doesn't let himself cry. He takes in a deep breath, steps into the hole, and out of my sight.

Mr. Mayflower stands over our graves as he slips on black gloves. "Thanks for making this easy. Promise to make it quick. And I won't shift into a wolf. Too violent. Too messy. Too unnecessary. I'll just snap both your necks. Easy and quite humane, I think." He finishes with the gloves, checks to see if his fingers have fitted through correctly, then folds those fingers together and stands taller. "Sad I have to do this, but it must be done. Are you boys ready?"

"Bree will hate you for this," I say, bringing up the only sliver of hope that might stop this.

Mr. Mayflower reflects on my comment. "She will, but my daughter will be alive to hate me."

That's it. He's really going to kill us. Even if it means turning Bree against him. I prepare myself to die.

"Mr. Mayflower? Could you please tell your daughter..." Saying this will feel weird because of what's going on, but I still need to say it, and I hope Bree somehow hears it. "Tell your daughter that I love her." I close my eyes and feel the darkness closing in. "I'm ready, sir."

I wait for it.

And wait for it.

"How much do you love my daughter?" Mr. Mayflower asks.

I slowly open my eyes. The werewolf now sits on the edge of my grave, his two fists spiked into the ground and balancing his massive size.

"Would you die to protect her? Throw your life away in an instant to keep her safe?"

I nod. I would do that. Even if things came down to her or me, I would always choose her.

Mr. Mayflower picks up a clump of fresh dirt and crushes it with his palm, letting the pieces sift through his fingers. "Quite a problem I have with you two. Let you live, you might tell someone about us and then our enemies will find us."

"The Demon Skins?" I ask.

The man pauses, and glances at me. "Bree told you about them, huh? So you know how dangerous they are. You realize that anything that exposes my family to them...is a threat to their lives."

"If they're a threat to Bree, why would I risk telling someone about your family? Why would I risk Bree's life?"

Mr. Mayflower scratches his beard, thinking. "Damn fine point there, Aiden, but what about your friend here? How can I trust him?"

"You can trust me, Mr. Mayflower! Honest. I can keep all kinds of secrets," Issy's voice drifts over the top of my hole. "I've always thought about joining the CIA after college."

Issy a CIA agent? That would be awesome.

Mr. Mayflower strokes his beard again and, shoots a glance over to the next hole. "Son, I'm serious about this. You tell anyone and I'll kill you and go after your entire family." The man then gives me a quick little wink. He's bluffing.

"No, sir. I won't. I swear to Allah that I will never say anything to anyone for as long as I live."

"Maul you like a piece of sausage I will, son. Spit out your bones."

"I understand. Believe me, I so understand, Mr. Mayflower. My lips are forever glued together."

The man thinks about it again, taking his time.

"Then we have an agreement. One I expect you both to honor." Mr. Mayflower stands up and towers over the hole again. "Climb out of there, Aiden. Need to have a talk."

I scramble out of the hole and brush dirt off my jeans and coat.

"Do I get to come out too?" Issy asks.

"Few more minutes down there won't kill you." Mr. Mayflower guides me away from the hole. We get about twenty feet before he continues. "To protect my daughter and her identity, would you love her so much that you would break up with her and walk away forever?"

Wow. I...I don't know about that.

"Put it to you this way. My daughter considers you her mate for life."

Mate for life? That sounds important. Like she wants to get married. Marriage? I'm not even a senior yet.

"You make her happy, and a father always wants to see their daughter happy, but a father also feels protective about his daughter. When a father sees something which could hurt his loved one, a father will do whatever it takes to stop it from happening. Can't ask my daughter to stop seeing you because she will refuse. As the Alpha, I could order her to comply, and then my daughter would loathe me, possibly even run away, and then we couldn't protect her if she were discovered by the Demon Skins."

Mr. Mayflower kneads his hands together. "Nothing against you, Aiden. I like you. If you were one of us, I wouldn't have a problem with this relationship. But you're not one of us, and my daughter doesn't fully understand that. There are many stories in our history about werewolves falling in love with humans. Those stories always end the same way. The werewolf turns on the human and kills them. Usually over some jealous rage or a simple burst of anger that races out of control. The partnership has never worked," he says.

I see what Mr. Mayflower means. This afternoon was insane. I did fear for my life inside Bree's bedroom. And what about that other time we were horsing around in the forest and Bree knocked me down so hard I lost my breath? The wolf couldn't hold herself back then either. What other "accidents" will happen if Bree loses control again. It's always been lurking in the back of my mind. That random element of danger that could lash out at any moment. I always tried to ignore it, pretend that it's not important since Bree says she can control herself. But there's this old saying I remember reading one time...*Actions speak louder than words.*

So far Bree's actions make me doubt her promises to control that dark side of her.

"Need a few days to think about it?" Mr. Mayflower asks.

I don't know what to say, so I nod.

"Understand completely. I promise that if you do call it off, Bree will respect your wishes and never bother you or your friend ever again. I will make sure of that."

I clear my throat. "Can I ask a stupid question?"

"Ask away."

"Um...well...is there a way I could be turned into a werewolf? How does that work exactly? Do I need to ask someone to bite me?"

The big man shows a slight hint of a grin. "Appreciate the gesture, and I'd be more than happy to let my daughter bite you, Aiden, but that's an old human myth."

Of course it is. Why would it be true? That would only make me happy and solve all my problems. Sometimes I would love to give life a swift kick in the coconuts.

"Hello? Can I come out now?" Issy calls out from his hole. "There's a raccoon wanting to eat me."

CHAPTER TWENTY-NINE

AIDEN

Monday comes, and I'm not ready. Last night I stayed up all night thinking about Bree. Do I break up with her? Do I tell Bree that her dad wants us to break up? Would she apologize for Friday afternoon? Would I accept her apology? Would things be awkward between us now? Would she kill me if I broke up with her?

I couldn't decide on anything.

I'm glad Issy's driving us to school. I'm so tired I can't keep any part of my eyes open.

"Stop drooling all over my window," Issy says.

Damn. I fell asleep again. I feel saliva pasting my mouth to the glass. I use my shirt to clean it off.

School becomes a maze. I've been stomping down these hallways for two and a half years, but my sleepy brain sees them in a confusing new light. I bump into the water fountain. I bump into the football trophy case. And I bump into Bree.

She waits at my locker. Her long, dark hair is twisted into a ponytail. A hopeful smile on her lips. That smile hopes I forgot about Friday afternoon. I still don't know what I'm going to say to her.

"Hey," she says.

I nod, open my locker, and concentrate on pulling out books for my morning classes.

Bree grips a book to her chest and steps closer, like she wants to say something.

I hesitate.

"How's Issy?" she asks.

"Normal, I guess."

I don't know. Why doesn't she ask Issy?

Bree twitches her lips to the side and rocks back and forth. I fight the urge to lean against my locker and fall asleep.

"You look tired."

"Didn't sleep well," I say.

"We hunted deer last night. I always sleep well on a full stomach." She grins.

"Yeah, I didn't sleep well," I repeat.

Bree loses the grin. "Were you like really tired...or...were you so worried about something you couldn't fall asleep?"

I close my eyes. Do I want to talk about this now? Think I need to wake up first.

"Like really tired."

"Think you'll feel better at lunch?"

I shrug.

"All right," Bree says, taking one awkward step back. She flashes a crooked grin and heads down the hall, glancing back at me before she rounds the corner.

Like I said, I'm not ready for Monday.

The three of us eat lunch like strangers. It's weird. No one wants to bring up anything. But we all know what each person wants to talk about. I mindlessly play with my mashed potatoes like I'm four again. Issy breaks out his phone and plays a game. Bree can't finish her roast beef sandwich that she went off-campus to buy.

I scrape the sides of my new mashed-potato hill.

Issy kills things on his phone.

And Bree simmers like a volcano. She suddenly bangs her hands on the table, and our plastic trays jump. "I can't stand this." She's so loud the other tables stare. Bree lowers her voice. "Does anyone want to talk? Because I sure do."

"Talk about what?" Issy asks.
Bree zeroes in on me. "Anything?"
I sip my grape soda and shrug again.
"Really, Aiden? If you're mad at me, then say that."
"I'm not mad."
"Then you're what? Tired?"
"I have a lot to think about."
She lowers her voice. "What are you thinking about? Friday?"
"Your dad mentioned a few things."
"What things? Things about me? What did he say?"
"Don't worry," Issy interrupts. "We're not telling anyone about the wolf situation. Your dad made it painfully clear what those consequences were. Am I right, A-man?"
"No...there's something else," Bree says, picking up on my hesitation. Why are girls so good at that?
"Your father...um...he took me aside and said..." I stop. Issy is here, and I don't want to make it weird and awkward for him. "I'll tell you in Algebra, okay?"

As soon as I squish my butt in the chair, Bree flips around. "What did my dad say to you?"
I've never noticed the artwork on our algebra textbook before. There's this generic-looking school kid sitting at his desk. There's this bright square coming out of his head, opening up these "rays" of mathematical equations that fire off like rays of the sun. I can't tell what the art means. Is the artist saying that students can use their minds as powerful weapons to take over the world? Or is he giving us a secret warning that our brains will explode when teachers stuff too much math inside them?
Bree waves her hand across my face. "Hello?"
Oh yeah.
"Um...your dad said that relationships between..." I realize that we have more kids sitting around us. So I start over. "He said relationships between 'wolves' and humans have always turned out badly."
Bree absorbs what I said. "That was true in the ancient

days, but that thinking is from my dad's generation. The ones who still remember telephones with spinning dials? That will never happen to us. What else did he say?"

"That maybe we should take a break from each other."

Bree's mouth twitches to the side. "He didn't tell me that." She thinks on that. "All right. Since Dad didn't order me *not* to see you, then I will do what I want. So nothing has changed."

"You can't say nothing has changed," I blurt out.

Her smile melts.

"Welcome, teen scholars, open up those textbooks to chapter thirty-one because we have a lot of material to cover today. Avanti!" Mr. Strickland says.

Bree lingers. Her eyes want to rip into my head and see what I'm thinking. She finally pivots around and opens her textbook. Mr. Strickland plunges deep into his lecture while Bree rips off a piece of paper from her worksheet, scribbles on it, and then tosses it over. The tiny note flutters on to my desk.

It reads *What has changed?*

I rip off a sheet of notebook paper and reply...

You scared the crap out of me. You lost control, and you promised me that that would never happen.

I toss the note forward. Bree reads it, scribbles furiously on a new piece of paper, which lands on my desk...

I was weak. I explained that. Mating season is over, and I'm fine now. How many times do you want me to say I'm sorry? I'M SORRY!!!!!

Bree sneaks a glance back. I feel her anxiety. She wants me to reply, wants me to give her a pass for Friday. A side of me wants to go along and treat the incident like it's a glitch in our relationship. An accident. But the rest of me is still confused and not sure what to do. Mr. Mayflower could be right. Friday afternoon could repeat itself. And I might not be alive to forgive her. The only thing I'm sure about is…I need more time to think this all out.

I need to be alone for a while. Can we take a break from each other? All I'm asking is for some time to think about all this.

I throw over my reply. Bree reads it and doesn't say anything for a while as Mr. Strickland goes on and on.
He covers sections one and two and writes the equations on the white board.
I copy down notes as the minutes tick by.
Bree stares out the window that's across the classroom, her face numb. She's never that still. Bree's always so full of life, always bouncing around like a bird in a tree, but now I've taken all that energy out of her. Does Bree hate me now?
I write another note..._We are still friends!_
It lands on her book. She reads it, then wads it up and lets it roll off onto the floor. Bree doesn't look back at me for the rest of class.

* * *

That afternoon I hitch a ride home with Issy. We stop for a burger at the Sonic Drive-In that's near school. At first we talk about the normal stuff we always talk about, but then Issy talks about Mr. Mayflower, wondering if everything is cool between the three of us. I set my wing-man's mind at ease when I tell him Mr. Mayflower considers the problem solved. I don't bring up what happened in Algebra or what happened Friday afternoon. Issy would think I'm a loser for freaking out over a girl trying to have her way with me.
"What's happening here?" Issy asks, eying his rear-view mirror. I twist around in time to see Pamela's yellow Honda backing up into view. She then swings her car to the empty space next to my window. "That girl passed behind us, stopped, and backed up all the way to park here. I wonder why we're so special," Issy says.
Guess I should care, but I don't right now.
The Honda's driver-side window sinks down to reveal Pamela while a couple of her girlfriends wave in back. Wave? These are the same girls who giggled when Pamela made fun of me. What's going on?

"Hi, Aiden. What's new?" Pamela asks, like she actually wants to know.

Issy leans over me. "Chillin' out. What are you fine women doing here?"

"Ice cream run," she says. "Where's Bree?" Those long lashes blink in my direction.

"I don't know," I say.

Probably crying in the back of her car, and that makes me feel bad. But I wasn't lying to her. I do need time to think. I don't know why she can't respect that.

A short girl in the backseat pops her head out the window. "Do you guys want to buy us some ice cream?"

Whatever. Do we look desperate? Do we look like two losers who will do anything to humiliate ourselves in front of a carload of girls if there was even a sliver of hope that we can touch one of them?

"Sure, ladies. We'll buy whatever you want," Issy says.

Pathetic, dude. Really pathetic.

"*We* nothing. *You* are buying them ice cream," I say.

Issy rolls his eyes. "Then I get first pick."

"You can have all of them. I don't care."

One single wolf girl complicates my life enough, but a car full of girls? That's too much for me right now.

The car hop comes by with our order. Issy asks her to bring him the ticket for the car next to ours. What an idiot. Must be great to be a girl. Wink an eye and then brush up against a guy and he'll get all stupid and buy you free shakes and crap. What a scam.

The back door of the Jetta pops open. Pamela slides in. "Mind if I crash?" She giggles as she leans into the gap between Issy and me. "Some days I like hanging out with guys instead of girls."

You couldn't power spray the smile off Issy's face right now. "You're welcome in this car anytime you want," he says.

Pamela nudges my cheek. "You look sad."

"It's Monday," I say with strong non-interest. I free my burger from its paper wrapper and chow down.

Pamela stretches forward, and takes a napkin. "You're

messy." She dabs my lips while doing another crazy little giggle.

I lean away from Pamela, stuff my mouth with fries, then stare at the ice cream menu at the next stall.

She turns to Issy. "What's with him?"

"He's having girl problems."

"Why are you saying that?" I snap back.

"Easy, A-man. I noticed you and Bree had a weird vibe going on at lunch, that's all."

"A weird vibe?" Pamela asks.

I mess with the car stereo, dialing through the different EQ setups. Powerful. Vocal. Heavy Bass.

"Did you guys have a fight?" Pamela asks.

"Bree is a complicated girl." Issy eats a fry.

"Dude, would you shut up?"

My friend raises his hands in surrender.

"Bree acts so mysterious all the time," Pamela says. "What's she really like?"

Issy chuckles. I fire off a look.

"I should point out that if you need a girl's perspective on the situation, you have this golden opportunity sitting inside your car right now." Pamela poses for effect. It's kind of cute.

Maybe I should keep my options open.

"Bree and I took a break from each other, that's all."

"Oh, I'm so sorry," Pamela says with some genuine sympathy.

"It's not a permanent break-up. It's just...we need to work some problems out."

Pamela touches my shoulder. "I understand, and that's very mature of you to take a day or so off to think about what you want. Sometimes you can be attracted to someone and you get to know that person, and then something comes up that you don't expect."

"You have no idea."

I punch Issy in the arm, and he winces.

Pamela steals one of my fries. "Sometimes people are different, and when they try to become a couple, the pieces don't always fit. Maybe you and Bree are like that. You have this attraction towards each other. Yet in the end, the pieces don't fit. And you shouldn't try to force them to fit." She chomps on my fry. "Do you have any ketchup?"

Minutes later, Pamela is camped in the back-seat of the car with a pile of napkins full of ketchup that she uses to dip all the French fries she steals from me. But I let her. I can't help it. She smells nice. Plus she's hanging out with us instead of with her friends, who pig out on all that ice cream Issy bought them.

I like this. It's normal. What I should be doing. Not hiking around forests. Not watching a girl rip a deer's head off and eat it. That's not normal. Having a girlfriend who hates French fries or seafood or even fruit. Who hates fruit? Bree does. And the girl's unbalanced. I never know when she's going to go mental and turn into that wolf. So here's this normal girl, right? She's cute, popular, and so openly flirting with me that even I've noticed. Don't I want normal? I wanted it before I met Bree. Plus I can't ignore this great feeling in my chest since Pamela joined us in the back seat. This is the best I've felt all day.

But then her blond hair brushes my cheek. It makes me think about Bree.

Damn it. I still don't know what I want.

Pamela glances over at her friends. "I should hop back to my car. I bet my tribe misses me. Oh..." She grabs her phone. "What's your number?"

Should I give it to her?

Why not? Keep my options open, right?

I give it to her.

Pamela hits my phone with a text. "Do you have me now?"

I pause, save the new contact, and nod.

"Text me if you want to talk about anything." Pamela brushes her hand against my leg. "I'm a fantastic listener." The girl then salutes Issy with her shake. "Thanks." She kisses him on the cheek and giggles as she jumps out of the car.

Issy leans way back in his seat and releases a heavy sigh.

Pamela starts up her car and gives me a goodbye wave as

she backs out and takes her entourage home.

When Issy finishes his fries, I scoop up our wrappers and empty cups, then leave the car to find a trash can. A silver-plated one catches my attention long enough to feed it our trash.

"Bruce Wayne!"

At first I don't react to the voice, but then I feel someone behind me so I turn.

Three big seniors block out the sun. They go to my school. This can't be good.

"Any plans Saturday night?" the oldest senior with huge side-burns asks.

Why is he asking that? Why is he even talking to me?

"I don't know," I reply.

"You're coming to my party. That's what. Saturday night. Lots of awesome people will be there. It'll be at my stepmom's brand-new house with this arena-sized outdoor patio. Believe me, it will be a night of epic celebration, and I want Bruce Wayne to be at my awesome party."

Issy falls in behind me, no doubt curious about my new friends.

The senior with the side-burns...isn't his name, like, Josh? He points at Issy. "Oh, dude, you're Bruce Wayne's side-kick! I want you at my awesome party too."

"Robin. His side-kick's name is Robin," another senior adds.

"No, that's Batman's side-kick. Bruce Wayne's ward is Dick Grayson, and that's technically his side-kick." The third senior says, the comic-book reader in this group.

"Who cares?" Josh asks. "Bottom line. I want the dude who kicked Kirk Cummings' ass at my party. This Saturday. No excuses."

The three large seniors wait for my reaction. A senior party? I don't know about this.

"Of course he's coming," Issy says. "We wouldn't miss an epic party at an epic place with an epic dude like you. Let's do this." He fist-bumps Josh, and they leave.

"Why did you do that? I don't want to go to a party."

"Why not? You've been honored," Issy says. "Didn't you hear them? Those seniors were honored by *you* coming to *their* party. Best thing that could have happened to you."

I thought Bree was the best thing that had happened to me.

"A-man, you have to go. C'mon. Without you, it won't be as much fun. Plus, that senior might change his mind and not let me into his party without you. At least go for your wingman's sake."

He's waving the loyalty flag, knowing full well I never let down a friend. Unless he's getting beaten in front of a Mexican restaurant.

Crap. I still owe him, don't I?

CHAPTER THIRTY

AIDEN

Saturday night. The directions lead us to a mini version of one of those Southern slave mansions you see in the movies. A single, large crystal light shines over the front porch entrance, showing the circular drive crowded with cars. Issy parks the Jetta on the street. Even from way out here, I can hear the music thumping the walls. They must have one bitching sound system.

"Bruce Wayne!" Josh yells, waving a red plastic cup of intoxicating beverage.

Before I know it, he puts another cup of beer in my hand and parades me in front of the other seniors in the house while Issy trails along. I get tons of high-fives and fist-bumps. Girls smile. Issy jumps in to talk to them as soon as they're done talking to us, and then gets a slap when he says something stupid. Everyone talks about how I took care of Kirk and his buddies while single-handedly saving my best friend. Some juniors at the party tell me I should run for class president next year.

That concept blows my brain cells. Me? Class president?

Next year I should run for the biggest class joke. I didn't stand up to Kirk. I would have hauled my ass out of there if I could. Wearing this "hero" mask gets too heavy sometimes. My stomach burns every time I have to lie about it. Like I'm being punished every time I commit a sin. Can I keep up with being a fake for another year? Or will someone replace Kirk and try to test how tough I am? Bree might have to step in and protect me.

So pathetic. I shouldn't be letting my girlfriend do that. I'm the guy here, right?

I sip on my cup of cheap beer that I don't want, but everyone here drinks so I have to pretend that I like it. The smell of the crap makes me want to gag. I've grown to hate it thanks to Dad. Issy starts on his second cup of beer and acts even more animated than usual. He makes another round through the party, hitting on the new girls as they arrive.

Soon Josh leaves me alone outside on the giant patio. Other kids chatter and drink behind me as I stare out into the backyard with its tiny sculptures lit with small, fancy-colored flood lamps. It makes the grounds around the house look like some wannabe museum.

A hand slides up my back.

Bree?

I roll to my left, and a blonde in this seriously-short pink dress giggles.

"I bet you need a refill." Pamela raises two cups of beer, and offers me one, but I show her my cup is still half full. Pamela hands me the full cup, takes my half cup, downs the rest of the beer in it, and then slips her new beer cup into the old empty cup. "There we go." She smiles.

Well, she's no stranger to beer.

"Surprised to see you here." Pamela flashes a bright smile and drinks. "How's life?"

I shrug.

"A man of few words."

"Sorry. I usually don't talk a lot."

"No worries. I can do all the talking." She takes another drink. "I've narrowed my college choices down to five. My dad is this gigantic Oklahoma Sooners fan so, of course, he wants me to go there, but I honestly don't want to live in Norman. NYU is the one school I really want."

"Why NYU?" I ask, not caring about what she's talking about.

"Because they have a great film school, but I don't want to be a director or something like that. I'd love to be a producer or a studio executive. That would be so fun. Now my second choice is USC for the same reasons, but I think NYU has more of a reputation as a place for serious filmmakers. Plus, living in New York would be the bomb. Where are you going to college?"

College? That's like a year and half away. And who's going to pay for that? My dad? Forget it.

"I'm not sure yet," I lie.

She squeezes my shoulder. "You should go to NYU with me. It would be so fun. You could be like this shy, genius-student film director, and I could produce your movies, and we could win Oscars."

That's great if someone wants to make movies and wants to go to New York City. None of which applies to this kid. Guess I should think about the future, but I don't have any dreams. Not really. Okay, maybe one. I don't want to be a future asshole to a future kid like me.

"So you didn't call me," Pamela says, her eyebrows inching up.

"Call you about what?"

"Your girl troubles."

I peek into my stale beer.

"Still thinking about her, huh?" she asks.

I shrug. I feel weird talking about Bree in front of Pamela.

Pamela leans in. I catch a whiff of the beer on her breath, but I also catch her perfume, and it's the same one she wore the day I poured my heart out to her. I can still remember it. "Can I help you decide?" Her boobs press against my chest.

Would it be bad to give in? Shouldn't I be happy about this? Shouldn't I let everything go and be with the girl I've fantasized about for so long. A girl I don't have to hide from the world. Pamela doesn't have secrets. Not any big ones that need protecting. I've never been to New York City before. Maybe I could be a film director. That does sound interesting. Maybe Pamela would be the perfect girlfriend for a popular senior that might run for class president.

My lips feel wet as Pamela sucks on them. She's kissing me.

I gaze into Pamela's eyes and realize they're hazel. I never noticed that before. They look so different. I'm use to them being amber. And her hair is different too. I wish it was darker. Like Bree's. Pamela doesn't smell like Bree either. She's too fake, too artificial. Bree has this hint of honeysuckle in her hair, so natural and light. Only enough of a scent to remind you she was there. Bree never smelled like this. It's like Pamela jumped inside a tub of perfume.

I miss that honeysuckle. I miss that dark hair. I miss those amber eyes.

I miss Bree.

My stomach sours. It's the same feeling I get when I lie.

Is this a lie? Is what I'm doing false? Is this not what I want?

Pamela holds back, and studies my face. "What's wrong?"

I don't want this girl anymore. I don't *need* this girl to be happy.

"Where are you going?" Pamela asks.

CHAPTER THIRTY-ONE

AIDEN

The guest bathroom inside the slave mansion is this tiny box. Only large enough for a narrow sink on one end and a toilet on the other. I park my butt on the toilet. Someone turns the handle and tries the locked door once in a while, but otherwise it's a great place to chill and think.

I want Bree.

She's the only girl that makes sense. The only girl that I think about. The only girl I want to be with.

I should have handled Friday better. When Bree threw me on the floor, I should have trusted her. If her dad wasn't there to pull her off, Bree would have realized what she was doing and stopped on her own. I didn't trust her that night, and I should have. Love means trust, doesn't it?

I shouldn't be scared of someone I love.

After about twenty minutes I flush the toilet to fool people into thinking I've used it. Then I leave the bathroom to get back to the party.

Issy throws himself at me, smacking my back against a French painting hanging on the wall. "She's here!" My wingman slurs the words together while his beer-breath gives me another vomit reflex.

I shove Issy off me. "Who's here?"

Like a flag in a slight breeze, Issy wavers back and forth. I better swipe his car keys. There's no way I'm letting him drive like this. My friend drags me towards the living room and points.

Five senior guys surround a girl in a chair. Her back faces me, but that black hair looks too familiar.

Bree whips around, her silky hair following. She's wearing makeup, looking like that gorgeous girl I took out to the zoo. Her long lashes blink as those familiar eyes center on me.

I move into the living room to get a better view.

Bree wears this sparkling red dress that shines and shimmies under the lights. She crosses her legs and sips on a cup of beer. Her eyes follow me. Bree must have come in when I was in the bathroom. But why is she here? Did Josh invite her to the party? Did Bree invite herself? Is Bree stalking me?

Should werewolves drink beer?

The vibe of the party changes. When I first arrived, the party was spread out through the house and the backyard. Now everyone crowds into the big living room. The only reason I can think of is Bree. A group of dudes hover around her, wanting to eat her up like candy.

Bree sits there like a queen, radiating this confidence I know she has, acting like this room is hers to command. Why is she doing this? This isn't hiding. All these kids go to our school, and they'll talk about her. I thought Bree said it was too dangerous for her to stand out like this?

Guess Bree doesn't care anymore.

Not once has she flicked her eyes away from me, even as she drinks. It's unnerving. I know what a deer feels like now. Is she trying to make me jealous?

I think it's working.

A hand touches my arm.

"She has some nerve." Pamela leans against my shoulder. "You only wanted some time to think and here's Bree putting herself out there like she's available. What a bitch. You should leave her. You don't need any girl who treats you that bad."

Bree's mouth twitches to the side. She heard that.

One brave asshole kneels beside Bree and talks to her. She

concentrates on him and props her hand right under her chin, acting like she's mesmerized by every word this guy says. A spark of anger jolts my heart. I don't want him that close to Bree.

"Let's go somewhere else. You shouldn't torture yourself by staying here." Pamela leads me to the front door and pushes down on the stylized handle. The main door releases, exposing the night air. I feel a breeze rush in.

Bree's head snaps back to me. Her nostrils flex, taking in my scent from the breeze. That bold confidence on her perfect face...cracks. Her mouth opens slightly, as if she wants to call out, but what holds me are those eyes. Those beautiful amber eyes. They're so sad. So very sad.

That sour feeling in my stomach keeps my feet still. I can't hurt her. I'll hate myself if I hurt her. Leaving with Pamela now will hurt Bree too much. That face of hers screams it. I know this girl so well that I can read every crease on her face. Behind that proud wolf showing off in front of all those guys...there's a girl who desperately wants me back.

"You're bothering my girlfriend," I say to the senior asshole trying to dominate Bree's attention.

The senior stands up. He's two feet taller than me. "Oh yeah? I think she likes it."

Bree leans back with a large smile. "I was enjoying his company. And since you were occupied..." Bree throws an eye dagger at Pamela, who doesn't like what she's watching.

"She's only a distraction," I say. "I guess we're both distracting ourselves tonight."

Bree glances at her dress. Her mouth twitches to the side again.

"Do we have problems here?" Issy stands behind me, slurring his words. "Do someone here need to get Kirked?" Issy sounds so drunk, but I appreciate the back-up.

The asshole senior hesitates. "Are you Aiden? The guy that —"

"Kicks ass like a box full of Batmans? Hell yeah!" Josh yells. "This should be a sick fight. Take it out to the patio so we all can watch you get killed."

Fight? I don't want to fight anybody. Here we go. This will be the night I lose my reputation as a "tough guy." Goodbye senior class president.

"My bad, Bruce. Didn't know this was your girl." The senior, who's not such an asshole after all, backs away. His bravado fades. "Need another beer?"

I flick my cup, and some beer still sloshes around. "I'm good, thanks."

The tall senior leaves. The other guys scatter, leaving us alone. Did I do that? Did I *intimidate* those seniors? Amazing. I sit next to Bree.

We toss a few glances back and forth.

"Thought you were leaving," Bree says.

"Not with Issy so trashed," I say. "I can't leave him alone with a bunch of drunk seniors. Something bad would happen."

"Your date looks disappointed."

Pamela leans against a far wall, watching our conversation.

"I came with Issy. Not her." I listen to my fingers tapping against the plastic cup of beer. "Did you follow me here?"

Bree downs the rest of her beer and doesn't answer.

"Should someone like you be drinking?"

"I should be drinking more," Bree smirks, that werewolf swagger of hers coming back. She steals my cup and drinks whatever beer is left. "Refills!" She jumps up with both cups and sprints over to the beer keg as I follow her. A senior pumps the keg and fills up both of our cups. Bree hands me one and takes my free hand. "We need fresh air!" she yells, dragging me outside to the large back patio. Bree gulps down more beer as she watches me.

I sniff the new beer, and it makes me sick. "I don't understand. So you followed me here and then decided, 'Hey, I want to crash the party!'"

Bree sways a little. "Maybe. I did have to go home and change first."

"Why are you dressed like that?"

"Don't I look amazing?" The pride swells in her voice.

"Every boy here checked me out. I could hear them all talking."

"I thought your parents didn't want you standing out like this?"

"It's none of their business. And why do you care? You have Pamela now." Bree drinks more beer.

"I don't *have* Pamela."

"So then...you're cheating on me behind my back? Or did we break up already and you just haven't told me yet? I'm mystified."

"I told you. I needed some—"

"Time, yeah, whatever," Bree interrupts. "Maybe you don't need time because it's so clear to me who you want to be with." Her eyes water, but she strains against it. "I can't take this any longer. You're killing me here because I don't know what's going on and you're not talking to me and it stresses me out." She quivers and gulps down more fermented hops. "Say it, Aiden. Say you don't want to be with me and spare me this pain. Because it hurts." Her voice cracks on the last sentence as a tear runs down her cheek, a blemish on her otherwise perfect makeup job.

I brush her cheek and wipe the tear off. The wetness coats my fingers. I cup her chin with my hand. Bree doesn't flinch. "I trust you, Bree. I trust you with my life. And I'll give that life to you. If you still want to share yours."

This flash of electricity pours through Bree, making her eyes sparkle as bright as her dress. "Yes, I still want it. And I promise I will never let it go."

I hug Bree, and her body squeezes around me. She's so warm and soft. "I'm so sorry. I'm so very sorry."

"We both messed up. So let's just forgive each other. I'll start." Her lips press against mine, and we kiss. That familiar scent of honeysuckle is back, her dark hair brushing against my cheek, those eyes I love to peek at. That playful girl who nips at my ear and licks my cheek. I cling to her, not wanting to ever let go of her again.

We sway to the music coming through the open patio doors of the house. A private dance together. Only the two of us enjoying the other's company. The world making sense as long as the other is there.

I see all the seniors hanging out inside, drinking and laughing inside the house. But I see Pamela lying across the couch, bawling her eyes out. Issy cradles her head in his lap, letting the girl cry all over him when he could be working the room and hitting on more girls. People never give my wingman enough credit for being such a decent dude.

The party winds down. I keep Bree in the backyard, hidden away from the others. I was right. Girl werewolves should never drink beer. At least Bree stopped licking me. She's licked my nose, my ears, my forehead, my hair, my shirt, my fingers. I'm dripping wet with wolf-girl saliva. And when I try to stop her, Bree just giggles. Three times tonight I've talked her out of changing into a werewolf. She says everyone will think it's funny. I know the sober Bree wouldn't want to do that so I'm forced to protect Bree from herself. Or her wolf self. I only hope I can keep Bree human enough to take her back home.

Now Bree bites my earlobe and...ouch. Pulls it.

"Would you stop?"

Bree giggles again.

I lifted Issy's car keys so I can drive him home. Since everyone drank more of my beer than I did, I'm good to go driving-wise. Drinking a huge one-third cup of beer tonight won't impress anybody here.

Issy comforts Pamela on the couch. They're both drunk, but my wing-man calmed the girl down, and they've been talking all night, which amazes me. Maybe they'll hook up. That would take the sting out of hurting Pamela's feelings if my wingman gets a girlfriend out of it.

I check my phone. One in the morning. Better collect some friends for the ride home. I guide Bree over to an outdoor lounge chair that isn't covered with vomit. I brush back the hair from her face. "Stay here, okay? I'll be right back."

Bree licks my hand and curls up on the chair. I leave her

there and slip inside the house.

A lot of kids have left, but some sleep on the floor instead of driving home. Josh removes his hand from a half-eaten bag of loaded-baked-potato-flavored chips and gives me a salute. "You outta here, Bruce?"

"Yeah. Grabbing my crew first. Great party. Thanks for the invite," I say.

The senior burps. "You're welcome. Do it again next month, right?"

"Right," I lie as I head to the couch. Issy and Pamela look up. "You ready to go home?" I hold up Issy's keys. "I'm driving."

Issy smiles. "Wonderin' where I put those." He slides his arm around Pamela. "Give my girl here a ride too."

Oh yeah. Pamela. I also have to take Bree with us so...this could get awkward. The way Bree is now, she might do something weird in front of Pamela. Like kill her. If I put Bree in the trunk, would she remember that? The girl is slap-happy drunk.

I better not do that. Bree might remember, and that would piss her off.

What if I put Pamela in the trunk?

Guess I'll have to chance it. I get Issy and Pamela to their feet. The two of them hang close to each other. Like two magnets you can't pull apart. They follow me outside to collect Bree.

The lounge chair sits empty. Lying on the ground is one shimmering red dress, two pieces of girl's undergarments, and a set of heels. Did she...?

A howl pierces the backyard.

Damn it, Bree.

Then I see her. She prances into the back-yard with her tail high in the air, her gray fur bristling for some reason. I notice her movements aren't graceful like normal. Her four legs quiver, and her body sways back and forth as if she can't get her balance right. Her wolf head tilts at a weird angle, and her tongue hangs out to the side of those scary fangs of hers.

But this scary-looking werewolf trips over a flood-light

and tumbles over like a two-year old.

I don't believe what I'm seeing.

Bree stumbles back to her feet, shakes her head, and wobbles towards the house.

Pamela squints. "Whose dog is that?"

I chase after Bree as she weaves for the open patio doors to the house. "Bree! No. Stop. Heel, girl."

Under her fangs I see the wolf grinning as she moves faster and slips through the doors.

Bree!

I run inside the house, expecting screams, people running, and general mayhem.

But I see Bree's snout inside a bag of loaded-baked-potato-flavored potato chips. Josh holds the bag in place for her. I take it back. Now *this* I don't believe I'm seeing. Doesn't Josh realize that he's feeding a...?

"I love dogs!" he says to me. "My mom would never let me have one because she says they pee all over the house." The senior pets my girlfriend, his eyes glazed over. He's still drunk. Amazing.

I do a quick check around the room. Everyone is either sleeping or in no condition to care about "the dog."

Two girls walk into the living room. Crap. I prepare for the blood-curdling screams that are sure to come.

"Puppy!" One girl wraps her arms around Bree and gives the werewolf a hug.

Should I tell them?

The other girl pets Bree. "Well, aren't you a pretty doggie."

We better go. I tug on her gray fur. "Let's go, girl. Need to take you back home."

Bree stops eating and whimpers. She stands on her hind legs and licks my face off again. Yuck. Her wolf breath mixes with digested potato chips, and it's disgusting.

"You have a cute dog," the first girl says, completely oblivious.

I wrestle Bree off and get her to follow me back to the patio doors, where Issy and Pamela stand waiting.

Issy laughs. "Bree is a cute doggy."

"Dude, shut up." I toss a look at Pamela, who tries to make out what the hell is next to me. This isn't good. I only hope she's drunk enough not to remember any of this.

Bree growls at Pamela.

I kneel in front of Bree. "Stop that. You've been a very naughty...um...girl. Go into the bushes and change back or I won't...pet you anymore."

Bree whimpers and looks sad as she rushes into the bushes.

Pamela squints again. "Do you know that dog?"

"Issy, why don't you take Pamela out to the car." I push them in that direction. "I'll meet you there."

"No problem," Issy slurs. "I got Pam. You got the wolf."

"The wolf?" Pamela asks. Her mind seems hazy, but not as hazy as I'd like.

She and Issy stumble slowly up to the patio doors.

Bree skips out naked and still giggling like a little girl.

Pamela stops, gestures to Issy and asks in her loud, outdoor voice, "Why is she naked?"

Issy shushes Pamela. "That's a secret," he yells, and they disappear into the house.

Bree slips her clothes back on, but it takes a while. I guide her to the Volkswagon and make Issy sit in back with Pamela. I put Bree next to me so I can keep an eye on her.

Bree cuddles up to my shoulder as I drive. I glance through the rear-view mirror and catch Pamela whispering something to Issy, who has this big smile on his face. Wonder what she's talking about. I hope she's not piecing things together. Pamela sneaks a look at Bree, says something else to Issy, and he answers. *Please don't tell her.* Let her be drunk and confused because that's our only defense tonight.

"Aiden?" Bree asks.

"What?"

"I can't feel anything."

"What do you mean?"

"I can't hear very well, or smell very well, or...I can't feel my tongue."

"It's the beer. It numbs your senses. Trust me, I have

experience in this."
    Wish I didn't.
    Bree clings to my arm. Her voice quivers like she's about to cry. "Is it going to stay like this? Will I never be able to smell or hear anything again? I'm freaking out."
    I bring my arm around and squeeze her towards me. "Don't worry. The effect will wear off."
    "Promise?" she asks.
    "Promise."
    All the muscles in her face relax, and a thin smile peeks out. "Are you hungry? I'm famished."
    "I could go for tacos," Issy says, sounding more coherent.
    "If I eat tacos right now, I'll get sick," Pamela says.
    Bree snaps up in her seat and twists to follow the voice. Her mouth twitches to the side. "What are you doing here?"
    Before the girl can answer, Issy puts his arm around Pamela. "She's with me."
    Bree hesitates, and flicks her eyes at me for confirmation.
    I nod.
    She moves them back to the new happy couple in back. "Oh." She turns back around and taps me on the shoulder. "Did I miss something?"

CHAPTER THIRTY-TWO

AIDEN

Issy wakes me up. I stretch and yawn. My wingman scratches himself as he sits on the edge of my bed. He's already rolled up my sleeping bag that I let him use last night. The clock says it's noon, and Issy wants to head back home. He had the brilliant idea of calling his parents before the party and telling them he was staying at my house for a Death and Valor 4 marathon. Issy calls Pamela to see how she's feeling. She wants Issy to come over later. I give him a fist bump.

"Are you in-sync with this, A-man?"

"Why wouldn't I be okay with it?"

"You were into her at one time, and I don't want you putting the hate on me for making a move here."

After last night I know who I want to be with for the rest of my life. And I know she feels the same way. And it's pretty damn awesome.

"You and me are solid, dude. Make your move."

Issy takes a Tylenol pill for his headache before I escort him through the living room. Dad watches football as he snacks on some Doritos. Issy and my dad exchange some awkward head nods before my friend leaves. I close the door and snap the deadbolt.

"Late night, huh?" Dad asks, more cheerful today than usual.

I didn't tell him about the party last night. He might have

tagged along so he could drink all the free beer. "We were up late playing D and V so Issy decided to crash here."

"Yeah, swore I heard that GameMaster of yours going late last night."

Dad must be hearing things. Doesn't matter. He's not suspicious, so I can go back to sleep and forget about it.

"Game's on," Dad says. "We can order pizza for lunch if you want."

I need more sleep not pizza, but I plop on the couch and watch football anyway. We get pizza delivered. I chow down, filling my belly with pizza that only multiplies the sleepiness by a factor of ten. Catch myself falling asleep a few times. But I stop fighting the urge and drift off.

A loud boom wakes me up. It's a distant boom like... thunder? I look over at Dad, and he's drinking. Great. The second football game of the double-header starts on television. There's a tornado watch icon at the corner of the screen thanks to our local station.

When they hit the next commercial break, a severe weather animation blasts across the screen. A weather guy shows a line of heavy thunderstorms on the radar heading our way. Dad finishes his bottle, then yells at the weather guy for interrupting his game. He's slurring his words already.

Time to hide in my bedroom again.

I close my door and do some homework. Rain pelts my window. At first it's a gentle tapping, like leaves blowing against the glass, but then it increases. The rain smacks against the glass with force. The wind slaps the trees around, making the branches twist and turn. The thunder grows louder. The time between the flash and the boom shrinks. That means the lightning is closer to our house. I unplug the laptop. Last year Issy lost a computer during a storm when lightning fried the circuit board.

The wind increases, punching the trees outside. The rain pours down.

Outdoor tornado sirens wail in the distance.

Damn.

I run to the living room. The weather guy on television says something about a tornado warning for Tulsa County. It might be already on the ground. They track the tornado on the radar map, and it's heading for our part of town.

Dad fumes at the television with his whiskey voice. "Stupid dumb-asses. Don't know shit. Tryin' to scare us. That's all. Cuttin' over the game fur this shit."

So much for having a responsible parent around.

"Dad, the sirens are going off. Don't you think we should go into the closet?"

The interior hall closet is the only kind of tornado shelter we have. What about Bree? Did she hear about the warning? I should call her, but first I need to get Dad's drunk ass into the closet.

"Dad?"

He doesn't answer.

The wind blows hard now, making the house creak. I don't like this.

"I think we should go in the closet."

"Shut up," Dad says.

"This is serious."

"Go runnin' to the closet like some little girl. Be my guest," he slurs.

A part of me wants to leave him. Let him die being a drunk asshole because it would serve him right. But he's my dad. Even though he's messed up...he's still my dad.

I grab on to his arm and pull him off his chair. "Let's both be girls, then." I hope the joke lightens him up as I work Dad towards the closet. I get him to the hallway, but he works his way out of my grasp.

"Get off me."

"But Dad..."

He throws a punch that connects.

I stumble back.

"Don't think your man enough to boss me 'round. 'Cuz you ain't. Stop being a wuss. Sleep all God damn day and then get all scared 'bout rain. What kind of man did I raise? Huh?"

The surprise hurts more than the pain in my cheek. I'm

used to the pain. A sudden flood of emotion pushes against me, and I try to fight it off, but then I feel tears streaming down my cheeks.

Dad strikes me with the side of his knuckle. "Stop cryin' like a wussy boy, you soft piece of shit."

The hit makes me cry harder.

He hits me again. "You gonna go to the bathroom and kill yourself now?"

The insult burns in the pit of my stomach. The pathetic kid hides inside that crevasse. My nose stuffs up as the tears pour out of me. I can't stop them. I want to stop them, and I can't. I am a wuss. Men don't cry like this. Why can't I shut it off?

"Stop crying." Dad slaps me.

The house shudders. The wind sounds angry. I hear metal clanking against metal, but it's not coming from outside.

Dad holds the iron poker from next to the fireplace. "Want somethin' to cry about, you little girl?"

I hold my hands out to block what's coming.

Dad slams the poker across my hands, knocking them down. Searing pain goes through my arms. Dad swings again and strikes the side of my cheek, and pain fires up my jaw. God, it hurts. I collapse to the floor. I'm bigger than him. I should get up and beat the crap out of him, but the pathetic turd inside me curls up to take his punishment like he's supposed to.

But Dad drops the poker, which clangs against the floor, and retires to his bedroom.

The wind calms down.

The rain stops.

The tornado never hits us.

I crawl to my bedroom, lock my door, and climb into bed. My head and cheek throb with pain. But somehow I fall back to sleep.

CHAPTER THIRTY-THREE

AIDEN

I drift awake. The morning sun blinds me, forcing me to squint at the clock. Issy will be here soon to pick my butt up for school. I slide off my bed and stumble into the bathroom. I do a double-take in the mirror. Crap. Purple shades my right cheek that's swollen and looks like I'm holding a melon inside my mouth. I also feel a headache coming on. Standing only makes it worse. No way I can go to school looking like this. Dad will be pissed if I skip, but if I go to school like this, everyone will know and call the cops. Better go ask him what I should do.

Dad watches television in the living room. He's not dressed in his work clothes, so I guess he's not going in today because of hangover #365. I ask him about calling in sick for school. Dad doesn't even try to look at me. He only nods his answer.

I head back to my room, call Issy, and tell him I have the flu. He buys my story and tells me Pamela wants to hang with him today. I give him a congrats before I let him go. I text Bree. Her parents finally bought her a new smart phone after Bree schmoozed them for weeks. It does a crazy amount of cool stuff, much more than my phone can do.

Bree calls me. "You have the flu?"

I give her the same sad flu story.

"That sucks. Will you be all right?"

"Yeah, I only need to live in bed for a while," I say.

"I so promise to come over after school."

"No," I say with too much force. "It's contagious. Believe me, you don't want this junk."

"Really, Aiden...I can skip school and come over to take care of you."

"But you'll get sick."

"The flu can't kill me, and so what if I have to suffer a little. I don't mind."

I do. I can't let her see my face. I can't let anyone see it.

"Maybe tomorrow you can come over. Seriously, I feel out of it. If you come over, all you'll do is watch me sleep all day. I only need peace and quiet. Not that I don't love your company, but..."

"All right. I'll check on you tomorrow, then. Do you want me to bring you anything?" Bree asks.

"I'll let you know."

"Love you," Bree says softly before she lets me go. Her sweet voice makes me regret saying no.

I mess around in my room for hours, mostly watching YouTube videos. I go into the kitchen and make some macaroni and cheese out of a box for lunch. Dad makes a sandwich, then grabs a handful of barbecue chips. I don't offer him any mac and cheese. Dad doesn't ask for any. I take my pile of cheese and pasta into the bedroom and stuff my face.

Ouch. But I have to chew on the opposite side of my melon bruise. I play a few levels of Death and Valor 4 online with some adult gamer friends who have night jobs and no social lives during the day.

I finish our mission and then go take a piss. I miss the bowl and aim lower, hearing that satisfying sound of liquid hitting water. Then I realize my headache is gone. Maybe eating lunch helped. Still, my swelling cheek looks bad in the mirror. Guess I should take some Tylenol for that. I shake the plastic bottle and hear no pills inside. Issy must have taken the last one Sunday morning. I check Dad's bathroom, and he doesn't have any Tylenol. I find plain old aspirin, but I don't think that's gonna cut it with this melon I have. I tell Dad that I'm going out.

He nods again, but still doesn't want to look at my face.

The gray sky from yesterday's storm still lingers as I coast my bike downhill, thinking about what I'm going to tell Bree tomorrow. I'll have to come up with another good excuse why I won't be at school or why she can't come over. How long will my face be like this? Surely it'll look better in a week, right? I bet it will. All I have to do is keep my friends in the dark this week. Somehow. I'll find a way.

I wheel into the Drug Stop Pharmacy parking lot and chain up my bike. The aisles inside have all kinds of stuff like chips, makeup, and crap to make your garden grow. Spring is almost here and so what? I'm looking forward to summer. Bree and I talked about getting summer jobs together. It would be awesome to work at the same place. Hopefully we can find somewhere fun that pays us a butt-load of money.

Extra-Strength Tylenol. Now we're talking. I grab a bottle off the shelf. This should help reduce the swelling. I check some of the other brands to see if there's something stronger that might work better. Nah, forget it. I'll stick with the Tylenol. Oh, and I could use some cheese balls and a candy bar too. That way I won't have to leave my room until dinner. The lady at the counter bags my stuff, and I'm out the door.

I kneel down and unchain my bike.

"Feeling better?"

That's Bree's voice.

I freeze and glue my eyes to the bike. Damn. What do I do? I can't look up or...

"I...I needed some Tylenol. Shouldn't you be at school?" I ask.

"It's 3:15," Bree says. "And, like, shouldn't you be in bed?"

"I needed Tylenol," I repeat.

"You should have texted me. I would have brought it for you." Bree sounds a little hurt.

"I needed to get out of the house."

If Bree was a human girl, I would accuse her of stalking

me because how else would she know I was at the pharmacy? But with that Lycan nose of hers, she must have caught my scent and tracked me here.

"Why are you staring at the ground?" Bree laughs. "Are you suddenly shy around me now?"

What do I do? Guess I'll have to hop on the bike and hope she doesn't get a good look at me. I roll my bike away from the rack while keeping my head turned away. "I got a headache still, and the sun hurts my eyes, but I swear I'll call you later." I jump on my bike, and aim it towards the street.

Bree touches my arm. "If you're feeling that bad, let me drive you home. You can put your bike in the trunk."

"I just...I can't...I..." I'm running out of excuses.

"What is it?"

She's suspicious. And I've got nothing.

Her fingers touch my chin and guide my eyes into hers. Bree's mouth drops in absolute shock.

"Okay, I'm not sick with the flu," I stammer, trying to sidestep. "I fell and hit my face, and I'm totally embarrassed, okay? I didn't want you to know."

Bree strokes my lip, and I stop. "This isn't from a fall, is it?"

I don't know what's worse on the embarrassment scale... lying to Bree that I fell, or admitting that I'm a loser who can't take a punch. So I don't say anything.

"Who did this to you? Was it Kirk?"

I shake my head. "I fell. It's true. I fell."

Bree's mouth twitches to the side. Her red eyes darken as the wolf slips into them. That scary girl who attacked me in Bree's bedroom glares back. "It was your dad, wasn't it?"

"I fell." My words sound a little stronger; still, I don't think I'm convincing enough.

"How long has this been going on?"

I swallow. "Bree...please."

"Don't lie to me. Not about this." Bree leans in, her red eyes piercing through her bangs. "Does your dad hit you? Like all the time?" The anger inside her swells. I can see it on her face. The tug-of-war between girl and werewolf. Right now the wolf is winning.

I hold in the pain. I'm not going to cry in front of my girlfriend. It only proves that Dad is right about me. I hear myself draw in a deep sigh. I don't want to say anything because it's going to cause trouble. A lot of trouble. But her soft fingers resting against my cheek make me feel ashamed for hiding anything from her.

"Dad only hits me when he's drunk. He's got a problem with alcohol. He needs help, and I want to get him help."

Bree gnashes her teeth. "Being his punching bag is not giving him help, Aiden."

"Dad wants to stop. I know he does. He always hates himself after he does it. He always apologizes."

"And then keeps doing it?" Bree asks. "Your dad beats the crap out of you, and then he pities himself? Poor guy. While he pities himself, your face swells up like a bowling ball."

I strain to hold back the pain. "I ask for it sometimes."

"Really, Aiden? How do you *ask* for this?"

Pain leaks around the wall I've put up. I can't prop it up anymore. Still, I'm not going to f-ing cry.

"Dad drinks because of me. Because I disappoint him. If I were more of a man, he would respect me."

"That's crap," Bree yells. "There is no good reason for him to beat you. None." Bree rips herself away and paces back and forth in front of the store. "I can't believe he did this to you." The anger in her voice burns through every syllable. It's like this rage. Something I've never seen from a girl before. Yeah, I've seen girls pissed off...but this is on a whole other level.

"I'll kill him," she says.

Kill him? Whoa.

"Chill out a minute. I didn't ask you to..."

In a snap, Bree hovers inches away from my face. "Don't worry. I'll take care of it. You won't have to worry about your dad hurting you *ever* again."

Damn.

"Bree, leave it alone."

She kisses my forehead and backs away. Bree's eyes are

on fire, the burning so intense that I can see the fury behind them. The fury of the wolf. It scares the hell out of me because....I know what she's going to do. It's written on her face.

She's going to kill my dad.

I climb off my bike. "Stay here with me. Please, Bree. Don't!"

This darkness takes over my girlfriend's face as she opens the door to her car. "I have to do this for you. Because you won't do it for yourself."

That hits me below the belt. *Because you won't do it for yourself.* And she's right. And I hate it that she's right. It's like Kirk all over again. My girlfriend fixing all my problems that I'm too much of a wuss to fix myself.

"I know my dad is screwed up, but I don't..." I trail off without finishing my sentence.

Do I want him dead?

No. He's sick. Dad needs help.

"You don't need him anymore," Bree says, her voice low and raspy, like that time she was on the verge of changing. "You have me and my family now. The pack protects each other from all outsiders. Anyone who hurts a wolf, hurts the pack. And we always protect our pack."

She slips into the Oldsmobile. The big car screams out of the parking lot. The growl of the motor echoes off the buildings and then fades.

I have to stop her.

CHAPTER THIRTY-FOUR

AIDEN

I pedal as hard as I can out of the Drug Stop parking lot and up the long hill. There's no way I'm going to make it back home in time to stop Bree. I could call Dad, but what do I say to him? Get out of the house because my girlfriend wants to kill you? Or do I tell him Bree is a werewolf coming to rip him to shreds? Dad would laugh and hang up. Do I call the cops? They wouldn't be there in time.

I try to call Bree. If she picks up, I might be able to talk her down.

But she doesn't answer. I make a quick plea on her voice mail and beg her to call me back before she does anything.

My phone then chirps. Is that Bree?

No. It's Issy.

Couple blks away. Got ya a choc shake if u want me 2 drop it by.

A couple blocks away from my house?

I call Issy.

"A-man, how you feeling?"

"Listen to me. Bree is rushing over to my house right now to kill my dad." I pause, barely able to breathe and get the words out. "You have to get him out of the house, like, right now."

"What did you say?" Issy asks. Too much info, I guess.

"Dude, Bree is pissed and going to my house to kill my

dad. I'm not home, and I can't get there fast enough. You have to get my dad out of there, Issy. I'm being serious as hell."

"Why is she going to kill your dad?"

"Zero time to explain. Get to my house as fast as you can. Make up any excuse, but get my dad out of there."

"Damn, you're being serious."

"I can't stress how much," I say.

"I'm pulling up to your house now."

"Do you see Bree's car?"

"Not yet."

Thank God.

"Please save him, Issy."

"I'm on it. Pamela's with me, and we'll make sure he leaves with us. I'll call ya back."

The line goes dead. My heart beats slower, but it's still on edge. I have to get home.

It takes forever to reach the first turn into my subdivision. I pedal down to the third right, and lean in hard for the turn. My bike flies as fast as I can push it. I put my back into it, breathing hard, wiping the sweat dripping into my eyes.

I finally get to my street. No sign of Bree's car, but Issy's Jetta is parked on the driveway. Did he not get my dad out? What's he waiting for? I jump the curb and let the bike fall on the grass as I run into the house.

The living room is a mess.

The coffee table is busted, some of the furniture ripped with claw marks...

Bree did make it here.

"Aiden!" a girl's voice calls out.

Pamela kneels on the floor, cupping Issy's head in her lap. My friend's body is stained with blood. His eyes flutter in and out of consciousness. I run over to them.

"I called 911, and they're on the way," Pamela says in between sobs.

"Issy? Can you hear me?" I ask.

He swallows and coughs. "Yeah. I...hear ya." He sounds so weak.

"Stay with us, okay? The EMTs should be here any

second."

Issy nods, and I see real pain on his face. Will he die? Damn it. I look around and try to make sense out of what happened. And then it hits me.

"Pamela? Did you see my dad anywhere? Another man inside the house?" She looks shaken up, and at first she doesn't even acknowledge my question. I tap her shoulder. "Have you seen another man around the house?"

Pamela snaps out of it. "I think...I think he went into one of the bedrooms."

I jump to my feet and check my bedroom first. Nothing. I check the spare one. Not a thing. Next I check Dad's bedroom. I see him on the edge of the bed, staring into space. His hands quiver, like he has Alzheimer's or something, but Dad looks okay. No wounds or blood that I can see.

I slide next to him. "You okay?"

He doesn't answer, only shakes. I stand in front of him.

His eyes crawl up to take in my face. Dad nods, hesitates, then says, "God sent a demon after me."

Or maybe he's not okay.

"What?"

"A demon came through the doorway. A demon with fangs. It came for me, to take me to Hell. It stared at me with those red eyes. It wanted to take me. Take me down to hell with it."

When did Dad get so religious? I can count on one hand how many times he's gone to church. My dad bends his neck, slowly, like his world moves in slow motion. It freaks me out.

"God sent me a message." Dad nods to himself. "I'm gonna heed it, Aiden. I'm gonna do what he wants me to do."

I have no idea what Dad's talking about. But he's not hurt, so now I have to go help the one who is.

Back in the living room, I kneel with Pamela and Issy. "How's he doing?" I ask her.

"He keeps wanting to close his eyes and sleep, but I don't think that's a good idea. On all those medical shows they always try to keep the injured person awake. I don't think it's good for them to fall unconscious."

We take turns talking to Issy, trying to keep him awake, and alive when the sound of a siren comes. The ambulance pulls up with two paramedics, who get to work on Issy. They stabilize him enough to load him into the ambulance. I take Pamela to the Jetta and open the door for her as the ambulance races off with sirens wailing. I get behind the wheel and drive off towards the hospital.

What if Issy dies?

Do I tell the cops about Bree? Do I convince her to turn herself in? Would her family even let Bree do that? Would Bree's dad want to bury the problem by killing all of us?

But how can I worry about that? My best friend might die.

No! Issy can't die. He has to hold on. I should be the one in that ambulance. I'm the one who exposed him to Bree. I'm the one who made him go over to my house to confront a pissed-off werewolf. I'm the one who killed Issy. I should turn myself in and tell the police I murdered my best friend.

"Where's Bree?"

Pamela's voice and sudden question snaps me back out of my brain.

"Huh?"

She sniffles as she wipes a tear off her cheek with Kleenex. "Your girlfriend. Where is she right now?"

Does she suspect her? Did Pamela add up all the weird things at the party and come up with Bree's secret identity? But should I still be protecting my girlfriend who's a murderer?

"I don't know where she is," I say, which is true.

The traffic light shines the green arrow, and I turn left.

"After Issy got off the phone with you, he said your father was in danger and we needed to get him out of the house," Pamela says.

Maybe I shouldn't be too honest yet. "There was a gas leak. I left a gas burner on in the kitchen, and I was away from the house. Issy texted me and mentioned you guys were in my neighborhood. So I asked him to get my dad out in case the house exploded."

Pamela thinks about that. "And then some random wild

animal crashes into the house and attacks Issy?" She pauses. "The same wild animal that was at the party Saturday night."
"That was a dog."
"It was bigger than a dog. More like a wolf. A big wolf. Like the one that attacked us." Pamela stiffens. "You're not telling me something."
I pretend that I'm too busy driving to answer.
"Aiden? What really happened in the school parking lot with you and Kirk?"
I peek over. Pamela has her arms crossed, her face skeptical. She's putting it together. I don't know what to do, so I shut up.
"Kirk told the truth, didn't he? Bree was the one who beat him up and threw those boys like they were paper wads." Pamela leans closer. "What is she?"
"I can't say."
"She tried to kill your best friend."
"No, she was going after my dad." I press my lips together. I shouldn't have said that.
"Bree can turn into a wolf?" Pamela sits back, thinking. "Is she a...?"
"Werewolf. Yes." There's no use lying about it now. This girl is smarter than I gave her credit for.
So I tell Pamela everything.

We track down Issy's hospital room. It's large with a window that has the drapes closed, allowing the overhead lights to cast a bluish hue over the cold linoleum. Issy lies in bed; his eyes open when he hears us come in.
Pamela kisses him on the cheek. "What did the doctor say?"
"The cuts and puncture marks didn't go in as deep as they thought. So they've cleaned out the wounds and are keeping me under observation to make sure I don't have an infection. I'll have to get a rabies shot if they don't find the dog." That frown is for me. Even after she attacked him, Issy is still keeping Bree's secret. But that face says that he resents it big time.

"It wasn't a dog. It was Bree," Pamela says.

"Told her, huh?" Issy asks.

"I figured it out," she says proudly. "You should call the police right now so they can arrest Bree."

"Wait a second," I object. "We can't call the police on Bree."

"She attacked Issy."

"Bree was upset."

"Duh," Pamela says.

"No, she probably feels awful about all this. Bree was only doing it because of what my dad..." Damn it. I don't want to bring that up too.

"What did your dad do to get Bree so pissed?" Issy asks.

I press my lips together again. I don't want to say it. It's my business. They don't need to know about that. No one needs to know.

"I lost half my blood saving your dad from a werewolf attack. You owe me an answer. This is me. Your wingman. We don't keep secrets."

"If you say you're Issy's friend, you'll tell him the truth," Pamela says.

Like I need even more guilt right now. I brush the curtains to the side and take in the view. We're up high in this hospital tower. I can see most of South Tulsa from here.

"Can I only tell Issy, please?"

I wait until I hear the door open and catch sight of Pamela closing it behind her. I move over to Issy, grab a chair, and take a moment.

This is hard. I'm embarrassed to tell anyone, especially my friend. I don't know if he'll understand the crap I've been going through. But if I want to keep him as a friend, guess I have no choice now.

"Does this have anything to do with your face?" Issy asks. "Because when you first came in here, I thought you were a zombie coming to eat my brains."

That makes me laugh. I can't help it. Issy always makes me laugh.

But then I tell him. I tell him about Dad's drinking. I tell him about the way Dad hits me. I tell him it's been happening more often. How it gets harder and harder to hide the marks Dad makes. Issy listens. He doesn't crack jokes. He doesn't tell me I'm a wuss. He only listens.

And before I know it, I'm also telling him about my attempted suicide. And the girl who triggered it.

CHAPTER THIRTY-FIVE

AIDEN

The sky spits water on me. The gray clouds try to produce rain, but fail. They only manage a few stray drops, one of which nails me in the face. I stand in front of the Mayflowers' house, wondering how my life became so damn complicated. I drum my nervous fingers against the fender of Issy's Jetta. I still can't believe he said to keep the keys and take good care of his car until he's out of the hospital. Issy's trust blows my mind. The guy should hate me for what I've put him through this year.

I stare up at Bree's bedroom window on the second floor. I haven't seen her peek out once yet. She must be getting a whiff of me out here.

I ring the front doorbell anyway.

Mrs. Mayflower answers. "How is your friend?" she asks as I walk in the house.

"He'll be okay. They're just keeping him for observation," I say.

"Good. Very good news." Mr. Mayflower's voice echoes from the staircase as he takes the last few steps downstairs to join his wife. "We were worried about him."

"She's upstairs in her room," Mrs. Mayflower says. "She's been up there all afternoon."

"My fault. All of it," Mr. Mayflower says. "Should have shut it all down the moment Bree told us about you. Went against every instinct I had. Now this calamity. Your friend tell the police yet?"

"He won't, Mr. Mayflower. He hasn't told anyone."

"Issy will eventually, or his parents will drag it out of him." Mr. Mayflower frowns at his wife. "We'll have to move again. Soon as we can."

Mrs. Mayflower sighs. "Where else is there to go? Another city? Another country? And what do you want Bree to do? Ask her not to make any more friends?" Mrs. Mayflower pauses as her voice quivers. "Will there be any more young werewolves left alive for her to be friends with?"

Mr. Mayflower hugs his wife tight. "Shhh. Don't say such things."

"Bree is so happy here," Mrs. Mayflower sobs.

"I know she is. We'll talk about it first. Promise you that." Mr. Mayflower lovingly pets his wife's long hair. I've never before seen parents act so...good...to each other.

I excuse myself and head upstairs toward Bree's room. I knock on the door. Bree sniffles like her nose is stuffed up. A sad, weak little version of her voice then tells me to come in. Bree lays on her bed, clinging to Rocky and Bullwinkle. She's curled around a pillow and her stuffed animal friends. Her eyes are swollen, like she's been crying for days. At the sight of me, a new wave of tears rolls down her pink cheeks.

"I know you hate me," Bree sobs. "I would hate me too." She gasps for a breath. "I can't believe I killed Issy." Bree breaks down, and cries hard.

It breaks my heart seeing her like this.

"Issy will be okay. He's not going to die."

"But don't you understand? *I tried to kill him.* I jumped on top of your dad, and I was ready to bite into his neck, and then I was going to snap it. But Issy kept trying to pull me off. Over and over again he tried, and it distracted, me and I got mad at him. So mad I swung around and attacked him." Her watery eyes find me. "Issy struggled, but there was no way he could throw me off. I was so pissed that this human was trying to stop me. I could see it was Issy, and still I couldn't stop myself. I treated him like he was just another animal I was going to kill."

Bree sniffles. The tears stream down. "When my fangs bit into him, Issy screamed, and his voice...his voice made me hesitate. His scream rattled me so much that I wrestled back control from the wolf. And then, I was so horrified over what I'd done that the fury I had to kill your father was gone. I used that guilt to push myself out of the house and run away."

Bree closes her eyes, squeezing out more tears. I sit on the bed next to her and gently stroke her long hair. The strands feel soft between my fingers.

But she yanks my hand away. "You should stay away from me."

"I'm never leaving you," I say, meaning it.

Bree pushes herself away. "No. You so need to stay away. I'll hurt you. One of these days I'll hurt you like I did Issy. I'll get mad, and then I'll freak out and hurt you on accident. I might even kill you. And so help me...if I do that I will kill myself."

"You would never hurt me. You said so yourself."

"My dad's right. There is no way we can live with humans."

My heart freezes. I don't like that sentence. "You made a mistake and now you feel real guilt about it. That's a good thing. That's a human thing. It means being around humans is good for you."

"I can't take that chance. Not with your life. I don't want to stand over your body some day and realize that I was the one who killed you."

"It's my life, isn't it? I'll take that risk to be with you."

Bree shakes her head. "You were right the first time. We both need time to think about this."

I don't want to think about it any-more. I love her. I want to be with her. Doesn't she know that without her I'll die anyway? How is she going to protect my life by destroying the only thing that makes it worth living?

MY GIRLFRIEND BITES

I go back home tired. The last few hours have kicked my butt, and I'm at the point where I need to chill. Home isn't the most relaxing place, but I don't have anywhere else to go right now.

I shut the front door. Cheap, all-purpose cleaning fluid stinks the air. Mom's old carpet shampooer stands near the entrance to the living room. I haven't seen that machine out in years. Pressed into the newly-cleaned carpet are rows of imprints from the heavy machine. That old smell from the carpet reminds me of Mom. I still miss her.

Dad watches television, but the television isn't on. He stares at the blank screen. His eyes catch me. "A policewoman came by to fill out a report. Says she'll come by later to talk to you."

"Why were the police here?" I ask.

"Animal attack report."

Okay. That makes sense.

"Did she say when they would come back?"

Dad shrugs. "Later."

Not helpful. But right now, I don't care. I need to relax. Crap, I need to take some of that Tylenol before my head swells up and explodes.

"I'll be in my room." I head for the hallway.

But something in the kitchen makes me stop. A dozen empty liquor bottles stand on the counter. I move to the kitchen and see empty beer bottles placed in a ring around the sink. No way. Did Dad pour all that liquor down the sink?

I shake my head. Too much wishful thinking. He'll forget that he did this and then waste the money buying new beer.

"How's Ishmail?" Dad asks.

I fill him in on Issy's condition. Soon Dad goes on and on about demons and how God is punishing him. It's bad enough I have an alcoholic for a father. Now he's a tortured follower of Jesus. I don't need this today. Before I reach the door of my room, Dad actually says...

"I love you."

My swollen cheek throbs.

Yeah, Dad. Love you too.

I down the Tylenol with water, flop on my bed, and fall asleep.

* * *

When I wake up, it's dark outside my window. My phone tells me it's a handful of minutes past six in the morning. I flip a light on and check my face in the bathroom mirror. The swelling has gone down big time. My melon is only a slight bump. Plus the throbbing pain is gone. I hear some activity in the kitchen.

Curious, I sneak into the hallway.

Dad eats breakfast at the table. He's clean-shaved, sober, and ready for work. What is that about? It freaks me out because it's like two hours before he needs to be at the airport. He never gets ready this early. Amazing.

Instead of heading back to bed, I go into the kitchen for some breakfast.

"I'll call the school and confirm that you have the flu," Dad says.

I nod and pour cereal and milk into a bowl. The silverware clanks as I open the drawer to take out a spoon. I hesitate. Will Dad say anything else? Mention it at all?

He stares at the wall and eats.

I take my breakfast to my room.

Around noon I drive the Jetta up to the hospital to visit Issy. One nurse stands at a big desk, working on something and not paying any attention. Just in case, I hide the paper bag I'm carrying. It holds Issy's present, and the nurse might take it away if she sees what it is. I poke my head into my wing-man's room. He watches television while a couple machines next to him beep and monitor stuff. I think of something funny to say.

"Has that nurse given you a sponge bath yet?"

Issy cracks a smile. "Francesca is the only cute one, and she works nights. Now if she volunteered, I would be forever in her debt."

"You could ask Pamela."

"Yeah, right. I don't wanna mess up a good thing, you know?"

I drop myself in a nearby chair. The rough cloth scratches my back. "So you're serious about her, huh?"

Issy thinks about it and nods. "Yeah, I like her. Who would have thought that a year ago."

"Lots of strange things have happened this year." I prop my sneakers on the corner of his bed.

Issy wants to add something, but doesn't.

"Bought you a present." I toss the paper bag in his lap.

My wingman digs inside and brings out the burger wrapped in thick paper. "If this is what I think it is, I might give you my car for the rest of the month."

"Seriously?"

"No." Issy unwraps the paper that hides a chili-cheese-covered nirvana. The frito-pie burger. Issy's favorite. "You are a god, A-man," he says before his mouth attacks the burger. We talk about all kinds of things as Issy stains his cheeks with chili and cheese. It's like nothing has changed between us.

He wipes off his cheeks and takes a break. "I can't eat anymore, but I'm saving the rest for later. Thanks."

The room grows quiet.

Issy cleans up the remnants of his burger.

I know what I need to say, and maybe this is the time to do it.

"Dude, I'm sorry about yesterday. I really thought Bree would back down if you were there. And for what it's worth, Bree feels awful about what happened."

"You have to get away from her." Issy sounds dead serious. "Dump her now. Use this as an excuse. If she's really sorry, Bree will accept that."

Dump her? She made a mistake. She was angry, unable to control herself. Bree hates herself for doing this. Why can't Issy see that?

"But I like her."

"She's a werewolf, dumb-ass. The girl turns into a monster that kills things. Someday that monster is going to turn on you."

"Wait a minute, you loved the idea I was going out with a werewolf. You thought it was awesome."

"That was before she tried to kill me."

"Dude, stop exaggerating."

"Screw you. I saw those eyes of hers, and she wasn't playing. If I hadn't distracted Bree, your father would be dead right now." Issy pauses and sighs. "Look, if me and you still want to be tight, you can't be dating Bree anymore because I don't want to be anywhere near her. If you got half a brain, you shouldn't be anywhere near her either."

But I love her. How do you walk away from something so perfect? How do you leave something that you know in your heart will never be this good again? Is Bree complicated? Yes. But are the complications worth it?

The door creaks open as the subject of our discussion slips in.

Was Bree listening all this time?

Issy straightens in bed. His jaw locks as his eyes glare at the intruder.

Bree looks extremely sad. She carries a plate of cookies wrapped in plastic. Bree tries to smile, but her mouth only does a weak bend. Her eyes shift to Issy. "I made these cookies for you," she says, looking for somewhere to put them. I clear off a place near some flowers, and Bree sets the plate there. She slowly approaches Issy, her hands clasped together and twitching slightly. She's nervous and probably feeling guilty. I feel so sorry for her.

Issy inches away from her, moving to the opposite side of his bed.

Bree hesitates at this, feeling the hostility. She decides to stay put. "Issy...words can't state...how deeply sorry I am." Her eyes begin to water. The devastated girl in the bedroom yesterday comes back. "Nothing I do can take away the pain and the suffering I've caused. All I can say is...I hate myself. I hate that part of me that I can't control. I'm working on it.

Believe me, I'm trying to fight against it so hard..." Bree stops, as if something is caught in her throat.

"Are you done?" Issy asks.

He doesn't care. That face has already made up its mind. Bree shifts her stance. She reads it too. "But the thing is...I stopped. When I realized it was you, I was able to stop myself. The wolf pushed me hard to keep going, but I boxed it up and contained it. That's why I stopped, and I have you to thank for that. If you weren't there, I don't think—"

"Bree, I don't give a damn about your problems being a werewolf," Issy says. "As far as I'm concerned, I never want to see another werewolf for the rest of my life."

Why is he being so hostile to her? Didn't he hear what Bree said?

Tears squeeze out of Bree's eyes. I put my arm around her back. Her glassy eyes look into mine, and they make me melt all over the place. I hate seeing her cry.

"She said she was sorry," I say, with too much anger.

"Screw her and her apology. Take the cookies, too, because I'm not touching them."

"Don't talk to her like that."

Bree touches my chest. "Aiden, please." She moves over to the plate of cookies and picks them back up. She makes her way to the open door and hesitates there. "I'm still sorry for everything." Bree lingers for a moment, then walks into the hallway.

I can't believe Issy did that. How sincere can a person get? Bree's obviously sorry, and the least Issy could do is acknowledge that. But no, he'd rather make her feel like crap.

I stop Bree near the elevators.

She wipes tears off her cheeks. "It's all right. He hates me, and I can't blame him."

"He'll come around. Just give him some time."

"I tried to kill him. He's not going to just come around." Bree bites her lip. "This isn't going to work, is it?"

"What are you talking about?"

"Thinking I can be a human like everyone else. I'm fooling myself."

An elevator chimes as its doors open. I step in with Bree. She pushes the hold button. "You should stay with your friend."

"But you're the one crying," I say, trying for a light joke.

"Go be with your friend. He needs you."

The doors try to close, but Bree hits the hold button again. But I don't want to leave.

"Aiden, go be with your friend."

I take the plate of cookies. "If Issy doesn't want them, I'll eat them."

Bree nods, but doesn't smile. I step off the elevator. Bree releases the hold button. The doors close, shutting me off completely from her.

CHAPTER THIRTY-SIX

AIDEN

Something doesn't feel right, and it bugs me. I need to go to school today. I need to talk to Bree. Yesterday I called her phone a few times, and she didn't answer. I sent a few texts with no replies.
    This morning I call Bree, and she answers. I offer to pick her up and buy her breakfast for once, like a man who wants to take care of his woman. I should have done this a long time ago. But since I have Issy's car now, I can make good on all those free rides Bree gave me.
    I also want to tell her that I love her. That I believe in her. That I know she's trying hard to be human, and if there's anything I can do to support her, I'll do it. I want her to know that I don't blame her for what happened to Issy. She only did it because she wanted to protect me from Dad. Her motives were good. It was only the way she responded that went a little too violent.
    Bree says she wants to drive herself to school. Alone.
    That's not the answer I want.
    I park the Jetta in the student parking lot and wait for Bree's car. But Pamela's Honda parks next to me instead.
    She slides out of her coupe. "I swung by the hospital to see Issy, and he told me Bree came to see him. She has got a lot of nerve."
    "She came to apologize because she feels awful about

what happened," I say.

"I still can't believe all this. A werewolf at our school. It's like some dumb horror-movie cliché." She leans her body against the Jetta.

"You can't tell anyone. You know that, right? If people knew about Bree, it would be dangerous for her."

"We *should* tell someone. Bree almost killed your best friend and your dad."

"Issy will be fine. Everyone will be fine. It will all go back to normal."

"Normal? I saw what she did to Kirk and those other boys. What if by accident some girl pisses Bree off? What if a teacher makes her mad? Don't you see? Everyone at school is in danger."

"I don't believe that. Bree would never—"

"Hurt your best friend?"

That shuts me up.

"We should tell the police."

"No, we can't do that. The police will tell the FBI, and the FBI probably has some super-secret-paranormal-werewolf division that hunts down people like Bree."

Pamela narrows her eyes. "Super-secret-paranormal-werewolf division?"

"I don't know what it's called, but the government probably has something like it."

"If they do, they have it because *werewolves are dangerous*."

"Swear to me that you will not tell anyone at school."

Pamela crosses her arms.

"Please? At least let me talk to Bree. Maybe she can convince you."

"Keep that girl away from both of us. If she doesn't stay away, I will tell the cops that she attacked him."

The familiar rumble of the Oldsmobile increases as it rolls into the parking lot.

Pamela tenses up and heads for the school building.

Bree observes her movement through the windshield before getting out of her car. "What did she want?"

"She was updating me about Issy's condition. He's doing better."

Bree hesitates, shifting her weight on one foot and then the other. Is she still upset? I try to hold her hand, but she brushes it away. She walks toward the school, and I follow. Bree lingers near the main doors as her hand rests on the door handle. Like she doesn't want to pull it open and walk inside. I pull the other door and hold it open for her. She steps through it.

Bree acts more cheerful at lunch. She suggests we go to the mall, and I offer to drive. I open the passenger door for Bree, and she hesitates again as her nostrils flare. She then realizes I'm watching and glues on a quick smile before climbing in.

Driving to the mall, Bree gets quiet again. That early cheerfulness disappears. Why is that?

Her nostrils flare again. That's it. We're riding in Issy's car. Damn, I didn't think about that. His strong scent must remind her of what she did. I lightly squeeze her leg to let Bree know I'm here if she wants to talk. Again, she flashes another quick smile that's only for my benefit.

Bree orders the lamb-stuffed gyro, the same thing she ordered the first time we went to lunch together. I decide to get the exact same order at the Tex-Mex place next door. Bree doesn't pick up on the irony. We eat and talk about random school stuff. All of it trivial and nothing I want to talk about. When I try to bring up the attack on Issy, Bree shifts to another subject.

In fifth hour, Mr. Strickland writes a new equation on the white board as we plunge into the exciting world of algebra. I can't concentrate. I have to know what Bree is thinking about. My fingers wander up her back, slip under her hair, and gently massage her neck. I've done this a few times in class. When Bree wears her long hair down, it conceals my hand. Bree purrs like a kitten when I knead those neck muscles. But this time she leans forward from my hand, takes out a fresh piece of paper, and writes. Bree normally doesn't bother taking notes in Algebra. She always waits for me to explain what Strickland is really talking about.

Bree finishes and hesitates again. What's with that hesitation stuff? If she needs to say something to me, why doesn't she...

Bree suddenly turns around, gives me a folded piece of paper, then turns back around.

I unfold it and read.

Dearest Aiden,

You mean the world to me. Without you, I don't think I would have survived at this school. You've shown me that humans could accept us. Even to the point of falling in love. And boy, have I fallen for you. I love your scent when it stays on my clothes. I love hearing your voice from a distance because it means I'll be close to you again. I love your gentle touch on my skin and when it strokes my fur as I howl through the forest. You love me the way I am, and because of this, I owe you the world. Which makes it so hard to write this. I've made up my mind. What happened Monday proves that I'm too dangerous to be around humans. I shouldn't be at this school. And I shouldn't be around you. Hurting you on accident would devastate me. So I asked my parents if we could move. They agreed. So I'll be leaving in a few days. I'm so very sorry, but I can't see you any more.

Please don't hate me.

Love always,
Bree

The classroom becomes black and white as all the color in the world bleeds out of it. The sentences sting. At first they contain phrases I've always wanted to hear, but then comes the sucker punches that knock my guts around, making them cry for mercy. But there is no mercy. No relief from the pain. Mr. Strickland draws shapes and numbers on the white board. Students listen or yawn. The clock counts down the minutes and seconds. The classroom lights give out their usual buzz. Everything seems normal, routine, like another day at school. But in this normal world, I'm trapped in a hole of crap and choking on it, sinking down more and more.

How could she do this to me?

A drop of water stains the paper. The tiny circle of wetness expands. Then I realize it's a tear, and it's coming from me. I wipe my eyes and hold on to the pain. I refuse to cry in class. I shouldn't even be crying over a girl like some wuss. But I want to. Bad.

No. Hold it in. It's like holding on to a hot bar of metal as it burns your hands. You want to scream. You want to yell. You want to cry and say how much it hurts, but I stuff those feelings in a place deep inside. The only thing I can't fix is the numbness I feel, like my nerve endings are shot and I can't feel any sensation.

Class ends.

Bree turns around. Her eyes weaken when they see my face. She knows what I'm feeling. The girl's lips tremble. "I'm sorry," she whispers, almost choking on her words. Bree then gathers her stuff and rushes out of the classroom.

CHAPTER THIRTY-SEVEN

AIDEN

Sixth hour is meaningless. School is meaningless. Life is meaningless. I go through the rest of the afternoon in a haze. Unable to see the world around me. Unable to care if I did. After the final bell, kids wash around me as I spy on Bree heading for her car. Some kids nod at me and say hi. My popularity at school is still intact. My run for student class president still a possibility.

And I don't give a damn.

Bree slows. She twists around and locks her eyes on me. I don't blink. I don't look away. I stare right through her, as if my eyes could hold her in place and prevent her from leaving. Maybe they could even coax her back and make her change her mind. But Bree rips away from my stare and sprints to her car in seconds. The engine revs, and she drives off. Leaving me.

"What did she do?" Pamela asks, her voice behind me. She must have been watching.

"Nothing," I lie.

"Did you break it off with her?"

I don't want to talk to Pamela now.

"Did she break it off?" she asks.

"Leave me alone." I head off to the student parking lot.

Pamela trails behind me. "It's for the best, Aiden."

I ignore her.

The house is quiet when I get home. Dad is at work. The red stain of Issy's blood won't come out of the carpet no matter how many times Dad tries to clean it. The stain reminds me of death. Pamela reminds me of death. The shotgun that hangs above the fireplace reminds me of death. The long, metal shotgun shells feel cold and smooth in my hand. I swore to myself that I would use the shotgun next time.

But that was before Bree saved me. Before her light shined in my life. A light that gave me hope and a reason to hold on tight to life. Now that rope I held on to has vaporized. Rope.

Now even thinking about Bree reminds me of death.

I drift off to my bedroom, lie on my bed, and think. I did this very same thing that night in August. That night I was in the forest with the yellow rope. That night I thought about Pamela, thinking about how I couldn't go on like this. Tonight the feeling's worse.

Before, I fell in love with the idea of Pamela. The idea that she projects to everyone at school. I didn't know the real Pamela when I told her my feelings that day.

But with Bree I fell in love with the girl I found hiding inside. The inside I had to dig out to find. It's a feeling that buried itself inside my chest, becoming a part of me that's hard to rip out. How can I forget her now? How can I pretend that the last seven wonderful months didn't happen? The warmth I felt in my gut every time I was near her. The warmth of her body against my body. Our long walks in the forest when we would talk about everything. I should have told her about Dad. If I had explained things to Bree, maybe she wouldn't have freaked out.

I lie in bed and stare at the ceiling for hours.

Thinking.

The sky chokes off the sun. The dying embers of light fade from the window. A blackness consumes the furniture in my room. A blackness I live in. I don't turn on a light. I don't change clothes. I don't even get under the covers. What's the

point? Who cares about sleep? Who cares what time it is? Who cares about tomorrow?
Meaningless.
Everything is meaningless now.

CHAPTER THIRTY-EIGHT

AIDEN

My last day of school. For some reason I want to get there on-time, so I'm speeding. I only have ten minutes until the first bell rings. I swing the Jetta into the school parking lot, snatch my backpack, and run through the maze of cars, across the bus drop-off lane, across the small plaza with the two flag poles, and right inside the doors. Kids flood the hallways. I join the rush hour and head towards first hour.

I pass by a girl showing off her cute legs. She's bent over the water fountain wearing a skirt and some frilly top. Doesn't that kinda look like...

Bree stands up in a blink of an eye. Her gaze on me just as fast.

My feet stop.

Bree stares.

Kids move around us, wondering why we're creating a bottleneck in the hallway.

Bree's eyes fall away from me. The girl quickly disappears into the stream of students heading down the opposite way.

She's gone.

Just like that.

The pain comes back. The one I can't rip out. Seeing her triggers it. My heart craves her like she's some drug that I can't get out of my system. But I don't want her out of my system. I want to be hooked on Bree forever.

Two minutes until the first bell. I find Bree's locker, take out a folded note from my backpack, and push it through the slit right above the number plate. It falls inside.

There. It's done.

Since Bree used a note to break up with me, I decided my final good bye should be done the same way.

She'll wait until after school before visiting her locker again. And when she does, Bree will see her name written on top of the note and smell my scent.

If she loves me, Bree will race to my house and stop me. She'll have to save me again like she did the first time.

And if Bree doesn't love me, she will let me die in peace. It's the same choice she made in the forest that night. Either I'll be saved or my fate will be sealed. A fate that says I was always meant to die.

CHAPTER THIRTY-NINE

BREE

The water tastes cold and refreshing as I lap it up from the fountain. I'm thirsty today, and I don't know why. All morning long I thought about Aiden and what I've done to him. That awful look he gave me when he read that note I gave him in Algebra. It destroyed me inside. Hurting someone you love crushes your spirit, and it hurts worse than silver. I didn't want to get up this morning. I wanted my family to leave town today and make the break quick and clean, because if I'm going to be depressed, I'd rather be miles away from anything that will remind me of Aiden.
 Is that? I catch his scent. Strong. Masculine. My body heats up again as it acts on old stimuli. I must be dreaming. I've been thinking about Aiden so much my brain is planting false sensations. But my eyes catch the real Aiden standing nearby, watching me.
 I shoot up like a scared fawn. His eyes give me a once-over from head-to-toe. Those eyes want to touch me again, and the wolf wants him to. She wants to bury caution in the nearest hole and risk the danger. Who cares if I hurt Aiden, he wants me and I want him. So what if the wolf hurts him? Aiden knows what I am. He knows the danger involved. He's brave. He'll risk dying if it means being with me forever. The wolf loves this idea. A human risking their own life to be with a werewolf. A real mate would do that. One worthy of a girl-

wolf's love and admiration.

But the human in me won't allow it. It's too selfish, putting someone I love in danger to satisfy my own wants. That's not real love. It's self-satisfaction on a dangerous scale. I know how delicate that balance between girl and wolf is, and because of that, I'm not playing chicken with Aiden's life. I love him too much to ever do that to him.

So I turn away from Aiden as he stares. I make my shoes move, forcing them to go against my heart. I move away from him while still trying to convince myself I'm doing the right thing. The longer I keep myself apart from him, the more Aiden will get over me.

But doing this for five more days will kill me.

Aiden eats alone at lunch. I stand far away, on the other side of the cafeteria, and lean against the wall, sucking on a plastic bottle of water because I have no appetite. Some guys say hi to me, and one even tries to hit on me. Most of them think I'm acting like a diva because I'm ignoring them. I play along. What's the point anyway? In a few days they'll forget all about me and concentrate on some other girl. Another girl who can enjoy her senior year. Hopefully that girl will make lots of friends and have a wonderful time. Maybe she'll find a boy and fall in love. Or focus on school and go to college and become the awesome woman she wants to be.

I wonder if I'll ever get a senior year somewhere else. I bet after the failure of this little "experiment" Dad and Mom will keep me away from human schools. I'll either get a GED or maybe get lucky and find another werewolf pack with kids my age. Still, human school isn't that bad.

Pamela Osterhaus slithers over to Aiden's table. She pours too much dressing on her salad as the girl makes herself right at home beside my boyfriend. I should say ex-boyfriend. Pamela talks, and Aiden listens. Her hand touches his knee. I don't believe her. The second Pamela finds out that I'm out of the picture, she's now Aiden's best friend. Which is convenient since her other boyfriend's in the hospital.

Her hand touches his arm. Look at her! I don't care what

that girl says, she still likes Aiden. Pamela angles her body towards him, her legs crossed, her foot twirling around in the air. She's having a great time with my boy...my ex-boy. Oh, I so want to...
Bree, stop it. This is good. Aiden needs someone to love when you're gone.
But her? Not her! Not the girl that broke his heart and then laughed at him. She totally doesn't deserve him.
I do.
Bree, it's over. Stop hurting yourself over this. Let him go.
A drop tickles my cheek as a tear slides down. I race through the cafeteria, not even hiding how fast I'm moving. I shoot out the doors and sprint to my car, unlock the door, and park myself in the back leather seat. I let the tears fall without hesitation and squeeze Rocky and Bullwinkle tight, like they're both safety cables keeping me from falling over the abyss. I cry for a while, trying to get it all out of my system before fifth hour. I'm so dreading fifth hour.

Mr. Strickland gives us a surprise quiz, and I'm so glad. This will keep my attention on the quiz and not on Aiden. The quiz itself is easy, and I surprise myself by how quickly I get it done. I turn it in and actually feel good about it. It's amazing how much Aiden has helped me in algebra. Math was so puzzling to me, and without him I would...why did I have to bring up Aiden again?

As if on cue, he glances up as I walk back to my seat. His eyes linger, and it kills me all over again. I sit down and hold my stomach and rest my head on the cold desk. I'm feeling sick to my stomach, a result of all this stressing out and the fact that I haven't eaten anything in, like, twelve hours. Aiden's scent floods my nose, making it difficult to shut him out. Five more days of this? I'll have to talk to Dad. There's no way.

The final bell rings, but I stay upstairs and spy through the big glass window at the end of one of the hallways. Kids emerge from the main doors below and head for the busses and parking lots. It seems to take him forever, but I finally see Aiden make his way outside. His head droops as all that confidence he showed around me is gone. The boy who felt like a mountain when the kids called him Bruce Wayne has now run off, and it's all my fault.

Aiden drives off in Issy's car, and I take a deep breath. I can go to my locker now.

I bounce down the stairs and swing around the corner into the hallway. The afternoon sun pokes through the glass on the outer doors and casts a shine on the floor. I squint a little. Werewolf eyes are super at night, but during the day I could use a good pair of shades. I spin my locker combination and open the metal door. Aiden's scent hits me in the face, and I freeze.

A folded note lies on top of my books. It has my name written in Aiden's handwriting.

My heart jumps. Why is he leaving me a note?

Before I can read it, a shadow blocks the sunlight and pulls my eyes to the outer doors. That shadow is a man who stands very still. He wears all-black, and I see something glistening on his belt.

A silver knife.

The man gives off no scent, which is totally weird. I should be smelling him. Why can't I...

My backpack drops to the floor. The wolf senses danger, and she backs me away from the doors. That's not a man. It's not even human. It's one of them. It has to be.

Its cold, black eyes lock on to my face. The target.

I have to run as fast as I can, or I will get—

The glass shatters as the Demon Skin flies through the door and into the school.

CHAPTER FORTY

BREE

The wolf takes control. I force myself not to shift because if I stop to do that, the Demon Skin will be on me in seconds, stabbing me with that long silver knife.

I fly down one hallway and then another. So fast my brain can barely tell me where I am. Alarms scream. A school lockdown announcement comes over the speakers.

I turn a corner, and a security guard aims his pistol.

I skid to a stop as he frantically waves his hand, wanting me out of his way. I race up some stairs, and his gun fires.

I peek down the stairway to see.

The Demon Skin stops at the base of the stairs, a bullet hole in its chest. That dead, patch-stitched face has zero reaction. Another shot plows into its shoulder.

Nothing. It's like the guard is shooting a stack of hay.

School security can't save me. No one can save me.

I leap from step-to-step and reach the second floor within seconds. The Demon Skin pursues just as fast. At least the creature's footsteps make noise. I run down another upstairs hallway, and a teacher motions me to come inside her classroom for safety, but I can't. The more I stay in school, the more I'm risking everyone's safety. I have to get out of the building.

The window.

I streak through the hallway, make a fast right, and head

down the next hallway, where I see the big window I used minutes ago to spy on Aiden. I run as fast as I can, close my eyes, and leap right through. The sound of breaking glass shatters my ears as my toes feel air beneath them.

The landing hurts. My legs are too strong to break bones, but my nerve endings aren't numb. The pain shoots up both my legs, and I yelp. But I shake it off and run across the outside plaza and past the waving flags.

A shadow flies across the pavement. The Demon Skin lands with a thud on the concrete.

Instead of chasing me, it swerves away and runs parallel to me. What's it doing?

I pull out my car keys and then realize I parked in the student overflow lot. That's why the Demon Skin swerved off. It's between me and my car that it must have found. I swing around and head towards the bus loading zone.

The Demon Skin increases its speed. It's super fast, and I can barely keep ahead of it. Something metal pings near my feet. I glance down and notice something spinning away. A silver throwing star. I look behind me. It throws another one that bites my shoulder.

The silver burns, and I hear myself scream. I try to pull the star out of my shoulder, but as soon as my fingers touch it, they burn too. Still, I manage to pull the star out, and it dings against the ground. My fingers swell up from the contact with the silver.

Only a few busses are left. Many have kids on board, so I can't take any of those. But there's an empty bus at the end. I race up the stairs and pant in front of the bus driver, who is reading something on his phone.

"We're broken down, honey. The replacement should be here any—"

"What's wrong with the bus?" I interrupt.

"The brakes don't work right."

That means it'll move.

"Sir, I'm so sorry." I toss the poor man off the bus, and he falls right on top of the Demon Skin as they both tumble to the ground.

I shut the door to the stairs and jump behind the wheel. I scan the controls. Parking brake. I pull that, and the air brakes release. I put the bus in drive and jab the pedal. The bus accelerates through the bus loading zone. I check the huge side-mirror. The Demon Skin runs after me.

I swerve on to the main road and pick up speed. I glance at the mirror again. There's no one back there.

Did I lose the thing?

A thump on the ceiling. That would be no. It's on the roof.

I turn the big wheel and try to weave the bus back and forth. The sound of metal sliding across the roof tells me the Demon Skin has trouble hanging on.

I push the bus as fast as I can towards an intersection and then make a hard right.

The tires lift off the pavement as the bus flirts with tipping over. The tires on the left side squeal against the weight of the bus.

I hold my breath.

The Demon Skin slides across the roof and flops over the left side of the bus, its legs pumping the air, but still the dumb thing holds on to the edge of the roof.

I finish the turn, and the vehicle bounces on all four wheels, causing the Demon Skin to slam against the bus. Its ugly body fills my side-mirror. If it's that close to the mirror —

A silver knife crashes through the window and slashes my arm. The silver burns my skin and eats muscle tissue. The pain is so sharp I drop my hand off the wheel. Wish I could lick the wound, but I would lose my tongue.

There are trees on the opposite side of the street. That will work. I aim the left side of the bus towards the trees, and they slam against the side. Their scaly bark rips across the Demon Skin as thick branches spear and poke at its body. A human can't take that kind of abuse.

But it can.

I run out of trees, but there is a building.

I flip the wheel and side-swipe the bricks hard. Bus windows shatter as metal scrapes against brick, creating this awful racket that makes my wolf ears almost bleed. Surely this will peel that creature off the bus if it doesn't crush it into small pieces first.

The building took out my side-mirror, so I have to look over my shoulder.

There's nothing clinging to the side. Thank the Goddess Luna. I can't believe I escaped from them. Again. This is insane.

An arm crashes through the windshield. Cold, hard silver cuts my chest, and a shock spreads across my body as the silver attacks it like cancer on steroids.

The Demon Skin crouches on the hood and shoves the knife deeper into my chest to make sure it does the job right.

I feel weak. My chest goes numb, the silver taking effect. Putting me to sleep. Forever.

I can barely move. I try to focus. My head is cloudy. That creature is on the hood. So...I need...to...get him...off.

I put all the energy I have into my foot and ram it against the brake pedal. The air brakes hiss, and the bus shudders.

The cold knife and the hand that holds it slide forward and tumble off the end of the hood.

The Demon Skin slides along the pavement, stops, and then stumbles back to its feet. I find the gas pedal and nail it to the floor. The bus accelerates and slams the creature down. Its bones crack as the bus rolls over it.

I speed up and check behind me. The creature is a little slow, but it rises from the pavement with two arms pointing in unnatural directions. Looks like it's trying to form the letter Z.

Of course I didn't kill it.

At the next intersection, I fling the bus into a left turn that plunges downhill and keep my foot down. I'm flying. I glance back again, and the Demon Skin halts on top of the hill I just came from. Bet crunching some of its bones caused it to have second thoughts about chasing me.

The bus sails downhill, and I start to feel better. Sure there's some silver in my blood that Dad will have to purge from my system, but at least that silver knife isn't still attached to my chest. I release all the tension in my body and try to relax. At the bottom of the hill there's another intersection. The light turns yellow so I push on the brakes. A buzzer sounds. The brake warning light shines.

Oh. So the brakes *are* bad. I pump the pedal, and there's no hiss of air. I must have used them up.

Jumping from a moving bus is not a problem. In fact, the wolf would love to try because it sounds fun and would be a huge adrenaline rush. But an out-of-control bus could cause a bad accident and hurt a lot of people. So I stay in the driver's seat and hope my wolf reflexes can handle what's about to happen.

I tune my ears to listen for cars approaching the intersection on either side. Left side sounds clear. Right side...

Car engine. Kids' voices. That's bad.

I'll have to time this perfectly.

I race into the intersection and spin the wheel hard to the right. I hear brakes squeal as a mom in a minivan desperately tries to avoid me.

The back of the bus swings away from the minivan, and the car clears us without a scratch.

But the bus goes into a skid and slides through the intersection sideways.

The wheels lift off the pavement again. And I feel the bus tilting so far over that...I grip the wheel as the side of the bus slams against the concrete. My head smacks against the metal frame of the window as I hear the high-pitched squeal of metal scraping the pavement. Bits of glass, metal, and gravel fly into my face, and I have to shut my eyes.

The bus slides forever.

Until it comes to a stop.

I open my eyes and find myself lying over a bed of glass, bent metal, and ripped seat cushions. Thanks to the impact, my head throbs, but I think I'll live.

For now.

CHAPTER FORTY-ONE

BREE

My parents freak when I call them. Dad leaves his financial services office immediately and picks me up on the way home. We rush into the house, where Mom has everything ready: food, cash, water, everything we need for a road trip. It's sad that my family has always been prepared for this. Dad grabs his things while I race upstairs to snatch some of my clothes. The pillow on my bed looks naked, and I realize Rocky and Bullwinkle are still in the back seat of my car at school. Piss on the sun. Wish I could go back and get them, but that's totally out of the question.

Aiden will take care of them if I ask him. I could also send him the keys to the Oldsmobile if he wants it. Maybe he could box Rocky and Bullwinkle and send them to wherever we end up.

No, I can't. What if that Demon Skin tracks down Aiden and tortures him for the new address? Who knows what those awful things will do to hunt us down? I'm not putting poor Aiden in danger. No, I'm better off not telling him where I am.

"Bree," Dad calls out, his alpha-male side coming out in full. The protector of the pack.

"Coming." I pick up the handle of my suitcase and my coat and do a final look around. I have nothing to hold on to. Nothing to remind me of the old pack. And if I leave this house, I'll leave behind my memories of Aiden too. I'm so sick of having nothing stable in my life.

"Bree?" Dad tries again, his voice frustrated.

I'm the last one out the front door as I throw my things into the back of Dad's Range Rover and hop in. Dad backs up and throws the car into drive. Soon we're cruising on the turnpike, heading west out of the city of Tulsa. Heading west towards an uncertain future I don't want to be any part of.

Dad stops at a service center on the turnpike to fill up. There's hardly any gas in the Rover since today's mass escape wasn't planned. Dad insists that Mom and I go inside the McDonald's and try to relax. I think it's more for me since I haven't stopped shaking since we left Tulsa.

My new phone rings, and I check the number. Aiden. I bet he heard about what happened. Should I answer it? The plan was to have a clean break, and I already told him goodbye. Demon Skins or not, I can't see him ever again.

The note inside my locker. Oh, piss on the sun. I never got a chance to read his note. Is that why he's calling me?

It rings again. What should I do?

I show Mom the number. "Should I answer?"

"He's probably worried about you," Mom says. "You should at least tell him you're okay."

She's right.

"Aiden?"

There's silence on the other end. Super weird.

"Don't worry. I'm all right," I say. "Everything's cool. We're leaving now so—"

"Bree?" Aiden's voice wavers. He sounds terrified. I sense it. Something's not right.

"Bree?" Aiden repeats.

"What's wrong?" I ask.

"It kidnapped me."

It? My heart freezes. The Demon Skin. Aiden doesn't even have to say anything else. I know. That thing must have tracked him down using that note in my locker. No one knows why, but the Demon Skins have a werewolf-like sense of smell.

"Are you hurt? Are you all right?" There's panic in my voice, and I can't hide it.

There's no answer.

"Aiden?"

A new voice takes over the phone. "If you care for this human boy, you will join us at the rose garden by the museum." Its voice is cold, unemotional, the words slow yet deliberate. It must be the Demon Skin. "You know the location. I picked up your scent there. Make your appearance at the rose garden, and I will let your human boy go. Unharmed."

That voice chills my ear.

"What do you want in exchange?" I ask, trying not to sound so intimidated, but I'm not too sure it's working.

"Only you. Ready for battle. The prizes for this encounter are simple. You win. You live. I win, and I have the privilege of adding another dead werewolf to my kills. The sun is falling now. When it disappears, I will kill your human boy. So you must not tarry or linger, little werewolf. Swiftness would be most prudent at this moment in time. I look forward to your attendance."

The line goes silent.

"What did he say?" Mom asks, reading my face.

I tell her. Mom closes her eyes and sighs.

"I have to go, Mom."

Her eyes snap open. "You will do no such thing. That's exactly what it wants you to do. It wants you to come so it can kill you."

"What else can I do? Maybe if the three of us fight it, we could kill it."

"Honey, we don't know if the one who attacked you was a scout or if it was working with a group of them. There could be a dozen of them waiting for us. Remember that it only took a dozen of them to wipe out the entire pack." Mom hesitates. "Besides, there's no way to kill those things."

"They have to have a weakness. Something we haven't

thought of."

"Your father has been following the on-line chatter from the other packs. No one has found a weakness. No one." Mom squeezes my hand. "All we can do is run and hope we can fight them on equal terms some day."

"Car is fueled up. Quarter Pounders smell good. Think I'll take a few for the road." Dad stops, his eyes finally noticing us. "Something else wrong?"

I tell Dad about Aiden, and he repeats what mom said. There's no way I can go back for him.

"These creatures only care about hunting down werewolves," Dad says. "That's the one fact about the Demon Skins we've discovered. Humans don't matter to them. So I find it highly unlikely that the creature holding Aiden will harm the boy if you don't show. It's a ploy to get you to come back."

"But how can we be so sure?" I ask.

Dad's massive form bends to one knee. His eyes soften as they look into mine. "I promise you that Aiden will not be harmed. If I thought he would be in any real danger, we would go back right now and get him. Trust me on that. But our enemy is ruthless and cunning; they will not hesitate to use our emotions against us. Don't fall for it."

Maybe Dad's right. Maybe Aiden is safe and that Demon Skin is only bluffing. That thought makes me relax as the scent of juicy burgers tickles my nose.

"How many Quarter Pounders do you want?" Dad asks, reading my hungry face.

I did use up a lot of energy this afternoon. "Two. No, better make it three."

Dad stands in line to order while Mom goes to the restroom. My thoughts drift toward Aiden again. I still hate the idea that he's so close to one of those awful things. But I trust Dad. If he thinks Aiden won't be harmed, I believe him.

My phone rings again. Aiden. My heart pumps faster as I take a moment to compose myself before answering.

The icy-cold voice returns to my ear. "It has occurred to me that you might require...incentive...to help your human boy. Therefore, I offer this..." A pause on the phone. My ears strain to hear the next sound.

Aiden screams.

I almost drop the phone.

Aiden screams again and again. Inside my head, I see his tortured face bending from the pain, and it kills me. What is it doing to him?

"Stop it," I yell into the phone.

Another pause.

"I have never flayed a human before. Their skin comes off...easily," the Demon Skin says, without passion or malice. Only stating things as facts. "Does that give you...incentive? I will continue this process unless you grace me with your presence, little werewolf."

It's a trap, and that's obvious, but how can I let that thing torture Aiden?

"No opinion on the matter?" it asks with a pause. "This human has another arm. The skin is soft and smooth. Pity to ruin it."

I imagine the blade resting against Aiden's skin. My friend terrified as his other arm hangs there limp, with the surface stripped of a layer of skin.

No!

"Stop it. Stop hurting him. I'll come, all right? I'll meet you there, but only if you stop hurting him."

"A wise decision. I will do as you ask. But the sun touches the horizon. Time is essential, and you are losing it."

The line goes dead.

I have to go. It's the only way to make sure Aiden is safe. Plus I'm the one who let him into my world. A world Aiden wasn't ready for. Now I've put him in danger once again.

I notice Mom's purse, and I dig through it to find her keys to the Range Rover. I press the key fob and jump behind the wheel. The SUV starts easily, and I quickly point it back towards Tulsa.

CHAPTER FORTY-TWO

AIDEN

A huge rose garden surrounds me on all sides with this sea of green and red. Walking paths criss-cross through the garden, chopping up the flowers into sections. Someone's effort at trying to tame and limit their spread, to present beauty in a controlled and accessible way. But those rose thorns remind me that embracing things that are beautiful comes with a price tag.

The sun hides behind clouds so it can't give me any warmth. My hands sink deep into the soft dirt, making my fingers cold. The ground is still cool from winter despite spring waking the roses and the trees from their deep sleep.

My kidnapper lingers around me. It's the weirdest thing I've ever looked at. Leathery pieces of skin laced together form its face. Silver chain-mail clings to its body along with a belt of silver knives and throwing stars. The handle of a silver pistol sticks out from a holster. It hides it all under this long, black coat that you would see on one of those old Western movies. Scars and bite wounds are carved into its face and hands. All of them deep.

But what's bizarre is its elbows.

For some reason, metal door hinges have been inserted over both elbows, each with six screws that dig into the skin. Almost like they were replacements for the joints that should be there.

The creature slipped inside my house without a sound. I heard no glass break. No door jimmied open. No door kicked in. The Demon Skin was as silent as a shadow passing over my wall as it entered my bedroom. I was lying on my bed, arguing with myself. Dad's loaded shotgun next to me with the fatal shot waiting in the chamber. I hesitated, wanting to give Bree more time. Wanting her to give me a reason not to do it. The pathetic me still unable to make a decision.

The creature grabbed me before I could even open my mouth, dragged me out of the house like a slab of petrified wood, and brought me here. I tried running away like Issy did against Bree's father, but the creature was too fast. It dragged me back here and sat me on the ground like a naughty child. It used a rope to tie my hands to an iron bench cemented into the ground. I feel the rope tight against my wrists, holding my arms behind my back.

I dared it to kill me. Begged it even. What do I have to live for? Nothing. But the damn thing refused. I hope Bree doesn't come. If she doesn't come, then this thing will have no choice but to follow up on its death threat. And then I'll finally be free.

The creature slides out a long, silver blade that scrapes against the scabbard. "Your companion has made her entrance."

Bree? Damn it. Why did she show up? I don't want her here. She's going to get killed.

A low growl echoes from one side of the bushes. I know that growl.

"I was convinced that you would not take up my invitation, little werewolf. Surely a she-wolf has no love for a human boy. They are such frail creatures compared to a powerful creature such as yourself. How can you love this... thing?"

No answer. But I know she's out there.

"Come, little werewolf, show yourself to your mate. Make his spirit fill with hope before I carve it out of him."

"Stay away, Bree. I don't want you to save me," I yell.

"This human lies. His feelings for you are intense. His

desire for your flesh is insatiable. He is even willing to sacrifice his life if he is not able to win your affections. I have read this in his note. The one he left for you to find, little werewolf. The note which led me to him." The creature orbits around me, its eyes hunting for Bree. "Is he not worth the trouble? Is this human not worth dying for? Time grows short, little werewolf." It lifts its blade to my neck. The sharpness presses a little into my skin. One flick will open me up like a broken piñata. "Perhaps I might change the rules to this encounter. Perhaps I might carve your mate up anyway. That impulse is becoming very appealing."

From a set of bushes, Bree the werewolf comes into view. Her fur bristles as she exposes her long fangs. Her amber eyes burn with hate while her muscles tense up like a spring ready to shoot her forward. She's poised for attack.

"Get out of here. I'm not worth it. You don't deserve dying for a wuss like me." My voice catches. Saying what I've been thinking for years hurts. It's hard to hear the words out in the open like this. But I have to say it. I have to save Bree from wasting her life on me. "If you love me, you will run and never come back."

The eyes of the werewolf soften. The girl who looks at me listens.

"It is too late to run. Your lover's fate will be decided by the end of my blade. My only question to you, little werewolf, is...which piece of your lover shall I carve off first?"

Bree launches herself at the creature's throat. Her teeth sink deep. They roll across the ground with her jaws locked on to him like a vise, but her wolf-voice whines in pain.

She releases it. The creature hops to its feet like it was only a nip from a kitten.

Bree hovers near the ground, shaking her head. The wolf's mouth hangs open as if she's eaten a mouthful of peppers that burn.

On the creature's neck are two large puncture wounds that mark the contact with Bree's fangs. Something oozes out of the wounds. The liquid isn't crimson like blood. It's shiny, almost...silver. They have silver running in their veins?

The creature orbits Bree, waiting for her to get up, savoring the battle as if it was bred to enjoy fighting.

Bree recovers. She flies at the thing in a quick, sweeping arc, grabbing her opponent and throwing him against a rock wall that collapses on impact, spilling rocks all over the grass.

The creature stands from the rubble with its one arm bent in a most unnatural angle at the collar-bone. With its good arm, it yanks the other one back into place with a crack. No pain registers on its face.

It throws itself at Bree, using the long knife.

Her paw rips the creature's arm away, but she yelps in pain as her claw tastes the silver chain-mail under its clothes.

The hesitation gives her opponent the edge. The creature drives the knife deep into Bree's furry stomach. Bree flinches from the pain, but tosses her attacker off, sending it tumbling along the ground.

Bree tries to stand on her hind-legs, but she's finding it difficult. She holds her stomach, which bleeds over her claws.

"Feel the silver, little werewolf? Feel the silver burning your hands and your mouth. Do you feel it consuming your stomach?"

Bree growls and jumps at her attacker.

The creature skillfully avoids her and rakes the knife across her back, making Bree yelp.

The pain enrages her. She snatches her opponent and thrashes it against the remains of the rock wall as if it was a fly-swatter.

One hit.

Two hits.

Three bone-crunching hits against the wall.

Bree stops. She looks tired. Her two paws shake like they're on fire. The soft pads under her claws blister and bleed.

The creature places its hands on either side of its head and snaps its neck forward again. Then it re-adjusts a bent leg.

Bree collapses to the ground, holding her stomach. The gray fur around it is stained red, and the skin blistered. The wounds on her back swell and blister too.

Her opponent hovers. "The burning is intense, is it not? The silver now invading your body, killing the tissues you need to survive. I will now show you mercy by ending your life. A life that is an abomination to the Creator."

I struggle with the rope binding my hands. I can't get out of the knots. I can't stand. I can't fight. This Demon Skin is about to kill Bree, and I can't do anything except watch.

Two angry howls pierce the darkening sky.

The creature stops and slowly turns. "My, my. What a day for surprises. Some friends of yours, little werewolf? Members of your pack, perhaps?"

Bree rips out a bone-chilling howl that everyone in the city must have heard.

The creature sniffs the air and reaches for the handle to its silver pistol.

Leaves and rose-bushes shake as something swims through them.

The silver pistol glistens out of its holster. The creature cocks back the chamber and raises it to fire.

Two werewolves race out of the bushes, both twice as large as Bree. One has white fur. The other black. It has to be Bree's mom and dad. They're here to rescue their daughter.

I only hope they're not too late.

CHAPTER FORTY-THREE

AIDEN

The creature fires off a few rounds, but the werewolves prove too quick. They attack it from opposite sides, taking the thing down to the ground. My heart soars. Surely two full-grown werewolves can kill it.

The black werewolf flings the pistol away from its owner. The gun bounces off some rocks from the broken wall. The fight between the three becomes a blur.

Hits and counter-hits.

Movements so fast I can't keep up with them. It's like a super-hero fight being fast-forwarded.

The creature gets behind the white werewolf and rips open the wolf's back with the knife, making it scream.

The black one tosses the attacker into the air. The creature lands on top of a bed of roses.

The white wolf falls to its knees as the black one comforts it, but the Demon Skin doesn't give them any time.

It jumps to its feet, launching throwing stars at them. So fast it's like bullets from an automatic rifle.

The black wolf shields the other wolf, taking hits from the silver stars that bite into its back. The black wolf grunts in pain, turns on the Demon Skin, and charges.

The long knife catches the wolf's mouth and splits its cheek open. The black wolf reacts to the pain, giving the creature another half-second to stab the wolf in the stomach.

The Demon Skin goes into a frenzy, stabbing and stabbing the wolf all over its underside. The swiftness and tenacity of the action leaves me stunned.

The black wolf collapses to the ground, the blows too much for the wolf to handle.

The Demon Skin leaps for the pistol and fires a few rounds into the white wolf, making it cry out. The black wolf cries with the white wolf, animal sympathizing with animal.

Somehow the black wolf gathers enough strength to charge again.

But the silver bullets get to him first, making the mighty black werewolf fall to the ground.

He doesn't get up again.

Oh my God.

Bree and her parents lay across the grass. The deadly silver inside them still on the attack, burning up their insides, slowly taking them out of this world forever.

The Demon Skin moves to the iron bench in no particular hurry. It unties the knots of rope and flings them away. "You can go, human. Your purpose is at an end."

At first I don't move. I was convinced this creature would kill me too, its taste for violence not satisfied by the elimination of three werewolves. But the Demon Skin ignores me and floats near his prey, watching them die.

I'm free to walk away. I'm free to go back to my room and stare at that shotgun again. I'm free to kill myself again.

That doesn't make any sense, does it?

So what the hell do you want, Aiden? Do you want to live? Or do you want to die?

Live.

With Bree.

Life would be priceless with her in it. Spending every minute of every day with this girl would be my heaven on earth. But my chance for that slips away. That hope rests inside her heart that I must keep beating.

Bree's eyes beg. They want me to help. They want me to fight.

But the coward shakes me hard...*Three werewolves*

attacked this thing. Werewolves! What are you going to do against it? You can't even beat up a couple of bullies let alone take on this soldier from hell. Guns don't even hurt this thing. Guns! Run away, Aiden. It gave you a choice to live, so run away!

But something different simmers under my skin. An anger. A fury at what this Demon Skin did to Bree and her family. This new sensation forces the coward aside and drives me towards the creature.

"I said you could depart, human."

I make a fist and pound the creature's face. It feels like punching cold mud. I attack with my left fist. Another right. Another left. I keep whaling on the Demon Skin, beating it like a sack of flour, anger fueling every strike. Fury powers my arms with more and more energy. I slam my fist into its mid-section and stomach. Over and over and over. I don't know if I'm hurting it, but damn, it sure feels good.

The creature tosses me to the cold ground. "Silly human, your crude display of violence is rather pointless. Move along. There is nothing more you can assist with here."

My knuckles hurt and bleed, but my pride stings even more because I'm so damn weak against this thing.

But I still can help Bree. I run over to her and bend down. Her weak eyes follow me as I stroke her fur. "What can I do? Is there anything that can reverse the effects of the silver?" I ask.

Bree wants to say something, but her wolf lips can only whimper.

I hear a cough from where the black wolf went down. But now a man lies there. Mr. Mayflower. He found enough strength to change back. His will is so damn strong. "Aiden!" he manages to say.

I run over to him.

Mr. Mayflower grabs my collar. "In our car...inside a tin can...there's a salve...it can dissolve the silver from our tissues." He sucks in some air, grimaces in pain. "Use it on my daughter. Save her."

I rise to my feet.

The creature grips my shoulder. Its hand feels cold. Its lifeless eyes take me in with no emotion. "Do not get involved. My master's war is with the wolves. Not with the humans. Nevertheless if you attempt to assist the wolves," I hear the click of a pistol hammer being cocked back, "then you are an ally to the abominations, and thus, I will be compelled to kill you."

I start walking.

Soon that walk breaks into a run as I hurry to the parking lot.

The Range Rover is easy to spot because the doors have been left wide open. Lucky for them the grounds surrounding the museum are in a nice neighborhood. I search through the glove box and the door bins. Nothing. I check under the seats. Nothing. I rip through all the baggage that's loaded in back. Sure enough, buried inside one suitcase full of mens' clothes I find one round tin can. It seems to be really old. Like from the 1950s or something.

I remove the top. There's this gummy substance inside. It has the touch and feel of petroleum jelly with a strange fruit-like smell. What is this stuff?

Whatever it is, I hope it will save Bree.

I screw the lid back on the can, shut the car doors, and run over to the path that will take me back to her.

My feet slow down as the coward takes back control. I lean against a nearby tree as my legs go soft like Jell-o. My stomach twists.

I don't want to go. I don't want to die now. The coward wants to run. The same coward who didn't want to die in the forest or use the shotgun in his room.

A real man is not afraid of death. He would risk his life to save Bree.

A real man wouldn't run away from his problems or try to escape from them.

A real man would confront them.

The sun drops below the horizon, inviting the darkness to creep in. I sprint to the Range Rover and search for some type of weapon, anything I could use against the Demon Skin.

I find a tire iron. Normally that would be a good choice, but that creature would laugh the moment I tried to use it on him. I could use the Range Rover itself, but I don't know where the keys are.

Do I attack the Demon Skin with a tire-iron and hope I somehow kill it?

That creature is too fast. I don't stand a chance.

I need something to distract it long enough for me to strike a lucky blow that will kill it. Somehow.

Think. What do I have around me? My belt. Can't choke it. I don't think the creature took in one breath of air that I remember. Let's see. The Range Rover has an engine. Tires. Well, I'm not strong enough to throw a tire at it. Bumpers. Gas tank.

Wait a sec. Gasoline?

What are those bottles called? Mr. Jenkins mentioned them in World War II history class. Damn it. The Finns used them against the Russian tanks.

A Molotov cocktail. Yes! A glass bottle full of fuel with a cloth stuffed inside with part of it hanging out as a wick. The Finns would light the wick and drop the bottle on the tanks. The glass bottle would crash, spilling fuel everywhere while the lighted wick ignited the gas vapors and fuel into a ball of fire.

What if I lit the Demon Skin on fire?

That's a much better idea than a tire iron. I better hurry.

I search for a glass bottle inside the Range Rover and find nothing. I look around the parking lot and have similar luck. I spot a trash can and dump out the contents. An empty wine bottle clangs against the concrete. Score. I'm lucky that someone took their girlfriend out for a picnic.

Now to siphon gas out of the car. I jog along the bushes and find a short garden hose attached to a faucet. I yank it off and put one end into the open fuel door. I saw this done in a movie once. I wrap my lips around the end of the hose and suck in air. I have to do it a couple time before—oh, crap.

I spit out gasoline and cough as the fumes go up my nose. My tongue burns. That's horrible tasting.

Gasoline spills from the hose, and I quickly guide the tube into the wine bottle. Clear and smelly gasoline splashes inside it. I fill up the bottle, take out the hose, and gas spills everywhere. I finally pull the other side of the hose out of the tank, making the flow of gas stop.

I need a wick to light the bottle with. I grab a shirt out of the Mayflowers' baggage and rip a large piece of cotton off. I stuff the material deep into the bottle with plenty of cotton hanging out. It's kinda crude but it might work. Now I need something to light it with. Do werewolves smoke?

Wait, didn't I see...I hop into the driver's seat and dig inside the door bin. I pull out two plastic tube-like containers. Some Spanish words and a logo are stamped on the side. I open the end of one and there's a cigar inside. Bree's dad must smoke. So if he has cigars...I take a more careful look around the front seats and find a lighter.

I put the round tin of salve in the front pocket of my pants. I place the tire-iron against my lower back and slip it under my belt in case I need another weapon.

With the Molotov cocktail in one hand and the lighter in the other, I head towards the path that will take me back to Bree.

CHAPTER FORTY-FOUR

AIDEN

My pace slows as I hear the low, agonizing whimpers of dying werewolves. I glance at the lighter and realize I can still smell the gas fumes. Wait a second. Can fumes ignite too? I thought I heard that somewhere. What if I light it and the bottle blows up in my hands? Imagine burning gasoline frying my skin like a crispy chicken nugget. Oh, that would suck. Getting shot doesn't seem so bad.

Why worry about that when Bree is dying?

Have to risk it.

I'll rush in there quick. Surprise it. That will be my only chance to nail it with the bottle. Otherwise, bang, bang, I'm dead.

Time to step off the cliff. I light the wick, and it glows a fiery orange.

Then I run and break out into the clearing. There's Bree, her father in human form, and the white wolf still on the ground. All dying. Where's the Demon Skin!?

Damn it.

"My warnings were clear."

The voice comes from behind me. It sensed me coming.

"Now you will share your lover's fate."

I cock my arm back and spin around, like I've done countless times in dodge ball.

The creature raises its arm with the silver pistol.

I hear myself yell as the wine bottle leaves my hand. The flaming wick lights up the face of my target, who hesitates at the fiery spectacle.

The bottle smashes against the creature's chest. A wall of flame roars to life as the rose garden shines in this brilliant orange. The Demon Skin becomes a walking bonfire, but it doesn't scream or yell.

It talks.

"Human fool. I do not feel pain. Your gesture is only a token one that will not prevent me from killing you." The creature of fire lunges for me.

And I run as fast as I've ever run in my life.

The path I choose leads me out of the rose garden and plunges downhill. It's dark, but I see perfectly thanks to the huge fireball that lights up the world. Running along the grass, my puny shadow looks like it's being chased by Hell itself.

The acid in my muscles begs my legs to stop, but I grit my teeth and force them to keep going. The path I follow curves uphill at a steep angle as it leads to the small forest that surrounds the museum grounds. I do my best to reach the top as fast as I can.

My legs are killing me. My lungs scream for air. I'm forced to stop at the top of the small hill. I look down.

The flaming creature slows as it struggles going up the hill.

But the Demon Skin stops and raises its arm. Its hand grips the silver pistol. The muzzle points to my face.

I'm going to die. There's no way I can dodge a bullet.

I brace for it.

The gun doesn't fire. The Demon Skin pulls back its arm to examine why. I look closer. The silver in the gun melts to the creature's hand. No wait, the creature's whole arm melts. Seriously, it's dripping off like candle wax. Wait a second. The Demon Skin has silver all over it, right? And silver melts at high temperatures, right? And all that dead skin must be feeding the flames, making the fire so hot it can melt the silver in its blood. The creature's muscles, tendons...they all must have silver inside them.

I free the tire iron from my belt. Time to go on the attack.

Moving downhill, I gather speed and race towards the ball of fire. The Demon Skin raises the melting arm to fend me off. I take a swing and knock that arm right off its body. Amazing! The creature stumbles back, and tries to use the other arm, but it falls right off its melting body.

The Demon Skin crumples to the ground as its legs melt away.

I feel the intense heat of the mini inferno. I back away as the flames rise higher and higher. The creature's human form changes into a mass of goo as the silver and dead skin liquefy. The sight is so weird I can't take my eyes off it.

Bree!

I rush back to the rose garden. Bree's wolf eyes are closed, her furry body still. Am I too late? I open up the round tin can, scoop a generous helping of the salve, and rub the substance over her wounded stomach. Her eyes flutter open. She's alive!

"Bree, stay with me. Fight. Please fight it." I touch her back and spread the substance over her wounds there. I use the salve on every cut I can find and see relief in her eyes. I caress the fur on top of her head. I hear a faint whimper from her mouth. I whisper in her ear, "Don't you dare leave me. I need you. I need you to stay in my life because you are the only girl in the world I love. The only girl in the world I understand. And the only girl in the world I can never replace." I lightly kiss her fur.

A new spark dances in her eyes. One that wants to live.

I rub my hand down her side and notice Bree's stomach wounds are healing rapidly, as if the salve not only dissolves the silver but also reverses the effects.

Bree moans when I stroke her body.

"Aiden! Stop fondling my daughter, and bring me that salve."

The gruff voice of Mr. Mayflower pulls me over to him.

"Put that salve on my shoulder wound," he commands. "No hope for my arm. Have to chop it off to keep the silver from spreading." The skin on his affected arm looks like petrified wood.

I apply more of the substance to his shoulder, and soon Mr. Mayflower can move it around. He scoops out a glop of salve. "Go to my wife, and tend to her wounds."

I rush over to the white wolf and slather what remains of the salve on top of all her wounds.

Sirens wail in the distance.

"Someone must have seen the fire," I say.

"Best fire I've seen all year." Mr. Mayflower smiles. "We'll have to get out of here." The huge naked man grimaces as he rises to his feet. "Piss on the sun, that hurts."

"Can you walk?" I ask.

He nods. "I'll carry my wife. You carry Bree."

I bend down and lightly place Bree's head against my chest as I lift her up into my arms. Damn, she's heavy, but I'll manage. Her eyes blink at me while a wet tongue licks my cheek. I catch myself laughing. This only encourages Bree to keep licking every part of my face.

We put Bree and her mom in back of the Range Rover. Mr. Mayflower shows me where the keys are and then slumps across the back seat. I drive the Rover out of the parking lot just as the first fire truck rolls in and passes by us.

CHAPTER FORTY-FIVE

AIDEN

Something wet touches my cheek. I open my eyes. Bree floats inches away from my cheek with a big smile. "Hi."

"Hey." I sit up and shake my groggy head. My back aches as I re-adjust myself on the uncomfortable wooden chair I slept in last night. Bree's bedroom window lets in the morning sun that lights up her purple cotton robe with polka-dots all over it. "How long have you been up?" I ask.

"An hour or so," she says.

"How are you feeling?"

"Awesome squared. That salve works miracles."

"Where did that stuff come from? It looked old."

Bree flops on her bed. "The healing salve is an ancient recipe. One the Elders created centuries ago. It's made from some extremely-rare elements and a tiny bit of witchcraft. Dad was lucky enough to find some friends on-line who could send him a can."

"Good thing he did."

"I know, right?"

"Aiden? Are you hungry?" Mrs. Mayflower calls out through the closed door. My voice is loud enough for all the wolf ears in the house.

"You should go eat something. I have to change anyway," Bree says.

I slip downstairs to the kitchen, where Mrs. Mayflower

bakes biscuits. Whoa. Biscuits? She's fully dressed and doesn't look injured at all. Almost like last night didn't happen.

"Mr. Mayflower went to the store and bought some human food. We have eggs, cheese, bread...oh, and I'm baking some biscuits out of a can, but I don't know how those will turn out because I've never baked anything before." Mrs. Mayflower moves over to a new toaster in a box. "And my husband bought this, too, so if you want any toast, let me know and I'll break it out."

They bought a toaster for me? Why?

Mr. Mayflower's giant hand slaps me on the shoulder blade, and it hurts like hell. "Sleep well?"

I nod and then notice he's missing his arm.

Mr. Mayflower follows my gaze. "Yeah, had to cut that off, but I should grow another arm in a few weeks."

"Are you serious?"

"Yup. Lucky it wasn't my head." Mr. Mayflower grins and motions toward the living room. A man wearing a crumpled suit and glasses stands up from his chair. Who's this guy?

"Aiden, this is Robert Doubleday from the FBI. Mutual friend, you might say. He flew in early this morning to fix some things for us."

The FBI? That's bad, isn't it?

Agent Doubleday looks me over. "Is this the kid?"

"That's right," Mr. Mayflower says. "Burned that thing up like a candle."

"Can he be trusted?"

"Completely."

The agent shakes his head. "Why the hell didn't we think of burning them?"

"Because we think with our fangs and not our heads. Still...not every werewolf carries a flame-thrower in the trunk."

"We might have to start." Agent Doubleday checks his phone. "I have to go meet with the police chief to start building this story up. I'll send your daughter and the boy here statements that they'll need to memorize word-for-word."

"They'll know it by heart," Mr. Mayflower says.

The agent walks towards the front entryway, but pauses. "Are you sure that you want to stay here? Scuttlebutt says there's a few Siberian packs that haven't been attacked...yet."

"Freeze my furry ass in Russia? Don't think so." Mr. Mayflower glances at his wife. "Think we're through running."

She smiles and nods.

"I'll build a pack right here in the middle of the city if I have to. Invite every displaced wolf to join us."

"Hell of a risk," Agent Doubleday says. "All that will do is put you farther up the target list. If you're not already."

"Know how to kill them now. We can fight back."

"Look, Mr. Mayflower, I don't mind helping a brother out smoothing things over with the humans, but if you want me to risk exposing my pack to carry out a war against the Skins. I'm not doing that."

"Didn't ask you to. Just saying that we *are* fighting back. Joining is optional."

Agent Doubleday nods. "I'll go clean up your mess now. Stay strong, brother."

"And you too, brother." Mr. Mayflower shakes his hand and the man leaves.

"Is he...? I mean, he's really from the FBI?" I ask.

Mr. Mayflower drapes his massive arm around me. "Pretend you never saw him. Now, let's you and me talk in the living room while you eat breakfast."

Mrs. Mayflower places a dish of heavily fried eggs, dark brown biscuits, burned toast, and a well-cooked piece of steak on the coffee table in front of me. I thank her and start on the steak.

Mr. Mayflower strokes his beard as he eyes me across the table of food. "I'm not a wolf who uses a lot of big, fancy words. Like to talk straight and to the point. Wanted to say thank you. Thank you for saving my family last night."

Bree comes in and leans on her mom.

MY GIRLFRIEND BITES

"Both these ladies are worth their weight in jewels to me." Mr. Mayflower's voice cracks a little. He realizes and clears his throat. "Only want to say that...what you did was brave. Something I would swear I would never see in my lifetime. A human saving the life of one werewolf is extraordinary. Saving three...I don't think my fellow wolves would believe me if I told them. Agent Doubleday is still a little suspicious."

Mr. Mayflower rests his hand on my knee. "Son, as far as this family is concerned...you are a member of our pack. And I promise we will be here for you, anytime you need us."

His words strike at something deep inside. Here's this man, who's not even my father, treating me like his real son. Not someone who takes care of him when he's drunk. Not someone who becomes a big punching bag at the end of a rotten day. But someone who's happy that Aiden Jay exists in this world.

"Thanks, Mr. Mayflower. I appreciate that."

The man checks with Mom and Bree, and they nod.

"Aiden...Bree told me about your situation at home."

I can feel myself withdraw. Just the mention of "home" puts me on the defensive.

"My good conscience can't let you go back into that situation. Which leaves me two options. Either call the police and have your father arrested, or you could stay here and live with us."

That's amazing.

I glance at him, then at Bree and her mom, who both smile.

"Go ahead. Eat breakfast. Don't have to give us an answer right this second. Think about it." Mr. Mayflower stands. His wife wraps her arm around his waist as they walk into the kitchen. Bree plops herself on the couch. She nibbles on a piece of my burnt biscuit and spits it out.

I laugh.

She laughs.

And it's like we're friends again. Just being ourselves with no one hiding behind lies or secrets.

Bree steals a piece of my steak and eats it. She shows me

that devious smile of hers. And it's the most beautiful thing ever.

Mrs. Mayflower drops us off so we can pick up Bree's car that's still parked in the overflow lot. Wiley Post High School looks like an abandoned building this morning. The main parking lot only has a handful of cars in it. Weird. It's, like, Friday morning, and there should be a ton of kids here. But the broken upstairs window and the big wooden board that replaces it shows the main reason. The morning news said school was canceled today as a precaution, giving everyone an awesome three-day weekend while school officials and the police get a handle on what actually happened yesterday. No one was hurt. Only some property damage. They probably will never figure out who the madman was that came into the school. But they'll probably question Bree about why this guy was chasing her. And why she had to "borrow" and crash a school bus.

Bree might get a longer suspension than I did.

But the Mayflowers aren't too worried about it. Agent Doubleday created a great story for the chief of police, involving the FBI witness protection program...a Russian mafia hit man bent on kidnapping a precious daughter for leverage against the father...and the National Security importance of keeping all the details on a "need to know" basis so the FBI can conduct its own investigation headed up by Agent Doubleday himself. Guess it's good to know werewolves in high places.

My girlfriend unlocks the car as I study the wooden board upstairs.

"Do you think they'll come back?"

Bree opens her door, and hesitates as her face darkens. "They will, but I hope we can figure out who's creating the Demon Skins so we can put an end to all this."

"I was scared last night. Really damn scared," I blurt out. The words come out easier around Bree. Like I can tell her anything without having to censor myself.

"Me too." Her eyes find mine. "I've never faced death before. Lying there on the ground last night, I could *feel* death coming for me. Creeping towards me like this black mist that I couldn't escape from. I always thought werewolves were invincible. That there was nothing in this world that could kill us. But if those Demon Skins and their creators win, I don't know if I'll even live to be twenty-one."

* * *

"Want me to go in with you?" Mr. Mayflower switches off the engine to the Range Rover parked in my driveway.

"Nah, it's okay, sir." I pop open the door and step out.

"My ears will be open. If he even raises his voice, I'll be coming in there."

I walk up the driveway, get out my house keys, and twist them in the lock. The deadbolt clicks away as I push the door open.

Dad isn't in the living room. I check his bedroom. No sign of him. Maybe he's out doing some Saturday morning errands, acting like a normal adult for once.

I head into my room, and take my backpack and a weekend suitcase I once used about ten years ago. The year Mom bought it for me. I stuff some T-shirts, jeans, and other essential clothes into it. I have some room in my backpack for small things, mostly keepsake stuff. I unplug the GameMaster, stuff a couple controllers into my backpack along with some game discs, and then tuck the GameMaster console under my arm. I'll have to come back another time for my computer.

I move across the living room. The patio glass door slides open, revealing Dad. He notices my baggage, and his face goes into confusion mode. I'm not looking forward to this.

Dad shuts the patio door and locks it. "Drinking some coffee outside. The weather's nice." He scans the suitcase and backpack again. "Where you going?"

I glue my eyes on the 737 aircraft painting. "Dad...um..."

The words fail to come out. Either I'm too scared to say them or I'm too afraid of what he might do.

"Running away from home." Dad grins, thinking that was funny or too wild to believe.

After this week nothing is too wild to believe.

"Yeah. I mean, kind of. I'm going over to Bree's house."

"Don't think her parents will love the idea of you playing sleepover with their daughter."

"It's not like that. The Mayflowers offered to take me in for a while."

"Without asking me? That's arrogant of them, ain't it?"

I hesitate. "They know, Dad."

That's all I can get out. The closest I've ever come to bringing up the subject in front of Dad.

"They know what? What do they know?" Dad asks with this hint of suspicion.

"You *know* what." I fire back. A sudden anger builds up in me. I don't know where it's been hiding. "You pretend like it doesn't happen, but it does. All it takes is one drink and you forget everything. But I do remember. I always remember *everything*."

Dad steadies himself on the back of the sofa. "You shouldn't have told them. That's none of their business."

"I can't hide it anymore. I can't...protect you anymore."

He doesn't say anything.

"And I shouldn't protect you. But I always got scared. I would ask myself, '*What will I do if my dad gets tossed in jail? Where will I go? A foster home? Or be homeless on the street—?*' And a real stupid part of me hoped you would just stop drinking." I check Dad's face. "But that's not ever going to happen, is it?"

Dad stands very still. Quiet. His face is tired and old.

"So that's why I'm leaving." I wheel the suitcase around and head for the front door.

Dad clears his throat. "I talked to someone from Alcoholics Anonymous yesterday. I'm going to a meeting tomorrow."

"It's too late for that."

"Now wait a minute. I...I would like you to come with me."

"Don't you understand? I can't stay here anymore."

His eyes widen, not in anger, but more in surprise. Dad hesitates. "You're right. The drinking has gotten out of hand." He takes a moment to rub his face. "I was so out of it that one day. I didn't even remember letting your friend inside and leaving the door wide-open. And that dog came in through that open door, and I was suddenly inside this nightmare, and I couldn't do anything but watch it happen." He glances at me. "I know you think I'm crazy for saying this, but I do believe that animal was a sign to change my ways. It shook me. Shook me to the core. Shook me so much I was forced to look at myself. And right now, I'm not liking the person staring back at me."

"Okay...so let me get this right," I say. "The moment you realized things were out of control, the moment you realized that you needed help was *not* the moment when you were beating the crap out of me?"

Dad freezes. His eyes scrape the floor.

He has no answer for that.

"Fuck you." I slam the front door shut.

* * *

Today Issy gets released from the hospital. And like a good wingman, I promised to pick him up. Bree insists on driving, saying it's the least she can do for him. Her guilt about what she did still bothers her. I think she wants Issy to forgive her, and Issy eventually will. I mean, how can you stay mad at Bree? She's awesome.

We take the elevator up to Issy's room. He's all packed and ready, but loses his smile the moment he sees Bree.

I try to ignore it and pick up his backpack. "This all your stuff?"

"Yes, and I have to be in this dumb wheelchair when you take me down because they have this dumb—"

"Hospital rule. Yeah, they made me do the same thing

when I was here." Suddenly I feel weird talking about it. They both know, but still, it's weird to just...say it like that.

"I'll wheel you out. Bree? Why don't you carry his stuff."

She brightens and takes the backpack from me as I roll Issy out of the room and down the hospital wing. Bree taps the button that calls an elevator. I push Issy inside. The doors close. The digital readout counts down from the ninth floor.

Bree flashes a big, friendly smile at Issy. "Did my dad take care of everything? With the hospital?"

Issy sticks his gaze on the featureless wall of the elevator. "Yes. My dad was a little confused, but he didn't argue when they told him he didn't owe anything."

"Awesome." Bree touches his arm, but Issy moves it off the armrest. This makes her frown and withdraw her hand.

The doors open, and I wheel Issy into the familiar first-floor lobby with all the buffaloes, Indian art, and other Oklahoma stuff clinging to the walls.

"I'll get the car," Bree says. The morning sun brings out her amber eyes and her long, dark hair. She almost skips as she exits through the glass doors, her pink cotton skirt bouncing on every step.

"We're riding in her car?" Issy asks, his voice tight. "Thought you were going to borrow your dad's truck?"

"Well, Bree wanted to help."

"I should have let my parents pick me up like they wanted."

"Dude, are you still pissed at Bree? You know she still feels awful about what happened. And she promises it will never ever happen again, and you should believe her. I thought you were cool with everything."

"You want me to trust Bree because she apologized? Feel grateful that her family picked up all my medical bills?" Issy climbs out of the chair. "Wake up. That girl is dangerous, and it's only a matter of time before she loses control and does something else she's 'sorry for.'"

Bree can adjust. She's learned so much being around humans already. She needs me to guide her, that's all. I can help her cope and not resort to violence. I know I can change her.

"You underestimate Bree."

"And you trust her too much," Issy says.

The familiar hum of the Oldsmobile reaches the hospital lobby. The large black car stops in the loading zone as Bree waits for us to come through the automatic doors.

"I won't go inside that car with her." Issy sits down and wheels himself away from the doors.

"Are you serious?"

He folds his arms and doesn't look at me. I've never seen Issy act like this. So serious. So rigid. It pisses me off. Why can't my wingman trust me on this? I know Bree much better than he does. Why does he have to act like such a dick head?

Whatever.

I leave his sour ass at the hospital.

CHAPTER FORTY-SIX

AIDEN

A robin sings, perched on some random tree in this random forest that has no name. I only know it as the forest I tried to kill myself in with a yellow rope and a broken heart. Fingers of sunlight pour through the green leaves. Velvet-soft grass brushes between my toes as I walk barefoot. A second pair of feet keep pace with mine as I hold Bree's hand. Today is an anniversary of sorts. A remembrance of the past and a celebration of the future. Our future.

I lay the picnic basket next to the rotted tree trunk I wobbled on top of during the worst night of my life. I can still feel that rope clinging to my neck, ready to bite the moment I jumped off.

Today, I didn't bring any rope.

Bree snaps a white table-cloth that we picked up at the dollar store. She drapes it across the trunk, covering the decay underneath. I grab two plates and put them on top of the trunk. It's a tight fit, but it'll work for our little celebration. We sit on the grass, taking out two bowls of salad we made up before coming out here. I squeeze a packet of blue cheese dressing all over mine. Bree's salad is filled with fresh spinach...on top of a pile of ham and bacon bits. After our salads, I bring out the box of chicken tenders we bought through the drive-thru at Ragin' Cajun. I've turned Bree into a fan of chicken, believe it or not. She can eat the

tenders if she smothers them in sweet barbecue sauce.
It's a start.

"You know something? I don't think I've ever thanked you...for that night." I gesture to the branch that held the yellow rope.

Bree licks barbecue sauce from her lips, thinks about it, and brightens. "I should thank you. You're the dude who saved my whole family. Me and you are even." She tosses a small piece of chicken that bounces off my nose.

I flick a crouton at her. Bree catches it in mid-air. Gotta love those animal reflexes. Her eyes narrow. The wolf comes out to play. She tosses it at me, and it bounces off my forehead.

"Ouch." I joke.

"Like that hurt."

"Don't make me chase you through these woods."

She stretches her legs. "Like you could catch me."

"I bet I could."

Her eyebrows perk up as a devious smile curls up her lips. "Try it."

She's messing with me. The second I move, Bree will be halfway to the car. Still, it'll be fun to keep Bree honest.

I jump to my feet, hop over the stump, and fall on top of Bree.

What? She didn't even move!

I pin her down to the ground. Her amber eyes watch me with this fire inside them.

"Did I seriously surprise you?" I ask.

"Not at all. But you were assuming I didn't want to be caught." Bree relaxes as I keep her down.

Suddenly those wolf eyes give me flashbacks from that night in her bedroom when she wouldn't let me get up. I release her arms and roll over on my back, feeling the cool grass under my T-shirt. Bree snuggles against me. Her nails skate aimlessly across my chest. Her touch is the most soothing thing in the world.

And we lay there for a while.

Listening to the grass and the trees sway with the wind.

The sweet smell of spring fills the air as the warm sun coats our clothes and skin.
And I want it to last forever.
I want *us* to last forever.

THANK YOU FOR READING

Dear Awesome Reader,

I hope you enjoyed *My Girlfriend Bites*. To be honest, I never thought I would ever write a paranormal romance. First off, I'm a guy. Second, vampires don't interest me and I think my favorite witch was Samantha on that 1960s TV show *Bewitched*. But I do like werewolves, like in the 1980s movie, *An American Werewolf in London*.

So why did I write this book? One word. ***Twilight***. I read the first two books and didn't like Bella Swan's character. I felt she was too passive and let Edward control her to the point where she couldn't do anything without him. It bothered me enough to start writing this book, asking such questions as: *What if the girl was strong and the boy was weak? How could she help him and how could he help her?* Soon the story of this novel took shape and I had to write it.

Reviews are so important to authors! If you have time, I would love a review of this book on the website of your bookseller of choice. Love it or hate it. Doesn't matter.

What did you think about the novel? I'd love to hear from you! Write me at **doug@dougsolter.com** or visit **www.dougsolter.com** for more options to stay connected.

Thank you again for reading *My Girlfriend Bites*!

All the best,

Doug Solter

ACKNOWLEDGMENTS

This book was a struggle to complete with numerous drafts at different times and in-between different projects. I almost deleted the novel a few times out of frustration because I didn't know how to fix the middle which was not working at the time. But Aiden and Bree stuck with me and refused to die. Big thanks to my friend Joe Kinkade, for convincing me not to delete the manuscript.

Jules Howe, LM Preston, Laura Benedict, and Kate Tilton, for being excellent beta readers. They were my story editors and made great suggestions on improving the book. Thank you.

Travis Pennington, for doing another fantastic job designing and doing the layout for the book cover and jacket.

Kate Tilton, again for all her support and marketing advice. Kate rocks to the second power.

Editor Pauline Nolet, for doing a great final proofread of the manuscript. Highly recommended.

Max Adams, for her continued support and for making me a better writer.

And for their support...Nancy Bilyeau. Pamela DuMond. Sonia Gensler. Karen Larsen. Christie LeBlanc. C.K. Kelly Martin. Anna Myers. Helen Newton. Cheryl Rainford. Courtney Summers. Amy Tipton. Angela Townsend. The Oklahoma chapter of SCBWI. All my friends from the Academy of Film Writing. All my friends and family. And anyone else I might have forgotten.

And another big thanks to my dad, Don Solter, for putting up with all my writing shenanigans.

ABOUT THE AUTHOR

Doug Solter has worked behind the scenes in local television for over twenty-five years. He has directed rap music videos and short films. Doug respects cats, loves the mountains, and one time walked the streets of Barcelona with a smile. Doug lives in Pennsylvania and is a member of the Society of Children's Book Writers and Illustrators.

Subscribe to Doug's email list...

www.dougsolter.com/subscribe

Connect with Doug through his website...

www.dougsolter.com

ALSO BY DOUG SOLTER

Keep reading for a sample from the first chapter!

MY GIRLFRIEND BITES AGAIN

SAMPLE

AIDEN

I brace for the most insane thing that I've ever attempted... entering Skull Mountain castle with only my gold sword, an annoying forest elf named Mutt who is about as useful as a surf board in a blizzard, and my trusted dragon Periwinkle. Having a dragon as an ally is great in a fight. Trouble is, Periwinkle was tricked into drinking a warlock's magic potion which chilled his gut furnace. So he can't even belch up smoke let alone a cloud of fire that could lay waste to Azeus and his evil army of zombie lizards.

Normally I would wait for the spell to dissipate, but Azeus is about to march his army out of Skull Mountain castle and down into Sweet Valley to slaughter the peasants who paid me in gold (six harvests worth) to defend them from the evil warlord. I can't let these peasants down.

But first I need a snack.

I pause the game and the heroic music stops, allowing silence to settle inside the large and open living room-kitchen combo. I stretch on the leather couch and eye some peanut butter cookies waiting for my mouth on the counter near the oven. I'm the only one in the house who eats them.

I find a clean glass in the dishwasher and open the large fridge. There's a pool of blood on the bottom shelf, thanks to all the raw meat inside. I wish the Mayflower's would clean that up. I know it doesn't bother them but...at least Mrs. Mayflower puts an open box of baking soda inside to help with the smell.

I take out the half gallon of milk and pour a cold glass. Since I don't want to die of cross-contamination, I wash my hands before taking my two cookies and milk into the living room. I devour cookie number one and wash it down with milk. I'm so glad God invented peanut butter. Let's just say I'm a big fan.

I grip the GameMaster controller and start the game from my save point. My loyal companions and I begin our march inside Skull Mountain castle to attack Azeus. The minute we get inside, Periwinkle burps and fire shoot out his nose.

Amazing! If the magic potion is wearing off, maybe I have a chance in this fight if Periwinkle recovers.

Azeus unleashes his zombie lizards and I'm hacking away at them like a madman as I hear the backyard door open behind me. But I'm too focused on the fight to pay attention.

A werewolf with gray fur pads into the living room. Its large sharp teeth drip with saliva as its dark red eyes stare.

"Hey," I say to the werewolf. My thumbs quickly hit buttons to set up a combo attack on one zombie lizard. Boom. That lizard didn't know what hit him.

The werewolf glances at the screen, then hops on the couch. The wolf flops down and snuggles its head under my arms and on to my lap. It's distracting my attack big time.

Azeus shows himself upstairs. His arm cocks back and he hurtles a bolt of lightning. Ouch. That knocks my life force down by half. Hurry up, Periwinkle! Burn that sucker to ashes. Mutt the forest elf is hacking away with his knife and doing quite well. The little son of a bitch can fight after all.

The werewolf on my lap shivers as its fur changes to skin. Its bones crack and reform as they change from wolf to girl.

My character's life force drops to 10 percent so I find a hiding place. Periwinkle is still blasting the lizard zombie army with fire. This should give me enough time to recharge and return to the battle.

"Did you miss me?" Bree, the former gray werewolf asks. I look down and my girlfriend is totally baby-naked. Like wearing nothing at all.

At this point, I lose interest in fighting zombie lizards.

"Hey, um...how was the hunt?" I ask.

"So, you didn't miss me?" Bree's mouth twists to the side.

I lean down and kiss her. She looks amazing. She always looks amazing.

"Bree!" a male voice roars behind us. "Put on some clothes. What have I told you?" Mr. Mayflower hovers over the couch. The large man is slipping on a T-shirt.

Mrs. Mayflower shows up and tosses a bath towel over Bree. Her daughter pouts as she rolls off of me and wraps her naked body in cotton.

"He's my boyfriend," Bree says.

"And when Aiden has a teenage daughter, he can raise her how he wants. But you're my daughter and we all agreed during this arrangement to follow my rules. You don't see Aiden running around here naked, do you?"

"He could if he wanted to."

"That's okay," I say. "I like wearing clothes."

Bree cuddles up to me as her parents head upstairs. "Did Periwinkle recover?"

"Yup. He's roasting lizards and it's amazing," I say. My health force is good now so I maneuver my character back into the fight with a killer combo attack.

"Wish we had a dragon to fight the Demon Skins with," Bree says.

"I was hoping you would tell me dragons actually existed."

"Sadly no," Bree sighed. "But there are bright boys who know how to use fire to their advantage." Bree kisses the side of my cheek. Another thank you for saving her life.

I love her little thank yous.

But then I feel a sharp pain. She's biting my ear again. She thinks it feels like a nip, but the girl has some sharp teeth.

"Bree," I protest.

She giggles and licks my ear to make it all good.

I know, Bree's a little different than most girls. But that's what I like about her.

Bree watches as Periwinkle burns a path for me and Mutt to charge up the staircase to attack Azeus.

"You should pack sunscreen for tomorrow," Bree says. "Your human skin is so fragile and I don't want you to get stupid skin cancer."

Tomorrow is that hiking trip. I forgot all about it. Well, I wanted to forget all about it.

"Why don't we stay here and play Death and Valor 5?" I ask.

"You need to get outside more," Bree says. "Besides, it'll be gorgeous this weekend."

"Remind me. Why are we doing this again?"

"To do something fun and to meet other people. I still don't know half the kids that go to our school and I'm already a Junior."

"I'm sure they're not worth knowing."

Bree ignores me. "The hiking club is the only group that does anything outside school. They're very active and they have like a hundred members. Lots of seniors. And we were invited to join. Shouldn't we see what it's all about before being so negative?"

"I like being proactively negative."

Bree's chin rests on my shoulder. Her soft hair brushes my cheek. "For me, can you be positive instead?"

Since having a girlfriend, I'm learning that there are some fights that are worth losing.

"For you, yes."

"Thank you," Bree whispers in my ear, then gives my earlobe another love nip.

With renewed spirit, I attack Azeus with my sword. His multiple lightning bolts burn through my life force and I have to retreat down the stairs. Azeus turns his attention on Periwinkle and kills him. The next victim is Mutt who takes a lightning bolt through his back. I hide again to recharge my life force. But Azeus sends in his special zombie lizards who can fly.

My character soon dies.

Available February 2023

ISBN-13: 979-8-9871263-1-8

For online book links: www.dougsolter.com

Also by Doug Solter

My Girlfriend Bites Again

My Girlfriend Bites Me (March 2023)

The Gems Young Adult Spy Series

Skid Young Adult Racing Series

Made in the USA
Monee, IL
29 April 2025